The BLACKSMITH *Brides*

4 Historical Stories

AMANDA BARRATT
ANGELA K. COUCH
PEGG THOMAS
JENNIFER UHLARIK

BARBOUR BOOKS

An Imprint of Barbour Publishing, Inc.

Worth Fighting For ©2020 by Pegg Thomas
Forging Forever ©2020 by Amanda Barratt
A Tempered Heart ©2020 by Angela K. Couch
A Malleable Heart ©2020 by Jennifer Uhlarik

Print ISBN 978-1-64352-422-1

eBook Editions:
Adobe Digital Edition (.epub) 978-1-64352-427-6
Kindle and MobiPocket Edition (.prc) 978-1-64352-426-9

Cover Image: Priscilla Du Preez / Unsplash

Published by Barbour Books, an imprint of Barbour Publishing, Inc., 1810 Barbour Drive, Uhrichsville, Ohio 44683, www.barbourbooks.com

Our mission is to inspire the world with the life-changing message of the Bible.

ecpa Member of the
Evangelical Christian
Publishers Association

Printed in Canada.

WORTH FIGHTING FOR

by Pegg Thomas

Dedication

This story is dedicated to the ancestors in my father's lineage who fought on both sides of the Revolutionary War. Both sides of his family came to the colonies in the mid-1600s. His father's side—the Lewis (Lewes) side—were Loyalists who moved into Canada following the war. His mother's side—the Yale side, which goes back to the royal line in Wales—were Patriots and include the surnames of Yale, Munger, Case, and Young.

May we all have their passion and
conviction to stand firm for what we believe.

Chapter 1

Meg McCracken plopped onto the padded velvet seat next to her mother. She glared at her three older brothers as they squeezed their bulky frames through the narrow door and sat opposite her in their father's coach. Her father, Callum McCracken, climbed in last and quirked an eyebrow at her crossed arms.

"Now, Meg—"

"Do not 'Now, Meg' me, Father. 'Tis they who need a talking to." She tilted her chin toward her brothers, who had the gall to grin back at her.

"They are your brothers. They do only what any brother would do for his sister."

"Is that so? And would you have me be a spinster then? Because no man can get within a rod of me without one of these great lummoxes planting himself in the way."

"Those who back off are not worthy of you, I say." Jamie, the middle of her older brothers and her favorite, winked at her.

"He is correct, you know," Father said. "You would not respect a man who ran off at the first sign of trouble. You have too much spunk for that. Just like your mother."

The look that passed between her parents added to the heat in the carriage. A sigh slipped from Meg's lips. She'd grown up watching these two people who were so much in love. Was it any wonder she wanted the same for herself? Those hulking brutes crammed onto the coach's other seat, however, had blocked every possible suitor so far.

"Was there someone special in attendance tonight? Someone who has caught your eye?" Mother asked.

Meg scowled across the coach. "Even if there were, he would have needed a battering ram to get close to me."

"I thought not. I did not see anyone new there tonight. So this discussion, 'tis not necessary, is it?" Ailsa McCracken hadn't raised five children, four of them boys, without learning how to diffuse an argument.

Meg gritted her teeth when Jamie winked at her again before he turned the talk to what the men always talked about—war. The ride home would only take a few more minutes or she'd be forced to listen to them rehash every quarrel with England since the Puritans first stepped onto the American shore. What was it about men that made them want to fight over any plot of land for any reason imaginable? Or for none at all.

She let her head rest against the plush interior of the coach. For all their tendency to be quarrelsome, she still wanted a man of her own. She was seventeen years old, more than ready to have a home and a husband. A man who loved her and looked at her the way her father looked at her mother.

Was that too much to ask?

⌐

Meg followed Jamie into the parlor, his rant against the king filling the space around them but easily ignored since she knew it by heart. She pulled off her long gloves and dropped them on the side table next to a blue vase full of fresh flowers. The scent teased her nose, a welcome change from the stuffy ballroom and crowded coach.

"I tell you, the colonies will not stand for any more oppressive acts. 'Tis past time we made it known to King George and everyone else in England. It cannot happen too fast for me," Jamie said.

She'd heard it before, from all of them, David, Jamie, Andrew, and even Robbie who was asleep upstairs, still a year too young to attend the dance.

Her brothers formed a line facing their father across the room. Their iron-haired patriarch turned to pin David, the oldest, with his frown. " 'Tis time to make preparations, is it not?"

"Preparations for what?" Meg asked.

All three brothers stared at her as if she'd said something stupid.

She clamped her hands to her hips and tilted her head. "Whatever is wrong?"

"Did you listen to nothing that was said tonight?" Jamie shook his head and snorted.

"Little sister, there was more afoot tonight than I think you know." David looked from her to their father.

"Don't be hard on the lass. What girl her age wants to listen to talk of war when there are handsome men to be danced with?" Her father's gaze softened as it lingered on her for a moment.

Father was a man to be reckoned with, but Meg knew he harbored a soft spot where she was concerned. Mother stepped beside her and wrapped an arm around her shoulders before leading her to a settee and sitting down beside her. A cold feeling gathered somewhere in Meg's middle. What had she missed? They always talked of war, but it never happened.

Did it?

Father turned back to David. "You shall need a soldier's kit before you enlist. The militia has no funds of its own to outfit the men. I doubt the new army will either."

David nodded. "We have some time, several months at least. The Continental Congress will not officially raise an army until King

George finishes laughing over this last feeble attempt by the Loyalists to divert the war."

Meg gasped. They were serious. Mother's grip on her shoulders tightened.

"It pays to be prepared." Father pivoted and faced his wife. They stared at each other, the silence dragging out as a message only they understood passed between them. "I shall do my best to keep Robbie out of it."

"Robbie?" Meg's voice came out little more than a squeak.

Mother drew in a shaky breath. "Sixteen next year. I know not how you shall keep him back."

"I would rest easier knowing he was here to watch over you and Meg."

"But you shall be here, Father," Meg said. "We shall be safe with you."

Jamie rolled his eyes at her.

She stood and faced her father, a slippery thread of fear coiled in her throat. "Will you not?"

"I wish I could, lass, but since they already deem me a traitor to the Crown, I must fight."

Mother stood beside her. "We shall be prepared. Meg and I will gather what you need to take with you. There is cookware for over a campfire and cups and. . ." Mother turned her face away and drew in a ragged breath.

It was real, this threat of war, not just talk anymore. Meg's brothers were planning for war. And Father. How could this be? Her throat tightened. Mother's shoulder trembled next to hers. Meg had to do something. She'd help her mother gather what the lads would need.

"I shall visit the blacksmiths tomorrow and inquire about soldier's kits." Her voice wobbled a bit on the last word, but she lifted her chin and met Father's nod of approval.

"A good thought, lass. We should each have a new knife as well."
A knife. Something with which to cut bread. . .or British soldiers?
Meg shivered.

⌒

Heat from the forge blew into Alexander Ogilvie's face. He wiped his
brow with a gritty sleeve. September usually brought cooler tempera-
tures to Philadelphia, but it seemed reluctant this year. Maybe it was
all the talk of war. It sure heated tempers around town. The people
remained divided between those who lobbied for independence and
those who wanted to repair relations with England.

Alexander stretched and glanced through the open double doors
toward the west, toward the distant mountains he couldn't see from
his father's blacksmith shop. If he had his way, he'd pack his belongings, meager though they were, and move west, leaving the rest of the
population to fight things out among themselves. He'd have enough
money saved soon.

He wasn't unsympathetic to the Patriot cause, but squabbling
over who collected his taxes didn't matter much to him. As long as
he stayed here, he'd be just one more blacksmith mending bean pots
and fixing broken hinges. The gentry could talk of their high ideals,
but for a working man, it mattered little whose plow he repaired.
Independence to him meant leaving the city and building the life he
wanted on the frontier. A life in which he took care of himself and
answered to no man for it.

He picked up his hammer and tongs when a tall lady with
a blue-and-gold plaid shawl draped over her elbows crossed the
street and headed toward the smithy. She wore a white lace cap
over the most vivid red hair he'd ever seen. She stopped at the
wide double doors. Eyes the blue of a peaceful sky and a chin
that came to a slight point reminded him of a pixie escaped from

Grandda's stories of the Scottish Highlands.

She cleared her throat, releasing him from whatever spell she'd cast.

"May I be of assistance, mistress?" He laid aside his tools, wishing soot and sweat didn't cover his hands. Or the rest of him for that matter.

"I hope so. I have been making the rounds of blacksmiths in town." Worry lines crinkled the corners of her eyes.

"Allow me to guess. You have a soldier to kit out for the militia." Probably a husband. How could any woman that beautiful not be married?

"How did you know?"

"You are not the first to come by." He pointed to a neat line of fire irons and hooks on the table across the room.

"Of course." She plucked at the fringe along the edge of her shawl. "How silly of me."

"Not silly at all. Everyone is busy with war coming." The droop of her shoulders tugged at his heart. "I can make what you need. One more kit shan't much matter."

"Oh, but I need four."

"Four?" He blinked.

She nodded. "For my father and three brothers."

"No husband then?" He wished he could grab those words back as soon as they left his mouth. What had possessed him? He fully expected her to leave in a huff. A grimy smith like him, asking such a thing of a lady like her. 'Twas the height of impertinence. At least the heat from the forge already had him flushed enough to cover his embarrassment.

She, on the other hand, blushed a rosy hue as she studied the ground at her feet. "Nay. No husband. But I should order five kits."

For the man courting her, of course. He pushed aside the

disappointment he had no right to feel.

" 'Tis all but certain that my younger brother will enlist as soon as he can."

Alexander drew in a deep breath. Another brother, not a suitor. "For you, I can make five."

She offered him a hesitant smile, the merest curve of her lips, and yet his heart squeezed. He'd make her order first. No. He'd drag it out so she might come back more than once.

"I'm not sure what they shall need, exactly. Father said to order knives. They shall need something to cook with over a campfire. . . ."

"I know what to make. Leave it to me."

She blinked those incredible blue eyes at him. "Thank you for taking my order. The other smiths were too busy."

"Aye. War keeps the smithies working."

She nodded and half turned as if to leave.

"I need your name to put with the order."

The pink in her cheeks darkened. She looked toward the street for a moment. "Of course. 'Tis Meg. Meg McCracken."

Her eyes met his, and he was lost.

"When may I collect them?"

"As soon as I have finished the order."

Another smile tugged at her lips, drying his mouth. "And have you an idea when that might be?"

He blinked. How could any woman be so beautiful? Had she just asked another question? He hiked his eyebrows, hoping she'd repeat whatever she'd said. Without thinking him a simpleton.

"When might they be completed for me to collect?"

"Ah, well, I've a list of orders ahead of yours, but shall we say two weeks?" He swallowed. "I could deliver them." But he really didn't want to. He wanted her to come back and get them herself. He didn't want to drop them at a back door with some housemaid.

"No need. I shall fetch them myself."

Thank heaven.

She took a step toward the doorway then stopped and glanced over her shoulder. "Which smith should I tell my family has taken our order?"

He sketched as close to a courtly bow as he knew how. "Alexander Ogilvie, at your service."

She nodded once and left.

Alexander leaned against the anvil and watched her walk away, glad that the wide doors of the smithy left him such a view. The scent of lilacs lingered in her wake. Lilacs and charred cotton.

Charred cotton?

With a yelp, he grabbed an old rag and beat at the side of his shirt where it smoldered in back of his leather apron. There must have been a live coal left on the anvil. Now there was a hole in his shirt.

If he wasn't careful, he'd have a hole in his heart to match.

Chapter 2

Where have you been?" Robbie caught up with Meg as she turned the corner from the smithy. His unruly brown hair escaped from its leather tie and blew across his ruddy cheeks. Was it only a year ago she'd tousled that mop? Now she had to raise her eyes to meet his.

"I placed our order with a smithy on South Street."

"Did you order five kits?" Hope shone from his hazel eyes.

Her heart squeezed. "I did."

"Good, because I have been thinking. The army will need young men for the drums and fife."

"Robbie. . ."

He stopped at the edge of the street and pulled her around to face him. Wagons rattled past. Dust shifted and settled at their feet. A stray leaf, already the gold of autumn, tumbled by.

"Listen, I know I shall have to try out, but I play the fife better than our brothers ever did. 'Twill be easy for me to earn a spot in the army."

"But Mother and I—"

"Father knows you shall be safe here in Philadelphia. Boston is where the action will be. He shall come around to my way of thinking. What if the lads need to hear the fife, loud and clear, so they know which way to move? What if one of our own gets disoriented in battle, and there's no one to guide him to safety?"

Meg pressed her hand to her forehead. She didn't want to think about the realities of war. She for sure didn't want to think of her older brothers, or her father, involved in any way, and certainly not Robbie. How could he fight in a war when he was too young to even attend a dance? The ache behind her eyes threatened to spill into tears.

She needed to change the subject. "I turned around, and you were gone. Where did you disappear to?"

"Oh." The sheepish grin that so often endeared her younger brother to her spread across his face. He dug into his waistcoat pocket and withdrew a small bag of boiled sweets. "I stopped at the general store for these."

Candy. One moment he talked of war, the next he grinned over a bag of candy. She'd never understand men. She accepted one of the sweet treats, and they continued home.

"Which blacksmith did you order from?"

"Alexander Ogilvie."

"Never heard of him, but he sounds Scottish. Father will like that."

She nodded. There'd been no hint of a Scottish burr in his speech, but there wasn't much in hers either. He had a charming smile, dusty-gold hair, and an intriguing cleft in his chin. A smile tugged at her lips. Not that she'd looked at him all that closely. But he'd asked if she was married, and a girl just naturally had to look at who was asking such a thing.

She shook her head and elbowed her brother. "You would have met him if you had been escorting me as you were supposed to. Be glad I do not mention that to Father."

"You wouldn't, would you?" His wide eyes pleaded with her.

She linked her arm with his. "How could I? I would have to admit that I lost track of you too."

His sigh of relief widened her smile until she remembered their errand. They weren't children anymore, out on a lark. Their lives were about to change.

And only the Lord knew how it would end.

$$\backsim$$

Alexander placed a repaired and cooled bean pot on the workbench when Thomas and William, his older brothers, stomped into the shop.

"Wrapping up for the day?" Thomas asked.

"Aye. And ready for supper."

"Sorry to leave you with all the work these past few days, but we bring good news." William rested his hip against the table and crossed his beefy arms. "There's a store of iron northeast of us. 'Twill have to be loaded on barges and brought down the river, but it should not take long to arrange that."

"The problem is"—Thomas stifled a yawn—"we'll need to move fast before someone else snatches it up. Iron is getting as scarce as hens' teeth these days."

"You are leaving again at first light, I take it?" Alexander stretched his shoulders, stiff from a day spent hunched over the anvil.

"That's the way of it." William clapped him on the shoulder. "I best get home to Catherine and the bairns. We've a long trek tomorrow." He left the shop.

Thomas watched him leave then pointed to the line of fire irons on the table. "You have kept busy?"

"Aye. While you were gone, talk of the coming war has poured through like water over a fall."

"The militia's men will need that equipment."

"Good for business, I suppose." Alexander banked the coals in the forge.

Thomas cleared his throat. "Now that war is almost upon us, I suppose you are planning on joining the militia."

Alexander paused then straightened and looked his oldest brother in the eye. "Nay."

Thomas's eyebrows rose to his hairline. "Truly?" Relief colored that single word. " 'Tis a weight off my shoulders, little brother, that I can tell you."

Could his brother be the only person who understood where Alexander's heart lay?

Thomas clamped a hand on Alexander's shoulder. "Da is too old to run the forge by himself anymore. Armies need blacksmiths to be successful. Never was a war won without a blacksmith close by. I say the blacksmith is as important as the doctor in times like this. Maybe more so."

Alexander closed his eyes and took a deep breath. Maybe nobody understood him, but he had to try at least one more time. "I still plan to head west to the mountains in the spring."

"Even if war breaks out?" Thomas's hand fell from Alexander's shoulder.

"Aye."

His brother pressed his fingertips to his temples. "I know you have harbored a fascination with the frontier, but 'tis a boy's fancy. You are a man of three and twenty years. You must be practical. How would you survive?"

The words stung. Anger roiled deep inside Alexander. This was no boy's fancy. Why couldn't his family see that? This was his chance to make something of himself. To own land like the gentry. He'd have to claim it, work it, and hold it against the Indians, but he knew he could. He wanted his life to be more than he'd ever have here in Philadelphia.

His family would never understand.

"I want to make my own way."

"You are a blacksmith."

"Aye. But 'tis not all I am." Alexander struggled for the words to make his brother understand. But how does one explain the pull of the wilderness on a man's soul? The driving urge to better himself? To Alexander, it was as inexplicable as the pull of a pair of brilliant blue eyes shining under a crop of hair so red he wondered if it might burn his fingers.

Some things defied words.

"What of our da? You know I shall be moving with Ruth and our bairns north to be near the Schuylkill Iron Furnace. We colonists must make our own steel now, and soon. William will fight. He is hot for this war. I thought you—" He lifted his hand and then let it drop to his side.

"Mayhap the war will not come. Talk is the Continental Congress is sending another missive to King George to negotiate—"

Thomas snorted and shook his head. "War is coming. Make no mistake." He leveled a hard stare at Alexander. "And we shall all need to do our part."

$\backsim$

"You and Father left Scotland because of a war, did you not?" Meg sat across from her mother darning socks in the parlor, Meg's least favorite chore but one they couldn't neglect with five men in the family.

"We did." A faraway expression crossed Mother's face. "But not to avoid the war, you understand. Your father and I were falsely accused as Jacobite supporters, traitors to the Crown. If caught, we would have been unjustly hanged. We had no choice but to leave behind all we loved and flee for our lives."

Meg fidgeted on her chair. "If Father and the lads join the militia, that will make them traitors to the Crown, will it not?"

"Aye. 'Twill."

"So they will become exactly what you were accused of back in Scotland."

Mother laid her mending on the ornate table between them. "Do not think your father has not considered that, my dear. In fact, he has thought of little else these past months."

"Then why does he get involved?"

"Your brothers. Simply put, they are less British citizens than we were."

"I do not understand."

"They were all born here, in the colonies, as were you. This is their home like Scotland was my home growing up. Their loyalty lies here, on these shores, not with some king separated by an ocean."

Meg stared out the window and pondered her mother's words. How did she feel about a split with England? She understood the unfairness of the new taxes and other measures Parliament had taken recently. But did they truly affect her? They certainly did if Father and the lads joined with the Patriots.

"If the war goes not well for the colonies, could Father be in danger from the Crown again? And the lads?"

"They would all be labeled as traitors. And if caught. . ." Her mother's voice hitched and she couldn't finish.

"They would be hung." Fear snaked its way from Meg's heart to her hands until they trembled. "And what would become of us?"

"We would be tossed into the street, at the very least. All our possessions confiscated by the Crown. But I believe, my daughter, with all my heart, that your father is right to join with the Patriots. While Scotland will always be the home of our youth, our home now is here, with you and our lads and someday, God willing, our grandchildren." She leaned forward and touched Meg's knee. "Years ago, we had to run. But this time, we need to stand and, if need be, fight. Your father would fight against anything on earth for his children's safety and prosperity."

Her parents had struggled and triumphed to become the family they were today. It wasn't right that the war could strip that all away.

Pride filled Meg, and something more. Something deep and strong inside that fueled her desire for the same type of marriage, the same type of commitment with someone she could build a life with.

But war was coming, and war wasn't a time to think about finding a husband and starting a family. She heaved a sigh and then shrugged when her mother sent her a questioning look. How could she put it into words someone else would understand? The war would come, and her family would fight. Some might die.

And so might her dreams.

⮂

Alexander buffed and smoothed a skillet for Mistress McCracken's order. He should have closed the shop an hour past, but he wanted the items for this order to be special. Not that it would do him any favors. A lady like Mistress McCracken belonged to a class far above a lowly blacksmith. Especially the youngest son in a family of blacksmiths.

"Your mam has supper on the table."

Alexander startled and almost dropped the skillet. He fumbled it into his grip and looked up at Da.

Thick white eyebrows rose over a surprised pair of steely blue eyes.

"I did not mean to unsettle you, lad. Just wondered if you planned to join us for supper."

"I was lost in thought." He set the skillet aside, away from those made for other orders.

Da approached, lifted the skillet, and ran a gnarled finger across the ornately twisted handle. He grunted. " 'Tis awfully pretty work for a soldier."

Warmth climbed Alexander's neck. "Aye."

"Do you suppose he shall need this fancy piece to fry his salt pork and heat his bread over a campfire?" Da's eyes held a twinkle.

The warmth flowed across Alexander's cheeks.

"Och, laddie, what is this all about now?"

"'Tis a special order."

"That much I can see for myself. Who be it for?"

"A family by the name of McCracken."

Da set the skillet down and studied it, one hand stroking his chin. "Canna say I know any McCrackens personally, but there's that architect who builds houses for the wealthy side of town. The one who designed the bridge across the Schuylkill a few years back."

"It may be the same."

"You are not sure?"

"Nay. 'Twas a lass who came and placed the order."

"That explains much." The twinkle in Da's eyes returned. "A bonny lass then?"

"Aye. But not for the likes of me." Alexander stared at his dirty hands. Working hands. Not like someone who designed buildings and bridges.

Da pulled a stool closer to Alexander's and perched on top of it. "We are about to enter a war that may change all that, lad."

"How?" Wars changed some things, but not social status.

"Mark my words. When we break from England, and 'tis my belief we will, this country will be like nothing the world has ever seen. A man will be what he makes of himself here. He shall not be owned by any king, or laird, or baron."

Da stood and tilted his head toward the door. "But he can still be scolded by his mam if the supper burns while awaiting him." With a wink, he left the shop.

Could it be true, what Da said? He glanced west. Maybe not here in Philadelphia, but what about those mountains where no king, laird, or baron had ever set foot?

If he were to be something more than one blacksmith in a city with dozens, the frontier was the place to make it happen.

Chapter 3

Knitting socks ranked only slightly higher than darning them for a way to pass the afternoon. At least Meg's brothers wore trousers instead of breeches, so she didn't need to knit over-the-knee stockings. She let the tangle of wool yarn and thin needles drop into her lap. If only she weren't knitting them for brothers who would soon be off to war. Gray skies and low-hanging clouds outside the tall windows did little to lift her spirits. With her needles silent in her lap, only the wispy squeak of the treadle on her mother's spinning wheel broke the stillness.

"Would you like some tea, Mother?"

Mother's eyebrows rose, and then she tucked her chin, giving a look only a mother can give. Her foot didn't hesitate, however, and the relentless squeak continued.

Meg huffed and scooped the yarn and needles from her lap. "No English tea. A pot of chocolate then."

"I know 'tis difficult, but soon tea will be unobtainable anyway. We might as well get used to doing without."

"I know. I'm sorry for my churlishness." Meg understood about the tariffs imposed by England on the colonies that made buying things like socks and tea almost impossible, but that didn't mean she had to like it. "I shall make us a pot of chocolate."

"Cook can do it."

"I do not mind." Meg tossed the words over her shoulder as she escaped the parlor.

She returned carrying a tray with a chocolate pot, thin china cups, and some of Cook's buttery biscuits.

"That looks lovely, and I'm ready for a break." Mother rose and stretched, a hand pressed against her back.

"I know not how you sit and spin for so long at a time." Meg placed the tray on a table between two high-backed chairs. "My fingers were almost numb from holding the knitting needles."

" 'Tis knowing that my labors will comfort my family in the months to come. Men fight the wars, but it falls to their women to prepare the practical things."

"What of the men with no women to see to them?" For some reason the blacksmith she'd met on South Street popped into her mind. Meg stirred the chocolate and poured it into the cups.

"Their lot is a sorry one, I fear." Mother took a sip from her cup and smiled. " 'Tis delicious."

After a taste, Meg did her best not to grimace. It wasn't terrible, actually, but it wasn't good British tea. She set her cup down. "I have been thinking."

"Aye?"

"What if I put together a packet of herbs for each of the lads? Medicine for a cold, something for a headache or a fever, maybe a mixture for a poultice."

"I think 'tis a fine idea. You have a good understanding of herbs and their uses. There is a new herbalist in town that I have heard of. You could visit her shop and find what you need." Mother took another sip. "She might have a recommendation for a local substitute for tea. But I must say I am learning to enjoy the chocolate."

"Would you mind if I visited the herbalist this afternoon?" Any excuse to leave the house was more than welcome, and she truly enjoyed working with healing herbs.

"I think 'twould be a nice diversion for you. The shop is on South Street, I believe. I'm sorry I cannot remember the name."

Meg's pulse did a little skip. South Street, the same as Alexander Ogilvie's smithy. She could stop there and ask directions. "There cannot be too many herbalists on South Street. I shall saddle Gulliver and ride over this afternoon."

"Why don't you take Robbie along?"

"Robbie went with Andrew on some errand for Father. They shan't be back until supper. I'm sure I shall be fine on my own."

Mother balanced her cup on its saucer, a frown gathering on her brow. "I prefer—"

"I know, but I shall be fine. You rode without a chaperone in Scotland, did you not?"

"That was an entirely different situation—"

"Please?" Meg held her breath. She understood why her parents were so protective of their only daughter, but she was far too old for a nursemaid, and she didn't want one of her brothers tagging along when she visited the smithy. Mr. Ogilvie wouldn't even look at her if one of them came.

Her stomach tightened at the thought. She'd rather liked how he'd looked at her.

Mother glanced out the window. "It looks like rain."

"I shall take my cape."

"I suppose—"

"Thank you." Meg bounced from her seat and kissed her mother's cheek. "I shall be back before Father or the lads."

She half ran to her bedroom to change into her riding habit, reveling in this newfound freedom. It had been days since she'd saddled Gulliver. The exercise would do them both good. And it was the perfect excuse to stop by the smithy to see if their order was finished.

After all, Mother said they needed to do their part. She grinned as she pinned on her straw hat.

⮒

"I shall go with your brothers to settle the iron off the barges." Da slipped off his leather apron and set it aside. "Sorry to leave you with all the work again."

Alexander shrugged. He didn't mind staying behind and working on the orders for those joining the militia. Especially those for the bonny lass with the sky-blue eyes. He'd hoped to have more of them done by now, but the miller had needed two gears repaired this morning and then the tanner a huge kettle to mend. He'd been busy. He wiped the black from his hands onto a rag. At least it was cooler today, feeling more like late September should.

" 'Tis fine. We need the iron."

"Aye. Unless something changes between now and December first."

"Then you think the trade with England will truly shut down as they say?"

"Why else have we been scrounging for iron wherever we can find it?"

" 'Tis one thing to talk about war, 'tis another for the thing to come about."

Da clamped a hand on Alexander's shoulder. "I know it. I wouldn't wish war on anyone. But this one is justified, I believe." He strode out of the smithy and into the street.

Alexander rubbed the back of his neck. What made a war justified? The king wasn't treating the colonists like full citizens of England, that much was true. But was rebellion against the Crown truly justice? Did two wrongs make a right? Yet even the preacher seemed in favor of war. Every Sunday, he expounded on the sins of

King George particularly and of Parliament in general.

Did it matter to one Alexander Ogilvie, lowly blacksmith, the third son of a working man's family? Be they redcoats or colonists, he'd still be fixing their gears and mending their pots when the war ended.

Unless he headed west. The frontier was like raw iron, unformed, undecided, full of boundless opportunities for a man to be something special. He wanted a place in it, a part in shaping it, the thrill of being one of the first of something.

He picked up one of the skillets for Mistress McCracken. Da had teased him about the fancy handles, but a woman like her deserved pretty things. He snorted to himself. Not that she'd notice. She'd hand them off to her brothers without a look. Or maybe not. What did he know about young ladies of quality?

He sighed and returned the skillet to the table before grabbing a new length of iron to work.

"Pardon me."

Jerked out of his thoughts, Alexander spun around and looked into the eyes that had haunted his dreams this past week.

"I did not mean to startle you." Errant locks of hair escaped like flames from under her straw hat.

"Mistress McCracken." Alexander swallowed a gulp. He put down the iron rod and scrubbed his hands on his leather apron. "I have yet to finished your order."

A slight smile tugged at her lips and danced in her eyes. " 'Tis only that I was riding by. I thought to stop and inquire, but did not mean to seem hasty regarding my order."

"You ride?" Of course she did. Wasn't she standing here in front of him wearing a fetching green riding habit? Did she not hold a riding crop in her gloved hands? Could he think of nothing intelligent to say?

"Of course." Her smile broadened. " 'Tis one of my favorite occupations."

" 'Tis one of mine as well."

She lowered her lashes and fiddled with the crop in her hands. "Seems we have something in common then."

"Aye." Alexander wanted to say something witty, something clever, something to bring her eyes back to where he could drown in them. His tongue clung to the roof of his mouth. The moment stretched to the breaking point.

"I should not have disturbed you, Mr. Ogilvie. I'm sure you have many important matters to attend to this day."

"Nay. That is, I do, but you are not a disturbance, mistress." But she was. In all the best ways.

Her eyes met his again, the glint in them hinting at humor. Was she laughing at him?

"And yet you frown," she said.

Did he? He rubbed at his forehead.

"I'm looking for an herbalist my mother heard had opened a shop on South Street. Do you happen to know where it is located?"

"Aye. Madam Richardson's shop. She is two blocks down on the right. A large clump of dried weeds hangs beside her door."

Her sweet laughter filled the smithy, lightening the dingy day. "I'm sure Madam Richardson would not appreciate you referring to her herbs as dried weeds."

Heat drifted from under his collar. "Nay. I daresay she wouldn't."

"Then we shall not tell her. 'Twill be our secret."

They shared a secret. Mistress Meg McCracken was standing in his father's smithy talking to him and sharing a secret. He tapped his fingers on the anvil. It felt real. This wasn't a dream. "I suppose those weeds are good for something."

"Most herbs have many useful purposes. I plan to put together packets for my brothers to take with them. . ."

"When they go to war."

"Aye." She dropped her eyes for a moment.

"You know herbs then?"

" 'Tis an interest of mine. I like concocting potions and poultices to help when someone is ill."

"A handy thing to know." Especially on the frontier. Not that she'd ever go there, of course. But a man could dream.

Thunder rumbled in the distance.

"I best be on my way. Thank you for the directions."

"You are most welcome, mistress."

"I shall return another day for my order. 'Twill be ready. . . ?"

Alexander stared at her for a moment while her unfinished question hung in the air between them. "Oh." He looked at the forge and then back at her. "Week's end, most likely. If the tanner doesn't crack another kettle beforehand."

"Until week's end then." She blinked those amazing eyes at him and left.

"Aye." Alexander stood as if he'd grown roots. They shared a secret. Now if he could just remember what it was.

⌒

Had she truly flirted with the blacksmith? She'd never flirted with anyone before. Never wanted to, even if her brothers would have allowed it. What was it about Alexander Ogilvie that prompted her to do so? He was a fine figure of a man, there was no denying that. And those tawny eyes of his. . .

Meg kicked Gulliver into a trot and let the breeze cool her cheeks. She fought a wild urge to return to the smithy and try flirting again. She was a full two blocks past the herbalist before she remembered it and reined Gulliver around.

The steady gelding tossed his head as if to remind her of the thunder and his dry stall in the direction they had been going. A jagged spear of lightning split the sky to the west.

"You are right, Gulliver. We shall visit Madam Richardson another day." She reined the horse back around and let him lengthen his stride. She could return to the herbalist's tomorrow. And ride past the smithy again. Nay. That wouldn't do. It was one thing to offer a slightly flirtatious smile. It was quite another to return the next day. What would Mr. Ogilvie think of her?

What did she want him to think of her?

The breadth of his shoulders. The tawny eyes that almost matched his hair. The cleft in his chin. The timbre of his voice. What little she'd heard of it. He was a man of few words, that was certain. But was he a man who would stand up to her brothers?

Her shoulders sagged. He was a blacksmith, not the type of "fine young man" her father spoke of. Men who attended dances and worked at jobs behind large desks in paneled offices. He was a blacksmith with dirt on his forehead.

She smothered a giggle with her gloved hand. When he'd rubbed his brow, he'd left a smudge. What would he have said if she'd mentioned it to him? Would it have flustered him? She thought so.

For some reason that pleased her.

Chapter 4

Alexander suppressed a grimace when William thumped the oak table, rattling their mam's sturdy crockery dishes.

"Are you aware that Alexander refuses to fight?" William didn't shout, but his voice filled the room. "Is our family to be branded with a coward? Or worse, a Loyalist?"

"Enough." Da leaned back in his chair, the only one at the table. He tamped a pinch of tobacco into his pipe. Mam brought him a taper from the hearth, and he sucked on the pipe until it lit. She returned to her rocking chair on the other side of the cottage's main room, next to Alexander's two sisters who were working on a pile of mending. He and his brothers sat on wide benches that boxed in three sides of the table.

Alexander fought the urge to thump his fist on something, possibly his brother's head. Instead, he relaxed each muscle in his body, one by one, as he'd learned to do when sitting in the forest waiting for deer to come to the stream for a drink. Tension clouded the mind and increased the likelihood of making a bad shot, or a bad decision.

"Alexander is no coward, nor a Loyalist." Da took another draw on the pipe, releasing a breath filled with its pungent smoke. "He has expressed his desire to head west, which is nothing new. Has he not said as much for the past year and a half?"

"But the war. We shall need every able-bodied man to whip the

British." William's normally ruddy complexion practically glowed in the candlelight. "To turn and run now—"

"Hold on." Thomas grabbed William's forearm. "He is not running away." Thomas turned to him. "Are you lad?"

Alexander looked from one brother to the other. Thomas shared his blond hair and easy manner, so at odds with William's feisty temper and quick wit. Neither agreed with his decision, but Thomas would always be fair.

" 'Tis like Da said, I have been planning to leave in the spring. I do not see that the war changes that."

"So you shall leave it to the rest of us who are willing to fight, securing your freedom, while you gallivant off into the wilderness?" William dragged his hand through his russet hair, leaving ends spiked up along the way.

"Aye. If that is how you want to interpret it." He squelched the urge to argue with William. It would do no good. His brother was like a snapping turtle on the end of a stick. Nothing would make him let go of his beliefs.

"And how would you interpret it?"

"I want to be one of the first to open the frontier. I want my shot at being a landowner. What does it matter to me if the hinges I make are sold to the Crown or a Patriot? It changes nothing for me."

Da raised his hand. "But think on this, son. The war will need blacksmiths. Can you not stay and work the forge? Can you not postpone your adventuring until the war is over?"

Alexander let his chin drop to his chest for a moment before meeting Da's steady gaze. "I think not." He ignored William's snort. "You have said yourself that this war could drag on for years. Most do. Other men are already pushing west, and they are also in need of blacksmiths. I want to be in the company of those who go first."

"Is it so important to be the first?" Thomas's fair brows drew down into a straight line. As the firstborn, it was unlikely he'd understand.

"Aye. For me 'tis."

Da raised his hand again. "Before you speak, William, remember that you are not the youngest son. I understand some of what Alexander is feeling. As the youngest of seven, I made my way here from Boston to build something for myself." Da rubbed his thick fingers across his chin. "There is no cowardice in striking out on your own. Of course, I had your mam with me every step of the way." He shared a fond smile with Mam. "I would feel more settled about you leaving, Alexander, if you took a wife before you left."

"There be plenty of young ladies at church who would jump if you crooked a finger at them." Mam's knitting needles never ceased as she cast a glance his way. Janet and Isabel, his younger sisters, both giggled over their mending.

"At least think on it, lad." Da stood. "We shall talk no more about this tonight." He pinned William with a narrow-eyed stare.

William pushed away from the table and stalked out the door, leaving it open in his wake.

"He shall come around." Thomas rose and walked to the door. He turned to look at Alexander. "I know you are no coward, little brother, even if I cannot understand your desire to go to the wilderness. Me, I'm glad I have a wife and bairns in a snug home down the street." He pulled the door shut behind him.

At least Thomas would accept his decision, if not agree with it.

"Why do you not take yourself off tomorrow and do some fishing? The lads and I can carry on for the day. You have earned a bit of fun," Da said. "And I have a taste for a fish supper."

He should finish Mistress McCracken's order at least, but a day spent fishing along the Schuylkill River was too mighty a temptation. He nodded.

"You could use the time to think on some of those young ladies your mam mentioned." Da winked.

He would think on it. There was good sense in what Da said. The Bible talked about a wife as a man's helper. In the wilderness that would be a valuable thing. But Alexander knew none of those ladies would match up against the blue eyes and flaming hair of Mistress McCracken.

⮑

"Where are you off to this morning?" Father glanced up from his breakfast as Meg breezed into the dining room.

"What makes you think I'm off somewhere?"

" 'Tis a new fashion then, to wear your riding habit to breakfast?" He quirked an eyebrow at her.

She laughed. "You have caught me out. I plan to saddle Gulliver and take a ride along the Schuylkill."

"By yourself?"

"Of course. I shan't go far, I promise, and I shall stick to the path along the river."

"I do not know—"

"Mother allowed me to ride out on my own the other day, only the rain turned me back sooner than I'd hoped."

"Maybe Robbie—"

"Where is Mother?" Meg looked around the room, hoping to distract her father.

"Still upstairs. She awoke with a headache. I think 'tis from all her spinning and knitting late into the evening. 'Tis stressful on her eyes."

"You could be right, but 'twill not stop her."

"Not your mother." He grinned. "Now about Robbie, he—"

"He is already off with David to pick up that order of timbers you need from the docks."

Father pushed back in his chair and eyed her up and down. "Seems you have this all planned out."

"Oh Father." She came behind his chair and wrapped her arms around his shoulders, still as straight and firm as a young man's. "You shall have to admit that I'm grown and can take care of myself."

He growled and leaned his cheek against hers. "That doesna mean I have to like it." His Scottish burr thickened at times when his emotions were stirred.

She kissed his cheek. "Part of me will always be your wee lassie."

Half an hour later, she mounted Gulliver and wavered a moment between heading west or north, but she'd told Father she'd be along the Schuylkill River, and Mr. Ogilvie had said the order wouldn't be done until week's end, two days away. With a sigh, she pointed Gulliver to the north.

"I'm surprised Father let me go so easily." The sorrel gelding tossed his creamy mane as if in agreement. "But I could not knit another sock. After two days of rain, I needed to get out of the house. I bet you needed out of the stable too." She patted his neck, already growing shaggy in preparation for winter.

Meg rode through the residential streets. She nodded to several acquaintances without stopping to chat. Even so, it took half an hour to reach the path along the river. She reined Gulliver to a halt and turned her face to the northwest, letting the breeze wash over her. It smelled faintly of fish and muddy banks with a hint of fall's decay. Several golden leaves slipped from their branches and floated to the water's surface as she watched.

She nudged Gulliver, and he stepped out smartly, eager as she was for a canter along the river's well-worn path. They settled into a steady rhythm, and she let her mind wander. It annoyed her that thoughts of the coming war pushed their way into her morning, so she mentally shoved them aside. Much better to think of Mr. Ogilvie.

What was it about the blacksmith that piqued her curiosity? He certainly wasn't like the well-groomed dandies who frequented the dances. Nor was he a dashing swain with rustic charm. He was a blacksmith with dirt smudged across his forehead. Not at all the type of man she should give a second look. Even if his eyes did match his hair to perfection.

They'd gone about a mile when the path dipped closer to the river. Gulliver slipped down the muddy slope, and she slowed him to a walk. The soft ground swallowed the sound of his hooves. There was an opening ahead where she and Robbie had stopped many times to let the horses drink. Gulliver's ears perked, and she patted his damp neck. He was no doubt thirsty. They followed the path around a dense patch of willows, and the opening appeared in front of them.

Someone was already there.

Broad shoulders spread beneath a black hat and tapered to a trim, but solid waist. Dusty-gold hair escaped its leather tie and clung to the back of his coat. Booted feet were planted wide and the fishing pole in his hands bent toward the water. The fisherman's attention was riveted to the action playing out before him. A fish flipped free of the river, its scales flashing golden in the sunlight.

"You caught one."

$$\backsim$$

Alexander jerked at the sound of her voice, and the fish, already free of the water's drag, flew past his nose and over his shoulder, no match for a startled blacksmith's muscles. A horse squealed, and then a flash of yellow caught the corner of his vision before the telltale *thwap* of something—somebody—landing in the mud made him cringe.

Mistress McCracken. He wouldn't have startled so at just any voice. It was her voice. Now he'd rather face a firing squad than turn around. He blew out a breath, closed his eyes for a moment, steeled himself, and then turned, prepared for the dressing down of his life.

Mistress McCracken sat in the mud, hands behind her holding

her upright, hat askew, knees drawn up, mouth a perfect circle only slightly larger than her eyes. . .while his fish flopped in the yellow folds of her gown.

Her horse stood a few feet away, its head hung almost nose to the ground, as if chagrined at dumping her in the mud.

Alexander sympathized with that feeling. He'd never felt more helpless—or inept—in his life.

She lifted one hand and then the other. Mud oozed down her sleeves, slid off her gloves, and plopped onto the ground beside her to disappear into the puddle in which she sat. Then she grasped for his fishing line tangled around the fish in her lap. Securing it, she held the fish aloft and aimed her blue eyes straight at him.

"Yours, I presume?"

He wanted to die. Right there. Right then. What on earth was he supposed to do?

Her lip twitched.

To his horror, his did too.

Then she laughed. Not a polite little twitter or a controlled guffaw, but a deep belly laugh that sprouted tears in her eyes.

He joined her laughter for a moment until the possibility that she might have become unhinged alarmed him. He came forward and took the fish then offered his hand to help her stand. She grabbed it with her muddy glove, and he pulled her to her feet.

She dabbed at her face with her sleeve, leaving a smear of mud across one cheek.

"Are you harmed, mistress?"

After another muddy swipe at her face, she gained control over her laughter. "I am, I believe, all in one piece, and you have plucked me free from the mud. 'Twould seem I have escaped harm." She spread her arms and looked down at her ruined gown. "Although I daresay this riding habit will never be the same."

"If you will allow me to replace—"

Her hiked eyebrows stopped his speech. Then she smiled and shook her head. " 'Twas entirely my own fault. Riding up behind a man and startling him while he fishes. My brothers will not let me hear the end of this, I can assure you."

"Let me, at least, escort you home."

She blinked, and her eyes softened. "I should like that." She blinked again, an impish glint sparking in her eyes. "If you do not mind being seen with such a hoyden as me."

"Never." He knew she jested, but he meant it, from the bottom of his soul.

He dumped the wayward fish in his wicker basket with the others he'd caught and gathered his fishing gear while Mistress McCracken washed the worst of the mud off her sleeves and gloves in the river.

When they were finished, he extended his hand. "Let me assist you onto your horse."

"I have not needed assistance to mount Gulliver since I was eight." Her pert chin lifted a notch.

"Perhaps, but with all that mud on your—" Heat flooded his face. "The saddle—the mud—if you should slip. . ." He bit his tongue before he could say anything more foolish.

Pink the exact shade of his mam's roses splashed across her cheeks. "Aye, well. Perhaps you have the right of it. One spill is quite enough for today."

He heaved a sigh and resisted the urge to wipe his forehead before making a stirrup of his hands. Her dainty foot securely in his palms, he boosted her onto the fancy sidesaddle. When she was settled, he untied his horse and mounted, joining her on the path back to the city. To escort her home. His chest expanded at the thought and then deflated.

It would be just his luck if all four brothers and her father were home to see him return her in this condition.

Chapter 5

Meg straightened her hat as best she could and kept her chin high as they rode through the neighborhoods north of her home. What had seemed a lark on the banks of the river with just the two of them seemed less so under the stares of several matrons they passed. Matrons who were friends of her mother.

Although she'd gotten rather good at hiding her escapades with Robbie by sneaking in the back door and up the servants' stairs, that wasn't going to happen today. This was a bit more drastic than her normal larks. Her gown was ruined, she suspected her layers underneath as well, and her saddle would need a thorough scrubbing and oiling.

She flicked a glance at her silent companion. What must he think of her? She'd jested about being the hoyden, but in point of fact, she'd been too close to the truth. The only girl in a family of brothers, she'd grown up more rough and tumble than a girl ought. Perhaps, instead of laughing, she should have cried and wailed like the proper young miss she was supposed to be. Her lips twitched again, and she smothered a chuckle.

He rode closer to her, his fine bay's shoulder practically rubbing against Gulliver's. "Is something amiss?"

Either his hearing was exemplary, or she didn't conceal her mirth well enough. "As good as can be expected, parading past my mother's friends in a ruined gown with, I suspect, mud on my face."

The poor man couldn't look more stricken. His eyes brimmed with concern. For her. Not the smothering kind of concern she got from her brothers. Something more. . .unsettling. Her mirth melted away on a tide of warmth that blossomed somewhere deep inside. She shifted in her soggy dress on her now equally soggy saddle, but barely noticed either.

She looked at his hands, free of gloves and free of the black soot from the forge. Broad, capable hands that had lifted her onto her horse as if she weighed no more than the fish he'd flung through the air. His coat sleeves hugged arms sculpted by hours pounding iron into submission. No wonder the poor fish hadn't stood a chance.

Gulliver turned to the left, and she realized they'd reached her street. She reined him to a halt. "This is my street. You needn't escort me farther. 'Tis only a few houses down."

"I shall see you all the way home."

She bit the corner of her bottom lip and wondered if her father had left the house yet. While everything had a perfectly reasonable explanation, she was fairly certain he wouldn't be of a mind to hear it after looking at his daughter.

"Really, I—"

"Which house is it?"

⇌

She must be ashamed to be seen with him. He didn't blame her for that, but whatever she'd said, this was his fault. He wouldn't leave her to face her family alone. He nudged Asa forward, and her horse followed.

" 'Tisn't necessary."

He looked into those incredible blue eyes filled with emotions he couldn't decipher. Exasperation? Concern? Uncertainty? Maybe an alloy of all three.

Before he could ask again which house was hers, a tall young man about his age with hair nearly as red as Mistress McCracken's came across the lawn to their left.

"For the love of all that is holy, what have you done this time, Meg?"

"A fine morning to you too, Jamie."

Her chin lifted higher as she rode past what could only be one of her brothers. Jamie snagged her rein and stopped the horse.

"I'm serious now. How did you come off Gulliver?" He eyed the sorrel gelding as though searching for any sign of injury to the beast. "Are you both well and sound?"

"Quite well." Her mouth tightened and her eyes narrowed.

Alexander was relieved that look wasn't aimed at him, but it didn't seem to bother Jamie.

"Mother will have something to say about your gown."

"Thank you for pointing out the obvious." She twisted in her saddle. "And thank you, Mr. Ogilvie, for seeing me home." She jerked the rein from Jamie's hand, startling poor Gulliver into motion. They disappeared behind the house.

Jamie turned to Alexander and gave him the same cursory once-over he'd used on the horse. "You are not covered in mud, so am I to assume you simply found her in that condition?"

"Nay."

Jamie's eyebrows fell into a flat line over a hard stare any laird of Scotland would be proud to own.

" 'Twas my fault she came unhorsed."

Jamie crossed his arms over his chest and planted his booted feet wide on the lawn. " 'Tis a story I should like to hear." A man to be reckoned with.

Alexander drew in a deep breath. "I was fishing along the river." He motioned to the fishing gear he had stashed behind his saddle. "Mistress McCracken came along just as I was battling a fish. I heard not her approach, and when she spoke. . ." He ran his finger around the collar of his shirt. "I overreacted."

"In what manner?"

"The fish had jumped free of the river, and when I pulled on the line, she was right behind me."

"Are you saying you flung a fish at my sister?"

Misery filled Alexander from his boots to his hat. As awful as it was, it sounded even worse when her brother said it aloud.

"I'm afraid so. The horse reared, and she lost her seat. With the recent rains. . ." He shrugged. " 'Twas muddy."

Jamie glared at him for a full minute.

Sweat gathered between Alexander's shoulders and trickled down his spine.

Then Jamie bent double and howled with laughter.

Was the entire family daft?

⇔

"You should have seen her, Father. She looked like a salamander escaped from the creek. Enough mud on her to chink a cabin."

Meg wanted to throttle Jamie. Slowly and painfully.

David and Andrew were out for the evening, so she was thankful to only be humiliated in front of half her brothers. Robbie's grin promised more of the same when they were alone. She squeezed her hands into fists under the dining room table to keep from throwing something at him.

"And the man who saw her home, do we know him?" Father twisted off a bit of roll and popped it into his mouth, his attention on Jamie.

"I can tell this story." She pinned Jamie with a stare meant to scorch his hair. "Without any exaggeration, since it happened to me."

Father paused mid-chew and turned his attention to her. His brown eyes revealed a twinkle of humor. "Very well. Proceed."

"When Gulliver and I arrived at the watering spot, Mr. Ogilvie was there fishing. He was battling a fighter. I saw it leap from the water and. . .I shouted."

Jamie covered his face with one hand, but it did nothing to muffle the laughter. She wished they sat closer so she could kick him under the table.

"With my attention on the scene before me, I did not realize how close Gulliver and I were to Mr. Ogilvie."

One more gasp out of Jamie and she didn't care what Mother said, she was going to fling the water in her glass at him.

"He jerked the line, and the fish, well, it shot straight back and struck Gulliver in the neck. He reared, poor old thing, and slipped in the mud. I lost my seat." She muttered the last with her head bowed, waiting for the scorn from her father.

"He must be a strong man to have sent the fish flying like that."

She looked at Father. Compassion filled his eyes beside their smile creases. Jamie started to speak, only to break off with a yelp. Mother raised an eyebrow at him. She was close enough to deliver the kick Meg had so wanted to send. Robbie's mouth dropped open as he looked between Mother and Jamie.

Meg sat a little straighter in her chair. "He is a blacksmith."

"That would explain it." Father popped another twist of roll into his mouth, indicating he was satisfied that nothing untoward had happened.

"Is he not the one you placed our order with?" Mother cocked her head and leveled one of those looks only a mother can give straight at Meg.

"He is." Meg pushed her potatoes around her plate, her face heating as she avoided her mother's eyes.

⌒

So much for sneaking away without an escort. Meg shifted on the seat of the wagon next to Robbie. He flicked the reins over the backs of Father's matched pair of black coach horses. They high-stepped down South Street after leaving Madam Richardson's.

"You may as well stop sulking." Robbie cast a glance toward her.

"I'm not sulking." She sat straighter. "I just do not see why you must come with me."

"You've never driven the team."

"I could have ridden Gulliver."

"That did not turn out so well for you the last time." The lingering smirk in his voice brought heat to her face. "How would you have carried all five kits home behind the saddle anyway?"

She crossed her arms and clenched her teeth. It irked that he was right. But Mother's careful watch over her these past two days had irked even more. Mother hadn't even let her come to the herbalist's by herself. Did she truly fear that Meg would run off with the soft-spoken blacksmith?

The smithy came into view and her pulse tripped.

A man walked into the smithy as Robbie halted the team out front and set the brake on the wagon. He wrapped the reins around the brake handle while she climbed down on the other side. They entered the smithy as the man spoke.

"Name is Boone. Daniel Boone."

Robbie dropped the coin purse he'd been holding. The metal clink when it hit the dirt floor drew everyone's attention. He scrambled to retrieve it, his mouth still agape.

Who was this man that Robbie should know his name?

Alexander's eyes met hers for an instant before he looked back at the man in front of him. The fellow, Boone, had a long rifle in his hand and leaned on it like a staff. He was dressed head to toe in buckskins with fringes hanging long down his back and swinging from each sleeve.

He looked like a wild man.

Meg pulled her shawl tighter across her shoulders.

"I'm looking for Alexander Ogilvie," Boone said.

Alexander wiped his hands on a rag. "I'm Alexander. This is my brother, William." He nodded to another man near the forge, one with a similar strong build, but sharper features and a thatch of dark red hair. "How can we help you?"

"Talk is you have a hankerin' to head west across the mountains."

Alexander glanced at his brother then back toward Mr. Boone. "Aye."

"Fact is, I'm headin' that way myself come spring. I have been asked to open a road into the wilderness. I aim to choose a spot and start a settlement."

"To stay?" Hope filled Alexander's voice.

Robbie grabbed Meg's arm in a grip that threatened her circulation.

"This country is about to burst its seams. There's land across the mountains for those who can take it and tame it."

William stepped forward. "What about the Indians?"

"Oh, there's plenty of them. Cherokee and Shawnee mostly."

"Are they friendly?" Robbie asked.

Daniel Boone turned and nodded at Robbie. "Depends on the day, son. But mostly you have to earn their respect. Injuns do not think like white people."

"War is coming." William crossed his arms, a stubborn angle to his jaw.

"There's always a war comin' or another one windin' down. Man is a fightin' critter for sure." Daniel Boone cocked his head. "I fought my share of battles, some against the French and some against Injuns."

William shook his head, skepticism written across the grooves of his forehead.

"What I'm lookin' for is a blacksmith willin' to settle in the Kentucke territory with me. If you reckon to go west, I would like to offer you a spot in my company."

To Meg's disbelief and dismay, Alexander extended his hand to Mr. Boone.

"I would be honored to travel with you, Mr. Boone."

They clasped hands.

" 'Tis Daniel. I have a mess of business to see to while I'm here. I shall return before I head south again to settle on a date and place to meet up come spring."

With that, the buckskinned man touched his fur hat and left the smithy.

"You really going to leave with Mr. Boone?" Robbie asked in a reverent whisper.

William stripped off his leather apron and tossed it aside. Meg couldn't hear what he said, but it was obvious he wasn't happy as he stomped out the door.

Alexander watched him go then turned to her and Robbie. "You have come for your order?"

"We have." Robbie looked over every piece Alexander handed him and asked questions about the pieces he didn't recognize. They talked, but Meg couldn't concentrate on what they said. The news that Alexander was leaving left her feeling abandoned. . .which was utterly ridiculous.

But the feeling wouldn't go away.

Chapter 6

After Alexander had explained all the pieces of the soldier kits to Robbie and showed him how they worked, the young lad had peppered him with questions about Daniel Boone and Kentucke. Questions he mostly didn't know the answers to. Questions he only half heard as he kept looking at Meg. Pale and silent, she avoided eye contact with him.

While he helped Robbie stow the kits in their wagon, she climbed aboard before he could offer his assistance, and then they drove away. Alexander stood beside the doorway watching until they turned a corner. She never looked back.

He returned to the horseshoes he'd been making when Daniel Boone arrived. It was easier to think while his hands were busy on a task he could do in his sleep.

The back door of the smithy squeaked open and then banged shut. He braced himself for William's return. Instead, it was Da.

"William says there was a distinguished visitor to our humble smithy."

"Aye."

"He said you agreed to join Boone's company in the spring."

"Aye."

Da scratched at his scalp over his left ear. "I know you have set your heart on leaving, laddie, but I must say, 'tis going to be hard to see you go."

Alexander laid his tools on the table and pulled one of the tall wooden stools from underneath to sit upon. "Are you asking me not to?"

Da took a second stool and drew it close, so their knees almost touched when he sat. "Nay. My heart says to keep you here, but my head says you have your own life to lead." He heaved a weary sigh. " 'Tis only life's justice, I suppose, for leaving my own mam and da when I was even younger than you."

"Have you ever regretted it?"

"Nay. How could I? Your mam and I have lived a good life here."

"It worries me to leave the work of the forge to you with Thomas moving to the foundry and William hot to join the fighters."

Da smiled and leaned closer, as if to share a secret. "Mark my words, William will stay and work the smithy with me if you leave. He knows the war will need this smithy along with all the others. Why do you think he is so against your leaving?" He sat back and winked. "His Catherine will be thanking you, your mam will too, for keeping him out of the fighting."

Alexander rubbed the back of his neck. That hadn't occurred to him, but with Catherine expecting their third bairn in early summer, having William in Philadelphia working the forge would be a blessing to her as well as Da. A pressure eased in his chest.

"Have you given any more thought to taking a wife?"

He had barely admitted it to himself, but after the incident at the river two days ago, the possibility of approaching Mistress McCracken's father and asking for permission to court her had plagued his mind. She'd shown herself to be no wilting hothouse flower, even if she was a young lady of the gentry. He admired both her spunk and her humor.

Her beauty didn't hurt either.

But today she'd all but ignored him. Perhaps she hadn't spoken to him because of her brother's presence. For sure it would be awkward with a younger brother along. He couldn't imagine speaking to someone with Janet or Isabel next to him. Certainly not.

"There is someone."

"One of the lassies your mother mentioned from church?"

"Nay. Remember the skillets you teased me for?"

"Those with the fancy handles?" Da's eyebrows drew down. Alexander nodded.

"But did you not say they were for a McCracken?"

"Aye."

"Och, laddie."

"You said yourself that the war will change things."

"I did, and 'tis my belief it will. But it has not even begun yet." Da shook his head. "You cannot bend iron that has yet to see the fire."

"She is different than you might think a high-born lady would be." He fumbled for words to explain but gave up with a shrug. "I have met two of her brothers, and they seemed to approve of me."

"As a blacksmith, aye. But not as a suitor for their sister." Da crossed his arms and leveled his no-nonsense stare at Alexander. " 'Tis one thing to work for a man, 'tis another entirely to try and enter his family. Nay, laddie, take your mam's advice. Look on the lassies from church. Any of them would be proud to marry a man like you."

A man like him.

Alexander clenched his teeth. He was bone weary of being seen as nothing but a blacksmith. He was so much more, or at least he could be. The frontier held all the possibilities he meant to fight for and hold to.

But he couldn't tell Da that, not without making it sound like he didn't appreciate the skills he'd learned at Da's elbow. He wasn't some ungrateful wretch. But he wasn't just a blacksmith either. He felt called to be something more. And as illogical as he knew it was, he wanted Mistress Meg McCracken by his side.

⇌

October's chilly wind blew down the street, the remains of fall's spectacular foliage skittering and twisting before it. Meg wrapped her heavy shawl around her shoulders and pinned it in place. It was woven in the McCracken tartan. She smoothed the fabric with her fingers, pride in her family flowing through her. It was an honor to wear her family's colors.

She'd thought a lot about honor these past two weeks with the sting of learning Alexander was leaving. The Patriots needed good men, men like her brothers and her father. She'd come to accept that now. So why would Alexander leave? They needed him, but he had chosen Daniel Boone over the Patriots, over her brothers. . .over her. That's what stung.

It didn't help that she knew she was being ridiculous over a man she'd seen only a few times in her life.

There was nobody she could talk to. Mother had finally lessened her hovering since the accident by the river. Meg wasn't going to risk stirring that up again by mentioning Alexander. Robbie talked of nothing but the war, except to extol the virtues of Daniel Boone, or laugh at her for not recognizing a man whom he practically idolized. She certainly couldn't speak to Father or her older brothers.

She shook herself out of those dreary thoughts and ran her fingers through Gulliver's creamy mane, the musky scent of him like a balm. "You listen to me, at least."

He swung his face her way. She slipped a piece of apple from her pocket and held it under his velvety white nose. While he munched his treat, she gathered the reins and mounted. With her skirts settled, she turned Gulliver toward town. She had nothing to do and nowhere special to go, but she craved the fresh air and exercise.

A wide-brimmed straw hat adorned with ribbons and feathers caught her eye in the window of the millinery shop. She stopped Gulliver to admire the gold-and-green creation.

"Watch out there. Out of the way!"

Meg twisted in her saddle. A coachman on a tall black carriage gestured wildly as he shouted again, his team of horses pounding toward her. Gulliver spooked at the shouts, stepping sideways and stumbling. Meg fought to regain her balance and turned in time to see a well-dressed elderly gentleman in the carriage tip his hat to her.

"Of all the nerve." She soothed Gulliver with one hand while watching the carriage speed down the road.

"Do you know who that was?" A matronly woman stood in front of the millinery shop, stretching to watch the carriage.

"Someone with very bad manners, I assume."

" 'Twas Mr. Franklin himself."

Benjamin Franklin? Meg looked again, but the carriage had disappeared from view. "He has returned to town?"

"Aye, poor man. You know his wife died last year. He must be terribly lonely now." The matron patted at her elaborate curls that puffed from beneath a frilly hat meant for a much younger woman. "And did you notice that he tipped his hat to me?"

"If you will pardon me, I must hurry along." Meg nudged Gulliver into a trot. Anything to get away from that gossipy old woman. Imagine, saying such things on a public street to someone she didn't know. And about Mr. Franklin no less, whom her father esteemed greatly as a man of wisdom.

Gulliver stumbled again. Meg pulled him to a stop next to the boardwalk.

" 'Tis his off front shoe, mistress." A young lad with straw-colored hair poking out from under his cloth cap pointed at Gulliver. "Half off, 'tis."

She jumped down and walked to Gulliver's right side. Sure enough, the shoe was twisted on his hoof. He must have caught it when he stepped sideways to avoid the carriage. Of all the luck.

"Thank you, laddie." She dug a coin from the purse that hung from her wrist. "Could you tell me where the nearest farrier is?"

"Closest be 'round the corner on South, mistress. Ye're almost there. Can't miss it." He offered a wide grin with a couple of teeth missing.

"Is that the Ogilvie smithy?"

"Aye, mistress, but they be a farrier if needed. I seen one workin' on a horse just this mornin', I did."

She tossed him the coin, and after catching it, he sprinted down the street.

Taking a closer look at her surroundings, she let out a huff. How had she gotten so close to Alexander's smithy without realizing it? Or had this been her destination all along, and she hadn't admitted it even to herself? However it had happened, Gulliver needed a farrier. She led him down the street and around the corner, wondering if it was only her horse that needed to see a certain blacksmith.

⤳

Alexander clamped onto the bar of iron and beat the glowing end to flatten it, only half aware when Thomas left his side to see to a new customer.

"Can I help you, mistress?" Thomas asked from the doorway of the smithy.

"I hope so. My horse has dislodged a shoe."

Alexander whipped his head around. Meg McCracken stood in a beam of sunlight, looking like an angel escaped from heaven. She'd returned. He'd kicked himself for a fool these past two weeks for letting her go without speaking to her the last time.

Now she stood before him again.

The iron bar slipped from Alexander's tongs and crashed into the hot coals of the forge. He fumbled the hammer trying to catch it, and the hammer landed on his boot.

"Pay no attention to my brother, mistress. I'll be happy to look after your horse." Thomas smiled at Meg and ran his hand down Gulliver's shoulder.

"Nay. I shall see to the lady's horse."

"I think not—"

"I said I shall see to it." Alexander stood as straight as he could on his throbbing foot, and glared at his brother.

Thomas frowned at him, looked at Meg and then back at Alexander. His eyebrows rose toward his hairline.

Eyes locked with his brother's, Alexander tipped his head toward the forge.

Thomas looked at Meg one more time then stepped away from Gulliver and mumbled, "Are you daft, lad?" as he brushed past Alexander.

Daft? Probably. But he wasn't about to lose another chance to speak with Meg. "'Tis a pleasure to see you again, Mistress McCracken."

She ducked her head and twisted the reins in her hands. "Gulliver and I were out for a ride when he took a bad step." She gestured to the twisted shoe. "We were not far from here."

Was she letting him know she didn't search him out on purpose?

He ran his hand down the gelding's shoulder and picked up the hoof. He pulled a pair of nippers from his apron pocket and cut the shoe away. "He has done no damage to his hoof, and the shoe is still in good shape. All it wants is to be reset."

Thomas stood near the forge but kept watch. Alexander turned

Gulliver around and tied him to the hitching rail out front. Away from Thomas's ears and eyes. He pulled a couple of nails from his apron pocket and settled Gulliver's hoof between his knees.

Why didn't she say something? Why did she stand on the other side of the horse?

He drove in the first nail then another, until the shoe was set. He clinched the ends and let Gulliver's hoof loose. The gelding stomped it once and flicked his tail.

"That's all he needed." Alexander patted the horse on the rump as he walked around him.

"How much do I owe you?" Meg reached into her purse.

He laid his hand over hers.

She gasped and looked up.

Her blue eyes stunned him yet again. His mouth dried while his pulse stuttered.

"No charge."

"But I must. I owe you something."

"You could meet me at the river on Sunday afternoon."

Chapter 7

What was she doing? Meg eased Gulliver down the slope where the river path neared the water's edge. She approached the watering spot like a bucket drawn from a well, powerless to change course. Her parents would shackle her to a chair in the parlor if they ever learned she'd sneaked out to meet a man. She looked over her shoulder, but no brothers followed, so she reined Gulliver around the last hedge of willows.

Alexander stood in almost the same place he had when they'd accidentally met here weeks ago. When she'd landed in the mud, and he'd escorted her home. But this time he wasn't facing the river or fighting with a fish. This time he was waiting for her, making her insides flip like the fish in the basket at his feet.

He took hold of Gulliver's bridle and offered her a hand to dismount. She bit back her usual retort about not needing assistance and placed her gloved hand in his bare one. He smiled, and the creases on each side of his mouth deepened. She slid to the ground next to him. He took a step closer.

"You came."

"Indeed."

"I'm glad."

His tawny eyes, shaded by his hat, lit with emotions that made her reclaim her hand. She turned and looked at the river as he tied

Gulliver beside his horse. His basket lay open, already half full of fish.

"You have been here for a while."

"Aye. 'Twas a short sermon this morning, so I got an early start. Yours must have gone on some longer."

" 'Twasn't easy to slip away."

A frown marred his brow. "I did not think you would have to sneak off."

" 'Tis only recently I have been given leave to ride alone. And since the last time here ended rather badly. . ."

He grinned. "I did not think it ended badly. Your brother did not challenge me to a duel."

Her cheeks heated at the memory. "Mother was less than amused."

"I can imagine."

He stepped closer.

She stepped away.

"Mr. Ogilvie—"

"Alexander."

"Mr. Ogilvie." She took a step toward the river and then turned and faced him. "I'm not sure why I came here today. Nothing good will come of it."

"Because I'm a blacksmith, you mean."

She wrapped her arms around her waist and drew in a deep breath. "Because you are going away. Because you are not joining the Patriots and fighting for our independence."

He dropped his chin against his chest for a moment and then paced down the riverbank a few steps. Just when she was sure he wasn't going to speak again, he squatted and picked up a smooth stone. With a flick of his wrist, it skipped across the surface of the Schuylkill.

"Do you think me a coward?"

"I know not what to think."

He plucked another river stone and skipped it after the first.

"How could you know?" Alexander stood and gave her a sad sort of smile. " 'Tis what most people will think. It does you credit that you did not assume. I thank you for that."

"But. . ."

"You wish to know why."

The answer to this had plagued her for weeks. She needed to know. "I do."

"I know not if this will make sense to you. Heaven knows my own family does not understand." He rubbed the back of his neck. "And you have grown up as part of the gentry."

"My father and brothers work. They build things."

"They lay out the plans. 'Tis the sweat of others that builds them."

She opened her mouth to argue but snapped it shut again. He had a point. Father didn't come home with hands covered in black, the way Alexander's hands had been the first time they'd met. Father directed others because he was smart and creative. She straightened and lifted her chin. "Someone must design and oversee such work."

"I agree. 'Tis something to be admired and. . .strived for."

"I do not understand."

"I'm not saying this well. I'm not good with words. But I want to be more than a blacksmith. I feel, deep in my spirit, that my destiny lies somewhere else. I'm not afraid to fight, but this is not my fight." He pointed to the west. "Over the mountains there is land. Raw land ready to be made into something new." He half raised his hands and dropped them to his sides. "I want to be a part of that. I want my chance to rise above being the third son of a blacksmith. I want something. . .of my own. 'Twill not be easy. 'Twill not be without its own dangers and battles. That is the fight I'm drawn to. That is my fight."

The longing in his voice sent tingles along her arms. For someone not good with words, he'd painted a powerful picture of the life he wanted. Not unlike her father, who had built a whole new life when they arrived on the American shores from Scotland. "I can understand that."

"Can you? When you have always been given whatever you wanted?" His eyes locked onto hers.

She sensed that her answer mattered to him. Mattered deeply. But he'd no idea what he'd just insinuated, surely. Whatever she wanted? She clutched her hands to her collar, beneath her chin, as she searched his face. "Mr. Ogilvie—"

"Alexander."

She closed her eyes for a moment and opened them again. "If I could receive whatever I wanted, my father and brothers would not be preparing for war."

⌁

She was right and Alexander knew it. It had been unfair of him to imply that her life was perfect, just because she'd been born into a wealthy family.

If he could have whatever he wanted, she'd come with him to Kentucke.

"Perhaps nobody receives whatever they want," he said. "I'm willing to work for what I can. And fight to keep it. I have no future here other than a life spent bent over a forge. No matter who wins this war, my lot will be the same. But I can build something for myself in Kentucke."

He swallowed, hard. If only he had William's glib tongue and quick wit. He took a step toward her. This time she didn't back away. That was a good sign, wasn't it? "Meg."

Her mouth dropped open at his use of her name.

"Meg, I want to know if there could ever be—" He cleared his throat. "If you could see a way—" Sweat gathered across his brow. "Would you be agreeable to seeing me if I approach your father?"

A blue jay winged overhead and landed in the willow thicket, scolding them with its raucous voice. One of the horses snorted. The breeze skimmed the water to ruffle Meg's dress and flutter the lace that flowed from the back of her hat.

After what seemed an age, she lifted her face. If only he could read the thoughts pulsing behind those incredible eyes of hers. He stood still, barely daring to breathe lest he interrupt her thoughts. She searched his face as if a map had been drawn upon it.

Pink stained her cheeks before she looked away at last. "We barely know each other, Mr. Ogilvie."

He suppressed a groan at her refusal to say his name. "Is that not what courting is for?"

She gave a nod, a single tiny dip of her chin. "Indeed."

"Then, you would be agreeable to getting to know me better?"

"But you are leaving."

"Aye. I want you to come with me."

Meg gasped and faced him. She pressed her fingers against her cheeks.

He refrained from slapping a hand over his mouth. Why couldn't he think before he spoke? Now he'd shocked her.

"Well, that is certainly saying it straight out."

"If I have offended..."

"You have not."

He took another step but she held out her hand, palm toward him. He stopped.

"My father, my brothers... 'Twill not be easy."

A wild rush of joy the likes of which he'd never experienced sluiced through his veins.

Saying it wouldn't be easy was more than just an understatement. But if the width of Alexander's smile was any indication, he wasn't to be deterred. If the pounding of her heart was any indication, she didn't want him to be.

What had started as her experiment in flirtation had moved, beyond all explanation, into something she hadn't expected. Hadn't even wanted.

Or maybe she had. Maybe this was what she'd longed for. Found in a place she'd never have imagined.

This man in front of her was like no man she'd ever met before. He wasn't as well-groomed, or as ready with a polished compliment, or as educated as the men she'd met at dances and dinner parties. But unlike those well-groomed gentlemen, this one wanted to ask Father for permission to court her. This one looked at her like she was priceless.

And that had her insides in a dance of their own.

What was it Jamie had said? That she needed a man who wouldn't back down from her brothers? There didn't seem to be any backing down in Alexander. He said he would fight if the fight was the right one. He'd have a chance to prove that in the confrontation to come. Not only was he a blacksmith, certainly not what her parents had planned for their daughter, but he intended to take her into the wilderness over the mountains. Her parents would not be pleased.

Was she?

He held out his hand, and she paused only a moment before placing hers in it. His shoulders blocked the sun from her. Even with his face cast in shadow, the wonder in his eyes shone forth. He raised her hand and kissed the back of it, his lips warm through the thin leather of her riding gloves. He stood, still holding her hand, and that wonder in his eyes warmed the rest of her.

It was the same kind of look that her father shared with her mother.

⮒

Their horses walked side by side, Alexander content with the dawdling pace. They shared about their families and little things about themselves along the way. Would this be what it was like to court a lady like Meg?

Meg nodded and waved to several pedestrians along the way, although Alexander barely noticed them. She'd know a great many people who lived on this side of town, of course. He sat a little straighter in his saddle when she turned her smile his way. They turned onto her street. When her house came into view, the reality of their positions in life slapped him in the face.

When he'd been here before, he had been too concerned for her welfare—and her brother's reaction to her condition—to notice the towering brick structure that sat back from the street. Her father's work, no doubt. It didn't take a master builder to appreciate the beauty and grace in the design of the house. The masterpiece was framed by sculpted hedges on both sides.

They rode to a hitching rail at the side of the wide steps leading to a pillared porch running the entire front of the house. He slipped off Asa and hurried to help her dismount. The smooth leather of her glove in his hand kicked his pulse to a high lope. She slipped her foot free of the sidesaddle's stirrup and shifted her weight but gave a small gasp as she started to slide off the saddle.

"My gown is caught."

Without a thought, Alexander spanned her waist between his hands and lifted her away from the saddle, freeing the fabric. He set her on her feet close in front of him.

"What's going on here?" A tall man somewhat older than Alexander stood on the porch at the top of the steps and frowned down on them, his arms crossed over his chest.

"Mr. Ogilvie has helped me off Gulliver. Surely you can see that for yourself." Meg stepped away from Alexander.

"Since when, little sister, did you require assistance getting on or off your horse?" One dark brown eyebrow rose above the other, then he swung his gaze to Alexander. "Just who is this man to have his hands on you?"

"Alexander Ogilvie, at your service." Alexander tipped his head in a slight bow.

"David McCracken. Whether or not I shall be at your service remains to be seen."

The oldest brother. He sized the man up and found much to his liking. Here was no dandy but a man to be reckoned with. Then it occurred to Alexander. . .

He would be the one facing the reckoning.

Chapter 8

If Meg didn't head this off soon, Alexander might not have his chance to speak with Father at all. "Is Father home?"

David's scowl turned back to her. "He is in his study. I'm quite sure he does not wish to be disturbed."

"Then I shan't take too much of his time." Alexander had tied his horse and Gulliver to the hitching rail. He offered Meg his arm. That wonderfully disturbing flutter his nearness brought tumbled around in her middle. She slipped her hand around his elbow, and he escorted her up the steps.

David's scowl deepened. "I do not see that you need to take any at all."

They stopped in front of David. Here came the first test.

While her brother was a tall man, Alexander topped him by a full inch made more distinct with his bulkier blacksmith's frame. However, side by side, the difference in their circumstances became evident. David's fine woolen coat and matching waistcoat were tailored to perfection. He wore the long-legged pants that had come into fashion. His polished shoes sported silver buckles. In glaring contrast, Alexander's coarsely woven coat, simple waistcoat, breeches, and battered boots made him appear what he was. A member of the working class.

Meg's confidence wobbled, but Alexander appeared completely at ease. She drew heart from that to push forward.

"Pray excuse us, David."

"Mother is in the parlor. Why do you not join her? I shall show Mr.—"

"Ogilvie." Alexander's name came out crisp and precise.

"Mr. Ogilvie to Father's study."

"But—"

"Mother waits for you, little sister." David took her arm and ushered her into the house with the authority of a general giving an order, no matter how genteelly delivered.

Meg glanced at Alexander. He nodded. With one last glare for her overbearing brother, she swept through the door and hurried to the parlor, her stomach knotting into a ball.

"Where have you been?" Mother looked up from her knitting. "You know I do not like you to ride off by yourself, especially without telling me where you are going."

"I'm sorry, Mother." Meg perched on the edge of her usual chair. "I should have said something."

Her mother nodded but gave her a narrow-eyed look. "What has happened?"

She'd never been able to keep a secret. One look and her mother always knew something was amiss. "Nothing has happened. . .exactly."

"Meg."

How could her mother pack so much meaning in a name?

"There is someone here to see Father."

"Oh?" A wealth of suspicion colored her mother's voice.

"A gentleman."

Mother set her knitting down. "What are you trying—or not trying—to tell me?"

That she was enamored with a blacksmith and toying with the idea of following him into the wilderness. But that wouldn't do.

Honesty may be the best policy, but honesty tempered with deference would go a lot further with Mother.

"You know I admire you and Father, do you not?"

"I should like to hope so."

"I do. And 'tis been my greatest wish to find someone whom I could share my life with in a similar manner as you and Father."

"Are you saying the gentleman is a suitor?"

"He would like to be. I would like him to be."

"Who is he, dear? Do I know him?"

Now came the sticky part. Meg drew in a deep breath and pasted a smile on her face. "You have heard of him, but you have not yet met Alexander Ogilvie."

"I do not recall anyone by that name."

"He made the soldier kits for Father and the lads."

"The blacksmith?" Her mother drew back into what Jamie would have called her high-court pose. Indeed, she could look as fierce as Father when she wanted to. And right now, Meg was getting it full force.

" 'Tis an occupation, Mother, not a life sentence."

"The blacksmith."

"He has plans to do more with his life. He plans to head west with Daniel Boone in the spring—"

"Then he obviously cannot be a prospective suitor, can he? If he shan't be here." Mother picked up her knitting. "I'm sure that will be your father's answer."

"But—"

"Your father will handle it."

Meg jumped to her feet. "Have I no say at all?"

$\backsim$

Alexander came to attention before Callum McCracken's desk. Meg's father stood beside a tall window that faced the street. He was everything Alexander had imagined. Tall and imposing with iron-gray hair and brown eyes that reminded him of a hawk on the hunt.

Alexander as the prey.

"So you wish to call on my daughter."

"Aye."

"Why?"

Alexander blinked. He hadn't expected that question. He'd expected to be asked about his occupation, his ability to provide for Meg, perhaps his family and their background.

"Why, sir?"

"Is that a difficult question for you, young man?" The thick gray brows drew together into a formidable line.

"Not difficult, sir, but 'twas unexpected."

"When you are ready then."

Alexander stiffened at the touch of arrogance in McCracken's voice. He would not be treated as a simpleton by anybody. Not even Meg's father.

"I wish to court Mistress McCracken in the hopes of winning her affection and persuading her to become my wife by spring. I head west then to start a new settlement in Kentucke in the company of Daniel Boone."

McCracken left his position by the window and stalked to his desk. He slapped his hands on the polished surface and leaned forward, supported on his stiff arms. "A war is coming. Are you a Loyalist?"

"I am not."

McCracken straightened and narrowed his eyes. "Are you a Patriot then?"

"Nay."

"Confound it, man. You must be one or the other."

"I do not believe that."

McCracken cocked his head, skepticism stamped on his features. "Those who will not fight, for one side or the other, are often labeled—"

"Cowards." Alexander crossed his arms over his chest. "But I am no coward, sir."

"So you say. But you will be branded one all the same. I shan't have my daughter's name dragged through the streets beside yours. Good day, Mr. Ogilvie."

"I—"

"I said, good day."

The study door opened. David stood in the hallway. Having obviously listened from the other side of the door, he raised his arm to usher Alexander out, his face a mask of smug satisfaction.

Alexander nodded to McCracken and pivoted to the door. He stopped in the doorway and looked back. "I shall return another day."

"You may waste your time however you wish, but I shan't receive you again."

Alexander ground his teeth together as he pounded down the hallway, David at his heels. The stony-faced butler held the front door open. Alexander snatched his hat from the man's hand and stalked out to untie Asa. Gulliver had already been taken away. Another sign that Meg was removed from him? He swung astride the horse and looked back at David. "This is not over."

David grinned and leaned his elbows on the porch railing. "You know something, blacksmith? I think you may be right."

⌒

With every intention of pounding his frustration on unsuspecting iron, Alexander entered the back door of the smithy the next morning. He cinched the leather apron around his waist, stirred up the banked embers in the forge, and threw open the large double doors facing the street.

Daylight poured in. The scent of frost tingled in the air. It wouldn't be long before winter clamped down on Philadelphia, and once spring arrived, he'd be traveling west. With or without Meg, he was leaving. He'd tossed and turned most of the night, finally praying for both wisdom and release from his turmoil. While he didn't hear the voice of God telling him what to do, he felt once again the confirmation that his future lay west.

A lone horse trotted down the street, passing shops that wouldn't open for another hour or so. Alexander stepped back into the smithy when the rider called out. He shaded his eyes from the morning glare as Daniel Boone approached.

"Glad you are open early."

" 'Tis good to see you again, sir."

" 'Tis Daniel, remember?"

Alexander nodded, still awed to be in this man's presence, although he'd better get used to it.

"Have you time to settle our plans? I would like to be on the road home within the hour."

"I do. Please, come in." Alexander pulled the pair of stools closer to the forge, its heat starting to fill the smithy.

"What I need most for this trip to the wilderness are strong men who can swing an ax. Somethin' I have a feelin' you can handle."

"Aye. I know one end of an ax from the other."

"Good. We shall be clearin' trees to widen an Injun path into a wagon road. 'Twill be hard goin', but once cleared, we shall have a reliable way to access the Kentucke Territory."

Alexander nodded.

"Once we have settled, we shall need a good blacksmith, but 'tain't likely to be enough work to keep a man goin' on that alone. Can you hunt? Grow crops?"

"I can hunt, fish, and I'm eager to learn more about farming."

"Dandy. Do I understand correctly that you are a trained farrier?"

"Aye. I'm a fair hand with the horses."

"We'll likely need your experience with that as well. Now to the details. We shall meet the first of March along the great wagon road where it crosses the Roanoke River. Do you know the place?"

Alexander had never been more than ten miles outside of Philadelphia. He knew where the great wagon road left the city, and he'd follow it until he found the river, if he had to ask directions in every town and at every cabin along the way. "I shall find it."

Daniel stood. "Bring whatever supplies you can. My sponsors will cover most of the necessities, but once in the wilderness, we shall have only what we bring and what we can make and mend for ourselves."

"I understand." Alexander stood and clasped Daniel's offered hand. As they turned toward the door, Alexander cleared his throat. "May I bring someone with me?"

Daniel faced him, eyebrows raised in question.

"A wife."

"You are married?"

"Not yet."

The thump on his back almost took Alexander's breath away.

"Pick out a good one, son. My Rebecca would love the company."

"Aye, sir."

Daniel Boone's approval was one thing, but how was he going to convince Meg's father?

⤳

A frigid wind lashed against the tall windows of the parlor, freezing rain spattering the glass. Meg looked out at the skeletal trees that lined the street, a cup of mint tea forgotten in her hands. Booted footsteps in the hall roused her from her melancholy.

The door eased open before Jamie poked his head around the corner. "Is it safe to come in?"

Meg gave him a wan smile. "Have I been that awful?"

"As a matter of fact. . ."

She heaved a sigh and set aside her cold cup. "I can always count on you to tell me the bitter truth."

He walked to her side and pulled her to her feet. "For what 'tis worth, I'm on your side, little sister."

"You are?"

"Indeed. I rather liked the fellow when he dropped you off all dripping in mud."

She didn't know whether to hug or strike this tall brother of hers. Her attempt at a laugh sounded more like a sob. He wrapped his arms around her, and she laid her cheek against his chest, dampening his shirt with her tears.

"There now. 'Tis not as bad as all that."

"Nay, 'tis."

"You honestly love this blacksmith?"

" 'Tisn't love—yet—but I believe with all my heart that it could be." She pushed away from Jamie's chest and took the linen handkerchief he offered to dab her eyes dry. "Each time I have been with him, 'tis as if—"

"How many times have you met him?" A scowl wrinkled Jamie's brow.

"First at his smithy, ordering your soldier kits. Once I stopped by to ask directions to the herbalist's shop Mother had heard about. By accident that day at the river when I. . .came home so disheveled. Then the day Robbie and I picked up the kits. And a few weeks later when Gulliver twisted off a shoe."

"That does not explain last Sunday."

"While he reset Gulliver's shoe, we talked. He asked me to meet him by the river on Sunday." She shrugged. "I should not have gone without telling anyone, but I wanted to see him again, and heaven knows you would have stopped me. Or worse, insisted on going along."

"So he asked you to sneak away—"

"That was my idea. I doubt he gave it a thought."

Jamie snorted, but he pulled her back against his chest. "If he was not leaving, it might be different with Father."

"He would still be a blacksmith, and that matters most to Mother."

"I think you are wrong about that, little sister."

She looked up into his unusually serious eyes.

"I think what matters most, to all of us, is that you are happy and safe."

She let her cheek rest against his chest again. Could she be happy remaining here, knowing Alexander was settling in Kentucke? Could she be safe if she went with him into the wilderness? Would she be safe anywhere with the talk of war on every tongue? Perhaps happiness and safety didn't go together except in fairy tales.

Chapter 9

Alexander squatted along the bank of the river. A fish toyed with his line, making the cork bob up and down. Another small one, no doubt. That's all he'd had disturb his line this morning. There'd be no fish for supper. He should care, but he didn't.

A brisk wind skimmed across the water and sent its chilled fingers around his neck. Its scent hinted of ice. He tugged his coat collar higher. This could be his last trip to the river for a while.

The cork disappeared below the water's surface, and he jerked the line. It flipped out of the water with neither fish nor bait on the end. With a low growl, Alexander pulled in the line and packed it away with his empty wicker basket. He tied both pole and basket behind his saddle and stood next to Asa, his forearms resting on the saddle, looking across the horse's back at the river.

He'd fallen in love with Meg so quickly and so completely. What was he going to do about it? What could he do about it? If only the river had an answer.

After untying Asa, Alexander mounted and fought the urge to run the horse all the way to the McCrackens' house. What good would that do? Her father wouldn't see him. He'd made that plain enough. The reins bit into Alexander's gloved hands until he heaved a sigh and slouched in the saddle. She wasn't for the likes of him. He'd known that from the start. If only that knowing could have protected his heart.

Meg paced between the tall windows in the parlor. She needed something to do. She'd organized the soldier kits and stowed them in leather satchels that could be secured behind a saddle or slung over a shoulder. She'd knitted socks for each of her brothers. She'd mended every piece of clothing that needed it. Now her hands were empty, and her heart was hurting. If she didn't find something to occupy her time, she'd break down.

"Why do you not take Gulliver out for a ride?" Mother stood from behind her spinning wheel and joined her at the window. "You could visit Madam Richardson and purchase more of that herbal tea I liked."

Madam Richardson was on South Street. Near Alexander. Meg gave her mother a searching look, but the older woman continued to stare out the window. Was she reading her mother's thoughts right? Was Mother offering her something to do, or pushing her toward the man who had left here weeks ago without a word and never returned. Nonsense. Why would her mother do that?

"You should pick up some herbs to make a medicine bag for each of the lads and your father, as we'd discussed before."

"I had forgotten about that."

"Purchase herbs for small ills like headaches, cuts and bruises, a sore throat. Things they shan't want to see an army doctor about."

"I bought some when Robbie and I were there. I shan't need to purchase much more."

"We should sew packets of oiled canvas to keep them dry."

"I will purchase some canvas at the mercantile."

"Then you should be on your way." Her mother turned and gave her a sad sort of smile. " 'Tis good to have something to do. Some small way we can help our men prepare. It keeps our minds off anything else."

Mother returned to her spinning wheel.

The gentle squeak of the treadle followed Meg out of the room. She made her way up to her bedroom, bemused by the conversation. Mother knew that Alexander's shop was just down the street from Madam Richardson. It was true that she loved the herbal tea Meg had purchased there many weeks ago when she and Robbie had picked up the soldier kits, but Mother wasn't the persnickety sort. She'd be happy with tea purchased at the herbalist a few blocks over just as well. Was it possible that her mother was reconsidering her objection to Alexander? Or was that simply wishful thinking? More than likely, Mother thought Meg must be over the blacksmith and felt it was safe to send her out on errands now. Meg pulled her new riding habit out of the armoire. It didn't matter what Mother thought.

Alexander had given up on her.

⇌

Gulliver picked up his pace as they left Madam Richardson's, the packets of herbs safely stowed in her saddlebag. Did he miss Alexander too? Meg shook her head. What a silly thought, especially since they'd turned the opposite direction. She was glad they didn't have to pass by the smithy. She was. And yet, she twisted in the saddle to look back that way. The door was open, as always. Even on a cold day the forge would keep the building warm.

She turned to face forward and a punch to the middle couldn't have stolen her breath any quicker. Trotting toward her was a familiar bay horse and a far too familiar rider. He rode with his head down, sitting listlessly in the saddle.

Whatever was wrong? His broad shoulders sagged beneath his coat. She reined Gulliver over to the other side of the street and halted him directly in Alexander's path. He'd have to stop or run her over.

Meg held the corner of her bottom lip between her teeth. What if he didn't stop, but rode around her? She lifted Gulliver's reins to move out of the way when Asa snorted and shook his head. Alexander looked up, and their eyes met.

The surprise in his eyes barely surfaced above the sadness.

Her throat constricted until she feared for her next breath.

"Meg."

"Mr. Ogilvie."

He ran his hand over his face and then around the back of his neck.

She wanted to run to him and fling her arms around him, right here in the street for the whole world to see. But she couldn't move. The pain on his face said more than any words. He didn't want to see her. Not now. Not ever again.

Despite her teeth holding on, her lip trembled.

"Oh Meg." He nudged Asa beside Gulliver and maneuvered both horses into an alley, away from the traffic on the street. He extended his hand, palm upward, and let it stop halfway between them.

He no longer blocked her path any more than she blocked his. He was giving her the choice to take his hand. . .or ride on.

She raised her eyes to his tawny gaze. A soft gasp slipped between her quaking lips. The longing in his eyes matched the one in her soul. She slipped her hand into his.

He drew in a deep breath. " 'Tis been a long time."

"Almost four weeks."

"Aye." He stared at their hands. "Your father would not accept me as your suitor." His fingers tightened around hers. "I do not blame him. I'm not good enough for you."

"Never say that." She wished he'd look up. His eyes, so expressive, would tell her what he was thinking.

" 'Tis true."

"I cannot agree."

He barked a short laugh without humor. "You are the only one. Even my brother called me daft."

"Does my opinion matter not? Even to you?" Her voice wobbled on the last word.

He jerked up his head, and their eyes locked. "Your opinion matters more to me than I can say."

"Well then." She coaxed a smile from her trembling lips. "Alexander. . ."

At the use of his name, he rewarded her with a wide smile. Then he sobered and loosened his grip on her hand. " 'Tis no use. I'm leaving for Kentucke in six weeks."

"Must you?"

"Aye. I gave my word."

She'd been there when he'd shaken Daniel Boone's hand. A man of honor would not turn away from that. She wouldn't respect him if he did. But her heart only knew that if he left, a part of her would never be whole again.

"Come to the house."

He shook his head. "Nay. Nothing has changed. I have no more to offer you now than I did the last time."

"But Father—"

"Told me he would not see me again if I returned." He let her hand fall away from his and gathered his reins. " 'Twas plain enough even for a simple blacksmith to understand."

"Alexander—"

"Nay." He closed his eyes and shook his head. "Unless I could offer you more—"

"I shall wait."

He looked at her, his jaw slackened. "You would?"

"Indeed."

He looked into the street and then back again. "It could be years before I have something substantial built in Kentucke."

"Then I shall wait years."

⌒

Alexander hardly dared to breathe lest he wake up and find himself in a dream. "Nothing on earth could inspire me to hurry and improve my lot in life more than that."

"Come by the house before you leave."

He started to shake his head.

"Please?"

The pleading in her eyes matched that in her voice, still tremulous despite the smile on her beautiful face. He wasn't worthy of her. He understood that even if she didn't, but he'd use every God-given talent he possessed to better his circumstances in Kentucke.

He took her hand again and raised it to his lips, watching—nay, drowning—in the blue of her eyes while he kissed the inside of her wrist, above the leather of her riding glove. Her quick intake of breath sent his heart pounding. He resisted the urge to pull her off her horse and into his arms, though her eyes told him she wouldn't object.

First, he would prove himself worthy.

"I shall see you home."

"I would like that."

They rode in silence, not the uncomfortable kind, but still he wished he had William's way with words. She flashed him a smile, no longer uncertain or trembling, but brilliant and—dare he hope— loving. If only he were leaving for Kentucke today. The quicker he got there, the quicker he would be back to claim Meg as his own.

They turned onto her street, and she stopped her horse.

"Nay. I shall see you to the door as a man ought."

"But—"

"Are you ashamed of me?"

She smiled and shook her head. "That is something I could never be."

He nodded, his throat tight, then swallowed and nudged Asa forward.

Her brother, Jamie, rode down the drive on a gray horse. His eyebrows shot up at the sight of them. As well they might, considering.

"Ho there, little sister, what is this?"

"What does it look like? Mr. Ogilvie is seeing me home." Her chin lifted to an angle that Alexander was coming to recognize as Meg at her feistiest. She was preparing to battle her brother over him. Verbally, at least.

"Then he is a brave man or a fool." Jamie's cheerful grin took any sting out of his words. "Or a bit of both."

With Meg bristling beside him, Alexander chuckled. " 'Tis likely you have put your finger on it."

Jamie nodded and touched the brim of his hat as he rode past. "Good luck to you."

Meg watched him go, her eyes wide and her mouth a circle of surprise. She looked at Alexander and shrugged. "I know not what to make of that."

He did. At least one of her brothers was on his side.

They rode around behind the house to the stable. He dismounted and helped her off her horse. Standing toe to toe with his hands still at her waist, the last thing he wanted was to let her go.

"You promised to come and see me before you leave."

"Aye." He pushed a stray lock of her silky hair away from her cheek, where the breeze had teased it. "You promised to wait."

Eyes glistening beneath a veil of unshed tears, she summoned a smile. "As long as I must."

He stepped back and turned to mount Asa. The fluttering of a lace curtain caught his eye. Someone watched them. Fair enough. He would never sneak around where Meg was concerned. He swung into the saddle and gazed down at her. "I shall come by on my way out of town."

"Six weeks." Her words barely reached him, so softly did she speak.

He nodded, his heart too full for words, and kicked Asa into a canter.

Chapter 10

He should have been happier. Alexander stood beside his new wagon, showing it to Da. A good stout wagon, strong enough to survive the primitive road they'd hack out of the wilderness. It included two extra wheels, a spare axle, and two water barrels mounted on the side. He had room to haul his new forge and anvil and as much scrap iron as he could scrounge in the bed of the wagon. His meager belongings would fit under the built-in cot.

"The canvas wants a good greasing to keep the weather out." Da thumped the side of the wagon. "Ethan Scribner has a well-trained pair of oxen to sell. He mentioned it when he was in last week."

"Ethan's a good hand with oxen."

"One of the best."

Alexander stared at his wagon, keenly aware that he was missing something.

"What is it, lad?"

Alexander lifted his shoulders in a shrug, but when his da tipped his head, he let them droop. "'Tis not how I would like to be leaving."

"'Tis the girl, I suppose."

"Aye."

"Some things are not meant to be. But I wish, for your sake, that it could."

He hadn't told Da about Meg's promise to wait for him. As the days had passed, he thought it less and less likely that she would. Not because she didn't mean it when she'd said it, but because life had a way of twisting and turning when one least expected it. Who knew what would happen with the coming war? Her circumstances—and his—may change too much to make it possible.

If only she could come with him now. He hadn't gone back to the McCrackens' because he had no argument to make that would sway Callum McCracken, and he knew it. He had nothing to offer a lady like Meg. He would see her before he left. One more time. Then only God knew what would happen from there.

"Will you deliver the gates to the Samuel Wetherill manor this afternoon? They are ready to go." Da shook his head. " 'Twould not surprise me to get them back in a year or so, to melt down for bullets to help the war effort. He is a true Patriot, Mr. Wetherill. Not like many in that section of the city."

Samuel Wetherill lived two streets down from the McCrackens. Even the chance to be that close to Meg made his heart skip a beat. He could detour past her house after the delivery. Not to stop, of course, just to be near for a bit. "I shall take them now. William came back with the buckboard. 'Tis still hitched out front."

"Need help loading them?"

"I can do it, Da."

Alexander hefted one of the ornate gates, his muscles straining under the weight as he carried it out to the buckboard. He returned for the other and grabbed a crowbar. He might need to pry the old gates loose. After removing his leather apron, washing his hands, finding his hat and gloves, he untied Da's team of horses and started down the street. Toward Meg's house.

"Do not do it, Robbie. Please do not go." Meg grabbed her brother's arm, but he shook her hand off without effort. When had her little brother gotten so strong? He was nearly as tall as David and looked more like Andrew every day. Right now, he was testing her patience.

"Of course I'm going. I shan't sit home to be thought a coward."

" 'Tis not cowardice to know when you are outnumbered."

"The lads and I will show those Loyalists who runs this town." He slapped a cloth cap on his head and jerked open the back door.

"Robbie!" Meg watched from the open doorway as he took off at a run. She clenched her fists at her sides. This was no lark. He was going to meet a gang of lads from his school who had been issued a challenge from another gang. Patriots against Loyalists. Just like their fathers. This town was ready to split right down the middle. Their neighborhood leaned Loyalist, and it was making life difficult for her youngest brother. For all of them. Hadn't Mother's garden club already divided along the same lines? And Father lost another contract just this week to a family who avowed their fealty to the Crown.

Hoofbeats stopped her from closing the door. Jamie and Andrew rode into the yard. Meg rushed out to meet them.

"Robbie just left." She pointed the direction he'd gone. "He has gone to join a fight."

"What fight?" Jamie asked.

"A gang of Loyalist lads from school has issued a challenge."

Andrew dismounted. " 'Tis just the way with lads at school."

She gripped his sleeve. "I think not this time. If you had seen him. . ."

"Come on, Andrew. I think I know where they will meet." Jamie looked down at her. "Do not worry yourself. We shall look out for him."

"Thank you."

Andrew grumbled but mounted on his horse. Jamie touched the brim of his hat and winked at her. Satisfied she'd done the right thing, she turned back to the house. She wouldn't tell Mother now. Not with Jamie and Andrew taking care of things. No sense getting her youngest brother into even more trouble.

⸏

The noise reached Alexander above the *clip-clop* of the team's hooves and the jingle of their harnesses. It sounded like the screech of a flock of crows in the distance, but then voices emerged above the din. Several young men crossed the street in front of him, another ran past his wagon. He kept the team at a slow trot but tightened his grip on the reins.

When he turned down the same street the young men had run to, two streets short of the McCrackens' house, bedlam spread out before him. His team pranced and tossed their heads at the noise and commotion. He pulled them to a halt.

A mob swarmed the street, lads who couldn't be more than twelve years old fought beside—and against—men his age and more. Clubs, branches, even broken bottles were swung as weapons. The mob surged toward him.

Da's horses danced in place until Alexander backed them up, intending to drive around another way to the Wetherills'. He managed to get the animals back to the crossroad when a lad came pelting across the street, his cap flying from his brown mop of hair and landing in front of the team.

Robbie McCracken.

With a growl in his throat, Alexander set the brake and tied the reins to the handle. The team wouldn't get far trying to drag the wagon with its heavy load. He glanced in the back and grabbed the crowbar.

"Robbie, wait!" He leaped free of the buckboard, but the lad was already too far away to hear him above the noise. Alexander ran after him, the boy's hair waving like a flag for him to follow into the crowd.

Pushing his way through, Alexander grunted when someone

planted a fist in his side. He shoved the offender, nearly tall enough to look him in the eye, into another man who rushed toward him with a club in his hand. He caught the club, twisted it away from the man, and tossed it aside.

What was this madness?

He caught sight of Robbie again, leaping into the fray with a half circle of lads his own age. The line of men facing them were both older and greater in number. No good could come of that. Another fist collided with Alexander's jaw and half spun him around. He jabbed back with the rounded end of his crowbar and heard the gasp as it drove the air from whoever had hit him.

He stayed focused on reaching Robbie's side. Already several of the young lads had fallen and lay writhing on the ground. Before Alexander could reach him, someone brought a club down on Robbie's bare head. He went down like a bag of wet sand.

"No!" Alexander shoved his way to the lad and stood over the top of him, wielding his crowbar like a scythe. He couldn't stop to check on the lad, but he could keep these hooligans from running him over or hitting him again.

"Robbie? Can you hear me?"

Nothing. Sweat broke across Alexander's brow and trickled down his back. He swung the crowbar and knocked a club from an attacker's hand. When the small man rushed him, Alexander grabbed him by the front of his coat and heaved him into the crowd. A space opened up around Alexander and Robbie.

"Robbie!"

Alexander whirled at the person calling Robbie's name and raised his crowbar, only to lower it slightly when he recognized Jamie leaping from his horse. The frightened animal bolted away.

Jamie skidded to a halt. "You are the blacksmith, are you not?"

"I am."

"Stand aside while I check on Robbie. And keep these fellows off my back, if you would."

"Gladly."

Another man pushed through the crowd toward them. Alexander stepped in front of Jamie as he knelt beside Robbie, and twirled his crowbar in readiness.

"He is my brother," the man shouted.

Jamie lifted his head. "That's Andrew."

"Who is the Viking with the crowbar?" Andrew took a hesitant step toward them.

"You can meet Meg's blacksmith later," Jamie said. "We need to get Robbie home. Now."

Meg's blacksmith. Alexander liked the sound of that. "I have a buckboard at the end of the street."

"You two clear a path," Jamie said.

Alexander nodded at Andrew, and they bracketed Jamie as he carried Robbie from the fray. They were almost to the edge of the crowd when a gunshot rang through the air.

"Hurry!" Jamie shouted.

They broke free and sprinted for the buckboard. Alexander vaulted onto the seat and untied the team. It took all his strength to hold them while the other two lifted Robbie into the back beside the gates and climbed in after him.

Alexander unlocked the brake, turned the team, and let them have their heads. The pair pounded down the street in a barely controlled panic. They took the turn onto the McCrackens' street as Alexander battled to bring the horses under control. He turned them up the McCrackens' drive and pulled them to a stop by the front door.

The door burst open and Mr. McCracken rushed onto the porch.

"What is going on?"

" 'Tis Robbie, he has been injured." Jamie jumped from the

buckboard, and Andrew handed him the limp form of their brother.

Mr. McCracken, his face drained of color, stood aside and let Jamie pass. He stopped Andrew with one hand. "Your horses just returned. I was coming to look for you." He pointed to his horse at the hitching rail. "Take my mount and fetch the doctor."

"We shall take the buckboard." Alexander met Mr. McCracken's gaze. The older man blinked, recognition setting in. "Hurry."

Andrew scrambled up beside him as Mr. McCracken disappeared into the house.

"Doctor Barlow lives on—"

"I know the place." Alexander slapped the reins over the team's backs, and they shot down the drive and careened into the street.

"Have a care, man. We need to return with the doctor in one piece."

Alexander gave the horses another slap and gritted his teeth. The lad hadn't moved since he was hit. They couldn't get to the doctor soon enough.

It was Meg's little brother.

⇌

Meg waited in the hallway at the base of the stairs where she could see the front door. She didn't want to be far from Robbie's bedroom where he lay in that unnatural stillness, the blanket over him barely rising as proof that he still breathed. But Alexander was bringing the doctor. She must see him and thank him for what he'd done.

Jamie had told them about the riot in the street. How he and Andrew had found Robbie already on the ground with Alexander standing over him, protecting him. Then how he'd driven like a wild man to get them home.

Tears welled in her eyes.

Her heart jolted at the sound of the team pounding up the front drive. She ran to the front door and tore it open. Andrew helped Dr.

Barlow from the buckboard. The poor man's hat was in his hand, wig askew on his head. She stood aside as Andrew hustled the doctor in.

Then she faced Alexander. He stood beside the lathered team. His coat torn, his hat missing, his jaw swollen and beginning to darken into a bruise.

He looked perfect to her.

She half ran, half slipped down the steps. He caught her at the bottom. She threw her arms around his waist, buried her face against his waistcoat, and sobbed.

"There now, lass." He put his arms around her shoulders.

"Robbie has not moved."

"The doctor will do all he can."

"I know." She wiped her sleeve across her face in a manner her mother would soundly disapprove of. "But he is my little brother."

"Aye."

She leaned back, still in the circle of his arms, and looked into his tawny eyes. "You protected him. You brought him back to us. Even if—" Her voice broke. She sniffed and tried again. "Even if we lose him, I shall forever be grateful to you for what you did."

"I only wish I could have reached him sooner. Before he took the hit."

"Come in the house."

"I cannot. The team. I have put them through much, and I need to care for them now."

Steam rolled in waves off the animals' sweaty backs.

"But you shall return?"

"Tomorrow."

"Promise?"

"Nothing could keep me away."

Which was a good thing, because nothing was going to keep Meg from loving this gentle giant of a man.

Chapter 11

Meg awoke to the sound of birds chirping outside her bedroom window, the sun's first rays peeking in, and the scent of bacon wafting up the stairs. Like any other morning. . .until the memories came crashing back.

"Robbie."

She threw back the covers and grabbed her dressing gown before dashing down the hallway, her bare feet slapping on the polished wooden floor. Robbie's door stood open, and she lurched to a halt outside. Her father held up his hand in a plea for her silence. Mother sat in a chair beside Robbie's bed. She leaned over the mattress, her head pillowed on one arm, her other hand holding Robbie's. Father rose from his chair across the room and met Meg in the hallway.

"How is he?"

"He is breathing a little easier."

"Has he. . ."

"Not yet. But the doctor did not expect he would come around until today, if then."

Or at all. He didn't say it, but she could see the truth in his eyes. Eyes that looked much older than they had yesterday. They matched the haggard lines drawn deep in his face, covered in gray stubble. He looked. . .old.

She hugged him, her face pressed against the side of his neck. "I love you, Father."

His arms tightened around her until she feared for her next breath. "Daughter, you mean the world to me."

He loosened his hold when Mother yawned and sat up to rub her eyes.

"Would you fetch your mother some tea? Have Cook brew some of the real tea, if there's any left."

Meg nodded. She stopped by her bedroom for a pair of slippers before heading down the stairs. Alexander said he'd be back. Her heart skittered beneath her dressing gown. She'd better hurry.

⌒

Alexander nudged Asa into a lope. The morning sun crested the trees, shining in his face. A hopeful sight. Would he find anything hopeful when he reached Meg's house? Robbie's limp form had haunted his dreams. Why hadn't he reached the lad sooner?

Meg's arms around him last night had filled him with awe. He loved her. He'd wanted to tell her that, but it wasn't the time. In three days, he'd leave for Virginia. There would be no waiting if he was to meet Daniel Boone when and where they'd agreed. Time was a luxury he didn't have.

He rode to the front door and tethered Asa at the hitching rail. Halfway up the steps, the door opened.

"I knew you would return someday, blacksmith, but I have to say, I did not want it to be under circumstances like these." David stepped aside and waved him into the hall.

"Robbie?"

"No better, but no worse either. According to Jamie, we have you to thank for that."

"I did not do enough. I did not reach him before he fell."

David thumped him on the back. "You were there and did what you could. I will—we will—always be grateful for that." He pointed down the hall. "Someone is waiting for you in the parlor."

David led the way to an open door and entered before him.

Meg stood by a tall window, the morning sun surrounding her, its glow a perfect backdrop for her fiery hair. She smiled when he entered and came across the room, but worry lines etched the corners of her eyes.

"I'm sorry about Robbie."

"I'm glad you came."

"I said I would."

"Indeed."

He wanted to say more. Her eyes told him she did as well.

David sat on the settee. "Have a seat, black—" He coughed a hollow laugh. "I cannot keep calling you blacksmith."

"Ogilvie. Alexander Ogilvie." Alexander took a seat on one of the dainty chairs and hoped it would hold his weight, although none of the McCracken men were small.

Meg sank into the matching chair. "We cannot thank you enough for what you did last evening."

Heat crept from under Alexander's collar. They wanted to make him out to be a hero, but he wasn't. "I wish I would have been in time."

"Trust me, we are all kicking ourselves about that." David leaned forward. "How did you happen to be there?"

"I was making a delivery to a house down the street."

Meg reached across the distance and laid her hand on his arm. "God put you where we needed you."

"My daughter is correct." Callum McCracken entered the room. His haggard face still bore the authority of the laird he might have been. "We owe you a debt we can never repay."

"You owe me nothing."

Meg didn't remove her hand, and her father noticed. His forceful look swung from Alexander to Meg and back again. "Today is not the day to renew our conversation from last fall. We will revisit it at another time."

Alexander stood. "I am leaving Monday morning. I meet Daniel Boone and his company in Virginia. We begin our journey to build a road over the mountains on March first."

A soft gasp came from Meg.

"Time is, indeed, very short then." Callum ran his hand over his gray hair, leaving it more disheveled than before.

"Father, come quickly!" The call was followed by footsteps pounding down the stairs. Jamie skidded into the doorway of the parlor. "He is awake!"

Meg's father and brothers rushed the door, but Meg stopped and grabbed Alexander's hand, tugging him forward.

"Nay, lass. Go and be with your family."

"You must come. You probably saved his life."

" 'Tis a time for family. Go. I shall return later."

"When?"

"This afternoon."

"Promise?" Her eyes filled with tears, a mixture of relief and joy sparkling through them.

"You are a lass who likes her promises."

"Because I know you are a man who keeps them."

The faith that shown from her eyes—faith in him—humbled him. "Aye."

He watched her scamper up the stairs behind her brothers, their father already gone into a room above. She looked back once, twice, and then disappeared behind a door. He sighed and left. He'd be back, like he said, and he'd get an answer. But would it be the one his heart desperately wanted?

Dare he hope?

$$\rightleftharpoons$$

Meg sat beside Robbie's bed, unwilling to leave for fear he might slip away again.

"They say he saved my life." Robbie's voice, although weak, was filled with awe. "Jamie said he stood over me like a Viking of old, swinging a crowbar and felling Loyalists like cordwood."

"Jamie has been known to enlarge a tale from time to time." Meg rinsed a clean cloth in cool water and placed it on the discolored lump that encompassed too much of his forehead. " 'Tis a good thing you are a hardheaded McCracken. A lesser man would not have survived such a blow." Pride in her family warmed her soul.

Robbie winced as the cloth touched his skin. He grabbed her hand. "They should let you marry him, you know. He is a man who can protect you, provide well for you. Even I can see he is in love with you."

Meg brushed her free hand across her heated cheeks. Such a conversation to have with her little brother. Not little. Not anymore. She squeezed his hand. "I believe you are correct."

"Do you love him?"

She dropped his hand and stood. "Such a thing to ask."

"Jamie says he is leaving on Monday. There is no time to be undecided."

"Jamie talks too much."

"I do not want you to go, really, but on the other hand, after the war, after we whip the British and send them packing back across the ocean, I would not mind seeing Kentucke."

His sheepish grin was her undoing, but her laughter was cut short by a knock at the front door.

"He's here." Robbie struggled to sit.

She pushed him back while her mouth dried and her heartbeat thundered. "You lie still."

"You will come straight back and tell me what happens, will you not?"

Voices drifted up. Alexander. Her father. Jamie. She patted Robbie's hand and then stood. "I have no doubt Jamie will beat me to it."

One hand pressed to her middle to stop the battle of nerves dancing there, she left the room and descended the stairs. The door to the parlor remained open, and from the voices, everyone but Robbie must have been in there. She pressed both hands to her stomach and breathed in through her nose. Back straight, she walked into the room. Every eye turned to her, but it was Alexander's she sought. He was there. Tall and handsome, solid and dependable as an oak.

"Come in, daughter." Father held a hand out to her, and when she took it, he drew her to his side. "This young man has come to ask my permission to court—nay—to marry you. To marry you Monday morning."

Her stomach lurched and settled as her heart raced. She stared at the toes of her shoes and felt the weight of her brothers' eyes on her. Mother came along her other side and wrapped her arm around Meg's shoulder.

"This is not the way I would wish for you to leave us, my daughter." Mother's voice wobbled on the last word.

"Nor must you, you understand." Father squeezed her hand. "Your mother and I will support your decision. But the choice is yours."

Mother nodded and smiled, no sign of disapproval on her face.

Meg scanned the room. Jamie winked at her. David gave a nod. Andrew grinned. She could almost feel Robbie's support from the room upstairs. At last she looked into the tawny depth of Alexander's eyes. What burned there needed no words, although she'd expect to hear them later, once they were alone. She tipped her chin down while her eyes remained locked with his, unable to stop the smile that pulled at her lips.

He answered with a dazzling display of white that caused her breath to catch. How could one man be so handsome?

He held out his hand. As she'd seen so often between her parents, there was no need for words.

She slipped hers into it.

He drew her to his side.

She turned to face her parents.

Father nodded while Mother wiped a tear from her lashes.

"This young man has proven himself worthy." Father looked at her brothers. "The war will be upon us soon. We cannot know what that will mean for any of us. Your mother and I have chosen to support the Patriot cause. If we lose. . ." He held up his hand to stop any forthcoming debate. "If we lose the war, we lose everything. The house, the money, perhaps our very lives. With this uncertainty hanging over our house, I give my blessing for Meg to marry Alexander and secure a future across the mountains. Perhaps for all of us."

Meg choked back tears as her brothers surged forward to pound Alexander on the back. Mother wrapped her in a hug. Father's eyes glistened, from pride she was sure, but maybe a touch of sadness as well. Then he pulled Mother back to his side.

"I believe Robbie will want to know what has happened. Your mother and I shall go tell him." He cleared his throat and lifted one gray eyebrow at his sons. "I'm sure you lads all have something to do?"

Jostling and laughter filled the parlor and spilled into the hall until Father closed the door behind them with a soft click.

It was just the two of them. Alexander took her hands and looked into her eyes. "I'm a man of few words."

"There are some a woman needs to hear." If she could hear anything over the pounding in her chest.

"Aye."

A shaky laugh tumbled from her throat. "That is not one of them."

His laughter rumbled in his chest. "I think I fell in love with you the second time you visited the smithy. The first time I heard you laugh."

"I think I started to fall in love with you that day at the riverbank when I fell in the mud. You laughed, but only after I did first."

"Well then." His fingers tightened around hers. He drew her closer. "May we build a life together that will be filled with love and laughter."

"Mr. Ogilvie, do you not have something you wish to ask me?" She wasn't going to let him off the hook.

"Aye." He knelt in front of her, their hands still twined together. "Mistress McCracken, would you do me the honor of becoming my bride?"

"Indeed I will, Mr. Ogilvie. Indeed I will."

He stood and his arms came around her.

As her mother and father had joined together and traveled to a distant land, so would she and Alexander. Her dream had come true despite the coming war.

She lifted her face as he lowered his. His eyes, hooded by thick lashes, took on a smoky hue. He pressed his forehead against hers and sighed. She slid her hands up the front of his coat and let her fingers graze the smooth hairs at the nape of this neck. His lips met hers. It felt like coming home.

Whatever lay before them in the wilderness of Kentucke, they would meet it together, with love and laughter.

Author's Note

The city of Philadelphia was a city divided. We often think of our staunch Patriots, but there were as many—if not more—Loyalists living there. The Intolerable Acts passed in early 1774 made British-made goods hard to come by in the colonies, including tea and textiles. Benjamin Franklin's wife died in late 1774 while he was stationed in England to try and keep the peace. He moved back to Philadelphia later that year. Samuel Wetherill, a strong supporter of the Patriot cause, was a Quaker and a businessman in Philadelphia. He was expelled from the Quakers and helped to found a new sect called the Free Quakers or Fighting Quakers. Daniel Boone blazed the Wilderness Road in the spring of 1775.

Pegg Thomas lives on a hobby farm in northern Michigan with Michael, her husband of *mumble* years. A lifelong history geek, she writes "History with a Touch of Humor." When not working on her latest novel, Pegg can be found in her garden, in her kitchen, with her sheep, at her spinning wheel, or on her trusty old horse, Trooper. See more at PeggThomas.com.

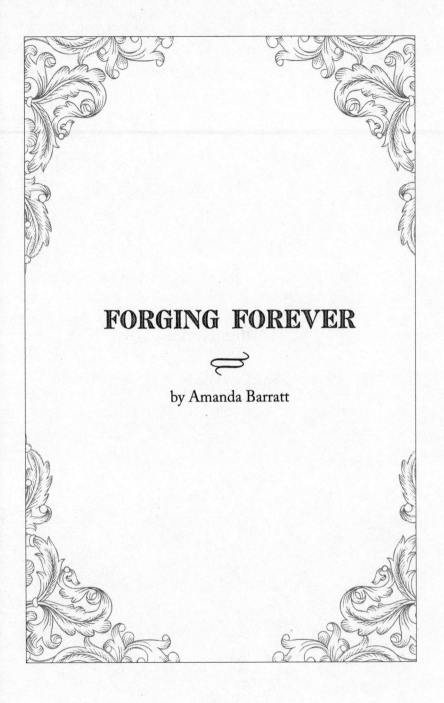

FORGING FOREVER

by Amanda Barratt

Dedication

Soli Deo Gloria.

Chapter 1

Breath rasped from Charles Bainbridge's lips, the cadence of each fading tendril indicating his departure from this world would not be long in coming.

Josiah Hendrick studied the face of the man lying in the middle of the immense bed. Bluish veins stood out against the translucent pallor of his flesh, the creases of his cracked lips lined in blood. One beholding him would think him aged well beyond his three score and ten.

A testament to death's power to sap all resemblance of what a man used to be.

The note delivered to the forge this morning, written in the maid-servant's uneven lettering, bid him hasten to Bainbridge Park, as its master was asking for him. Josiah had washed away the grime of the smithy and ridden as fast as he could, praying he'd not be too late.

"Charles." He leaned forward, close to the bed. "It's Josiah. I'm here, just as you asked."

At first, nothing. Then his eyelids flickered. Fluttered. "Josiah." The word was a gasp. "You came, my boy."

"Of course. Of course I did."

In the semidarkness of the chamber, a hint of a smile touched Charles's lips. "I. . .have something for you."

"I need nothing. Your friendship has always been—"

"A paper. On the table. Bring it to me." He made a weak motion toward the low table against the wall. Josiah stood and went to it. It held the stub of a candle in a silver holder, an array of bottles containing remedies that had proven powerless to effect a cure, and a folded piece of parchment. Josiah took it up, brought it with him back to his seat. Charles's gaze fell on it.

"Open it."

Josiah unfolded the paper and smoothed it on his knee. "Shall I read it aloud?"

"No. Read it yourself. . .quickly."

He scanned the lines. His breath caught. He raised his gaze to Charles. " 'Tis a deed for a share in Wheal Prosper. Yours."

"No, boy." Charles swallowed, the sound of it thick. "Yours."

"Mine?" Josiah frowned. "I—I don't understand."

"I'm giving it to you. You must. . .sign the deed."

"To me? But why?" He was not this man's heir. Of no connection save a long and abiding friendship. He'd no right to such a gift, a share in a profitable mine, worth upward of two hundred pounds.

"Because I'll not see it fall into the hands of that wastrel, Phineas." A spark of the man Charles Bainbridge had been before consumption eroded his lungs—a firebrand of energy, good humor, and determination—entered the dying man's voice. "And because you've a right to it. 'Tis your mine, boy."

"It *was* my father's. Once. Those days are long gone." Josiah stared at the paper, fine black script against yellowed parchment.

"Don't tell me you've not often rued the fact. I may be choking on my own blood, but I've not forgotten the past." A hint of color stained Charles's cheeks, and his voice grew stronger. " 'Tis a stake in what should have been rightfully yours. More than that, it transfers the share to someone other than Phineas. My estate is regrettably entailed to him, and I'll not have him receive a tuppence more than what's legally his due. That insolent puppy owns too much of Prosper as it is. What's needed in those shareholder meetings is a strong man with a desire to further the good of more than his own purse." A cough spasmed his body.

Alarm escalating, Josiah rang the bell to summon the servant, then poured water from a pitcher into a glass. He raised Charles's head, trying to help him drink, but the dying man shook his head. Blood trickled from the corners of his mouth, standing stark against the bed linens. "No," he choked. "Leave it."

The maidservant, a woman named Sarah, hastened in and rounded the side of the bed, gaze on Josiah. "Should we send for Dr. Creighton?"

Charles grimaced. "I've had enough of that man and his leeches. Can't an old man die in peace? Fetch my writing desk, girl. Be quick about it."

Sarah scuttled away, closing the door behind her. Charles lay back against the pillows. Silence fell, save for the ticking of the mantel clock, the snap of the fire in the hearth, and Charles's labored breathing. Hands on his knees, Josiah stared at the clock as the minute hand chipped away. It measured time, but not a life. None but God held power over the number of a mortal's days. Humans only owned so much control.

Sitting at three deathbeds in his thirty-one years had taught him those truths well.

The door opened, and Sarah returned. Charles roused enough to motion for the girl to hand the lap desk to Josiah. Josiah thanked her with a faint smile. "Leave us," Charles rasped.

The door shut. Josiah balanced the desk on his lap, the fine sheen of the wood beneath his calloused fingers.

"Charles, I cannot accept this. 'Tis too much—"

"Would you deny an old man the privilege of resting peacefully in his final hours, knowing his affairs are set in order?" Charles wore the same look as when he used to splay his cards upon the table knowing he had the winning hand.

Josiah shook his head. "Nay, but—"

"Then let me do this thing for you. Goodness knows your friendship has been a gift to me."

"As yours has been to me." The magnitude of both—this friendship and the gift—overwhelmed him. In the eyes of society, he, a mere blacksmith, merited neither.

He'd been blessed by the former. Did he dare accept the latter? It lured him, tempting, and not only for Charles's sake.

"Sign it. I've already done so."

Josiah opened the hinged lap desk. Loose papers filled its depths, the scent of wood and ink, his senses. He took out a sharpened quill and ink pot. Quill in hand, the deed on the desktop, he regarded his friend, lying prone on the bed, face nearly as pale as the nightshirt swathing his wasted frame. A glimmer of determination shone in his gaze.

"Sign it," Charles repeated. "Show Phineas who's master. Be the man you should have become."

Josiah's hand shook as he dipped the quill in ink. Slowly, he formed a *J* in the fine hand he'd been tutored in as a boy. The quill scratched as he wrote the rest. He blotted the signature.

"Done?"

He nodded. "Aye, sir."

"Good." A ghost of a smile edged Charles's lips. "You'll do me proud, boy."

And what of Phineas Trevenick? When he discovers his cousin has gifted me a share in the most prosperous of the Trevenick mines? When he is forced to grant me admittance to shareholder meetings? Can I bear sitting at the same table as the man who stole almost everything from me?

He must bear it. Hadn't he, in hidden moments he'd never have voiced aloud, imagined such a thing coming to pass? A sort of justice. A restoration of his birthright.

Though it wasn't what they'd once had, 'twas a kind of renewal. Wheal Prosper would never again belong to the Hendrick family. His father had forfeited that right in a desperation-fueled decision made on the turn of a card. He'd lost. Phineas's father won. Now, both men were dead. And their sons' lives couldn't be more different.

Josiah reached across and clasped a hand over his friend's. This same hand had held his at the age of twelve, guiding him in how to shoot a pistol, been a steadying presence on his shoulder at his father's funeral, lifted many a glass of canary in salute as they whiled away winter evenings to the tune of backgammon and firelight.

"*To perdition with polite society!*" Charles would bellow, downing the glass.

Now, the fingers were limp, the flesh clammy. Then almost imperceptibly, Charles squeezed back.

Josiah's throat tightened. "Thank you."

Their gazes held, man to man. Friend to friend. In the bedchamber, as shadows cloaked the room and twilight fell, Charles whispered words so low Josiah had to strain to hear them. But their impact settled within him and lingered long after he left Charles slipping in and out of consciousness, Bainbridge Park in the clutches of nightfall.

"*Make it count, boy.*"

Chapter 2

Cornwall, England
August 1798

Elowyn Brody followed her father through Launcegrave's wind-ing, close-set streets, breathless at the pace he set. Her stays pinched her waist, tendrils of hair falling loose around her face, her cheeks flushed.

Tradespeople hawked their wares with shrill cries of "Five for six-pence, pilchards!" and "Eggs, fresh eggs!" Women in serviceable grays and browns bore brimming market baskets from stall to shop, stopping now and then to exchange greetings or gossip. Children clung to moth-ers' hands round-eyed, or scampered toward the Punch and Judy show set up in front of a brightly decorated wagon. Men ambled from the swinging door of a public house bearing the name the Eagle's Head.

Her father strode through the village with a rare purpose, his steps, for once, unimpaired by the stagger of drink. He'd woken her hours before dawn, and they'd hurried through the black, cold night, path lit by the lantern in his hand. Sunlight had replaced the earlier chill, but she still wore her cloak, frayed ribbon knotted at her throat, the brown fabric threadbare and faded. Not that she cared. What use had she for a fine cloak, or a fine anything? All she sought was enough food to keep her stomach from gnawing emptiness and a roof over her head that didn't leak every time the sky so much as thought of rain.

Beautiful things were for those with lives to match. And any dreams of a life different than the one she possessed had all but died. Fancies made for miserable bedfellows.

"Where are we going?" She ventured the question now that they'd reached Launcegrave. She'd naught to fear from him with the crowd all around. Even he would not strike her in public.

"Ye'll see soon enough," was his only reply.

He'd brought nothing with him, as far as she could see. Perhaps if he'd something of value to sell, 'twas hidden in a pouch in his pocket. Or did he intend to seek out work in the town?

Nay. That notion seemed too good to be true. Launcegrave appeared a place more prosperous than Fawley, the smaller village an hour's walk from the cottage she called home. The majority of Fawley's occupants were no stranger to hunger and privation. Wheal Hervey might pay wages, but the pittance offered scarce deserved the name.

Sheep milled about in an enclosure in the main square. A throng of men were gathered round, listening to the auctioneer, who stood above the crowd on a raised wooden platform.

"Do I hear ten guineas? Ten guineas and sixpence?"

Her father stopped on the outskirts as the bidding went on.

Did he intend to purchase something? They'd no coin, not even enough for a meal of bread and cheese at a public house. She'd used their last few shillings a fortnight ago, when she'd bought flour in Fawley for bread to supplement the vegetables she grew. She'd earned the coins by taking in washing, and had hidden them in a hole in her straw mattress so her father wouldn't spend them on gin. Since losing his job at Wheal Hervey six months prior, he seemed more than content to let her earn their crust. He'd oft voiced his wish that she marry, so her husband might support them both, but the only suitor she'd ever had was Jonas Mason, and she refused to wed a man of sixty. What he lacked in teeth he made up in girth. And temper, so gossip said. Better the daughter of a wastrel than the wife of a man of cruel disposition.

She tugged on her father's sleeve to ask why he bided here, but he scarce heeded her, gaze on the auctioneer. The sheep were finally sold, followed by a mare and then her foal. Her gaze followed the foal as it was led away by a burly man. Hopefully its owner treated his animals well. The foal's glossy black coat shone in a shaft of sunlight. She read the skittishness in its eyes. Poor dear. Who could blame its fear at finding itself separated from its mother and sold to a new master?

"Well, that appears to be all for today, gentl'men," called the auctioneer.

Fingers tightened around her arm as her father made his way toward the front, pulling her along with him. She stumbled over the hem of her dress, but his bruising grip gave her no choice but to follow, half dragged through the press of men.

"Auctioneer." His booming voice startled her as they stopped before the man in the yellow silk waistcoat and high-crowned hat.

"Yes?" The auctioneer stepped to the edge of the platform. "Have you something to sell?"

"That I do, sir." He gave her a push forward. She stumbled.

"I beg your pardon?" The auctioneer's forehead creased.

"The girl. My daughter."

Her breath caught. She blinked, looking from her father to the auctioneer.

"What do you mean?" He came down the steps, gaze narrowed.

"I mean I wish to offer my daughter for sale to the highest bidder. She's a comely girl, a hard worker. Make anyone a suitable servant, even a wife." Her father's tone was matter-of-fact, his gaze on the auctioneer.

"Nay." The word rasped out. Panic scrambled in her chest. "He does not mean—"

Finally, he looked at her. Determination glinted sharp in his gaze, his weathered face unyielding.

Her stomach clenched. He couldn't be serious. This was a jest. A cruel one, but a joke nonetheless. In a moment, he'd turn to her and laugh that great bellow of his, and they'd continue on their way.

The ripple of conversation at her back increased.

"Stop!" She grabbed her father's coat, making him face her. "You don't mean this. You know you don't."

"How many times do I have to say it, girl? Yer no good to me. Ye refuse to wed Jonas Mason, and because of yer obstinacy have strapped me with the financial burden of yer bed and board. I'll stand for it no longer. Wife, maid, or whatever else they like to do with ye, ye'll not be my concern after today."

Her throat tightened like a fist strangled it. She'd never seen such a cold gaze. She turned to the auctioneer, praying, willing him to stop this madness.

"He can't do this." She forced the words past the grip round her throat. She wanted them to come loud, forceful, but they emerged barely above a whisper.

The auctioneer glanced between the two of them. He looked neither astonished nor horrified, simply perplexed. He rubbed his thumb across the scruff of his chin.

"This is most irregular."

"It's within my rights." Her father crossed his arms. "The girl is but eighteen. I've heard tell of men ridding themselves of wives in this very way. Why may I not do the same for a daughter? If ye'll not do it, I'll hold the auction here and now meself. But if ye do, ye'll get a share of the profits."

Her pulse roared in her ears.

Dear God, please, this can't be happening. This is a nightmare. I'll wake up soon. Dear God, let me wake up. She pressed her nails into the flesh of her palms, as if the pain might jolt her from slumber. But the sensation barely penetrated. And her surroundings remained as vivid as before.

"Very well then." The auctioneer took hold of her elbow.

"A moment, pray." She lifted her chin and met her father's gaze square-on. Hoping to find some shred of compassion there, a hint that this was her flesh and blood, the man who'd given her life. "If you do this thing, you'll not see me again. Ever. I'll be dead to you. Is that what you want?" Her voice broke a little.

His eyes, meeting hers—or rather, looking through her—were naught but stone. "Get on with it."

"Come along now." The auctioneer pulled her up with him onto the platform. Her breath shuddered in and out. Shame seared her cheeks as she faced the crowd. Mostly men, a few women. They regarded her with interest, whispering amongst themselves, gesturing. At the front of the crowd, her father folded his arms.

Would no one save her?

I'm a person, she wanted to shout. *Not an animal. Won't a one of you stop this?*

Still awaiting transport, the sheep bumped into one another in the pen and bleated. She stared at them, their gray bodies a blur. Bits of straw scattered the ground.

"Hurry along, auctioneer," a squat-chested man in the front called. "Let's see what a fine piece of flesh is worth."

Ribald laughter followed this remark.

There was no escape.

The auctioneer nudged her forward, so she stood in the center of the small platform. Wind blew tendrils of hair into her eyes, carrying with it the scent of offal and straw and sheep. She hugged her arms across her chest, drawing into herself. She would not cry. Not in front of this crowd that grew by the minute, as if news had spread like putrid throat throughout the village.

"Who will make an offer for this girl?" The auctioneer's voice echoed through the square.

Her eyes fell closed as a single tear slid unbidden down her cheek. *Dear God, deliver me.*

⌐⌐

He'd witnessed enough of the baseness to which humanity could stoop to make him oft wish to leave all mortals behind and live at peace in some deserted place.

But in all his days, Josiah had never thought to behold this.

He'd come to Launcegrave to deliver a kettle, receive payment, and purchase a few supplies at the market. He'd walked by the auction because Farmer Dudley was to sell his foal today, and Josiah was curious to see what price the fine animal would take.

Now. . .this. A girl. Forced onto the block by a man he didn't recognize and Mr. Fulkerth, the auctioneer, a man who'd sell his own mother if he thought he'd get a goodly commission for the job.

The girl stood in the center of the platform, arms hugged across her chest. Her height was only scant inches below Fulkerth's, but the way she drew her body into herself made her seem small. Fragile. Hair the color of honey fell in tangles around her face. Something glistened on her cheek. A tear. Josiah expected her to swipe it away, but she left it there, as if too spent to notice or care.

His heart clenched.

Surely this could not be legal. Permissible. Of course, the slave trade did exist, though he'd heard of a politician in Parliament doing his level best to get the barbaric practice abolished. But this was an Englishwoman of tender years.

The root of the matter. She was a girl. By law, the man's property, whether the man who'd brought her to Fulkerth was her father or husband.

A man could do what he pleased with his own property. Be it house, animal, or woman.

There wasn't a thing Josiah could do to stop it.

"Do I hear five guineas?"

In the middle of the crowd, men a shifting wave around him, Josiah glanced to see who bid. Several lifted their hands. He recognized most.

His fingers curled into a fist. They ought to be ashamed.

"Six guineas. Do I hear six? Seven guineas. Look at that hair." Fulkerth lifted a strand off her neck, pinching it between his fingers, the ends fluttering in the breeze. "Like gold silk, 'tis."

He expected her to shrink from the touch, but she stood, arms crossed, body motionless.

"I'll not part with her for less than ten," called a voice from the front. "She's a hard worker. Docile to yer bidding. A man would not find a better servant. Or wife."

"Do I hear ten guineas?"

Jeremy Wakely, the proprietor of the Three Swans, lifted his hand. Likely, the man wished for a servant at his inn, since he was happily wed to an attractive wife.

Would the young woman be safe in Wakely's employ?

"We have ten guineas. Do I hear eleven?"

The girl stayed motionless, gaze blank. As if she'd winged her soul elsewhere, leaving only her body behind.

Another man raised his hand, upping the bid.

"Good day, Hendrick." The voice—like hot tallow—sluiced over him.

He flicked a glance, all too aware of whom he'd see. Phineas Trevenick stood at his elbow, fingering the handle of his silver-tipped walking stick. Everything, from his beaver hat, to the intricate folds of his snowy cravat, to the sheen of his black leather boots, was the definition of dandified fashion. Surprising the man would dirty the soles of said boots to take in a public auction. Beside him stood Sam Byng, his manservant. Shadow, more like.

"Trevenick." Josiah's father had taught him to nod in deference to his betters, but he wouldn't acknowledge Trevenick any more than he absolutely must. He fixed his gaze on the auction as the bidding upped to twelve guineas.

"Interesting proceedings. I can't recall having seen the like before. Have you?"

Josiah said nothing. He curled his fingers at his sides, tempted to walk away and leave this wretched spectacle behind.

But he couldn't. Not until he was assured the young woman would be safe.

Somehow, though he didn't know her, a desire to protect her rose within him.

"She's a deuced pretty bit of muslin." Trevenick's remark sent a curl of disgust down Josiah's back. He dragged in a breath.

The bidding rose to thirteen.

"She is at that," Byng muttered.

"Pay what you must, Byng. It won't take more than a few guineas to outbid these Johnny raws. I've a wish to have her."

A cold sickness noosed Josiah's stomach.

In an instant, the memories rose to the surface. The paleness of her skin as her life ebbed out with her will. Mary's last, gasped-out words, her thready grip clinging to his, her eyes rolled back in their sockets.

What might our life have been, I wonder? Without him in it.

The weight of her day-old child in his arms, the babe's body stiff and cold. Following its mother after only hours, too frail and small to stand a chance. Josiah's shoulders shaking with silent sobs as he stood at the foot of the bed of his dead wife, holding her infant daughter in his arms.

"As you say, sir." Byng pushed through the crowd, toward the front.

"Fifteen guineas. Do I hear fifteen?"

Byng raised his hand, six-foot sinewy frame visible above the shifting onlookers.

"What think you, Hendrick? Will she prove a diversion? I've a... desire for one."

Slowly, Josiah turned, meeting Trevenick's gaze. "You disgust me." He gritted out the words.

"I don't see why." Trevenick plucked a speck off the cuff of his coat. "What else is the girl good for? And a man must take his pleasure where he can find it."

A slow heat rose inside Josiah's chest.

Phineas Trevenick had preyed on the defenseless one too many times.

This time, God help him, he could do something about it.

"Thirty guineas," he shouted, raising a hand.

The auctioneer, startled, glanced at him then recovered. Josiah had known the man for years. Many had looked down on the Hendricks when their fortunes had fallen. Fulkerth, himself hardly a gentleman, had been one of them. "We have thirty. Do I hear thirty-five?"

"Thirty-five." From Byng.

"Forty." Josiah's voice rose.

"Forty-five," Byng stated.

"We have forty-five. Do I hear fifty?"

Trevenick chuckled, shaking his head.

Josiah could not outbid Trevenick. None in the county could. The Trevenicks owned two mines, hundreds of acres of land, a town house in London, and an estate in Cornwall. Fortune had favored them second to none.

Bile rose in his throat. Trevenick would win, as he always did. Claim the girl, debauch her as he wished. Josiah could do nothing. Powerless. Again.

The share.

Six months he'd sat in shareholder meetings while Trevenick behaved as if Josiah weren't in the room. He'd reaped profits as the mine flourished, cast his vote when decisions were made, cast it for the benefit of the workers rather than the profit of Trevenick coffers. More than once the man had suggested—if a barely veiled threat could be called thus—it would be wise if Josiah let the Trevenicks buy him out.

He'd declined.

The woman's face swam before him. Even with her face ashen and arms hugged about herself, she was comely. And young. Too young to have her virtue stolen, her life destroyed.

"Make it count, boy." Charles, lying on his deathbed.

"Your goodness could not save me." Mary's grip loosening, going slack and weighted.

The two blended into each other, an echoing cacophony.

"Call off your manservant." He ground out the words.

"What?" Trevenick's eyes widened.

"Do it," he muttered. "I can guarantee it will be to your benefit." He stayed where he was, hands at his sides, while Trevenick cut through the crowd and asked the auctioneer to delay. Of course, Fulkerth did. Who would dare do anything but obey a Trevenick?

Byng and Trevenick returned.

"Well?" Trevenick arched a thin brow.

Josiah swallowed. "I'll sell." He cut his voice low. "Provided you step away here and now. A hundred and fifty pounds for my share in Prosper and your withdrawal from the auction."

Trevenick chuckled, shaking his head. "No."

Shock sluiced through him. *No.* After all the times Trevenick or Byng had cornered him after a meeting...

"A hundred," Trevenick said. "Not a farthing more."

Conversation hummed around them. The two men stared at each other.

The share was worth well over two hundred pounds. Prosper had become one of the best-producing mines in Cornwall.

"A hundred and twenty-five."

Trevenick shook his head. "Byng." He flicked a glance at his man-servant. "Tell Fulkerth to proceed."

"Right away, sir." Byng turned.

"Wait."

Trevenick and Byng stopped.

"I'll meet your terms."

Trevenick inclined his head. "Very well."

Giving himself no time to contemplate what he had just done, Josiah strode through the crowd, toward the front. "Fifty guineas." The words tore from his throat, loud and firm and surprising even himself.

The auctioneer looked askance at him, doubtless wondering at the change in bidders.

"Fifty guineas. Do I hear fifty-one?"

The crowd stayed silent.

Beneath the brim of his tricorn, Josiah fixed his gaze on the girl. She didn't look at him with a spark of hope, a trace of life returning to her eyes. Didn't look at him at all, in fact.

"Going once. Going twice. Sold"—the auctioneer slammed his gavel on the platform railing—"for fifty guineas to the man in the gray coat. That concludes our auction for today."

The crowd shuffled, drifting away.

"What're ye going to do with the woman?" asked a man with protruding, yellow teeth who stood nearby.

"That's none of your concern," Josiah muttered. Ignoring the gazes of all around him, he moved through the crowd. Trevenick and

Byng stood where he'd left them, apart from the rest.

"So the deed's done." Trevenick looked amused, as if the auction had been but a game of loo. "Don't you feel a bit like Esau, Hendrick? Selling your birthright in exchange for a bowl of pottage?"

Byng smirked.

"Payment, please."

"But first, the share." Trevenick held out his palm.

It was only by chance he'd brought the papers today. He'd meant to stop by the office of the attorney his father once employed and pose some legal questions to the man.

Now, there'd be no need.

Josiah withdrew them from his inner coat pocket. For a moment, he stared at the folded documents. So light in his hands. Yet, how he'd prized them and all they stood for.

He shoved aside the emotion rising up. He didn't have the luxury of feeling now.

He handed them to Trevenick, who opened and scanned them. "We'll need to sign a bill of sale." Josiah kept his tone emotionless. "But I've other matters to attend to today. Our agreed-upon price, if you will."

"Of course." Trevenick handed the papers to Byng and reached inside his pocket. He withdrew a leather pouch and passed it to Josiah. "Fifty guineas is all I have with me at present. I'll have the rest sent round to you."

Josiah stiffened, the weight of the pouch heavy in his hand. A half-smile curved Trevenick's lips. The emerald signet on his pinky caught the light and glistened. "Rest assured, you can trust my word as a gentleman."

Josiah pocketed the purse. "Then our business for today is at an end."

"One moment." Trevenick met Josiah's gaze. "What compelled you to do this?" Curiosity flickered through his pale green eyes.

To save an innocent woman as I could not save my wife? To redeem one thing in this mad, broken world?

But he wouldn't give Trevenick the satisfaction of hearing him utter those words.

"I bid you good day." He turned on his heel and strode away, gravel crushing beneath his boots. Around him, the village bustled. Two women who'd been in the crowd eyed him with open curiosity as he passed, their gazes asking questions they were too polite to voice.

He had no answers.

The young woman stood near the auction block. The auctioneer and the man who'd sold her, likely her father, waited nearby. But it was to the girl his gaze went. She stood, hands folded at her waist, the edges of her shabby cloak stirred by the wind, staring straight ahead.

He sucked in a breath as he approached.

God, I know not if what I've done is Your will. I scarce know what I've done at all. But please, I beg of You. . . Guide me in this.

Chapter 3

Stripped in body and soul, she was. As exposed as if she'd been physically undressed upon the block. There was only one thing she could do to shield herself and that was to go numb. Become as one who heard and felt nothing, who did not exist at all.

She stared into emptiness, the street a haze of movement she didn't really see. Breath pushed in and out of her lungs. A tangible sign life still tethered her to this earth.

"Miss?" The voice broke through the blur. Low-spoken. One might even say gentle. And. . .male. The last made her tense, her gaze jerk up.

He stood before her, but a pace away. A sturdy man with a height half a foot above hers. A tricorn topped his dark brown hair, his square jaw unshaven. She lingered on his eyes. Not their color, a blend of brown and green, but their depths. Men might regulate their countenances to put on a convincing show, but their eyes told the truest tale of their character. His did not hold anger, and bespoke the same gentleness as his tone.

"Yes." Her answer emerged as a breath.

"The name's Hendrick, miss. Josiah Hendrick."

"Elowyn Brody." Her voice came surer this time. Why did he approach her?

"Fifty guineas is the agreed-upon price," the auctioneer's voice cut in.

The truth slammed through her. Her breath caught. This man, this Josiah Hendrick, had been the one to. . .purchase her. She'd not noticed the buyer, nor heard the price until now. Fifty guineas. She'd never seen such a sum in all her life.

Her father had done well. Very.

"I have it here." Mr. Hendrick handed a leather coin purse to the auctioneer, who made a show of opening and inspecting it, before turning to the other person standing by. Tom Brody. She'd never again think of him as Father. The auctioneer counted out a few coins for himself, then passed the purse into Tom Brody's hand.

She'd not looked at him since she stood upon the block, but she did now. He pocketed the money in the depths of his loose-fitting brown coat. She'd mended that coat only last week.

The force of his betrayal sliced like a surgeon's knife through flesh.

"Good day to ye then." He bobbed a nod in the auctioneer's direction.

"Not quite." Firmness edged Mr. Hendrick's voice. "I'd like a bill of sale. That way you'll not return and seek her back again."

In the folds of her cloak, she clenched her hands together.

"Aye." Her voice surprised her as much as it did the men. She met Tom Brody's eyes in a direct stare. "There must be a bill of sale. For after this, there will never again be anything between us. Any claim you had on me is yours no more."

A flicker of pain entered his gaze, filling her with a flash of bitter satisfaction. She'd cut him, wounded him as he'd wounded her.

"I've pen and paper here." The auctioneer rounded the small table set near the platform. He nodded to Mr. Hendrick. "Sit yourself down, sir, and write it out."

For long minutes, he bent over the paper, quill scratching against its surface, forehead creased as he paused for a moment to think before he resumed writing. The three of them stood in tense silence, watching. In the distance, a child laughed. Footsteps sounded as townsfolk walked past. The sheep still bumped into one another and bleated in their pen. Doubtless the man who'd bought them was seeking help to herd them home.

Finally, Mr. Hendrick blotted the paper and looked up. "If you'll sign." His tone had gone from gentle to granite in a matter of minutes.

Tom Brody walked round the table. His graying head bent over the page as he dipped the quill into the pot of ink. Elowyn did not have to watch to know what he would do. His crudely formed X would seal the bargain.

Mr. Hendrick blotted the mark then folded the paper. Without another glance or word, Tom Brody turned and walked down the street, shoulders stooped, steps halting as if already impaired by the bottle. She gazed after his retreating form. A cold deadness filled her from the inside. Her heart drummed in her chest as he turned the corner.

He hadn't looked back.

She blinked, a stir of wind stinging her dry eyes.

"That concludes our business for today." She turned at the auctioneer's words. The shorter man stood looking between the two of them, as if he did not quite know what to make of it.

"Aye." Mr. Hendrick nodded. "That it does."

She regarded him, throat suddenly tight. Not with tears, but fear. He owned her with the bill of sale to prove it. What did he intend to do with her?

Her knees shook. She gasped out a breath. She'd never fainted in her life. She refused to start now. Spots danced before her vision.

"You look unwell. Come. Let's find somewhere to sit."

Mr. Hendrick put his hand on her elbow, supporting her unsteadiness, steps accommodating hers.

She'd been pulled through the night by Tom Brody, then hauled upon the platform by the auctioneer. Both had handled her roughly and with little care, like she were a mare in need of a harsher bit.

His was a touch truly kind. Still she stiffened beneath it.

She didn't know Josiah Hendrick. Yet she belonged to him. He could do what he pleased with her or to her. Over and over, that reality cycled through her.

Surely it can't be worse than what I left.

They made their way down the street. Launcegrave on market day had earlier seemed a festive place. Now, the squawking voice of the puppeteer performing the Punch and Judy show made her cringe. The wooden puppet Punch whacked at Judy, his wife, with a stick.

"Aye, Mr. Punch, you do beat me!" she howled.

The audience laughed.

Elowyn looked away. A group of men spilled out of the Eagle's Head, staggering almost directly into them, obviously well into their cups. Mr. Hendrick's fingers tightened around her elbow as the men passed.

They stopped before a weathered stone building near the end of the street. The hanging sign creaking in the wind spelled out the Three Swans. Mr. Hendrick opened the door and motioned her to precede him.

She stepped inside the low-beamed room. 'Twas dim-lit and dark-paneled, filled with square tables, most occupied by patrons. Mr. Hendrick removed his tricorn and hung it on an empty peg beside other hats.

A lad wearing an apron and carrying a tray of dishes stopped midstride. "Good day to ye, Mr. Hendrick." He jerked a nod.

"Good day, Mark. A table, please."

"Of course, sir. Right this way, sir, ma'am." The boy nodded again and led them through the crowded room to a table near the back next to a stone hearth, empty of heat on this summer day.

Mr. Hendrick pulled out a chair. She sank into it gratefully. 'Twas a relief to not have to bear her weight on her still-trembling legs. He took the seat opposite while the serving lad waited, having deposited his tray of dishes on a vacant table.

"Now then. What can I get for ye?"

"Are you hungry?" Mr. Hendrick folded his hands atop the table.

She shook her head. The scents pervading the room—greasy mutton and pipe smoke—made her queasy enough.

"Just tea, Mark. Thank you."

"Right away, Mr. Hendrick." Mark picked up his tray and headed toward the back.

The serving lad gone, Elowyn kept her gaze on the scarred wood of the table, hands in her lap. 'Twas not her place to press a conversation. Doubtless he'd tell her soon enough his reasons and intent for purchasing her.

She pulled in a steadying breath.

Peace, though, could not be drawn in as easily.

⇌

Elowyn Brody sat across from him, gaze on the table, curling tendrils of golden hair brushing her too-pale cheeks. Though she'd taken pains to conceal it, her unspoken fear hung about her like the cloak she wore. When they'd stood beside the auction block, she'd looked nigh ready to faint. He'd have picked her up and carried her—as slight as she was, he could have done so with little effort—but that would have only frightened her further and drawn the stares of all of Launcegrave. So he'd supported her as best he could and made for the Three Swans.

He swallowed, throat dry. He must speak, but what?

In the heat of the moment, he'd only thought to rescue her from Trevenick. Now the deed was well and truly done. What course he should next take, he knew not. He could give her a few pounds and give her liberty to go, but to where? Her father—a more worthless scoundrel Josiah had rarely laid eyes on—had abandoned her. If she'd other living family, he'd see she found her way safely to them at once.

If not? He could take her to his house as a servant. Yet 'twould hardly be seemly. Peter, the young man he employed at the forge, returned to his own cottage at night. They could not be the only two in the house. The impropriety of such an arrangement, even if his intentions were purely honorable, would set the town to gossiping. He'd not subject her to that.

He could wed her. Hadn't her father said that very thing—*a suitable servant, even a wife?*

After Mary, he'd consigned himself to spending the remainder of his life alone. Marriage had not served him well the first time, and he'd no desire to repeat any part of that past again. He'd no need for a wife and had become accustomed to doing for himself. Contented, even.

What of her, this slip of a girl named Elowyn? What did she need? He could provide for her. Offer her respectability, a home, a comfortable and secure life. The tender feelings that usually accompanied marriage...

After Mary, he'd cobbled together what remained of his heart to not forget those around him in wont of kindness and compassion. But love? That he'd left behind.

Dear God, I beg Your sovereign wisdom to guide me.

Mark returned with a tray and laid two cups on the table, along with milk and sugar. Josiah thanked him and gave him sixpence. The lad grinned.

Elowyn cupped her hands around the blue patterned cup like it was a cold day and she meant to warm them. She lifted it to her lips and took a tentative sip. Josiah ran a finger along the base of his cup but couldn't bring himself to taste the steaming tea.

Cup clinked against saucer as she set it down. Her gaze met his. She'd eyes the color of a storm-battered sea, a mingling of blue and gray. They fixed on him now, trepidation evident in their depths.

He cleared his throat, shifting in his seat. "Have you any family besides that man?" Brody did not merit the title of father.

She shook her head. "Nay. None. My mother died when I was a child. I had a brother, but the fever took him too."

"No other relations?"

"None that I be aware of, sir." The candles on the mantel behind them cast soft shadows on her finely boned face. Her features were delicate, but there was strength there too. And beauty. He looked away, suddenly ashamed for noticing.

Her lack of relatives left him with the only other option. To make her his wife, provide her a home. With a father like that, doubtless she'd had little before.

God, is this what You ask of me? Was it a coincidence I walked by the auction just as it took place? Could You have meant me to give this young woman a home, my name?

A settling certainty in his spirit gave all answers as yes.

His heart pounded like a hammer against an anvil.

"I've a cottage not far from here. There's a forge there where I work as a smith. It isn't a grand place, by any means, but 'tis comfortable enough, secure when it rains and in winter. I'd see to it you lacked for nothing 'twas in my power to provide. I don't see any other way round you staying there though, unless. . .unless we marry."

Other than a sharp intake of breath, she made no sound.

"I'm truly sorry for what happened to you. I can't offer much, but I can promise to do my best to be a kind and generous husband. I'm not asking for love, but mayhap we could come to. . .like each other in time." He kept his voice as gentle as could be. The magnitude of the shock she'd undergone must be almost unbearable. Beneath the table, his fingers tightened into a fist. What manner of man could deal thus with his only daughter?

She blinked. "You wish to wed me? To take me to your home as your honest wife?"

"I'd not take you there as anything else." He met her gaze, hoping she read strength there, that he was a man who, once he'd set his mind to something, did not back down. He made a promise, he upheld it. He took a vow, he kept it. Always.

But to bind himself for a lifetime to a woman he'd known less than an hour? Could he, they, truly do this thing?

She bit her lip and seemed to be working out the matter inside herself. Conversation mulled around them. The *tromp-tromp* of boots sounded. The door banged shut. He kept his eyes on her.

Slowly, she nodded. "Aye then." Her gaze and tone remained steady, candlelight a soft glow on her features.

Relief drained through him, though he wasn't quite sure why. "I'll do all I can to see you do not regret this." Whether or not he would harbor regrets of his own remained to be seen.

To that, she made no response.

"The parson, Mr. Wingfield, and his wife are friends of mine. He will give us the license. We can be wed tomorrow." Tomorrow. That still left tonight. She'd have to stay somewhere, and he wouldn't chance getting her a room here. Though 'twas not a disreputable place, she'd be alone, and ofttimes in the evening folk got rowdy after one too many pints. "I'm sure Mistress Wingfield would not object if you stayed the night with them. She's a good woman."

A hint of a grateful smile crossed her lips. "I'd appreciate that."

He stood, pushing back his chair, their tea mostly untouched and growing cold.

"Let us away then. The parsonage is a ten-minute walk from here.

Can you stand the distance?"

She nodded and stood.

He left payment for the tea on the table, and they wove their way through the room to the entrance, where he retrieved his tricorn. He pushed the door open and held it for her, then followed.

The swell of high afternoon had faded, replaced by dusky light, a stillness to the village, the remnants of market day packed away.

Side by side they walked, through Launcegrave's familiar streets.

If only the future awaiting them was as well charted as the path he now trod.

Chapter 4

Sleep had not proven a friend. Instead, she'd lain awake most of the night, coverlet twisted round her, staring at the ceiling in the chamber the Wingfields had lent her. Thinking. Wondering. Fearing. Morning, it seemed, had come in both a blink and an eternity.

She poured water into the basin and washed herself with the cake of lavender-scented soap, then put on the dress she'd worn yesterday. 'Twas her best out of the two she owned. Once, it had been a dusky shade of rose, but time had faded the color to a lighter hue, and the garment had been mended in several places. She'd altered it from a gown of her mother's, taken from the bottom of a trunk when she'd turned sixteen and needed a gown befitting a woman, not a child.

'Twas a blessing she'd worn it yesterday. Her other dress, left at the cottage she'd shared with Tom Brody, was in far worse condition and held not the sentimental value of this one.

A knock sounded on the door. Elowyn turned, running her fingers through the untamed curls of her waist-length hair.

"Come in."

The door opened. Mistress Wingfield stepped in, matronly frame garbed in a deep green dress covered by an apron that matched the snowy white of her cap. A tray laden with tea, toast, and a bowl of porridge filled her hands. Though the parson's wife had asked Josiah to stay for dinner last night, he'd declined, for which Elowyn had been thankful.

"Good morning, dear." Mistress Wingfield set the tray on the chest of drawers with a clink. "Did you sleep?"

Thankfully the woman had not asked if she'd slept *well*. "Aye. A little."

"It's quarter past seven, and we're to be at the church by nine. So you've plenty of time to have your breakfast."

"Thank you. That's very kind." Elowyn tried for a smile. The aroma of rich tea, buttery toast, and milky porridge wafted from the tray. Her stomach churned. She'd do her best to eat something, so as not to offend Mistress Wingfield, but 'twas doubtful she'd be able to handle more than a few bites. She pressed a hand to her middle, eyes falling closed, inhaling a deep breath.

Footsteps sounded on the creaking floorboards. A warm hand settled on her shoulder. She opened her eyes and found Mistress Wingfield looking at her, kindness in her gaze. "I know this turn of events is sudden. And after what you endured yesterday. . ." She pressed her lips together. "It's only natural to be shaken. But I've known Josiah Hendrick since he was a lad. He's a good man. You've naught to fear from him."

Elowyn nodded. But she could not trust in the certainty of the woman's tone and words.

To trust meant to let down her guard. To not expect betrayal.

How long had it been since she'd done either?

"Here. Let me help you with your hair." She motioned to the dressing table by the window. Elowyn sat while Mistress Wingfield opened a drawer and took out a brush. The woman gathered Elowyn's hair in her hands and pulled the brush through it with gentle strokes. "You have lovely hair." In the mirror, Elowyn glimpsed the woman's smile. "When I was a girl, I wished mine were the color of yours. Alas, it stayed the same shade of unremarkable brown, which has since faded mostly to gray." She laughed. "Five children and enough mischief to match will do that to a body, I daresay."

She'd met the four Wingfield children still living at home last night. The eldest girl, Lydia, had given Elowyn her chamber for the night, and roomed with her two younger sisters. When Elowyn had protested that she didn't want to be a bother, the sixteen-year-old had laughed and said 'twas no bother and the room was really a guest room that she occupied only when they didn't have company. The carefree way the young woman teased her father and bantered with her siblings had startled Elowyn. Lydia Wingfield could likely speak to her father about any concern without fearing the back of his hand. What must it be like to be encircled by such love and openness?

"What do you think?" Mistress Wingfield smiled, setting the brush aside. She'd swept Elowyn's hair up in a knot, leaving a few curls hanging free around her face. Never had her wayward curls looked so polished, her own fumbling efforts usually leaving much to be desired.

"It's lovely." Elowyn returned the smile. "Thank you."

"Happy to help. With three daughters, I've plenty of experience. Speaking of them, I'd best leave you to your breakfast and go back downstairs. Lydia does try, but she's a bit scatterbrained when it comes to playing the lady at table. Is there anything else you need before I go?"

"Nay. Thank you. You've been very kind."

"I'll be up in a little while." Mistress Wingfield rested a hand on Elowyn's shoulder for a moment before turning, her footsteps receding, the door shutting behind her.

Elowyn twisted one of the curls round her finger, staring at her reflection. The neatness of her hair didn't hide the circles beneath her eyes or the paleness of her face. Though what did it matter? This wasn't a usual wedding, nor was she a usual bride. When he'd asked her yesterday, she'd been lured by the gentleness in his gaze, the words he spun... " *'Tis comfortable enough. . .secure when it rains and in winter. . . lack for nothing."*

His roof didn't leak. The thought had popped into her head as he'd spoken. She could endure the gnaw of hunger in her belly, the grueling work of scrubbing laundry in exchange for a few pence, but blast it all, the drip, drip, dripping of rain and slush onto the floor, onto her bed, despite the buckets she placed beneath the cracks, drove her nigh to distraction.

She'd agreed to wed a stranger because he owned a cottage with a roof that didn't leak.

A hysterical laugh escaped.

For a blacksmith, he must make a goodly living. How else could he have afforded the price of fifty guineas? Others had bid for her, but she'd steeled herself and heeded neither faces nor voices.

Why had he purchased her to start with? Why did he wish to marry her? She'd little to recommend herself. Perhaps marriage was the only way he could see to bringing her to his home. Men needed women to cook and clean and—

A wave of heat stained her cheeks.

Did he expect they'd be. . .fully married? Of course, as his wife, she'd have to submit to him in every way. It was his right, and her duty.

She leaned her forehead into her palms.

He'd promised to be kind, but as she'd learned with Tom Brody, 'twas foolishness to believe a promise made by any man. At least she'd known the extent of what Tom Brody was capable of. Or so she'd thought until yesterday. She didn't know Josiah Hendrick at all.

Nonetheless, this very day, she'd speak vows binding them together before God.

Nausea rose in her throat.

Once, she'd thought she'd known what it meant to be trapped. But she hadn't known, not truly.

Until now.

$\backsim$

He was no stranger to the solemnities of the marriage ceremony. He'd been wed before, in this very church, to Mary. Then, a goodly number of villagers had been in attendance to witness their vows, with a party after. On that spring day eight years ago, the world had seemed a fresh and new and gladsome place, Mary's laughter as they danced, the sweetest music he'd ever heard. The future, a thing of beauty.

Looking back, he saw himself, at twenty-four, blind with a love he believed made anything possible.

How wrong he'd been.

He waited to the right of the altar, Mr. Wingfield standing front and center. Save Mistress Wingfield and Peter, there were no guests or witnesses. He'd dressed in his dark blue coat and buff-colored breeches. He'd had a miserable time knotting his cravat. If he fumbled thus at the forge, he'd not be a smith worth his trade. Thankfully, Peter hadn't been there to see. He wouldn't have asked the young man at all, except they needed two witnesses, and on such short notice, he could think of no other. Peter sat in the front row, wearing his Sunday coat and waistcoat, tousled hair slicked back, face red from scrubbing.

The stone church bore the timeworn scent of buildings a century old. Morning sunlight filtered through the arched windows, dust motes sparkled in the air. The door creaked.

Josiah turned. His heart stammered in his chest.

Mistress Wingfield and Elowyn crossed the threshold, the older woman slightly ahead.

His gaze met Elowyn's. For a moment, her steps faltered. She looked as pale as she had yesterday on the block, the shade of her skin making her eyes stand out all the darker. She carried no flowers. He should have thought to pick her some. Yet how would she have taken it if he had, an ordinary gesture from groom to bride, when the circumstances of their union were anything but?

Mistress Wingfield took her seat in the front pew and Elowyn, her place beside him. He was acutely aware of the warmth of her shoulder near his, her lavender scent, the way her honey curls brushed her neck. She didn't look at him, gaze straight ahead, hands clasped at her waist.

Mr. Wingfield looked between the two of them, the *Book of Common Prayer* held in one hand, his white and black clerical robes brushing the floor. Earlier, the man had taken a few moments to speak to Josiah. Though he'd agreed to perform the ceremony, his words this morning had been cautionary.

"Marriage is a sacred institution, not to be entered into lightly."

"You think I am?" Josiah had replied.

"No. I just hope you realize the responsibility that will be yours when you pledge yourself to this young woman. This decision, solemnized in moments, must last you both a lifetime."

He'd not found words to answer the parson.

Now, the time for remonstrance had passed. Mr. Wingfield opened the book.

"Dearly beloved, we are gathered here in the sight of God, and in the face of this congregation, to join together this man and this woman in holy Matrimony. . ."

Ten years hence, twenty, what would he remember from this day? The way her gaze darted to and fro, as if seeking some way of escape, before voicing her almost inaudible "I will." How her hand shook as he slipped the simple gold band upon her finger—his mother's ring had been too tight for Mary, and she'd never worn it. It slid onto Elowyn's slighter hand easily. Cracks marred her skin, callouses her palm, making him wonder what sort of work she'd been doing up till now.

Would he remember the way the sacredness of the words sank deep inside him, each a vow he must keep before God? Or how the pronouncement that they were man and wife made his breath unsteady?

Most of all, would he remember this day as the start of a future filled with promise? Or the beginnings of a mistake that would cost them both dearly?

Mr. Wingfield closed the book, the ceremony at an end. Josiah turned to Elowyn. His wife. It would take time to think of her by that title. He paused, hesitating as to whether or not he should take her arm. Peter and Mistress Wingfield spared him by rising and coming toward them. Mistress Wingfield pulled Elowyn into an embrace.

"Congratulations, Master Hendrick." Peter's crooked teeth flashed as he grinned.

"Thank you, Peter. I appreciate you taking the time to come."

" 'Twas a pleasure, sir," the twenty-one-year-old replied, taking a step back.

"God bless you, Josiah." Mistress Wingfield clasped his hand. Her gaze fell on Elowyn in conversation with the parson. "I trust you'll be good to her," she said softly. "I know not what this girl's past has been, but I do know she needs love and tenderness more than most."

Her words found purchase inside him, much as her husband's had an hour ago.

Love and tenderness. He'd tried to give both to Mary, but he must have failed. For what else would make her seek the arms of another within a year of their marriage?

The past was the past. Elowyn was not his first wife.

"I will try," he answered. Mistress Wingfield's eyes crinkled as she smiled.

Motioning Peter to follow, he moved to where Elowyn stood a few steps away with Mr. Wingfield. "This is Peter. He works with me at the forge."

"Pleasure to make yer acquaintance, ma'am." Peter made a bow. "If there's anything that wants doing for ye, ye've only to ask."

"Thank you." Elowyn's smile brought a flush to Peter's already ruddy cheeks. "I'm happy to meet you."

He didn't fault Peter for being dazzled by her. She'd smiled easily at the young man, and the gesture transformed her face, revealing a dimple in her right cheek.

"Shall we sign the register now?" Mr. Wingfield broke in.

"Aye. Of course." They'd taken up enough of the Wingfields' time already. The man likely had pressing parish matters to attend to.

They made their way into the vestry where the thick black book sat on a low table, open to a fresh page. Mr. Wingfield handed Elowyn the quill and pointed to where she must sign.

As she bent over the table and carefully formed her name, one thing stood starkly apparent.

The smile had left her face.

Chapter 5

The wagon jostled along the rutted road, Launcegrave a memory in the distance. Elowyn sat, hands clenched in her lap, as far to the edge of the bench as she could manage. Despite her efforts, whenever the wheel hit a particularly large bump, it nonetheless threw her against Mr. Hendrick.

The man she must now call husband.

"We're nearly there." He held the reins loosely in his hands, handling the two horses with an ease that could only come from years of experience. The bracing wind pulled her hair back from her face. The air held traces of salt. They neared the sea.

Had this day not seen her pledged to a stranger, she'd have smiled at the prospect.

"Are there any beaches near your home?"

He glanced at her. The words were the first she'd spoken since her "thank you" after he'd helped her into the wagon. "Aye. There's one but ten minutes from the house. Are you fond of the sea?"

She nodded. "I've never lived such an easy distance to it though. It must be a fine thing to watch it in all its moods and seasons."

"It is at that." A smile turned up the corners of his lips, the gesture slightly crooked. His jaw was clean-shaven today, though his brown hair hung longer than fashionable and wanted a trim. She'd always tended to her father's. She winced at the slip of thinking of him as such. Some habits were hard to unmake. "I'll show you the way tomorrow. Then you can walk there whenever you wish."

"I'd like that." She gave a bit of a smile, wanting to thank him. He smiled back, wind riffling the edges of his hair beneath the tricorn. He had a certain wildness about him, despite his gentleman's garb. Thus far, he'd been naught but kind to her. But she'd not let herself hope this kindness would last. Sooner or later, mayhap even tonight, she'd discover the reason he'd done something so unlikely as purchase a wife at auction.

She only prayed when she did discover it, 'twould not entirely destroy her.

"The house is just ahead."

The wagon jostled onward, drawing them nearer.

Toward her new. . .what? Dwelling? Place of residence? Home? Could she dare think of it as such?

Nay. Not yet. Ever?

That did not bear considering now.

The softly sloped fields and meadows stretched all around, interspersed by trees. Green blended into the pale blue of the cloud-laced sky, as if the two touched each other. A limitless landscape.

They turned into a narrow drive.

'Twas like he had said. Three buildings—a forge, stable, the largest a cottage. The former two built of wood, the latter of stone. All larger than the dwelling she'd lived in before yesterday.

The wagon came to a stop. He jumped down, and she made move to climb down. But before she could gather her skirts, he rounded the wagon and held out his hands. She placed hers in them.

Wide and strong and calloused. The hands of a man unafraid of honest work. They steadied her as she descended, skirts aswirl as her feet landed on the hard-packed ground.

"Thank you," she murmured. Her hands fell from his.

He nodded and started toward the house. Uncertainly, she followed up the slightly overgrown path, which led off in two directions, one to the forge, the other to the house. The exterior of the stone cottage was weathered with age and elements, but it looked solid, the thatched roof in good repair. Firewood leaned against one side in a neat stack.

He took a key from his pocket and unlocked the door. It creaked open.

He went in first, leaving her to follow. She ducked through the door and stepped over the threshold, fingers fisted in her skirts. Semidarkness coated the room, and she blinked, adjusting to the difference in light. Mr. Hendrick stood near a hearth, fumbling with flint and steel. A spark caught, and he lit a candle, then another, placing both on the mantel.

The room was low-ceilinged and of middling size. An oaken table sat in its center, a finer piece of furniture than she'd expected a blacksmith to possess. Three chairs sat around it. Another table stood against one wall, and behind it hung all manner of pots and cooking utensils. A cupboard against the same wall likely held more. Two windows let in light through panes in goodly need of cleaning.

She sensed his gaze on her. Likely he expected some response. "It's. . .nice."

"I hope you'll find yourself at home here." He took a step toward her, eyes meeting hers. Somehow the size of the room made his shoulders seem wider, his height, taller.

She swallowed, the space suddenly close, all too aware that 'twas but the two of them alone, in his house, and she his wife. Any answer or thanks she might have voiced died on her lips. Her gaze fell to the worn floorboards and the hem of her skirts.

"Look about at liberty." The words were perfunctory, as if her lack of an answer had somehow displeased him. "I'd best see to the horses." He moved past her, ducking through the doorway. The door groaned shut.

A closed door stood to one side. Though he'd given her leave to look around, opening it felt rather like trespassing. A small chamber held an unmade bed, covers rumpled and turned down as if the person who'd last slept there hadn't bothered to do more than climb out of it this morn. Heat burned her cheeks at the intimacy of the sight.

Would she be expected to share it with him?

A chest sat at the foot of the bed, a chair against the wall. A shirt lay tossed against the back of the chair, along with a pair of trousers.

By nature, men were not tidy creatures. At least the ones she'd known. Mr. Hendrick was not proving an exception. Though the house was sturdy, it lacked the gentler touch that, though she'd had precious little to work with, she'd always given the various cottages she'd shared with Tom Brody.

Perhaps this was why Mr. Hendrick had chosen her. He'd sensed the lack in his life of the refinements a woman could provide. Hot meals. A tidy house. Mended clothes.

If so, she'd not fail. She'd clean and scrub and mend and bake, doing everything she could to earn her keep. She might have faults aplenty, but being bone-idle had never been one of them.

She pressed a hand to her middle, the room's scent unfamiliar and altogether masculine.

If only she could be certain that was all Josiah Hendrick expected of their marriage.

$$\backsim$$

Silence, thick as a foggy night, hung over their first meal together. She'd asked if he wanted her to cook, but he said he'd picked up something yesterday in Launcegrave. She could scarce swallow the cheese, and the crusty bread lodged itself in her throat like gravel. She drank tea, both hands wrapped around the cup, and eyed him across the table. He ate and said little. Perhaps because every time he did speak, her answers came out short and halting. After finishing his meal, he left, saying he had things to attend to in the forge. She washed the few dishes with water carried from the pump outside, glancing toward the forge as she filled the bucket and then emptied out the dirty water. She swept the cottage and considered washing the windows, but by the time she'd finished sweeping, her eyes had grown heavy, fatigue weighing every muscle in her body.

Still Mr. Hendrick had not returned.

The night had grown chilly, so she made up a fire and sat before it, staring into the snapping flames, their pop and crackle a soothing, familiar sound. Yet she could find no comfort in it tonight. She twisted her hands in her lap and tried to steady her breathing.

Her mother was dead, her father had abandoned her, and she was to share a cottage belonging to a man who now legally called her wife.

For so long, aloneness had been a shadow at her heels, a companion in the evenings when Tom Brody fell asleep after coming home from the public house sated with too much drink. She'd sat by a fire much like this one, worrying about how they were going to eat, the state of the roof, what to do after he'd been dismissed from the mine.

But now, she was more alone than ever. The truth seeped down to her bones.

She tried to pray, as she'd often done, but no peace descended upon her spirit. Perhaps this was her punishment for some sin she'd committed, the wicked thoughts she'd entertained about her father, the times—God help her—she'd wished him dead. The Bible did say children were to honor and obey their parents, and though she'd obeyed him in most things, except in the matter of marriage to Jonas Mason, she'd not honored him in her heart.

Her eyes fell closed, and she leaned her head against the back of the chair, praying for forgiveness, if indeed there was any to be had. To hear the parson at the church she'd irregularly attended, God's vengeance was a fiery thing, crushing both sin and sinner.

Minutes later, the door scraped open. Heart thudding, she

started and opened her eyes.

Mr. Hendrick stood inside. He'd changed into a worn shirt, loose in cut and rolled to the elbows, and a pair of faded trousers. His gaze took her in. She lifted a hand to her hair. It fell in mussed tangles around her cheeks, Mistress Wingfield's handiwork dislodged by the wind and the day's exertions.

She rose on shaking legs. He took a step toward her. Firelight shone on the raw-hewn angles of his face and the graze of stubble on his jaw.

Her chest tightened. Breath all but refused to come.

She knew little of the intimacies of marriage. Her mother had died when she was still a child, and she'd had no woman friends to speak of.

Yet here she stood, in a dimly lit room on her wedding night. Her pulse thudded in her ears. If she could push past him and flee into the night, she would.

His eyes darkened with inexplicable emotion as he regarded her.

"I just came in to fetch some things," he said quietly. "I'll be staying in the smithy."

"You mean. . .you're not. . .we're not. . ." The words came out ragged.

His brow furrowed, as if with confusion. Then understanding dawned on his features, bringing a stain of red to his cheeks.

"I'll not ask anything of you you're not ready for. Have no fears on that score."

For a moment, she just stared at him. Then a sob emerged, choked, unbidden. She clamped a hand against her mouth to hold it back. Hot tears slid down her cheeks. Her shoulders shook. She swiped at her eyes, trying to check herself, but she only cried harder.

A touch rested on her shoulder. She looked up through a blur of tears. He stood but a step away, concern in his gaze.

"I'm. . .sorry," she gasped out.

"Don't be." He pulled her against him, encircling her with his arms. Gulping sobs shuddered her body. She cried from the pain of what Tom Brody had done to her, from the tension and exhaustion of the past days, of the past year, of her life. From relief that she'd not have to endure conjugal duties, along with everything else. She cried like she hadn't done in years, since childhood, likely.

He let her. Stood there, surrounding her with his arms, while she soaked his shirt with her tears. Whispered words brushed her hair, so soft she couldn't make them out. Minutes passed. Her sobs subsided. He smelled of woodsmoke and leather, and his arms were strong and warm. The cadence of his heartbeat filled her ears. Steady. Even. Safe.

Reality doused her. Had she taken leave of her senses? What was she about, seeking comfort in his arms?

She pulled away, taking a step back, wiping at the tears on her cheeks. The fire crackled. Silence hung between them.

"Will you be all right?" he asked, as if he doubted she would.

She nodded, flushing. Had she actually broken down and bawled like a child in his arms? What had she been thinking? She hadn't been. She'd been overcome in the moment and let her guard down.

"I'll be fine." Should she thank him? If so, for what? Not having his way with her? Letting her cry, and comforting, not rebuking her?

All of these were on her tongue, when he walked past her, toward the bedchamber. She turned and stared after him, listening to the clomp of his boots and the sounds of rummaging as he gathered what items he needed.

A few minutes later, he emerged, arms full with blankets and a pillow.

He nodded to her. "Good night." His footfalls echoed as he crossed to the door, opened it with one hand.

"Good night," she whispered too late.

Chapter 6

Drafts of cold air seeped through cracks in the smithy walls. The floor of the forge was no place to seek a decent night's rest. Josiah's aching neck protested as he sat up the next morning, bedclothes covering his bent knees.

But rest upon it he must. Every night. Come winter, he might ask if Elowyn minded if he slept in the main room, in front of the fire. Else he'd likely catch his death.

He scrubbed a hand across his jaw, shoulders lifting in a sigh.

He'd begun to question any sanity he'd ever possessed. What had he been thinking, binding himself to a woman he didn't know on a decision made in less than a day? He could have secured her a position as a servant in the village, given her ten pounds, and let that be that. Wouldn't rescuing her from Trevenick have been enough?

Trevenick.

Not only had he surrendered Charles's gift, made with the express purpose of keeping the share out of Trevenick's grasp, he'd surrendered his chances of ever again owning a claim in Prosper. Trevenick was now the majority shareholder, and if one of the other shareholders decided to sell, 'twould almost certainly be to him.

He'd failed Charles. He didn't believe in ghosts haunting the living, but there was a kind of haunting nonetheless in the knowledge he'd betrayed the trust his friend had in him. Although Charles, rough exterior belying his tender heart, would have likely come to understand why Josiah had done what he had.

And in doing so, he'd relegated himself to this. A forge. An anvil. Pounding on metal the rest of his living days. After acquiring the share, he'd intended to continue his work in the smithy, but as his profits from the mine increased, use those profits to seek new opportunities for investment. In time, he'd hoped to give up blacksmithing and let Peter take over the forge.

Now none of that would come to pass.

'Twas not the work he despised. There was satisfaction in crafting a fine piece of workmanship out of raw material, mending something broken. But mining was in his blood. Though shareholder meetings had been a poor substitute for going into the bowels of the earth to seek out precious ore, looking over maps and diagrams, deciding which route to take, which vein to throw one's efforts behind, it had been something. The talk of lodes and copper and prices had thrilled him, notwithstanding Trevenick's glare across the table.

Of course, he'd only known mining up until the age of sixteen. The rest of his life had been spent at the forge. After his father lost Prosper at the gaming tables, they'd sold their manor house to pay off their creditors, and his father drifted, as if he knew not how to reckon with himself. Particularly when Prosper began to flourish under Trevenick ownership. With his ailing mother in need of care, Josiah had not been afforded the leisure to drift, and rather than seek employment at the mine and put himself in Trevenick's power, he'd sought it with Ned Coggin, the smith. For two years, the aged man had taught him the trade. When Ned died, Josiah had ransacked their savings and bought the cottage and forge.

His work, coupled by his father's eventual assistance, had gained the respect of Launcegrave, and the surrounding areas. After his father's death, the year before he'd wed Mary, he'd taken on Peter. The lad's weak lungs were no match for going down into the mines day after day. Peter insisted Josiah had saved his life by teaching him a smith's trade, and in return, the young man had served him well.

Memories from last night washed over him. The look of stark fear on Elowyn's face when he'd first entered the room. At first, he'd not realized why. Then it hit him. She'd thought him a brute who'd insist upon his rights as a husband, be she willing or no. The fault was his. He should have assured her earlier that their union would remain in name only.

Then her tears. Wracking sobs, cried out as her slight frame shook in his arms. He'd comforted her as best he could, but left feeling it had not been enough. The miseries she'd endured were an ocean of depths that it would take time to plumb.

Aye. He'd done the right thing, despite his doubts. Not the easy thing, mayhap, but the right one.

He rose and folded his blankets then strode into the day. Dawn's light brushed the sky in hues of peach and pale blue. Wind rustled through the grass, reminding him of his promise to show her the beach. He went through the motions of morning chores, feeding the horses, milking the cow. Chores complete, he crossed to the pump and pulled off his shirt, the icy water prickling his skin as he pumped water over his head, the stream cascading across his chest and shoulders. Having brought no towel, he pulled the shirt back over his head and picked up the milk pail then went round the side of the house to the front. At the door, he paused. It was his. He needn't knock.

But somehow, barging in didn't seem right.

He raised his fist and rapped on the wood, then waited. Beads of water dripped from the ends of his hair, falling onto his shirt. He rubbed a hand across his jaw, the roughness there reminding him he'd forgotten his razor in his rush to clear out of the bedchamber last night. He'd gotten out of the habit of shaving every day. Even though he'd spent six months as a shareholder in Prosper, he'd not bothered to acquire a gentleman's polish.

Yet now, with Elowyn's presence, he'd do well to reacquaint himself with the practice.

No voice or step greeted his knock, so he tried again, louder this time. As before, nothing. He shifted. He had to have something for his breakfast and Peter's. The sun told him it was already half past seven. Peter would be here within half an hour to eat before starting work. One couldn't get an hour's work, let alone a day's, out of a hungry young man. His own stomach chose that moment to protest.

Make that two hungry men.

He opened the door and peered inside. Quiet and empty. Mayhap she was still abed. He didn't fault her after the day she'd had yesterday. She'd endured enough miseries to warrant a fortnight of slumber.

He'd be as quiet as he could, getting his breakfast and Peter's. She need not even know he'd come in. Gently, he set down the pail of milk.

The door to his bedchamber—hers now—stood half open. Taking care with every step, he crossed the main room as quietly as he could, inching toward the door. If he shut it, 'twould be quieter for her while he was fixing the victuals.

He reached for the knob.

The mattress creaked.

He froze.

Footfalls sounded, soft but audible. The floor creaked.

She was awake. And he stood outside her bedchamber, half hidden by the door.

He spun on his heel. Hang breakfast. He'd not embarrass her—or him—by coming upon her in a state of...well, never mind what state.

A muffled gasp sounded. He turned. Elowyn's face appeared in the crack of the door, which she'd pushed almost closed. From what little he could see, she was wrapped in the coverlet from his bed, her fingers holding the fabric closed near her chin. Her hair tumbled around her shoulders.

"Good morning." It sounded daft, but 'twas all he could think to say.

By the frantic look in her eyes it was most assuredly *not* a good morning. "What time is it?"

He rubbed the back of his neck. "Half past seven."

Her eyes widened. "That late. I must have overslept. I'm so sorry."

"Don't be—"

"You must be wanting your breakfast. 'Twill be but a moment, and I'll fix it." The door shut before he could assure her he didn't need her to cook every meal for him, that he'd make breakfast for all of them, that it was understandable and natural to be tired.

But only the closed door remained to witness any of those statements, so he went back outside, brought in an armload of wood, and stoked the fire. The flames crackled, warming the gooseflesh on his skin from his morning wash as he stirred up the blaze.

The bedchamber door opened. She'd donned her dress—the only one she owned, he realized—but her hair still fell loose about her shoulders, and bare feet peeped from beneath her skirts.

"You've started the fire."

He nodded, poker in hand. "Milk's over there. Got a full bucket today. Jinny had a calf this spring, but I sold the calf last month." At an admittedly low price to the Darter family, whose growing children sorely needed the milk the animal would provide in time.

She crossed the floor and hefted the milk bucket in both hands. "Your breakfast. . .it will only be a few moments."

"I can wait." He hung the poker on its rack. "Help, if you like. I'm no stranger to the kitchen, though I'm not much of a cook."

"Nay. I can manage." She set the milk on the floor near the cupboard.

He pulled out a chair and sat at the table, hands atop the wood, folding and unfolding them. She scurried about, rummaging through the cupboard, pulling out a bag of oats, rushing to the pump for water, running back in again, hauling a pot to the fire and hanging it there. Firelight gilded her loose hair golden, flushed her cheeks.

Leaving the pot of porridge to bubble, she hurried across the room. He'd offer to help again, but for some reason, she didn't seem to wish it. So he stood and retrieved the family Bible from the mantel.

A cry. A clang. A thud.

He turned, the heavy book in hand.

Elowyn sat sprawled on the floor in a spreading pool of milk. The tin pail lay on its side.

Enough was enough. He set the Bible on the table and strode across the room. She stared up at him, bare feet sticking out from beneath her milk-splattered skirt, lips parted with shaking breaths, eyes wide with. . .terror.

He held out a hand to help her to her feet. Instead of taking it, she recoiled, body trembling as much as her voice. "Please. 'Twas only an accident."

"I'm not angry with you."

"Then why would you strike me?" she whispered.

Strike her? What? "I was going to help you up." He held out his hand again. This time, she took it, her grip moist with milk. He lifted her to her feet. When they stood at nearly eye level, her hand still in his, he gazed at her for a long moment. She stood still, chest rising and falling. "I would never strike you, Elowyn. Never."

"It's just. . .I overslept and spilled the milk and was altogether careless."

He shook his head in disbelief. "What manner of man do you think you've wed?"

She ducked her chin. "I don't know."

He'd given her no cause to think him a brute. Still she came to such a conclusion. Past experience. The only teacher one had.

He swallowed, her hand small in his. "Did your father beat you?"

At first, nothing. Then she nodded, cheeks stained with shame.

White-hot anger surged through him. He wanted to ram his fist into Brody's gut and see how that snake liked it, then bash his skull against the wall for good measure. To strike a defenseless woman, this frightened girl, his own daughter. A good many words came to mind for the blackguard, none of which the Lord would approve of.

"Hear this, and hear it well," he said quietly. She met his eyes. "I'm not that kind of a man. I may have faults aplenty, but you need never fear I would lay a finger on you in anger. I promise you, Elowyn." For the second time that morning, her name fell from his lips. "You're safe here."

⮌

"What manner of man do you think you've wed?"

Hours later, his words turned through her mind, coupled with the earnest yet firm way he'd voiced them. Her answer had been true. She didn't know.

When she'd laid her head on the pillow last night—one that bore the scent of the man who'd held her in his arms while she wept— she'd intended to rise early and have breakfast prepared, so he could eat a hot meal before going about his labor at the forge. With the breakfast, she'd make amends for her tears and weakness the previous night. Show him she was a hard worker who'd serve him well.

Instead, she'd overslept, exhausted from the two sleepless nights prior. She'd sought to salvage her error by rushing around, a mistake in an unfamiliar kitchen, and ended up kicking over an entire bucket of milk.

Tom Brody, when he was sober enough to notice, would have

strapped her for such carelessness and waste.

Her husband had done the opposite. He'd helped her to her feet, and then he assisted her in cleaning up the milk and dishing up breakfast in time for Peter's arrival. Noticing the state of her gown, he'd disappeared into the bedchamber and returned, a nut-brown dress draped over his large hands, saying she could wear it if she liked. She'd changed while the men ate, the garment baggy on her frame, but at least clean. It bore the faint fragrance of roses, making her wonder who'd owned the garment before, and why Mr. Hendrick had it in his possession.

When she returned to the front room, the men had left the table, bowls scraped clean. She ate her own porridge, washed the dishes, and then her gown, which she hung on a line outside to dry, listening to the sounds of clinking metal, staccato hammering, and the rumble of male voices.

After the noonday meal, vegetable stew and oatbread, which both men praised her warmly for between bites, they returned to the forge, while she washed the windows and attacked dust and cobwebs, cleaning the front room until it fairly sparkled. Hours later, footfalls sounded, and she turned from giving the room a final sweeping, broom in hand.

He'd washed at the pump, hair slicked back with water, droplets falling onto his white, open-collared shirt, the damp material clinging to his chest.

A flush filled her cheeks, and she swiped a tendril of hair behind her ear to distract herself. She'd rarely seen a man more powerfully hewn. While her father's middle had sagged with drink and idleness, there was nothing soft about this man's physique.

He stepped inside, boot prints tracking her freshly cleaned floor. She winced. But it wouldn't do to mention it to him.

"Shall we go down to the beach?"

"Aye." She nodded, excitement spiraling through her.

"Would it disturb you if I got a few more things from my...er, the room first?" He rubbed his stubbled jaw.

"Nay," she hastened. "Please, do."

"Thank you." He stepped past her. "I'll be only a moment."

She put away the broom and smoothed a hand down the bodice of the dress. It was well stitched, though worn and faded. What woman had worn it, and what relation had she been to her husband? Again, the question rose.

"Shall we away?" His voice rumbled behind her. He moved to lay a pile of items on the table, including a razor and towel.

"Aye, Mr. Hendrick."

He came toward her. He'd dried his hair and added a brown waistcoat over the white shirt, though no cravat. "You're my wife, not my servant. My name is Josiah. And I'd take it kindly if you used it." One corner of his mouth tipped upward. "Else I might think you're addressing my father."

"Aye, si...Josiah." His name on her tongue tasted new and time-worn both at once.

"That's better." This time, his grin was full-fledged, crinkling the corners of his eyes. Upon first glance, no one would have called him a handsome man. But at his smile, her heart tripped a beat.

They left the cottage and started side by side down the winding road. Birds twittered overhead, and the sun warmed her face and hair. As in Launcegrave, Josiah didn't walk ahead of her, but accommodated his steps to hers. Accustomed to hefting her skirts and hurrying after Tom Brody, she appreciated the thoughtfulness.

His mother must have taught him well. One wasn't wont to pick up such manners unless one was gentlefolk. Since he didn't seem averse to conversation, she decided to ask the question that had pressed her all day. "Who did it belong to? The dress?"

He glanced at her face then the dress she wore. "My first wife."

His first wife.

Another woman had lived in the stone cottage, cooked meals for a man who didn't mind lending a hand or cleaning up messes. Known the gentleness of his warm arms around her, his strong hands to help her up. Shared his bed. She pulled in a breath.

"Did she. . . ?" She couldn't finish the sentence.

"She died. Her child with her." He stared at the road ahead, steps without pause.

They'd had a child. Her heart twisted. The man who had wed her knew what it was to truly ache in spirit.

"I'm sorry." To her ears, the words sounded small. Inadequate.

A trace of pain filled his gaze. "It was over six years ago. A long time past."

The wind blew strands of hair into her eyes, the path growing steep and rocky. "Time may heal a wound, but that does not mean 'tis mended well and truly. Such a grief, 'tis a hard thing to bear."

He nodded. "That it may be. But life has a way of helping us move on. Mind your step, now."

Sensing that was her cue to abandon the subject, she focused her gaze on the landscape spread before her. The cliffs, craggy green and jagged stone, plunging downward. The sea, crashing against the rocks, foam white as fine lace. The sea. . .

Windswept. Raw. Beautiful. The waves coming in, lapping against the pale sand then falling away, into the turquoise of the water. Gulls cried overhead.

Her heart stirred at the wonder of it. They descended the path, reaching the beach itself.

"Althea Beach. What do you think?" Wind fingered his hair, tugging it over his forehead, into his eyes.

"I think it grand." The sweep of the waves muted her words.

"And so it is." A smile edged his lips.

She closed her eyes and tipped her face toward the wind, letting the music of the waves and the calls of the seabirds wash over her. Every indrawn breath of briny air lessened the tension in her chest, replaced by a measure of peace.

Lord, surely out of love for man You did create this place of beauty. And I thank Thee for it.

She opened her eyes. Josiah stood, watching her, the rugged cliffs a backdrop behind him.

"I must confess I could gladly stay here forever." She smiled. "Just me and the sea."

"I've ofttimes had the same feeling. Whenever I wish to think a matter through, this is where I come. I've spent hours staring out at the sea. Thinking. Praying. God seems as near here as He does in any church."

Her gaze held his. "So He does."

He held out his arm to her, and she placed her hand upon it, fingertips brushing the swell of muscles beneath his cotton shirt. For the first time, no fear stirred through her at his touch.

The sun slipped lower, painting sky and sea in golden fire. They made their way along the edge of the beach, the waves rushing in and fading away, the wind on their faces, the endlessness of it all swelling through her like rich music.

For the first time since that morning walk to Launcegrave, a spark of hope rose within her chest, caught tinder, and remained.

Chapter 7

Two Weeks Later

The familiarity of the forge wrapped round him like a cloak on a winter's day. Tools he knew by touch, movements ingrained into the very fabric of him.

If only all aspects of life could be so clear and plain.

Josiah put the iron into the flames, forehead furrowed as he assessed the temperature. Sweat slicked Peter's face as he manned the bellows.

"What say you?"

Peter squinted at the piece of iron immersed in the fire. "Looks to be ready."

Though Peter was only hired help, not an apprentice, Josiah used every opportunity to teach him the trade. At first, his inexperience had been good for little else but pumping the bellows, feeding the fire, and other tasks that required little knowledge of the craft. But as time went on and he grew in aptitude, Josiah had begun instructing him further in the skills required to be not only a passable smith but an artisan. As old Ned Coggin had once taught him.

He drew the iron out with tongs and carried it to the anvil. Peter handed him his hammer, and he raised it.

Clang-clang.

Sparks flecked off red-hot iron with every strike.

'Twas not merely a hammering out but a shaping. Every hit made with the finished item in mind. He'd learned early on that control, not mere strength, was the mark of a good smith. He fell into the timeworn rhythm.

"Fetch more coal, will you?"

"Aye, sir." Peter headed off. "With a thump and a sound—Old Clem! Beat it out, beat it out—Old Clem!" He sang the familiar smith's tune, which imitated the measure of hammering out iron. But as usual, Peter's key was off, giving the song a lopsided air.

Josiah shook his head with half a smile as he hammered away, examining his work after every blow. One too many would bend the iron too far, and it would have to go back into the fire. 'Twould never do to rush the task. Still, he hoped to take Mistress Rundell's poker to Launcegrave today, along with a few items he'd finished yesterday. The delivery of the pieces would provide the excuse he needed for the trip.

Peter returned, hauling a bucket of coal. He set it down and watched Josiah work as he shaped the curved handle of the poker. One more strike, carefully placed, and...there.

He plunged the piece into the slack tub. Steam hissed upward, clouding the air. He let it cool while he pulled his leather apron over his head and hung it on its peg. His shirt stuck to his skin with sweat, his hair damp and sticky. He needed a wash and a clean shirt to be presentable enough to set foot in Mistress Lampton's shop.

Pulling out the finished poker, he surveyed his work, the finely curved handle making the piece not only useful but elegant. He held it up for Peter's inspection.

"That's fine." Peter nodded, a tiny grin creeping over his lips. "Shall I start on the haft for George Allen's shovel? He do wish it mended by Saturday. Then there's the handle for Will Trigam's plough."

"Aye. I'm away to Launcegrave this afternoon to deliver Mistress Rundell's poker...and conduct some other business."

"Must be glad business for ye to wear that look." Peter grinned at him over the slack tub.

Josiah scrubbed a hand across his face. Was he really so obvious? "'Tis for Mistress Hendrick. A surprise."

"I be that glad ye wed her, if ye don't mind my saying so." He looked up, hair falling into his eyes. "She sings nice. And her tattie pie is better than me own mother's."

Josiah chuckled. "I'll be back in a few hours." He grabbed towel and soap from his pile of belongings and headed toward the pump. As September neared its midpoint, the nights grew chillier, but warmth still pervaded the afternoon air.

I'm glad too. Perhaps more than I've a right to be.

Setting soap and towel on the grass, he began to pull off his shirt.

"Finished for the day already?"

He started at Elowyn's voice and hastily pulled his shirt back down over his chest. She stood on the grass, two mugs in hand.

"I'm away to Launcegrave."

"Oh. I was just bringing you something to drink." She handed him the mug, their fingers brushing over the handle. Wind stirred her hair. She'd taken to wearing it up, a kerchief banded round it, loose tendrils falling round her cheeks. With every day, she seemed to grow lovelier.

"Thank you." He downed the water in two gulps, relishing the coolness, and swiped a hand across his mouth. "I'm sure Peter will appreciate it too. What have you been about this morning?" He handed her the empty mug.

"Laundry."

"Did you not need help managing the kettle?" He'd always helped Mary. 'Twas no small task to haul water for washing, heat it in a great kettle on a fire outside, then beat the clothes with a wooden mallet until all the dirt and grime had loosened. Fresh water had to be gotten for rinsing then the clothes run through the mangler to wring out excess water.

Elowyn shook her head. "I've managed for years and am not like to stop now." Her tone was matter of fact. "It's all washed, and drying on the line." She pushed a strand of hair behind her ear with a reddened hand. "I felt almost idle, with so little of it to do, I washed the bedclothes too. I used to take in laundry, when. . ." She didn't finish the sentence.

Truly, she must be stronger than she looked. Her slight frame didn't appear sturdy enough to accommodate the labor of a laundry maid. Her father had been no kind of man to let her work thus without lifting a finger.

"Will you be wanting something to eat before you go? Because of the laundry, I haven't prepared anything, so it might be awhile." Hesitancy flickered in her gaze. As if he were her master and would scold her for being remiss in her duties. Thankfully, in the past two weeks, the look had dwindled from fear to hesitancy. And each time he coaxed a smile from her, warmth unfurled in his chest.

"Nay. Not hungry. Is there anything I can fetch you while I'm in town?" He'd offer to take her with him, so she could choose household stuffs for herself, but 'twould ruin his surprise.

She bit her lip, a sure sign she was debating whether or not to voice her request.

"Write up a list. I'll collect it after I've made myself decent enough to set foot upon your floors." It had taken three times of him tramping across her freshly scrubbed floors before he took the consternation on her face to mean he'd best see his boots were clean or take them off at the door.

She flushed. His grin broadened. Unsuccessfully hiding a smile, she turned and walked toward the house. He stared after her. Her hips swayed as she walked, Mary's dress altered so it molded to her slighter frame. He swallowed.

Two weeks of marriage had slipped by, the familiarity of his old life blending with the newfound cadence of Elowyn's presence. Flaky pasties for the evening meal, a drink of something cool brought to the smithy, wildflowers in a vase on the dining table.

The way her nose crinkled as she laughed at Peter's jokes. Her soft singing as she washed the dishes. The rapt wonder in her gaze as they watched the sunset at Althea Beach. Her hand in his as they sat round the table while he blessed the food. Looking up after, to find her studying him with a hint of a smile, something indecipherable in her sea-hued gaze.

Frigid water poured over his skin as he cranked the pump.

After Mary's death, he'd thought he'd never again have a heart whole enough to bestow upon another. Now, here he was, after a union made in the most improbable of circumstances.

Finding himself slowly, day by day. . .giving his heart to her.

⌒

Elowyn's needle slid through cotton as she mended a hole in the sleeve of one of Josiah's shirts by the light of fire and candle. She'd noticed the rent while hanging clothes to dry this afternoon. Now, several hours later, the cotton baked by the sun, she could rest her back and turn her hand to a less arduous task.

The quietness of this new life settled in her soul like a balm. Days of work that left her with a satisfied weariness, walks along the beach watching the sun sink lower, ribboning the waves in gold, nights curled up on a real mattress in a sturdy bed. The folk who stopped to drop by items for repair, request a piece made, or pick up a finished one had been curious when Josiah introduced her as Mistress Hendrick, but mostly friendly. On walks to the beach, those they passed greeted Josiah with tips of the hat and respectful greetings or hearty handshakes and friendly words, stirring something akin to pride in her chest that 'twas she on his arm. When she'd walked beside Tom Brody, they'd been greeted with naught but derision.

Most noticeable of all, Josiah never stumbled in with drink on his breath, nor fell asleep at the table with gin dribbling down his chin. Not once had she seen him drink anything stronger than coffee. And she recognized the scent of liquor well enough that he'd not have been able to mask it.

Aye. 'Twas a peace she knew not how to reckon with, but had begun to bask in nonetheless.

The door creaked open. Josiah came in, arms laden with packages. She set aside her mending and hastened to him. He laid the parcels on the table. He wore his gray coat, his tricorn. Clothes betwixt the garb of a gentleman and a smith.

"It looks like your trip was a success."

"So it was." He handed her a parcel, a smile playing at the corners of his mouth. "Open it."

"Why? What is it?" She turned it over in her hands uncertainly.

"Open it and see." From a man who measured every word and showed his feelings but moderately, he looked fair to bursting with anticipation.

She untied the twine, letting it fall to the table as she undid the wrapping. That too fell away as fabric unfolded in her hands.

"'Tis a cloak," she breathed. Of deep green, thick and buttery soft, the ribbons at the throat a match to the rest. She'd seen ladies decked in such garments, but had never dreamed they were so warm to the touch, so smooth and fine.

"'Tis yours."

"Nay, Josiah." She shook her head. "'Tis too fine. . .too grand for the likes of me." What miner's daughter glimpsing the finery of the prosperous hadn't imagined wearing such a thing in her heart of hearts? As a girl, she'd been no exception, gazing wistfully as open carriages bearing ladies and lords passed by. As a woman, she'd thought she'd outgrown such fancies. She smoothed her fingertips across the ribbon.

She hadn't.

"Do you like it?"

"Aye, but—"

"Then it's yours." His eyes crinkled with a smile. "As are the contents of those other two parcels." He pointed to the largest one. "Come. Let's have a look."

As she undid the wrapping, a gasp escaped.

"Hold it up."

She did. 'Twas a gown of burgundy, lace trimming the square neckline. Though simple in cut and made of cotton, not silk or velvet, never had something so new, so beautiful been hers. Her breath caught as she held the dress against herself, turning so the skirt swayed.

"Well? Does it suit?" His voice brought her gaze up.

Her first instinct was to fling her arms around him. She took a step toward him then stopped herself. 'Twould be childish to do so, hardly seemly.

"It's beyond anything." Did the fullness in her heart make its way into her voice by half? Carefully, she folded the dress and laid it in its wrapping.

"There's another parcel there."

Like a child at Christmas, she tore it open. A pair of fine stockings and embroidered garters caught her gaze before she flushed and folded the parcel, realizing exclaiming over underthings would hardly be proper. She refolded the parcel.

"But why?"

"Cannot a man buy presents for his wife?"

She stilled at the gentleness with which he said the word. *Wife.*

When she'd wed him, she'd thought to be a well-treated servant, given food and shelter in exchange for work, but little else. Certainly not luxuries like cloaks and gowns.

"I suppose so." She flushed, but surely 'twas from the firelight.

His boots sounded on the floorboards as he crossed to her, standing a pace away. "I know naught about these matters, fashion and suchlike. But I do know you cannot go to church in that old dress, and your other gown is little better." His scent overwhelmed her senses, wind, soap, a hint of leather. Close as they stood, bathed in firelight, she noticed the nick on the corner of his freshly shaven jaw, the shades of dark and light in his eyes. "I didn't want you to feel out of place," he said softly.

"Thank you." The words seemed gossamer in the face of his kindness toward her. Surely there was something she could do for him.

"I'll be going to church come Sunday. I hoped. . .with the clothes, you might join me."

She nodded. "I'd be glad to."

Something she could do for him. . .

Did she dare? Would he take offense if she asked? But—she took in the ragged ends of his hair—it truly needed to be tamed.

"Shall I. . .would you like me to. . .that is. . .I really do think I ought to trim your hair." This time, she couldn't blame the fire for the fierce heat of her blush.

His eyes widened, then a grin crept across his lips. "You do, do you?"

"Aye." She folded her arms across her chest. "I do."

He took off his tricorn and ran a hand through his crop of unruly strands as if assessing its state. "Very well then. Saturday night, you may do just that."

Chapter 8

As he sat by the fire, hair wet from his bath, a towel draped round his shoulders, Josiah questioned yet again the wisdom of agreeing to Elowyn's request. And kept on questioning as she approached, hair damp and loose about her shoulders, a pair of scissors in one hand, a comb in the other.

He glanced at her. "You're sure you know what you're doing?"

She nodded, firelight soft on her features. "Of course I'm sure. I tended to my. . .Tom Brody's many a time. Now, turn round." 'Twas the first time she'd given him an order, especially in a voice that brooked no refusal. He instantly obeyed.

"So long as you're sure."

A giggle escaped. "What are you so afraid of? Are you Samson, afeared you'll lose your strength?"

He liked the sound of her laughter, even if 'twas at his expense. "Of course not. It's just. . ." He frowned, unsure how to phrase it. "I usually manage myself. Not since my mother has anyone ever. . ." His words trailed away. Did this woman ever have a way of making him tongue-tied, stumbling over the simplest of sentences. If she knew, she'd likely think him a half-wit.

"I understand." She worked the comb through the thick strands of his hair. Her hands were gentle, and as they every so often brushed his neck, the side of his jaw, he relaxed.

For long minutes, the only sounds were the snip of her scissors and the crackle of the fire. 'Twould have been a peaceful way to fall asleep, had he not been acutely aware of every time her fingertips brushed his skin.

"Have you always been a blacksmith?"

"I learned the trade when I was sixteen."

"Your father taught you?"

"He took to the trade in time, but nay, 'twas not he. Ned Coggin, the smith here before me. I worked alongside him for two years."

"Keep your head still and tilt it forward, so I can make the back even."

He dipped his chin toward his chest. Her lavender scent washed over him as she bent toward him, scissors snipping. He drew in a breath of it, then another. 'Twas delicate yet defined. Like the woman it belonged to.

"So what did your family do before blacksmithing?"

A piece of wet hair fell down his collar, making his back itch. Yet 'twas her question, not the tickle in his back that made him uncomfortable.

"We were in mining. My grandfather and father both."

"What changed? You can put your head up now. I'm done with the back." She walked round and clipped at his right side.

"After my grandfather's death, the mine fell on hard times. We were attempting to break through to a new level when we suffered a flood, which took months of time and resources to restore. During which the workers labored for not even an ounce of copper. My father did the best he could, and truly, threw everything he had into restoring our fortunes. But in the end, it came to defeat. He—" He swallowed, the words wooden on his tongue. "He wagered the mine on a card game, in the hopes of regaining enough to pay part of his debts. It did not end well." He jumped as the scissors nipped a corner of his ear.

"I'm sorry, Josiah." Her hands stilled. He turned to look at her and sensed 'twas not for snipping him that she apologized. Compassion shone in her gaze. "Misery piled upon misery. 'Tis not an easy load to bear."

"Nay, but learn to bear it we must. For misery is part and parcel with life." His ear tingled, though the skin hadn't broken. He stopped himself from rubbing it.

She moved to the other side and resumed trimming, curlings of hair falling onto the towel and to the ground. "What happened then?"

"My father's mind was in no state to think of work, so I filled the gap. Old Ned Coggin took me on. We sold our house, rented a room in town. My. . .mother died." The door he stared at became a canvas, painting pictures he'd rather not see. His father's crumpled expression as he clutched his mother's hand atop the coverlet, powerless to stem the tide of her life. "Ned died not long after, and we scraped together enough to buy his forge and cottage. Two buildings in sorrier repair, I've rarely seen." He gave a dry chuckle.

"And mining? Do you miss it?"

Perhaps scissors in her hand emboldened her. When she wasn't being timid, she could ask questions direct enough to rival a magistrate. " 'Tis in my blood. A thing like that doesn't change overnight. Nor ever, if truth be told. But we made do, my father and I. Forged a life."

"A goodly one." She picked up a hand mirror from the table and held it up. "Well, what do you think?" A smile played about her lips. Slightly parted, the color of strawberries. A curl dangled near her neck. He ached to capture it with his fingers, tuck it behind her ear. Touch her skin as she'd touched his.

I think you are beautiful. I think I'm in a fair way to falling in love with you.

His gaze held hers. A beat passed. She kept smiling, a look of expectancy on her face.

"Do you not like it? I only trimmed it up a bit."

He glanced in the mirror. She'd trimmed the edges of his hair with such deftness, leaving no traces of the raggedness his own efforts had always achieved. One would almost think him a gentleman.

"It looks. . .fine." What else was he to say? That he cared little about the state of his hair or the reliving of his past. He only wanted more of this nearness, to unravel the mysteries of the woman he'd wed. "Thank you."

She pulled the towel from his shoulders, bits of hair falling to the floor. "You're welcome." She walked across the room and took the broom in hand.

He stood, rolling his shoulders and rubbing a hand across the back of his neck. The broom swished against wood as she swept up his hair.

Two weeks. That's all that had passed.

He stared at her, moving about his house with the assurance of one who'd dwelt there for years, humming a low tune in time with her sweeping.

Two weeks since she'd come into his life. . .

And made him wonder if losing his heart again might be worth the risk.

⁓

'Twould be their first outing as husband and wife. Besides church, that is. Though they'd been wed a month, they'd spent most of the time at home, except for the occasional trip to Launcegrave for errands.

Mistress Elowyn Hendrick, the blacksmith's wife.

A role that still seemed strange to her, but one she'd begun to slowly settle into.

The village fair had been going on since morning, but they'd remained at home until early evening. Josiah had labored in the forge alone, Peter having secured the day off to spend at the fair.

Autumn's breath hung in the late September air as they approached the green on the outskirts of Launcegrave. The wind bore strains of merry fiddling high onto the air, blending with laughter and voices, woodsmoke and roasting meat.

As they drew near the crowd, her fingers tightened atop Josiah's arm. She'd never been fond of crowds or parties. But she intended to do her best for Josiah tonight, so he'd have no cause to be ashamed of her. For she did take pride in being on his arm.

Most of the stalls that had earlier held dairymen selling cheese or hagglers' bits and ends had emptied. Beneath a tent, folk sat and ate at long wooden tables, while in the center of the green, couples fligged up in their finest skipped to the lively tune of a country dance. The dance ended as they approached. Lydia Wingfield hurried toward them on the arm of her partner, cheeks pink and eyes sparkling.

"You came!" She disengaged her arm from the young man's at her side and hugged Elowyn. "I'm so glad."

"You look radiant."

Lydia beamed. "So do you in that lovely gown of yours." She turned to the young man at her side. "Allow me to introduce you to Thomas Custance. He's a clerk at the bank. Mr. Custance, these are my friends, Mr. Josiah Hendrick and his wife, Mistress Elowyn Hendrick. Mr. Hendrick is the blacksmith."

"I believe we've met before." Thomas held out his hand to Josiah. "You mended that hearth crane for my mother. She was quite pleased with how it turned out."

"I'm glad to hear it. Are you enjoying the festivities?"

"Indeed." Lydia looked up at Thomas, and Elowyn would swear stars filled the girl's eyes. "It's been a lovely evening."

Mr. and Mistress Wingfield strolled toward them arm in arm,

their two youngest daughters at their heels.

"Elowyn, dear. How wonderful to see you." Mistress Wingfield embraced her warmly.

"As it is to see you." Surrounded by the Wingfields, her unease faded. She could fit into this life, with these people, couldn't she? In time, mayhap, 'twould be as if she'd always been there. Fully belonged.

How her heart craved such a feeling.

Lydia and her beau chatted with her family a while, then went off to join the dance, along with the other two Wingfield girls.

An elderly man approached their circle, shaking hands with the Wingfields and Josiah, who introduced him to her as John Martin, an old friend.

"A word with ye, Hendrick?" Mr. Martin asked.

"Of course." Josiah turned to her. "Excuse us a moment?"

"Certainly," Elowyn answered.

Josiah and Mr. Martin moved away, heads bent in conversation. She watched him disappear into the crowd. Of course he'd no need to cling by her side all evening.

Still, his presence had given her a kind of mooring. Without it, some of her earlier awkwardness returned.

"Shall we sit down?" Mistress Wingfield asked. Mr. Wingfield offered Elowyn his other arm, and the three of them made their way toward the backless benches set up in a square around the dancing area.

"Mr. Wingfield!"

They turned at the voice. A boy dashed toward them. "Mr. Wingfield!" He skidded to a halt, panting. Tears tracked down his grimy cheeks. "I've been looking everywhere for ye." He made a noise between a gulp and a sob. "I went to yer house and knocked and knocked, but no one was in. So—" He gasped for breath. "I come here. Please, sir. Ye've got to come. 'Tis my mum." He swiped a hand below his nose. "She don't have long left, and she be asking for a parson."

Elowyn's heart cinched. The frantic tremor in the child's voice, the fear flashing through his too-wide eyes. Those were only the outward signs.

She was all too well acquainted with those that lay beneath.

Mr. Wingfield bent and laid a hand on the boy's shoulder. "I'll come with you straightaway."

"Are your little sisters with her, Jem?" Mistress Wingfield asked gently.

"Aye, mistress." Jem nodded. "Please, sir." He tugged on Mr. Wingfield's sleeve. "We'd best hurry."

Mistress Wingfield glanced at her husband. "I'll go with you, Edward. The little ones. . ." She turned to Elowyn. "I'm sorry."

Elowyn shook her head. "Nay. You'd best make haste."

The Wingfields followed young Jem away from the festivities. Elowyn stared after them, wind stirring her hair.

Be with Jem and his family tonight, Lord. Comfort them. The loss of a mother is a heartache no child of tender years should have to endure.

She slowly made her way in the direction of the dancing. Surely she could find Lydia and the Wingfield girls. What was keeping Josiah? The sky was fading fast, the night lit up by roaring fires and lanterns hanging from the trees. Fiddling blended with drums, the music loud and lusty.

Lifting her chin, she refused to allow herself the slightest stir of unease. Being unattended at a country fair was nothing compared to hauling Tom Brody home from the public house whilst foxed patrons pelted her with lewd comments.

Walking toward the dancing, she scanned the crowd for Lydia's auburn curls.

And collided with a solid object, the impact stealing her breath.

"I beg your pardon, sir." She looked up at the gentleman she'd run into. Or had he run into her?

"No harm done." Light flickered over his features. He stood tall and elegant in a double-breasted coat, a beaver hat atop his pale hair. In one hand he held a silver-tipped walking stick. His gaze met hers.

She flushed, ashamed to be caught staring. "Good day to you then." She dipped a fumbling curtsy and made a move to walk past him.

He stepped slightly to the side, blocking her. "I don't believe I've had the pleasure of an introduction," he said, voice cultured and smooth.

"Oh. I do apologize. I'm Elowyn. . .Hendrick." She'd almost said Brody but stopped herself in time.

"Phineas Trevenick." He bowed, hand resting on the handle of his walking stick. "At your service."

She curtsied again. " 'Tis a pleasure to make your acquaintance, sir." She'd never spoken directly to a member of the gentry before. How ought one behave?

"Hendrick." He raised a slender brow. "Are you any relation to the smith, Hendrick?"

"He's my husband."

"Upon my word, you don't say."

"Do you know him, sir?" She pushed a strand of hair behind her ear. At least her dress and cloak made her look the lady.

"I do indeed. Quite well, actually. We were boyhood acquaintances." The crowd milled around them, thinning out with the approach of nightfall.

She could hardly imagine a blacksmith would associate with a gentleman on social terms, so it must've been before Josiah's father lost their mine.

"Then I'm glad to make yours." She smiled.

"Are you here alone?"

She shook her head. "Nay. My husband's with me, but someone asked to speak with him. I was with other friends, but they had to leave unexpectedly."

"Then you are here alone. Allow me to wait with you until your husband returns. The rabble has a tendency to get out of hand after dark, and I wouldn't wish harm to befall a lovely woman such as yourself." A burst of raucous laughter nearby confirmed his words.

"Thank you, sir. That's most kind." She pulled the throat of her cloak tighter around her shoulders as a crisp breeze picked up. The flickering fires illuminated the forms of the revelers in a kind of eerie glow. She gave Mr. Trevenick a grateful look. She could have managed herself, but his solicitude was kind, and she welcomed the company. Ought she go in search of Josiah? But if she did, that could lead to her getting lost. Surely he'd look for her in this general area.

"How long have you and your husband been married?" He studied her face.

"A month."

"And do you—"

"Elowyn." She turned at Josiah's voice. Relief filled her as he came toward her. "I've been looking everywhere for you and the Wingfields." He clasped her shoulders, his touch warming her beneath her cloak.

"Mr. and Mistress Wingfield were called away unexpectedly."

He gazed down at her from beneath the brim of his tricorn, apology in his eyes. "Then you've been alone?"

She shook her head. "Nay. An old friend of yours, Mr. Trevenick, was kind enough to wait with me."

Josiah's gaze swung to Mr. Trevenick, standing a pace away.

"Good evening, Hendrick." He bowed.

"Trevenick." Josiah gave a brief nod.

"I happened upon your wife, and thought it only my duty to wait with her until your return."

"I thank you, but your duty is now discharged."

Elowyn frowned. For a boyhood acquaintance, Josiah greeted him with little friendliness. He glanced at her. "We should be going."

"Aye." She turned to Mr. Trevenick. "Thank you again, sir."

"I bid you both a pleasant evening. Mistress Hendrick." Mr. Trevenick nodded.

Josiah offered her his arm, and they walked through the dispersing crowd toward the road. Lanterns swung and bobbed around them as others made their way homeward.

She looked at him in the half darkness. "What kept you?"

Their steps crunched as they walked. "Martin wanted my advice regarding some difficulties at his granary. I'm sorry I was absent so long."

"You needn't apologize." The sounds of fiddling and laughter faded as they moved onto the road, the moon a glow against the darkness.

Silence fell for several minutes.

"What did you speak of with Trevenick?"

Josiah was not like Tom Brody, changeable in his moods. Yet there was a note in his tone she'd not heard before. "Very little." She tried to keep her own voice light. " 'Twas only a few moments before you came."

"For that, I am glad," he muttered.

His coolness gave her pause. "Why?"

But he did not answer.

Chapter 9

Tugging her shawl tighter round her shoulders, Elowyn hastened down the hillside. Delivering food to the Darter family, the mother laid in a churchyard plot but a week ago, had left her heartsore. Tears welled in Jacky Darter's eyes when she'd handed him the box of bread, freshly made cheese, a cloth-wrapped stargazy pie, and a dozen apples from the tree growing in back of the forge. He'd clasped her hand and called her a blessing, while young Jem and his sisters stood by, eyes hollow with hunger and grief. Before leaving, she'd bent down and hugged each in turn, despite the rank odor about them, their skinny arms twining around her neck. Jem's throat bobbed as he vainly held back tears, and she left the meager cottage with a knot in her own.

Wed to Josiah, she no longer had such lack herself and could begin to supply those of others. The needs around were great indeed, and what she could do seemed painfully little, but 'twas something.

A breeze nipped her cheeks as she headed toward home. Backdropped by the cliffs and the sea beyond, the great stone engine house of Wheal Prosper rose high. Men hauled laden cartloads, while the bal maidens sat, "dressing" or picking the ore by breaking it into pieces with hammers. Younger children sat at another table, sorting the pure ore from the waste. The wind carried their voices. Though the work was hard, 'twas at least not lonely. She'd have done such herself, if

Tom Brody had permitted her.

Onward she walked toward the forge. Tonight perhaps she and Josiah would sit in front of the fire and he'd read aloud while she mended, the deep notes of his voice lulling her into a warm daze. 'Twas too cold now for him to sleep in the forge, so he'd brought his bedclothes inside and bedded by the hearth instead. But not without first asking in his quiet way if 'twould discomfit her to have him in the house. She'd answered nay.

Never had she known such kindness could exist. Tom Brody had rarely made, much less kept, a promise. When Josiah said a thing he meant it, and did all within his might and main to see it carried out. He was generous with his customers, fatherly toward Peter, and of late, when they sat by the firelight, she caught him looking at her with such tenderness, her heart swelled. She'd begun to dream of a married life where a door did not separate them at night, imagined his lips against hers, their children playing on the beach, and Josiah sweeping them up in his strong arms, their laughter blending with the wind.

She turned down the lane and started toward the cottage. An unfamiliar horse stood tied near the forge. Voices drifted from the open window of the house. Elowyn stilled.

"What business have you here, Trevenick?" Josiah's voice.

Trevenick? Phineas? Her fingers closed around her skirt. Ought she go in or remain outside?

"To see about the repair of this toasting fork." 'Twas indeed Phineas Trevenick. Why was that gentleman here?

"You could have sent a servant."

"Perhaps I could have done. Is your wife hereabouts?"

Elowyn sucked in a breath.

"She is not." Steel was more yielding than Josiah's voice.

"Tell me, are you glad you acquired her?"

"I am glad you did not."

You did not? What did Josiah mean?

"Is that the reason then? What manner of misery did you think I would inflict upon her?"

Silence greeted that remark.

Elowyn's stomach twisted. Wind blew her hair round her cheeks, and she swiped it back with a shaking hand. Had Mr. Trevenick been at the auction that day, also bid for her?

"No matter. I got the better end of the bargain, of that I can be certain. You'll be missed, though, at the shareholder meetings."

Shareholder meetings?

"No doubt you'll be able to aptly compensate for my presence. Now, if you'll excuse me, I've work to do."

"Very well." Mr. Trevenick's tone remained as smooth as ever. "Your father chose an apt name, you know. Wheal Prosper is most certainly prospering, more than ever before. Pity, after so long, you might have enjoyed a portion of the benefits, if you'd not esteemed that girl more than your share." Boots sounded across the floor. "I bid you good day."

Heart a frantic clamor in her chest, she picked up her skirts and ran across the yard, toward the forge. She slipped inside the dimness and leaned against the back wall, taking deep breaths of air that smelled of smoke.

Nay. It couldn't be true. She pieced together fragments of the conversation, trying to come to grips with their meaning.

Josiah had owned a share in Wheal Prosper—*that* was the mine his father had owned? Then, on the day of the auction, he'd sold it to Phineas Trevenick, to purchase her and prevent Mr. Trevenick from doing so. No other explanation made sense.

Tears burned her eyes.

Why?

Why would he do such a thing for her, a stranger to him? Give up rights and profits in his father's former mine to save a mere girl? She'd thought his sacrifice great, but now the magnitude of it increased tenfold.

'Tis in my blood. A thing like that doesn't change overnight. Nor ever, if truth be told.

She wasn't worth it. Not the ruin of this good man's dream. Tom Brody had brought her to what should have been misery, and instead she'd been granted a home, a hearth. Happiness.

Aye. She'd been little acquainted with the meaning of the word till she wed Josiah Hendrick.

While she'd basked in the first happiness she'd known since before her mother's death, he'd borne this loss alone. And still he'd held her while she sobbed on their wedding night. Opened her eyes to the beauty of Cornwall. Given her a dress and cloak and smiled to see her joy.

From the beginning, he'd shown her love. A love deeper than fickle emotion steeped in feeling. A love she did not deserve.

The consequences of her father's actions were hers to suffer, not his. She didn't deserve redemption. Hot tears slid down her cheeks, and she clamped a hand against her mouth to muffle a sob.

What she did deserve was every dram of the guilt now weighing her down.

She inhaled a trembling breath, fighting for a calm that would not come.

She'd not rest till she found a way to repay him.

⌒

"You're quiet tonight." Throughout the evening, she'd scarcely said half a dozen words. He'd grown accustomed to their conversations about all manner of things. Books, childhood memories, his work at the forge, plans for next spring's garden. The topic mattered less than the woman he shared it with.

Tonight, she'd been as silent as on that first day.

"Am I? I hadn't noticed." She looked up from her knitting as the fire hissed in the hearth. He rose to stoke it then resumed his seat. They sat across from each other, chairs on opposite sides of the fire. But with this distance between them, they might as well have dwelt in different counties.

"Are you well?" Sitting forward, elbows on his knees, he studied her in the glow of firelight. Had she been that pale when she'd returned from Jacky Darter's? He'd been too riled from Trevenick's visit to notice. A visit he'd not told her of, nor would he. The less she had to do with that man, the better.

"I'm a bit tired." She laid aside her knitting and stood, chair legs scraping the floor. "I think I'll retire early."

He hoped she wasn't sickening with something. There'd been word of fever in the village.

"Good night, Josiah."

He met her gaze. For a long moment, she regarded him. Something brewed in her eyes, a look he couldn't cipher out. She turned away and crossed to the bedchamber.

"Good night."

The door clicked.

He stared into the flames. In the smithy, he was never at a loss. He knew how hot metal needed to be heated in order to be made malleable, how to strike iron so it bent without breaking, how to craft intricate curves and designs to make a piece beautiful, as well as useful.

But with the inner workings of the heart—hers, his own—he was well out of his depth.

He blew out a sigh and scrubbed a hand across his face. It had not been his best day. He'd drawn on every drop of self-control to keep from grabbing Trevenick by the throat and throwing his sorry carcass

out the door. That he'd dare to show his face on Hendrick property. . .
The man had come to gloat, like some feudal lord flaunting his riches
in front of his serfs.

Why would Trevenick concern himself with a lowly blacksmith?
Everything one might aspire to, Trevenick had. An old family name,
an estate, not only one mine but two, both of which he now held
complete power over, since all remaining shareholders acquiesced to
his bidding in everything. Servants, heaping coffers, luxury, grandeur.

Mary.

Heat rose in Josiah's chest. Grinding his teeth, he stood. For the
sake of his sanity, he refused to relive that past. Trevenick and his
power had already stolen enough from him.

He'd be dashed if he let that man claim a particle more.

Chapter 10

Good day, Mistress Hendrick."

The voice at her back made her start and turn. Phineas Trevenick stood behind her, studying her beneath the brim of his beaver hat.

She made a slight curtsy. Launcegrave bustled with the din of market day. Peter had taken ill with fever, leaving Josiah at the forge, rushing to meet a large order for nails without an assistant. She'd offered to make their twice-monthly trip to town alone and had ridden in, stabling the horse at the Three Swans while she shopped.

"Admiring the millinery?" He gestured to the window display of velvet-trimmed bonnets and plumed hats.

"Only for a moment. I'd best be on my way." She ducked her head and turned to walk away. She'd not soon forget Josiah's conversation with Mr. Trevenick two weeks prior. Truth be told, more than one night, she'd lain awake sleepless, thinking of little else. Why had Josiah not told her what he'd done? Or of Mr. Trevenick's visit? His silence had stilled her own tongue from bringing the matter up with him.

"Why the hurry?"

She'd have continued onward, pretending not to have heard him, but 'twould have been improper to cut a member of the gentry. Slowly, she turned back around. A horse and rider clip-clopped down the street, passing them.

"I've errands to attend to, sir," she said, voice cool.

"You look troubled." His brow furrowed. His coat was the color of plums, his cravat snowy white. She was surprised he'd dirty his polished black boots with the refuse of Launcegrave. "Have I offended you?"

She shook her head.

"Well, something seems amiss." He took a step closer, the scent of musky cologne wafting over her.

Did she dare? She'd vowed to somehow repay Josiah but had conjured no way to do it. Mayhap this man might provide a way. "I do confess, sir. I don't quite know what to think of you."

He arched a brow.

She swallowed back the dryness in her throat. "What I mean to say is, at the. . .um. . .auction, you did bid for me." Would he admit to it?

To her surprise, he nodded. "I did. When I came upon the scene in the square, I was quite naturally appalled. To think the auctioneer would have countenanced such a thing. So I did the only thing I could think to do. I had my servant bid for you. As a gentleman, I could not stand by and witness a lady in such distress without doing what I could to alleviate it. I thought after all was said and done, I could employ you in my household as a servant."

A servant? Such a life in a fine house like she'd heard Trevenick Hall was would have been bearable. Equally respectable.

I am glad you did not. What had Josiah meant by those words? Was Phineas Trevenick a monster? Josiah seemed to hold no fondness of feeling toward him.

"Then why did my husband prevent you?"

He shook his head as if equally confused. "I don't know. When he came to me and offered his share in the mine I already own the majority of in exchange for allowing him to win the bidding, I gave way."

She still didn't understand. Not Mr. Trevenick's motives, nor Josiah's.

"But what of the share? Is there any way it might be gained back?"

He took a step toward her. "Why do you inquire?"

She met his gaze. "I know Josiah was loath to part with it." But why then, had he? Mayhap he valued it less than she thought.

He gave a brief smile, eyes lingering on her face. "I understand your concern. And would welcome discussing the matter further, but not here in the open street. Would you wait upon me tomorrow for tea at Trevenick Hall? I shall be in all day."

"Would you like my husband to wait upon you as well?"

"That won't be necessary." He lowered his voice. "I should tell you, Mistress Hendrick, that your husband has harbored strong resentment toward me since his youth. Even at an early age, he showed aptitude for managing Wheal Prosper, and his father's loss of it to mine was a bitter blow. Since then, he's refused to meet me on civil terms. I think it would be best if you and I attended to this matter alone. To spare him any embarrassment, you understand."

That explained Josiah's behavior toward Mr. Trevenick the night of the fair. All men had their weaknesses. Tom Brody's was drink and debt. This harbored grudge from the past, Josiah's.

A gust of autumn air chilled her face, fingered beneath her cloak. She shivered. "If that is what you think best."

"Then until tomorrow, Mistress Hendrick." He tipped his hat and walked away. She headed down the street in the opposite direction, marketing basket in hand, cloak billowing behind her, exposing the lower part of her arms to the bite of the air.

Mayhap Mistress Wingfield had some insight into the matter. Before returning home, she could stop at the parsonage to speak to the woman. To gain answers. Not more questions. She'd enough of those.

A lifetime's worth.

Trevenick Hall stood at the end of the avenue, a towering edifice of caramel stone. Its very pillars seemed to proclaim the power and pride of its occupants.

Hurrying up the shrub-flanked avenue, breathless in the stay-laced confines of the burgundy gown, she felt as small as a child in comparison to the immense estate before her. The circular drive with a stone fountain at its center, the manicured lawn, the dozens of windowpanes winking in the sunlight, bespoke a manner of living that couldn't be further from the one she'd lived with Tom Brody.

What place had she to call upon the head of one of the foremost families in Cornwall? Mayhap she should turn round. Toward Josiah and the forge and safety.

Her steps crunched determinedly on the gravel. She'd not retreat. She'd come this far already.

Mistress Wingfield had been out, Lydia told her. So she'd not had a chance yesterday to speak to the woman about Josiah or her course of action. She'd slipped away from the house an hour ago, taking care not to let Josiah see her leave in her best gown. She'd left a note on the table, saying she was going to the Darters. Doubtless he'd wonder why she'd not told him herself.

She couldn't bother about that now.

Slowing her pace, she ascended the wide stone steps, walking between pillars that dwarfed her to reach the massive front door. She stared at the brass knocker shaped like a crest, a curved *T* in the center, before lifting her hand to take hold of it and knock.

A moment passed. Her heart thudded beneath the bodice of her gown.

What did she hope to achieve, exactly? For Mr. Trevenick to cede to her a share rightly his? Though he seemed a gentleman, such a request went beyond the bounds of courtesy.

He'd invited her. She'd not imposed herself.

She'd let him take the lead, see what happened.

A liveried footman opened the door. "Yes?"

"Mistress Hendrick to see Mr. Trevenick. He's expecting me," she added.

"Come in." He held the door while she stepped inside, then closed it with an echoing click. "Your cloak?" asked another servant in identical wig and livery.

Fingers unwieldy from cold, she undid the ties and handed over the garment. The footman laid it over his arm and disappeared down the hall, shoes an echo on the marble.

"Right this way." The first footman led the way, leaving her to follow. The house was called Trevenick Hall, but it seemed a palace, with dark wood paneling and gilt-framed paintings of stern-faced men in powdered wigs. He led her through an arched threshold, down a passageway, their steps an echo. He opened a door on the left.

"Mistress Hendrick to see you, sir."

"Send her in. And bring tea."

The footman held the door and nodded to her. She stepped inside. Mr. Trevenick rose from a settee in a room as elegantly appointed as the great hall.

He made a bow. "Mistress Hendrick. Good afternoon."

She curtsied. "Good afternoon."

"Won't you sit down?" He gestured to the matching settee across from his. She crossed the room and sat on the edge, her hands brushing the silk upholstery. He resumed his seat and crossed his legs, one hand leaning on the armrest. A ring with a green stone the size of a small robin's egg glinted on his pinky. The heat of the crackling fire warmed her chilled fingers and face.

"I saw you coming up the avenue. You walked here."

She nodded.

"Was that not strenuous? It is over two miles from the Hall to the smithy. I marvel at your strength."

"'Tis an easy distance." She didn't add that she'd had no other way of going to the Hall without attracting Josiah's attention.

The door opened and the footman carried in a silver tray. He set it on the low table in front of Mr. Trevenick's settee with only the faintest of rattles, bowed, and left the room.

Mr. Trevenick leaned forward, lifted the silver pot in one hand, and poured tea into a delicate cream-and-gold patterned cup. "Milk? Sugar?"

Had her stomach not been knotted with unease, she'd have answered yes to both, just to see what it tasted like. "Thank you, but nay. Plain is fine."

"A biscuit?" He gestured to the tray of round biscuits dusted in a powder so fine it looked like a scattering of snow.

She shook her head. "Nay. Thank you."

He rose and handed her the cup of tea. Beneath the saucer, their fingers brushed. "Thank you," she murmured.

His gaze held hers. "My pleasure."

He returned to his seat and poured his own tea, dropping two lumps of sugar into the cup with little silver tongs. She sipped the steaming drink. The tea's richness marked it as of the finest quality, even without milk and sugar.

But she hadn't come here for tea. Lowering the cup with a clink, she drew in a shallow breath. "Pray do not think me forward, but should we not get down to the reason for this visit?"

"Which is?" He set his cup on the edge of the table.

"My husband's share in Wheal Prosper. You did say we'd discuss the matter further." She tempered her words with a smile.

"So I did." He leaned back in his seat. "I regret I must tell you, much as it pains me, there's nothing to be done. Your husband sold the share to me, completing the transaction with a bill of sale. A fair and legal business matter. And unless he has the capital to pay me back, I'm afraid my hands are tied."

After she'd come all this way, that was all he had to tell her? He could have said as much yesterday. She pressed her lips together. "If such a sum could be got hold of, would you sell?"

"I'm afraid not." He stood and walked toward her, seating himself on the opposite end of the settee. "The truth of the matter is, I've long coveted that share. It was owned by a distant relation of mine, who, upon his death, gifted it to Hendrick. Parting with it now would be a matter of bad business."

Heat crept up the exposed skin of her neck. What a wasted journey. She'd been foolish to think any good could come of it. "Why did you summon me here if that was all you had to tell me?"

He took the cup and saucer from her hands and set it on the end table beside the settee. "I apologize if I've done so under false pretenses." He reached across and took her hand, holding it in both of his. She pulled away, but he held fast, his fingers trapping hers. "Since that night at the fair, I've been wondering how I might manage to renew your acquaintance. Meeting you in town yesterday provided the perfect opportunity."

"Why would you wish to renew our acquaintance? Surely you've enough of your own kind to associate with." She didn't care how angry her voice sounded. He'd tricked and misled her. He deserved all the ire she could mete out.

"Perhaps I do. But none are as beautiful—" He removed one of his hands from around hers and trailed his thumb down the side of her cheek. She sucked in a sharp breath. "—as you. I find my usual restraint has all but—" He trailed lower, brushing her bottom lip. "—fled."

Panic rose tight in her throat. She had to leave. "You forget yourself, *sir*. I am a married woman." The bravado in her words did not altogether hide the tremble there.

"You are mistaken, my dear." He leaned closer, his breath brushing her cheek, lips nearing hers. "I forget nothing."

She turned her face away.

"I could offer you a great many things. Fine clothes. Jewels. Luxury enough to make you forget you ever sought that paltry share." Honey purled through his voice. "A beauty like yours is in wont of ornament to enhance it. It would be my pleasure to provide such ornaments." His breath tickled her cheek. "In return for your favor, you'd find my generosity. . .boundless."

"You are greatly mistook if you think I am that kind of woman." She struggled against his grip on her wrist, teeth gritted. "I'm asking you to let me go."

He chuckled softly. "You're even more beautiful when your passions are roused." He leaned over her, his weight pushing her back against the settee.

She gasped, head jarring against the armrest. Pain shot through the back of her skull. Her vision blurred with the impact. "Stop! Release me at once, or I will scream."

"It will be of no use to you." He shucked off his jacket, legs pinning her to the settee. "There's not a soul here to come to your aid. Here, I am the only master." He leaned over her, hands reaching beneath her skirts, the scent of his cologne making her sick. "What I desire, I possess."

Her mind began to go blank, shutting out her surroundings, drawing into itself. The only shield she had. 'Twas happening again. Only this time, 'twas violation she'd suffer, not mere abuse. Bruises to her skin would heal.

Those to her soul would not.

Too many times she'd been a victim of the strike of Tom Brody's hand or the sting of his strap. Again and again, she'd endured the physical pain, weeping tears that went deeper than the marks upon her body. Beseeching God for deliverance. When none had come, she'd ceased to ask.

But now. . .

God, please, save me.

She would fight.

His breath heaved in her ear as his saliva-wet lips neared hers. Drawing on every ounce of strength, she raised her knee and drove it hard into the flesh of his stomach. Once. Twice. He reeled back with a yowl of pain and a muttered curse.

Heart pounding, she clambered off the couch. One chance. That's all she had.

She ran, not looking back, grasping the doorknob and flinging open the door. He called after her, his shouts echoing in her ears. Her footsteps slapped against the floor, her skirts fisted in her hands. Down the corridor, through the great hall. A footman stood sentry, but she wrenched open the door herself and fled down the steps. She flew across the gravel, lungs burning, hair flying behind her.

Escape.

That single word became her heartbeat.

She ran until she could run no more and Trevenick Hall was far behind her. Then she collapsed to the ground, gulping in breaths, tears streaming down her cheeks. Stones and dirt bit through her stockings, but she scarcely heeded the pain. Fire stitched her side, and she pressed her hand against the spot.

She was unharmed. His lips had not touched hers, and he'd not violated her. She should be overwhelmed by relief. And she was. Yet shame yawned deeper. Sorrow. She'd brought it upon herself by thinking she could somehow alter the course of events Josiah had put into motion when he'd sold his share. In the end, she could do nothing to get it back.

About so many of life's miseries, she could do nothing.

She'd wondered why her husband treated Mr. Trevenick with coldness. No longer. She'd thought him a gentleman. She could not have been more mistook. Likely 'twas not some petty grudge from the past that made Josiah cold toward him, but his knowledge of the blackness of Trevenick's character.

She must move past her fear and seek answers from the only one who could give them. Her husband. She'd tell him she'd overheard his conversation with Mr. Trevenick, and ask why he'd done what he had that day at the auction.

If he'd not rescued her, she could be trapped at Trevenick Hall, Phineas Trevenick, her master, subject to his violation.

Not only had Josiah saved her from Tom Brody; he'd protected her from so much more.

A tear trailed down her cheek. She brushed it away.

'Twas time to move forward. Josiah had treated her with nothing but honor. If he'd esteemed her enough to sacrifice for her, should she not accept his gift instead of doubting her worthiness to receive it?

Mayhap the God she'd so often petitioned had heard her cries and indeed granted deliverance. Both through Josiah's rescue and giving her the strength to fight today.

Thank You, Lord.

She picked herself up off the ground and moved down the road in the direction of home, though her legs still shook. Feathered clouds swirled against the blue of the sky, the grass browning as autumn overtook summer.

She'd give herself tonight to rest and gather herself enough to speak to Josiah tomorrow. She'd tell him the truth about everything, including confessing what she'd done today. If they were to have any kind of loving marriage, honesty and openness must come from both sides.

Oh, that he might accept her heart, bestow his in return. If she could but know she had a chance at attaining the love of this good and gentle man...

In time. In time, I can ask him all.

Onward she walked, filled with the strength of a plan newly made.

Chapter 11

Hoofbeats pounded the road. Stepping out of the forge, Josiah squinted into the glare of afternoon sun. Horse and rider turned down the lane. As they did, he glimpsed the face of the man atop the sleek brown animal. Unease stirred in the pit of his stomach.

Phineas Trevenick.

Likely come to pick up the toasting fork. Josiah should have clouted him with it. His jaw hardened. He still might. He stepped into the forge to the bench where he kept finished pieces and took the utensil in his hand. He'd extract every last farthing from this particular transaction. The man could have sent a servant to retrieve it, or tossed the toasting fork in the rubbish bin. They had enough in their coffers to have another sent from London.

Not bothering to wipe the sweat from his face or the grime from his hands, he returned outside. Trevenick dismounted and tied his horse to the hitching post outside the forge. He strode toward Josiah, standing out against the roughness of the smithy in his bottle-green riding coat and buff breeches. Worthless dandy.

"Good day to you." Trevenick inclined his head.

"Trevenick." He gave the barest of nods. "Your fork is mended. The cost comes to five shillings." Stating the price gave him momentary satisfaction. Usually he adjusted his fees to what the customer could reasonably pay, which meant he often took a loss. Today, he'd make certain his fee matched the worth of his work.

Trevenick took the fork and examined it without comment. He withdrew a coin purse from his coat pocket and handed Josiah a crown. Josiah exhaled a breath of relief as the man did an about-face and walked toward his horse. Good.

Instead of remounting, Trevenick put the fork in his saddlebag, the end sticking out, and turned back to Josiah. In his hands, he held what looked like a folded square of cloth. 'Twas a shade of rich green. Familiarity niggled the corner of his consciousness.

"Is Mistress Hendrick about?"

"Nay." Behind him, the fire in the forge snapped. Though that heat had naught to do with the one simmering in his chest now. Why did this man seek out Elowyn? Did he think to win her favor as he had Mary's, plying her with flattering words and gifts until she bent to his will?

"Pity. But no matter. I expect I can trust you to see this is returned to her." He handed the bundle over. Josiah took the fabric in his hands, and unfolded it.

Running her fingers over the softness, eyes wide with delight. Billowing behind her as she walked to church.

Elowyn's cloak. There could be no mistaking it.

"Ah, yes. You're wondering how I came by it. She left it at my house yesterday."

Yesterday? He frowned, trying to grasp some reality to anchor him. Elowyn had visited the Darter family yesterday. Though when she'd returned, she'd not said a word of Jacky or the children.

"You're mistook. My wife was nowhere near your house."

Trevenick emitted a low chuckle. "Oh, didn't she tell you? But of course, she would not have spoken of it. How foolish of me to assume you knew."

He took a measured step toward Trevenick. "Knew what?" So help him he'd—

"That your wife was with me yesterday. We had a most. . . entertaining afternoon together. Which reminds me. There's one more article I have yet to return." He reached inside his coat. An embroidered ribbon dangled from his fingertips, stirred by the wind.

One thick and blue, embroidered with white roses.

A garter. The very one Josiah had chosen for her.

White-hot heat consumed him. The cloak fell to the ground. He lunged forward, grabbing Trevenick by his cravat, shoving him against the forge. His fist tightened around the neckcloth, his jaw gritted. A thousand words fought for utterance, but none emerged past the vice around his throat.

Trevenick gulped for air, face turning red. "Unhand me."

Every muscle in him wanted to sate the fury, ram the man's skull into the wood again and again until he slumped lifeless. *Elowyn.* His Elowyn.

Mary. The coy tilt of her head as she turned to look back at Trevenick. The flush in her cheeks whenever she'd returned from one of her "walks."

It had happened again. A growl of rage, of disbelief, of madness rose from his throat.

"You forced her."

"I assure you she was most accommodating. Of course, you should know that. Or don't you?" The words were a rasp, but that did not lessen the impact. Josiah tightened his grip on Trevenick's throat, the man's pulse beating beneath his fingers. A gurgle emerged.

He drew back, fingers curling into a fist.

Mary.

Struck.

Elowyn.

The force of the blow reverberated through his arm. Trevenick's head slammed against the forge. Blood trickled from his nose.

Josiah stepped back.

"Come on." Breath sawed in and out of his lungs. He dug his boots into the dirt, feet planted wide. "Your lackey isn't around to do the job for you. Not this time. This time, it's just you and me."

Blood dripped from Trevenick's nose, falling in blots upon the ground. He leaned against the forge, wheezing for air.

"What?" A bitter laugh escaped. "Not man enough to sully your own fists? Nay. You just bed the women, to hang with the consequences."

"Your wife had to come to *me* to satisfy her needs. Now, who's the man?" Trevenick pushed off the wall and came at him. He swung. Josiah ducked. His fist connected with Trevenick's cheek. To thunder with that chiseled profile.

Rage, raw and feral. Fists against flesh. A strike to his eye. Lightning pain.

Elowyn.

Her name rose like a howl in his brain.

No matter what he unleashed upon Trevenick, it would not give him that which he most craved.

Not revenge.

Oblivion.

⌁

Elowyn hurried down the lane as the first droplets of rain fell from the sky. Though it did not assuage her guilt from yesterday over lying to Josiah as to her whereabouts, she'd truly been glad to visit the Darters today. Glimpsing the stark pain in Jacky Darter's eyes as he spoke of his wife had only reinforced her decision to be truthful with Josiah and seek his truth in return. Life was too short to live with doubt and secrets between them. Love, too precious to be wasted.

She gazed at a sky the color of slate, water pelting her face and hair. She pulled her knitted shawl tighter around her shoulders. It wasn't until late last night she'd realized she'd left her cloak at Trevenick Hall. Though she rued the loss of Josiah's gift, she gave thanks a garment was all yesterday had stolen from her.

Empty basket in hand, she pushed open the door to the house. It creaked. She hung her damp shawl on a peg and turned, blinking in the dimness.

Josiah sat at the table, shoulders hunched forward, face hidden from her. She forced a smile to her lips, despite the trepidation skittering through her. She'd not delay their conversation another hour.

"Rain's coming down hard."

He turned. She gasped. An ugly bruise darkened his eye. Dried blood coated his upper lip.

"Gracious! What's happened?" Dropping the empty basket to the ground, she hastened toward him, kneeling in front of his chair. "Who did this?"

He only stared at her. Hair fell over his forehead, tangling around his face. Particles of dried blood blended with the stubble darkening his jaw.

The look in his eyes was one she'd seen many men wear, but never he.

Darkness.

Her breath seeped out. Whenever Tom Brody had worn such a look, she'd kept herself scarce. Or suffered the consequences.

Josiah is not my father.

But still a tremble shook her.

"Josiah," she said softly. "Please. Tell me what happened."

"There are some items on your bed." The words were between a mutter and a breath. He didn't look at her, seemed barely to see her at all.

She frowned. "What?"

"Go." The command made her jump.

She rose, only vaguely aware of the ache in her knees from

kneeling, and crossed the room. The door to her bedchamber stood half ajar. The floor creaked as she stepped inside. Her pulse thudded in her ears.

Spread across the bed lay her cloak.

And a length of ribbon. Embroidered with white roses.

A wave of nausea heaved through her stomach. She'd realized when she'd arrived home that she'd mislaid her garter. Her mind had been in too much tumult to spare thinking of where. Who had brought these things here?

And what conclusions had Josiah drawn from them?

She looked over her shoulder, gaze falling on the slumped form of the man at the table. A man bearing the marks of a struggle. A man who'd regarded her with coldness in his eyes, where there had formerly been warmth.

On legs that no longer seemed her own, she returned to his side. He glanced up. His features might as well have been hewn in stone. Firelight cast angry shadows on his battered face.

Thunder rumbled, shaking the house.

Neither of them spoke. She stood before his chair, her body cold and still. Hating the silence, but afraid to break it.

"It's no use," he said, voice a low rasp.

"What?"

His rose, faced her, his hard-hewn frame making her small in the low-ceilinged cottage. "Our marriage. This mockery of a life together." He took a step toward her, gaze narrowing. "Is a faithful wife too much to ask?"

Her heartbeat tasted raw. "Do you think me unfaithful?"

"You were with Trevenick yesterday afternoon. You told me you were at the Darters. What else have you lied about?" His voice escalated. "How many times has it been? How many times have you given yourself to him? While I spared you my touch because I sought to treat you and our marriage with honor. Did the vows we spoke mean nothing to you?" He shook his head. "The fault is mine, I suppose. I should have noticed the signs. Instead I let myself be played for a fool."

Tears pressed against her eyes, his words slicing her. "I was *never* unfaithful to you." A sob choked her voice. "I've given myself to no man, nor ever would, except to one to whom I was bound in a holy union before God. Why would you think thus of me? Have I given you cause? Have I played the coquette? Have I done anything but seek to be a good and true wife? Answer me that, because if I have been at fault, I should like to know it."

He stared at her. His faded shirt hung untucked, open at the throat, the fabric spotted with dots of browning blood. "Trevenick brought by your cloak. He said you'd been to Trevenick Hall. The cloak I can understand. But how would he have come to have *that* if what you say is true?" His voice held disbelief. He thought her a liar and a faithless woman. The first she might be, to her regret. The second she'd never...

She swallowed. " 'Tis true I was at the Hall. He invited me there, to speak about...a matter. Yet 'twas all a ruse. He'd no intent of discussing it at all. He—" Her throat jerked. "He imposed his advances upon me." Tears slid down her cheeks. "He would have violated me if I'd not defended myself."

The color leeched from his face. His hands hung limp at his sides.

"I did wrong in trusting him, thinking his station enough to merit him the title of gentleman. If I can claim any fault, it is that. Not faithlessness." She drew in a shaky breath.

"I did not know." His voice was serrated, scarcely louder than a whisper.

"You did not know. Yet you immediately thought the worst of me? How can I expect to trust in any kind of stability if this is how you behave?" The words flew from her mouth, angry darts. "I can bear many things, but cruel suspicions and mistrust, I will not bear."

"How can I expect to trust in any kind of stability if this is how you behave?"

The same words she'd pressed back time and again in the face of her father.

"Elowyn—" He took a step toward her, but she backed away, holding up a hand.

"Nay. Do not." A driving ache throbbed in her temples. She couldn't stay here. Not to look at him, to face him, to recall what he had thought her capable of. "I think it's best if I go."

"Where?" Pain filled his gaze. She looked away so she did not have to see it.

"I don't know." She tried to pull clarity from the scrambled muddle of her mind. "To the Wingfields."

"For how long?"

"For tonight, at least. I need. . .some time." She moved past him, into the bedchamber. Of course, as his wife, legally he could prevent her. Would he? Nay. He'd never imposed anything upon her against her will.

Slowly, she gathered a few things and bundled them up in her old cloak. The new one she left on the bed. Carrying her makeshift bag, she walked back into the main room. He stood where she'd left him. He turned.

"It's raining," he said quietly. "You should take the horse."

"Nay." She shook her head. " 'Tis yours."

"Take it, Elowyn."

Too spent to argue, she nodded. She moved toward the door. There, she paused, looking back at him. Body taut, eyes haggard, like the cares of the world rested on his shoulders, and he could no longer stand to carry them. An ache speared her heart.

"I will return," she murmured.

And left him.

Chapter 12

He stood at the window as she rode away beneath an angry sky, down the ribbon of road, until horse and rider disappeared from sight. She was gone.

He was alone.

Josiah stumbled across the room like a drunken man and collapsed into a chair.

A vase of dried flowers sat in the center of the table. She'd picked them on one of their evening walks, bending down and filling her arms with the purple blooms.

"They're meant to be saved," she said, smiling up at him. *"Then, though their beauty may fade, 'twill never die."*

A cry rose deep in his throat. It shook his bent shoulders, another following on its heels, until he wept wracking sobs, tears sliding from his swollen eye, stinging the cuts on his face.

"Elowyn. . .I'm sorry. . .God. . . I'm sorry. . ."

"Yet you immediately thought the worst of me? How can I expect to trust in any kind of stability if this is how you behave? I can bear many things, but cruel suspicions and mistrust, I will not bear."

Her shattered gaze. The tears in her voice. Her upheld hand putting a barrier between them.

Elowyn was not Mary. But he'd pinned on her the same conduct, thinking this woman as faithless as the last. She was innocent, and he'd wounded her by deed and word.

And she'd left him.

The fault was his. He'd told himself he'd healed from the pain Mary had inflicted. But he hadn't. It lay beneath the surface, a cancer outwardly cured, inwardly spreading through his body and wreaking misery.

He'd asked God to help him forgive the wrong Mary had done him. But had he truly forgiven her? Or only told himself he had?

Memories clawed to the surface, taking form inside him.

He'd fallen for the miner's daughter with the flame-hued curls and spirit to match the moment he'd first laid eyes on her. When she'd agreed to wed him, he'd considered himself granted an unparalleled treasure. Being near her every day, watching as she twirled about the cottage humming a country dance, holding her at night, he'd thought no man could ask for a better life. But as the months passed, she became sullen and withdrawn, disappearing for hours on end, leaving him combing the countryside, worry-frantic, only to find her walking toward the forge, refusing to tell him where she'd been. He'd noticed other differences too. A pair of pearl earrings on her bedside table, a silk shawl.

It wasn't until the deed was done that he'd discovered the truth.

"Your wife is with child."

Even now, the memory of the physician's statement still had the power to wrest his breath.

The distance between him and Mary in prior months told him more than words.

When he confronted her, she didn't deny it. And when she spoke the name of her child's father, everything in him went cold. She'd tearfully begged him not to confront Trevenick, to claim the child as his own. Said Trevenick had wooed her with trinkets and gifts and promises of a grand life, until she'd succumbed to his advances. She hated him now, she said.

Josiah had done as she asked. As the months passed, Mary retreated into herself, becoming a shadow of the woman he'd fallen in love with. Hours after the premature birth, Mary died, the child less than a day later.

When she'd first told him the news, he'd pushed back his own emotions and focused on caring for her. After her death, his rage, long tamped down, had been all-consuming. He'd ridden to Trevenick Hall and shoved aside the servant who'd insisted Mr. Trevenick would not see him. He'd told Trevenick the truth, every last part of it, including the words Mary had spoken on her deathbed.

Trevenick had listened in silence, as the truth poured out of him in a half-coherent flood. When Josiah finished, Trevenick said one thing only, with a half smile.

"She was deuced good in bed."

Josiah had lunged at him, fueled by a level of fury he hadn't known existed. When Sam Byng came at Josiah from behind, he'd been unprepared to fend off the attack. The servant had shown the mettle of his strength, throttling Josiah into unconsciousness. He awoke in a ditch, body bruised and bloodied, three ribs broken. For weeks, Peter had managed the forge while he'd lain abed, recovering, trapped in the anguish of his thoughts.

The memories receded. Josiah exhaled a jagged breath, as spent as if he'd lived them all again.

Another's wrong did not make his own right.

He'd sinned.

Oh, he put on a good act, the kind neighbor always willing to lend a hand, the dependable friend. Even the steadfast husband. But deep inside, he'd harbored bitterness and anger. Toward his father, for the recklessness that led him to gamble away their mine. Toward Mary, for betraying him with body and heart. Toward Trevenick, most of all, for his air of self-important entitlement that stole from Josiah what he valued most—his mine, his first marriage.

Toward Elowyn. He'd fallen in love with her, the woman he'd wed in a moment's decision. She'd seemed everything Mary had not been, genuine, sweet, good. And he'd begun to cherish the promise of a future better than his past.

When he'd thought she too had betrayed him, his world had caved in.

Yet what, then, was his world truly built upon? If the actions of those closest to him could stop the turning of it and reduce him to a person he was ashamed of?

Conviction coursed through him.

"God." He lowered his face to his hands. "I'm not strong on my own. I need You. Not something from You, a petition granted, just You. Fill me with Yourself so I need nothing else, so my steadfastness lies in You, not this world and the people in it. Here and now, I make a decision to forgive those with whom I've dwelt in unforgiveness. My father. Mary." There, he stopped.

Trevenick had attempted to violate Elowyn. An act that, if he didn't have every judge and magistrate in the county in his pocket, could have seen him brought to trial. Josiah ground his teeth. He wanted to unleash a great many things upon that man. Forgiveness wasn't one of them.

"I cannot forgive Trevenick in my own strength, but I believe You can help me to find a way to do so in Yours. Help me to see him as You do." He paused. "Forgive me for the wrong I've done and the anger I've harbored." Again, his shoulders shook. "Forgive me."

The final part of his prayer was one he did not voice aloud.

For Elowyn. For her to be safe. For him to be granted another chance.

For forever to not be too late.

Would the tears ever cease falling?

"I'm sorry," Elowyn choked out between gulps. "I don't usually do this."

"It's all right." Mistress Wingfield's tone was soothing. "If you think you're the first who's cried on my shoulder, you're much mistook. With three daughters, it's a wonder our house isn't swimming in tears."

Her laugh came out more like a sob. She drew away, and Mistress Wingfield handed her a handkerchief. After attending to her nose and eyes, she clenched it in her lap. Rain pattered the roof, and candles lit the Wingfields' bedchamber.

"Now, do you think you can listen?"

Elowyn nodded, sniffling. Through her tears, she'd told Mistress Wingfield all that had happened.

"The story of Josiah's first marriage is not mine to share. Suffice it to say, there were things that occurred. Things that, if you knew, would give you a different portrait of his behavior today. He's suffered a great deal. Though that doesn't excuse his actions, it may perhaps help you understand them, and realize all he said was spoken in a moment of blind anger, out of a heart raw with past griefs."

She sat, wordless, twisting the handkerchief in her hands.

"If you ask him, I feel certain he'll tell you. Truth is a balm that, though it may not completely heal past wounds, will help to salve them."

Mistress Wingfield was right. They needed honesty, Josiah and she. But first, she'd have to be honest with him. She met Mistress Wingfield's eyes. "I went to Trevenick Hall because I overheard a conversation between Mr. Trevenick and Josiah. Josiah sold his share in Wheal Prosper to save me that day, at the auction. And I did not understand why he would do such a thing." She looked down at the handkerchief in her fingers. "He gave up a thing that he held dear for my sake, and I could not reckon with it. Until I went to Trevenick Hall and discovered the truth of its master's character." She shook her head. "Though he may possess the trappings of a gentleman, he is not worthy to be called by that name. Yet still, I cannot understand it. Why would Josiah do such a thing for a stranger?"

"He wished to protect you from"—Mistress Wingfield pressed her lips together—"Mr. Trevenick. That seems a reasonable enough motive, especially considering. . ."

Elowyn raised her gaze to the ceiling, face crumpled. "But why me?"

A warm touch rested on her knee. "My dear, I'm beginning to think your concern lies less with the sacrifice Josiah made and more with your own willingness to receive it."

The words sank deep inside her. Elowyn met the older woman's eyes. Fine creases netted their corners, speaking not only of her years but of the cares she'd borne in a life expended for the service of others. Compassion emanated from them now.

"Tell me: If the woman Josiah saved had been someone else, would you so utterly rue his sacrifice? Or would you think it an act of kindness? A redemption rendered?"

She looked away, fighting the truth.

She wasn't worthy. That belief had been seeded the day her mother died and Tom Brody started drinking. If she'd been, somehow, enough, to her mother and to God, her mother's life would have been spared. Her father would have learned to love her.

Neither happened. As time passed, he'd fallen deeper into the clutches of drink and poverty. She'd suffered in silence, her early attempts to mend his ways receiving naught but angry rebuttal. She'd begun to view herself as worthless, as he did, the state of mind chaining her to him as surely as if leg-irons shackled her. Mayhap she didn't deserve a better life.

Josiah had changed her circumstances. But though the voices from her past had dimmed, they'd once again risen to mock her.

"I. . .I don't know," she finally said, voice weak.

"It's not a question of your worthiness or unworthiness. None of us are truly deserving. Certainly not of grace, much less the promise of eternity. But yet, the Lord mercifully grants us both. It's an act of love, my dear. One not dependent upon merit, only acceptance. You don't have to attain worth to receive God's love. It's already yours."

Fresh tears rushed to her eyes. Somehow, Mistress Wingfield no longer spoke of Josiah, but of God.

"At my mother's funeral, the parson said the Lord loved only the truly good. That if we did not work every day in toil and sorrow to attain righteousness, we might as well give ourselves up to eternal damnation."

"And you believe that?"

She shrugged. " 'Tis all I've ever been told. I've wanted to fear God, and be loved by Him. Growing up, I didn't have much time for scripture reading, and what I read, all the stories of plagues and folk being turned into pillars of salt, well, it seems to be true."

Mistress Wingfield smiled. "God loves us enough to convict our sin, but He never condemns us for it if we seek His forgiveness. There is such a thing as judgment, but there's also grace. 'Where sin abounded, grace did much more abound.' That's in the Bible."

"I never found such in there." 'Twould take time to contemplate Mistress Wingfield's words, and more time still to change a way of thinking that had been hers almost as long as she could remember.

Help me to do both, Lord.

"I'll show you sometime." Mistress Wingfield's smile deepened. "As for your worthiness to accept the sacrifice Josiah made on your behalf, I believe 'twas no coincidence he did so. You are enough,

Elowyn, and you've no need to doubt your worth, or prove it. Least of all in the eyes of Josiah."

"Am I?" Her voice was weak. " 'Tis unlikely he thinks so now."

Mistress Wingfield shook her head. "Now that, I very much doubt. Marriage is by no means an easy endeavor, even in the best of circumstances. For two souls, each with their own brokenness, to find unity, can only be accomplished with the Lord's guidance. But that you have. And your husband does care for you. Very much, I believe."

"And I for him." With all her heart, she meant it.

"Then you have that too." She reached across and squeezed Elowyn's hand. "In time, I feel certain all will come right between the two of you."

Chapter 13

Waves sluiced over his body, his muscles burned, morning air prickled his face. Rightfully, these sensations should have dulled his mind into a lesser kind of torment.

They did not.

The feeble slant of sun didn't dissipate the cold of his morning swim, but Josiah didn't care. He welcomed the cold. Welcomed anything that would stop him from thinking of her.

Sleep had proved a miserable failure, so he'd risen early and stared blankly at the cottage. Remnants of her greeted him at every turn. The jars of preserves in the pantry, her knitting in a basket near the hearth, the fresh loaf of bread wrapped in a cloth. He didn't dare set foot inside her bedchamber. It held traces of her everywhere, her lavender scent a lingering wraith.

He'd made his own tea, choked on how awful it tasted, and succeeded in burning the porridge. He'd have to scrub for a week to get the blackness off the bottom of the pot.

He sliced through the water, pushing himself hard. Brutally, especially after his brawl with Trevenick. Physical pain be hanged. Better that than the perdition of his thoughts.

Usually a morning swim was all it took to clear his head. Today, it seemed swathed in cotton wool. Except for one pummeling reality.

She'd left him.

He dove beneath the water with a growl.

He'd come to the beach to prevent himself from walking to Launcegrave, pounding on the Wingfields' door like a madman, and begging her to come back.

I've been a wretched cur. I'm sorry. I beg you to forgive me. I love you, and if you let me, I will spend the rest of my days cherishing you. Every beat of my heart is a refrain of your name....

He came out of the water sputtering, water dripping from his hair. Thunderation, he sounded like a besotted addlebrain.

He *was* a besotted addlebrain.

He swam for the shore. His efforts to blunt his emotions by punishing exercise had done not a jot of good. Even if he had to grind his jaw and suffer every moment of every day, he'd leave her in peace. She'd said she would return. He had to trust her. Forcing her to act upon her words before she was ready would do no one good.

His clothes lay in a discarded heap on the sand. He walked barefoot up the shore and dressed. Peter was well enough to return to work, and Josiah needed to get back to the forge. Muscles thrumming after his swim, he lingered for a moment, wind scraping his face, staring out at the expanse of water.

Let my past not have destroyed my future. Make a way of redemption. And though I don't deserve it, Lord...bring her back to me.

Gulls soared overhead, dipping and diving toward the waves. The surf swept in, then out in froths of foam. Resolutely, he turned, back to the forge and his labors and surviving with a heart scrubbed raw.

His breath hitched.

A woman came down the beach. Her hair blew behind her in ribbons of unbound gold.

His heart, his thoughts, his world stilled, fixated on one point.

Her. Walking toward him.

She approached, moving slowly across the loose sand, gaze riveted to him. This, more than their wedding morn, was her bridal walk. He stood still, wind tangling his hair, untucked shirt billowing. Watching her as if she and she alone encompassed the whole of his universe.

A few paces away, she stopped. Her pulse thudded in her throat. Standing before him, her carefully formed words dissipated. The remembrance of what had passed between them when she'd seen him last weighted the air.

"I thought you might be here."

He made no response. Water dripped from the ends of his hair, the bruise around his eye dark, his jaw unshaven. But no anger filled his gaze. Only. . .brokenness.

"I came back"—she swallowed—"to tell you the truth. I heard what Trevenick said to you about the share. I know what you did. I went to see him because I thought I could somehow make it right. Because I couldn't fathom why you would make such a sacrifice for a stranger. And"—she drew in a breath—"because I didn't believe I could ever replace the loss of your dream. I took matters into my own hands, and chose dishonesty over coming to you. Whatever hurt or mistrust I caused you, I'm sorry." She stopped, waiting. Stripped vulnerable by her words, yet freer because of them.

He took a step toward her, and another, until he'd spanned the distance between them. He took her hands in his, gazing down at their intertwined fingers.

"My forgiveness is freely granted. You need not have asked it. It is I who must seek it from you. There is a part of my past you do not know. Mary, my first wife, chose Trevenick's attentions over fidelity to our marriage vows. She. . ." His throat jerked. Her own ached with unshed tears. ". . .conceived his child, and died shortly after bearing it, the child with her. After which Trevenick showed not the slightest scrap of pain or remorse. I was a younger man when it happened, and thought I had moved on, but I had not. I deeply regret my words and actions. Through them, I wounded a woman I've grown to love." His voice broke. "You speak of unworthiness. It is I who is unworthy of you. Of your trust. Your heart. A return of my feelings. I dare not ask it—"

A sound between a sob and a laugh escaped her throat. " 'Tis already yours. My trust. My heart. My love. All of it."

This man who had suffered fathoms of heartache in his past had sacrificed for her, proven himself by word and deed, and now voiced a love he'd already lived out in countless moments.

She could trust him. Truly. He wasn't her father. He was good and steadfast and aye, imperfect, but so was she. They both had scars, regrets, and parts of themselves they hadn't yet shared, but right now, none of that mattered.

"You're certain?" His gaze delved into hers, his voice ragged.

"I'm certain." A smile tugged at her lips.

For a long moment, he studied her, as if he wanted to drink in the whole of her. Then, as waves crashed and sun fell warm upon them, he lowered his lips to hers. He tasted of salt and held her tenderly, his strong hands tangling in her curls. She cupped the back of his neck, pulling him closer, fingers twined in his damp hair.

Love looked like scrubbing the floor after spilled milk, glancing up at her with half a smile as he plunged the rag into the bucket. It looked like cliff-side walks, cried-out tears in the arms of one who cared, evening haircuts by the fire. Her carrying water to the forge as he wiped his hands on a rag, a grin easing over his sweat-damp face. It looked like hard work to build a simple life, realizing that love wasn't easy, but that all worth fighting for was rarely so.

And it looked like this kiss. Gentle. Cherishing.

Josiah.

Minutes later, breathless, they drew away, his hands framing her shoulders. Her head spun from the sweetness of his lips against hers. Kissing him again was a temptation she'd not long be able to resist. But first, she must ask one thing. She took a deep breath, drawing in courage with it. "Do you think you'll ever regret the loss of the share?"

At first, he said nothing. Wind tugged her hair in front of her face. She didn't push it aside, eyes on him. "Nay." He shook his head. "At times, I may miss the mine, but not the share. Having any part of the Trevenicks could never lead to good."

"But if you're not content—"

"That day, at the auction, I felt a moment's loss at what I thought was treasure. But now I see it wasn't treasure at all, but a poor imitation of something I thought would bring back the life I once had." He cupped a hand against her cheek. "You are more to me than all the mines in Cornwall." A tear slid down her cheek at the fervency in his voice. "My wife." His mouth brushed hers. "My heart." He kissed her again then leaned his forehead against hers, hands framing her face. "My love."

Author's Note

The opening scenes of this story were inspired by Thomas Hardy's *The Mayor of Casterbridge*, where the dissolute Michael Henchard sells his wife and daughter at a harvest fair. I first discovered this story as a teenager and have since been intrigued by whether such auctions were a fictional license of Hardy's, or if they actually occurred in England. While researching this novella, I discovered records of several such sales, and historians give evidence to many more. Desperation and poverty, as well as family discord, led men to alienate themselves from their spouses and children in this drastic way. One hopes, as in Hardy's novel, the women found contentment with their new families.

A heartfelt thank-you for coming along to Cornwall with Josiah and Elowyn! I pray the journey has blessed and encouraged you as you dwell in the love of a heavenly Father who calls you His. Because you are His, you are worthy.

Blessings,
Amanda

ECPA bestselling author **Amanda Barratt** fell in love with writing in grade school when she wrote her first story—a spinoff of *Jane Eyre*. Now Amanda writes romantic, historical fiction, penning stories of beauty and brokenness set against the backdrop of bygone eras not so very different from our own.

She's the author of several novels and novellas, including *My Dearest Dietrich: A Novel of Dietrich Bonhoeffer's Lost Love*. Two of her novellas have been finalists in the FHL Reader's Choice Awards.

Amanda lives in the woods of Michigan with her fabulous family, where she can be found reading way too many books, plotting her next novel, and jotting down imaginary travel itineraries for her dream vacation to Europe. She loves hearing from readers on Facebook and through her website amandabarratt.net

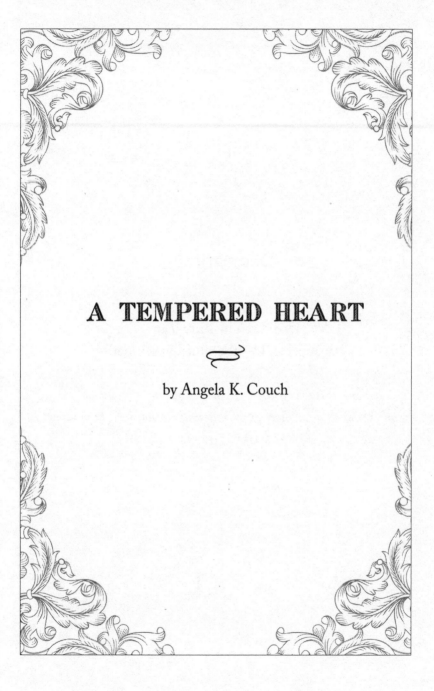

A TEMPERED HEART

by Angela K. Couch

Dedication

Dedicated to Terry Jean
An angel child—the aunt I never met.

For our light affliction, which is but for a moment,
worketh for us a far more exceeding and eternal weight of glory.
2 Corinthians 4:17

Chapter 1

Charlottesville, Virginia
April 2, 1861

Thomas Flynn coiled the chain onto the desk, its music a gentle *clink, clink, clink*. A haunting song, but what did it matter so long as another debt was paid, one more link loosened from the fetters binding him?

"Finest work I've seen." The station manager slid a drawer open and withdrew a slip of paper from his desk—the loan agreement Flynn had signed to fulfill his master's dying wish of having his remains returned to North Carolina to be buried in the town of his nativity. Relatives had seen to the burial but had not felt compelled to reimburse Flynn the cost of travel. What could they possibly owe him? After fifteen years of breaking his back for Matthias Leighton as his apprentice, there was no better reward than being handed the run-down shop and its heavy lease. And the debt.

The clank of coins dragged Flynn's attention to the station manager's purse, shaken to release a few coins to its owner's palm.

"A little something extra for the quality."

"Thank you, sir." Flynn shook the man's hand and took his leave. He was wrong to harbor hard feelings against his old master, the man who had taught him his trade, taken him in like a son. The closest thing he had to family since his own abandoned him in this town.

Outside, the warm spring air mingled with the hustle and bustle of commerce. Shop owners set their wares out to be viewed, peddlers parked carts along the street. A train's whistle hardly penetrated the din of shoppers and those who wished to attract their business.

"Flynn!"

Muscles tightening across his shoulders, he turned to see Dr. Paul Allerton's raised hand. He forced his feet in that direction. The one man he could not refuse.

"Sir?"

"Glad I saw you, Flynn. My daughter is to arrive." He looked to the engine's slow approach. "Give Eli a hand with the luggage."

It was all Flynn could do to keep his jaw from clenching. The man never asked. He bellowed orders as though Flynn were just another piece of his property. And yet it was not within his power to say no. "Sir." He moved several paces off, positioning himself between Eli, who waited near the wagon, and their mutual master. It hardly mattered what color a man's skin—it was easy enough to be bought and sold.

The squeal of iron on iron brought the engine and its cars to a stop, and smoke whooshed down on them. Flynn didn't bother covering his mouth and nose as many did. Smoke and fire were his livelihood.

He stood back from the bustle of people exiting the cars and scurrying across the platform to meet family and friends. Flynn had forgotten the doctor had a second daughter, an older one who had married a northerner long before his association with Dr. Allerton began. Eli nodded at him and moved to where luggage was being offloaded. Flynn stood back while Eli spoke with the men. Two large trunks and three smaller ones were set aside.

"I take it Dr. Allerton's daughter is planning a lengthy stay," Flynn mumbled as they lifted the first trunk.

"Returning for good, as I understand it." Eli's dark skin already gleamed with perspiration from the sun warm overhead. April had welcomed spring with vigor. "Her and a young'un."

"Not her husband?"

"He died. Left her with the boy and his fortune."

A grunt escaped Flynn as they hefted the trunk into the back of the wagon. Not because of the weight, but because in his opinion the Allerton estate already boasted enough wealth.

They were loading the second trunk when a shout rose from the door of the passenger car. "My bag!" The doctor spewed curses as he hurried away from the train, a child in his arms and a woman on his heels.

Flynn dropped his side of the trunk, and it cracked against the side of the wagon before rolling off. He snatched the dark leather medical case from the front seat of the nearby carriage, only paces ahead of Eli. By the time he reached Dr. Allerton, the child, a boy no more than ten, was laid out on a bench, breath rasping in his throat, his small hands slapping his chest.

"You're only making it worse." The woman, drenched in black silks, shoved past the doctor and dropped to her knees by the boy. One hand cradled his face while the other gripped his. "Charlie, you're all right. I'm here. You need to breathe slower. Breathe with me, sweetheart." She pressed her cheek to his. "Breathe with me."

She inhaled deeply, though less than steadily.

In. Then out.

And another. Whispers in between. Her large bonnet and its black lace blocked the child's face, making her all he saw or felt, his whole world. Flynn almost remembered when his mam had been that to him. Before she'd let him go.

Gradually, the boy's small chest took on the same pattern. Steadier. Stronger.

Something tugged at his hand, and Flynn glanced over to see the doctor take his bag. A sigh slipped Flynn's chest in rhythm with the boy and his mother.

Her smile was for her son alone as she withdrew to peer into his eyes. "That's better." She placed a kiss on his forehead and helped him sit. "All better now. Everything is all right. Nothing to be afraid of. We're finally home."

Flynn leaned into the station wall. His sleeves were rolled to his elbows, but he was hardly aware of the coarse brick. Neither could he remove his gaze from the woman and her brown ringlets losing their battle with the humidity still heavy from rain that morning. Rich brown eyes peeked from beneath her dark bonnet as she glanced at him. How long had she been widowed? How difficult had that time been, left with only her son? Smooth skin reflected her youth.

"Charlie gets excited and loses his breath. He doesn't need anything from your bag, Father. A dozen doctors have studied him, and offered nothing. Please, can we just go home?"

Home?

Father?

This was Dr. Allerton's daughter? Of course. Flynn almost laughed as he shuffled back a step. He had work to do. He stalked back to the wagon and stifled a curse. The trunk he'd dropped lay open on the street, its contents spewed across the dirt. Eli worked to clean the mess, and Flynn hurried to lend a hand. What better way to put a woman from one's mind than rummaging through her belongings? He groaned. Books. Quills. Gowns and everything that fit under them. Flynn tried not to think on that while shoving the silky fabrics into the trunk. He allowed one last glance as Dr. Allerton's eldest daughter helped her boy into the carriage and disappeared after him. She had her father and her late husband's wealth. What would she ever want with a blacksmith who hardly owned the sweat-ridden shirt on his back?

Esther Mathews pulled her son close as they drove away from the train station. She recognized the questions and answers chasing across her father's expression as he studied her boy. Always the same. Something was different about Charlie. He learned slower. Spoke slower. Wasn't the same as other boys his age. No one saw beyond to the gentle angel God had sent her. Not even Charles, his own father.

Especially not Charles.

"You never said anything in your letters." Father inclined his head toward her child.

"There is nothing to say." Flint edged her words. She would not discuss Charlie in his presence. His heart still raced under her hand. She'd not let anything more upset him today.

"I would like to examine him once you are settled."

Esther held her tongue. Speaking would only prolong the conversation. She would decline the request later. Charles already saw to it that the best doctors examined their son and always with the same results. There was nothing they could do. Her child was flawed, mentally damaged, physically inferior, and all anyone offered was his removal from her arms.

"How is Julia? I am anxious to see her." Esther forced a smile, eager for another topic.

"Your sister hasn't said a single intelligible thing since we received your letter. She's planned dinners, parties, and tea with half the ladies in the community."

Esther didn't know whether to smile or cringe. Hopefully he exaggerated. The last few years had made her quite content to remain at home with her own company. Far away from the whispers.

Charlie leaned to look out the window, and she compelled her hands to settle on her lap. Aided by his natural curiosity, Charlie's excitement was almost contagious. She didn't want to smother him under her fears.

"Mama, look!"

Esther leaned forward to see the usual bustle of busy streets, but with the addition of military uniforms—sore thumbs among those in regular attire. She couldn't be sure to what Charlie pointed, so she simply smiled and squeezed his shoulder. Sometimes she wished to see the world through his eyes. Without the cynicism that came so naturally to her now. The world had turned upside down since Mr. Lincoln won the election in the fall. Seven southern states had already seceded from the Union, and both sides were building their armies. What would the next few months bring?

Conversation was sparse on the journey to the large house her father had commissioned to be built shortly before she'd been introduced to Mr. Charles Mathews. She'd forgotten the deep red of the brick and the grandness of the peaks. Never mind the great chimneys that had once drawn her imagination to the castles of England. They seemed rather less impressive now. Though still very elegant. Boston boasted great houses, but her husband had liked living in the middle of everything, and so provided an elegant town house. Trapped in the center of the city, by the end it had begun to feel like a prison.

Would she find more freedom here?

Esther climbed the steps with Charlie's hand grasped tightly in hers.

He squirmed, pulling away. "Mama, too hard."

Instantly relaxing her hold, she slowed. "I'm sorry, sweetheart."

His grin beamed at her, offering complete forgiveness. If only this were the boy people saw.

"Esther!"

The feminine squeal pulled Esther upright. *Julia.* She rushed to throw herself into the outstretched arms of her little sister. Though not so little anymore despite the eight years between them. How old had she been, maybe ten, when Esther left? A decade had transformed a little girl into a woman. She'd noted the maturing in their letters, but to see it...

Julia held her out for a moment. "I'm so glad you've finally come. Far too long and not even a visit since that man stole you away."

"I'm here now." What little she had to offer.

"Yes. And to stay. You must tell me everything. Your letters left much to be desired." She gave another hug that slowly weakened. Julia withdrew, looking past Esther to Charlie. He stared back, blue eyes curious and smile in place, tip of his tongue showing between his full lips.

"*This* is Charles Jr."

Esther extended her hand, and he eagerly took it. "This is Charlie." She stooped to capture his gaze. "Charlie, this is your aunt Julia. Say *hello* to her."

"Hello."

"Hello, Charlie." Uncertainty hung in Julia's voice, but her expression softened. She glanced to Esther. "We should get you two settled and rested from your journey. There will be time for visiting later."

Esther nodded and followed; her feet felt almost as heavy as her heart. The journey had been difficult enough, but the reunion with her family laid her torn heart open. It ached for her little boy, ached to find others who would see him as she did, and love him the same.

Chapter 2

Flynn's hammer danced against the cooling copper until the red glow became dull. He set the tool aside and returned the thinning copper to the heat of the forge. A few minutes later, he pulled back and again laid it across the dip in his swage block. He used a smaller hammer to tap out the sway of the ladle. While the copper began to resemble the final product, he would spend the time necessary to smooth every crease and ridge and add ornamentation to the handle. His customers expected the best, and he would give it to them.

Despite the steady tap of his hammer, footsteps breached his concentration, sounding out across the floor of his storefront, to his smithy in the back. Usually a bell announced customers, but he had opened the door with hopes of a spring breeze. A large shadow blocked the light from the storefront as he finished his last strike. Flynn relaxed the ladle onto the block and rotated his shoulders to ease the tightness of his muscles.

"What can I do for you?"

Lyman Hastings, the gunsmith from down the street, offered his meaty hand. "For once, I would like to do something for you."

Flynn raised a brow. He'd never considered Hastings a friend, and the man never went out of his way in the past when Flynn needed the help. "What, exactly?"

Instead of answering, Hastings picked up the nearly formed ladle. "What is this worth? A few cents, perhaps? Hardly enough to get your head above water."

Flynn snatched the ladle away. "What do you want?"

"The army requires rifles, and there's money to be made. I just received an order that is worth over two hundred dollars. Part of that could be yours."

"You want me to build rifles?" He moved to a pail of clear water on the workbench near the door and dipped a cup inside. Better to not allow the other man a glimpse of anxiousness in his eyes.

"The barrels. I'll give you the specifications and provide the iron. It's the time I don't have. They want them by the end of May."

Flynn had enough orders to keep him occupied over the next six weeks, but he needed the money. "How much?"

Hastings scratched a hand across the side of his ruddy face and a day's growth of red whiskers. "Thirty-five if I am providing the iron."

"How's the quality?" Nothing more frustrating than trying to mold cheap iron that would do better as a wagon wheel or horseshoe.

"You think I would give our soldiers anything but the best?"

Flynn held his comment. "Forty dollars."

"Forty! Have you no loyalties to the Confederation?"

The month-old Confederation that Virginia hadn't officially joined? "I have loyalties to myself. Same as you, I believe."

Hastings frowned. "My final offer is thirty-seven."

"Forty."

He huffed out a breath. "Very well. I will have the iron delivered in the morning."

Flynn nodded and then walked toward the door, indicating their conversation was over. He had work to attend. Yet he lingered in the doorway after Hasting's departure. He closed his eyes and filled his lungs. If he could keep up with his usual work while forging the rifles, he might put a dent in his debts. It would require long days of hard hours, but for the chance to get ahead, he couldn't decline.

The murmur of women's voices drew his gaze to Dr. Allerton's daughters. Hooped skirts sweeping the street, they strode toward him with boy in tow. The elder sister, who had arrived a week earlier, glanced Flynn's way but with disinterest. Probably didn't recognize him from the station. He hadn't expected otherwise. There was no reason for the pang in his chest.

"Good morning." Julia Allerton paused and peered through his shop window, which showed little due to the haze of dust.

He made a mental note to wash the glass. "Morning, Miss Allerton. Is there something you wished to see?"

Her slender shoulder rose a degree. "I was going to send someone for a new broom and shovel for Esther's room, but maybe we'll pick one out while we are here."

Esther. Though the lady in question frowned at the suggestion, and her son pulled from her grasp, something in Flynn softened at the use of her name. His baby sister had been named Esther. Barely a year old in his memory, she'd be a young woman now at sixteen. Or was it seventeen? How could a memory so clear have happened so long ago?

"I'm hardly picky about what my fireplace broom looks like." Esther's voice rang with exasperation as she tried to drag her son from where he crouched to examine a stone. "And we are expected at the milliners."

Julia hooked her arm through her sister's. "It won't take very long, and you have yet to appreciate the artwork you'll find in this shop."

"Charlie is already tired." Esther's focus remained on her son who again reached for the stone. We've stopped at almost every door we've passed."

"We came to shop. You are the one who insisted on bringing the boy instead of leaving him with a nurse."

Esther's shoulders pulled back and her body stiffened. "I already told you how I feel about that." She took a step, boy in tow. "I think it best I take Charlie home."

"I want rock, Mama."

"It's dirty, sweetheart." She tried another step.

The boy's eyes, set wide apart and with a slight slant, filled with tears.

Her own face crumpled, and she touched his cheek. "I know you want it, but it'll soil your hands. We need to stay clean today."

"I stay clean, Mama," but he still reached for the stone.

Flynn crouched down and plucked it from the dirt. As ordinary as rocks came, but the boy seemed to place importance upon it. "I could wash the stone, ma'am. Would only take a moment."

She studied him for the first time, her expression showing uncertainty. At the same time, a smile bloomed across the child's face, transforming his whole countenance.

That was sufficient for Flynn. "I'll be back in a trice."

They followed him inside, past his display of wares to his workshop and the pail he used for cooling. Warm water washed over the stone, bringing out tones of red that had not been visible under the dirt. Flynn couldn't help but wonder what was wrong with the boy. He didn't act like others his age. Nor did he speak the same. His appearance was quite different as well—something about his face.

"See, Mama!"

Flynn turned. They stood in the doorway to his smithy. The large blue eyes of the boy scanned the fire, bellows, anvil, and table set with tools. Esther only took a fraction of the time to take in where he worked all day, before focusing on him and the stone in his hand. He couldn't tell which had earned the distaste rippling her brow.

He wiped a rag over the stone and held it out to her.

She plucked the rock from his palm and set it in her son's waiting hand. "This was very kind of you, sir. Charlie is very fond of stones. He collects them."

"Not an unusual pastime for a boy." Flynn offered a smile, hoping for one in return. She was so unlike her younger sister. Life pinched the corners of her eyes, and a worry crease seemed to have taken up permanent residence between two well-shaped brows.

"Thank you, Mr. . . . ?"

"Flynn."

Her eyes widened just a smidgen but enough to see the question and answer left unspoken. *Irish?* She gave an uneasy smile and backed into the storefront where her sister looked over his wares. He was used to the dismissal, the walls that rose when people learned the only thing remaining of his family, but the sting faded slower this time.

⮑

An Irishman? Her late husband had cursed the existence of them, and they had indeed plagued the streets of Boston. But this man did not speak with the same strong brogue. Looking at his wares, it was obvious he was a talented craftsman.

But Irish?

"Look at these fireplace shovels." Julia waved her over to a small selection leaning against the wall. Some simpler styles, while others sported intricate handles portraying hearts and vines. One spiraled upward from the base into an elegant hook at the top, a teardrop of bronze melded within. A matching broom stood alongside. A man who knew his craft.

She brushed a finger over the smooth handle. "Very nice."

"Is that the set you would like?"

"Should do adequately." The need for a fire in her room was almost gone with the warming weather, but this would appease her sister.

Julia motioned to Mr. Flynn, who stood in the doorway beside Charlie. "Can you set these aside, and I'll have someone fetch them."

His head dipped with a nod, but his azure gaze remained on Esther, stirring the strangest sensation in her chest. "I hope they will serve you well, ma'am."

Esther refrained from shifting. "I'm sure they will." She should tell him how beautiful she thought them, how much she appreciated the skill required. Instead, she opened her hand to Charlie. "Let's be off."

He came obediently, but she wasn't blind to the pat on the shoulder the blacksmith gave him as a send-off. Her core melted at the gesture. Most seemed eager to keep her boy at arm's length, as though his ailment would somehow pass to them. A boy with a heart as big as Charlie needed touch, needed acceptance.

The sun greeted them as they stepped onto the street, and Esther blinked at the noonday brightness, not allowing herself to look at the man who watched them from his doorway. Instead, she glanced to her sister. "When we're home, I'll give you the money to send. I see no reason for Father to take care of me as before I married. Charles left me a comfortable enough living."

"Nonsense. Father will not hear of you fritting away your living so long as you're here. Besides, Mr. Flynn has a debt with father. Anything we wish from his shop is simply deducted from that amount. Don't give it a second thought."

Esther held her reply, though she had no intention of backing down. She enjoyed her independence, and would allow Mr. Flynn the same. If he paid Father with the money she owed him, that was his right. Though what sort of debt would a blacksmith have with a doctor? Even if not as large a man as many of the blacksmiths she'd seen, the strength in his lean frame was impossible to ignore. Hard to imagine such a virile man sick. Perhaps a family member had fallen ill? For all she knew, Mr. Flynn was married with a dozen children. The Irish never seemed to do things by halves.

After the milliners, Julia led her to the dressmakers where she hurried about selecting ribbons and gushing over fabrics. Esther looked on, commenting as needed. Charlie ran his free hand over the dainty laces and different fabrics while his other gripped the stone so graciously cleaned.

A smile pulled at the corners of her lips at the thought of the kind gesture on her son's behalf. Perhaps the Irishman had a houseful of children after all.

"Madam Goshen is ready to take your measurements." Julia beckoned her toward the curtain at the back of the room. "I'll keep an eye on Charlie."

Seeing no other option, Esther crouched and squeezed her son's hand. "Mama's slipping away for a few minutes, sweetheart. Can you be a good boy for Aunt Julia?"

He nodded enthusiastically, "I be good!"

She kissed his head and joined the seamstress, who pulled a pencil from her bun, a coil of chestnut streaked with gray. While Madam Goshen measured everything from the length of Esther's arm to the thickness of her waist, they discussed patterns and fabric. With Charles gone over two years now, both Julia and Father insisted she set aside her black and grays for more cheerful colors. She would relent with a soft violet, and perhaps a dark green or blue. All the while, she kept an ear attuned to the other side of the curtain and Julia's chipper voice.

Esther compelled her shoulders to relax. She was silly not to fully trust her own sister with Charlie. He was a good boy after all. Generally quite patient and well behaved. Coming home was the right thing to do.

Final pattern decided on, Esther pushed through the curtains and straightened her hat. "I think we are ready." And not a minute too soon. The day's excursion left her exhausted. She glanced around for Charlie. Had he also gotten tired and found a place to rest?

"Julia?"

Her sister held royal-blue satin up to her chin while she gazed in a full-length mirror. "One moment. What do you think of this shade for my complexion?"

The shade suited her fine, but where was Charlie? Esther walked around the table of fabric between them.

"I usually stay with lighter colors, but this blue—"

"Where is he?"

Julia's nose wrinkled. "Who?"

Esther shoved past to search behind a display of ready-made gowns. Her heart skittered and her head spun. "Where's Charlie?"

Julia jerked as though waking and spun around. "I—he... He was standing near that display not a minute ago. I swear."

Perhaps, but he was nowhere to be seen now. Anger and panic flooded Esther with raging heat. She charged the door.

Her child was lost in an unfamiliar city, among people who wouldn't know him.

Chapter 3

The tinny jingle of the bell barely breached the clang of Flynn's hammer. He paused only long enough to holler that he would be another minute. The copper glowed, begging to be formed. His tapping gentled as the swoop of the serving spoon thinned into the indention. Finally, it was cool enough to set aside though not ready to join the matching ladle he'd formed that morning.

He pushed to his feet, but made it no farther. An inquisitive face stared at the half-formed spoon.

"Where's your mother?" Or the boy's aunt, for that matter? While most children his age might wander the streets on their own or in bands, Flynn gathered from their brief meeting that Esther Mathews kept a tighter rein on her son.

The boy pointed behind him but moved closer to the swage block. He reached for the utensil, and Flynn handed it to him.

His mouth formed a large O.

"Your name is Charlie, correct?"

A grin broke across his face and lit his blue eyes. "I am Charlie."

"You can call me Flynn." He extended his hand, and the boy took it, albeit briefly.

"You make this?" Charlie's full attention again settled on the spoon.

"I did. But it's not quite finished. Still needs a lot of smoothing.

Folks don't like snagging their mouths on barbs when they eat."

"I can. . . I can watch?"

Flynn arched his neck to see into the storefront. No sign of the child's mother. "Maybe just for a minute, and then we should ask your mother."

"Mama's busy."

"I'll bet she is. But that don't mean she'll not miss ya." He felt his speech relax, the familiar accent returning. Something he never allowed around his customers. Something this child would not judge him for.

The boy merely smiled. "She always misses me." His eyebrows rose to tell half the story.

Flynn couldn't hold his own smile. "I can't blame her." He took the spoon and began tapping out the rough edges, a wave of loneliness seeping through him as though he were a boy again. How often, with night's shadows upon the walls and sleep far from him, had he thought about his parents, wondered if they missed him as much. For the first few years, he had cried himself to sleep. He'd have done anything to go with his family, prove that he could be of use to them.

"You. . .are very. . .strong."

"I've been doing this for a long time." Over fifteen years ago he'd started as an apprentice. He'd not been much older than this boy.

"I want. . .to be strong."

Flynn looked up from his work and saw something flicker in the child's eyes. Something akin to determination.

"Then. . .Mama won't. . .worry so much."

Setting the hammer aside, Flynn laid a hand on Charlie's shoulder. "Worrying is something mothers do." Nothing stopped that. His had worried about food enough for the younger children and Da finding work. Though Mam had little choice, tears stained her cheeks when they'd left Flynn behind. "We should find yours."

"Can I. . .come back?"

"You'll have to ask your mother. But you are welcome."

The faltering smile returned, and he lunged to wrap his arms around Flynn's middle. Enough to knock the wind from his lungs—though not from the pressure of the hug. But from the heart of it.

When Charlie finally released him, Flynn tried to speak but had to clear the thickness from his throat. "Let's be off then."

Charlie slipped his hand into Flynn's larger, coarser one, before leading the way to the front of the shop. With a glance up and down the street, Flynn tried to recall the colors of the gowns both women wore. All he remembered was the charcoal of Esther's. The same shade of gray skirts hustled in the opposite direction, franticness in the movements.

"Come on," he urged Charlie and hastened after her. He had to slow his walk, so Charlie could keep up. Flynn was about to call out when Esther twisted around. She didn't immediately see them, but the relief in her expression displayed the moment she did.

"Charlie!" Instead of a reprimand, her arms engulfed the boy. Then her eyes narrowed, her gaze cutting to Flynn. "What are you doing with my son?"

An accusation more than a question, but he kept his voice even in reply. "Looking for you. He wandered into my shop a few minutes ago."

"But why—?"

"Why wasn't someone watching him closer?" he countered. "Or maybe you watch him too closely."

"Mr. Flynn, I have no idea what you mean to imply, but I suggest you know nothing of the situation."

"What I mean to say, ma'am, is your boy is very—"

Esther stepped in front of Charlie as though to block him from Flynn.

"Curious, ma'am. Your boy is curious and attentive. I don't mind him watching when he likes."

"I. . ." Her mouth fell open.

"Good day, ma'am." Flynn turned on his heel and started back to his shop. He doubted Mrs. Esther Mathews would bring her son anywhere near him again, and all the more's the pity.

⇌

Esther sat by Charlie's bed long after he slept, content to watch the soft contours of his face and the rise and fall of his chest. Too easy to recall the fear of hours earlier, the panic of missing her son. She now knew better then to trust Julia with him—she had remained almost indifferent through the whole ordeal. And Mr. Flynn. . . Esther honestly wasn't sure what to make of the Irishman and their exchange.

Curious. Attentive. Two characteristics no one had ever associated with Charlie. Both warmed her and granted hope.

A splinter of light angled across the room from the opening door and the lamp the housekeeper held. The light glowed upon her tawny skin. "Your father asks that you join him and Miss Julia in his office."

Esther leaned down and pressed her lips gently to Charlie's cheek. "Very well," she whispered. The office—not the parlor or the library. The office meant Father had something he wished to discuss with her. She was far too weary for more than a warm cup of tea and her bed, but she started down the great stairwell she had once raced up and down as a young woman, eager to throw herself into society's path—or at least the path of any eligible gentlemen. Nothing seemed to have changed since then. Except her.

Father hardly glanced up from the thick ledger laid across his desk. Julia sat straight-backed on an ornate chair upholstered in royal-blue damask. Stale pipe tobacco permeated the air.

"You wished to speak with me?"

Father pulled what appeared to be a letter over the ledger, and tapped a finger to it. "The boy is in bed?"

"Yes, *Charlie* is sleeping." She folded her arms across her stomach. Her father had yet to call his own grandson by his given name. Always *the boy* or *that child*. She held to the hope that given time he would begin to see more than Charlie's ailment, but perhaps he never would. Always the analytical doctor.

"Have a seat then. Julia was telling me of your excitement in town."

Esther sat in a chair matching her sister's, only a small table holding a globe separating them. Charles had traveled extensively after Charlie's birth and had insisted she accompany him. She and *only* she. Always, she had refused to leave her baby. She might have seen most of Europe by now, but she'd never regret her choice to remain behind. Only the distance that had grown between her and her husband. Only the animosity between them at the time of his death.

"I have found the perfect solution."

Esther jerked her focus away from the globe to her father, who held a paper out to her. She stood to take it, unease rushing to her center. "Solution? For what, exactly?"

Instead of answering, he waved for her to be reseated. "I know you feel you are doing what is best for your child, but it is not so. He needs proper care in a reputable sanitarium. I wrote to an acquaintance of mine in Richmond, and he is willing to take the boy."

Esther's attempt to lower into her chair faltered at his words, and she almost dropped to the floor. She staggered to right herself and find her seat—about the same time his words fully registered in her head. She shot back to her feet. "No one is taking Charlie from me."

"Surely you see you are not fit to raise him. He's not a healthy child, Esther. Will you spend your life playing nursemaid when you were born to so much more?"

The same old arguments. She had heard them a thousand times from her husband and friends. Until they had all abandoned her. Charlie was the only one who stayed true, who loved her freely. How could they all expect her to give her own child away to strangers who couldn't love him. Wouldn't love him. She'd seen how doctors reacted. And nurses. Indifference. Disdain, even. They saw him as a problem, and their duty was to make problems disappear.

"You have done everything you can for him." Julia stood and moved to touch her. "You must see this is for the best."

Esther jerked away. "Whose best?" She slammed the letter onto her father's desk, making him startle. "Yours, Father? You can't stand the thought of people seeing him as your grandson. It's only yourself your concerns are for."

"How could you say such a thing?" Julia sputtered.

Father stood as well, hands pressing into his desk. "He's not a healthy child, Esther. His heart. His lungs. Give him to someone who can see that he receives the care he needs."

"He needs me." Esther stalked from the room and up the stairs. She made it as far as the room where her dear, sweet Charlie slept. Embraced in the darkness of his chambers, she sank to the floor near his bed. What if she was wrong? What if holding him close only hurt him in the end? The years of weariness and worry leaked from her eyes, tears for her boy as she continued her prayer.

"Oh God, help me."

Chapter 4

After tapping the narrow mandrel from the center of the newly formed rifle barrel, Flynn set both aside and stretched his right arm. His shoulder and elbow ached from the steady pace he'd kept all morning. All for two barrels. The work required of him loomed over his head, but the agreement had been struck, and he would see it done.

Flynn slipped out the back to the well. A long drink of cool water and the breeze behind the shop worked to refresh him. In a few more minutes he would return to work. For now, he allowed his eyes to close and he leaned against the wall. Two faces rose up in his thoughts, as they often had in the past week. They pestered when he least expected. Esther Mathews standing like a she-bear over her young cub, and Charlie with his ready smile.

Grunting the image away, Flynn downed the last dribble of water from the bottom of the tin mug and turned inside to stoke the fire. He had no time for wasting thoughts on a woman so removed from him or a child he could do nothing for. With his family's wealth, young Charlie Mathews had everything he could ever want. Something most children never boasted.

Why then did Flynn ache to give him more?

Flynn shoved a flat slab of iron into the forge. Maybe what he felt was more akin to the desire for a family of his own—something he barely remembered anymore. A childless widower was the closest he'd had to a father after his own walked away, and it wasn't until the last few years of Leighton's life that Flynn had felt any warmth from him.

The iron showed red, so he pulled it from the heat and laid it over the deepest curve in the side of his swage block. He laid his frustration into the iron. Even if he desired it, he could not afford to take a wife or consider a family until the debt was paid. He didn't dare consider how long that might take. Most of his life, probably.

Heavy blows began to curve the iron in on itself, and Flynn paused to insert the mandrel into the center to maintain a place for the barrel. Matthias Leighton, whom he'd apprenticed under, had lingered five years with failing health, Flynn keeping the smithy going and seeing to all his master's needs. Unfortunately, the quality of the man's work had faltered before he'd stepped aside, and his customers had gone elsewhere, taking their money with them. First, Flynn had only been aware of the doctor's fees, but he had worked out an agreement. Business was picking up more each year, and he'd make good on the doctor's patience.

Little had he known of Matthias's other deficits.

Flynn pounded the iron with more fervency than needed. No wonder Dr. Allerton had insisted he add his signature to the loan. Matthias Leighton had died within the year.

A shadow hovered near the door of the smithy. Long skirts. Dainty boots.

One last strike and Flynn raised his gaze to the woman. His chest constricted with the strangest feeling. Bitterness? Remorse?

"Mrs. Mathews."

"Mr. Flynn."

Only then did he note the head peering round her full skirts with a full smile and dancing eyes.

"What can I help you with?" Flynn straightened and wiped a rag over his wet brow. How must she see him dripping with sweat, his clothes stained? And she immaculate in warm brown skirts. . .and having the same effect on him as a slow sip of coffee. The warmth passed through him, slowing his thoughts, filling his chest. "I assume your earlier purchase was delivered and is satisfactory."

"Yes. Thank you." She stepped into his work space, her gaze doing a thorough scan of the area. A small pucker formed between her eyes. "Charlie has spoken of little else besides his visit here. He's been quite anxious to return."

Much more anxious than his mother, 'twas certain. She glanced at her gloves as though afraid to have already soiled them since her entry.

"He is welcome to watch if he likes." Flynn smiled at the boy and was rewarded with a grin. Sending the iron back into the forge, he stole another glance at the mother. Though no longer a debutante, she wore her maturity well, with a grace that suited her. Dark waves lay across her neck, mutinied from where pins held her hair at the back of her head.

"Is there a chair I may use?"

Her question pulled him from his musings. "You mean to stay and watch as well?"

Her stoic expression was answer enough.

"Very well." He fetched her a chair from the far corner and placed it near the door for her.

She scooted it farther out of sight from the shop's door and windows before sitting, then guided Charlie onto her knee.

Flynn set the glowing iron on his anvil and tried to ignore the eyes burning just as hot from across the room. Despite the back door being wide, the breeze seemed to have died. He inserted the mandrel and took his hammer to the curve of the iron, closing it in on itself.

"What is that you're making?" the feminine voice asked.

"The barrel for a rifle."

"A rifle?" Her tone rose in pitch.

"Aye." He gave the iron another hit, though it cooled quickly now.

"I thought your work above such. I see no other weapons on display."

"The contract I have is with a gunsmith and for the Confederate Army." Removing the mandrel, he returned the iron to the heat, which allowed him a glance at his guest. Charlie appeared enthralled. Esther looked mortified.

"Then you support the Confederates. And slavery."

His spine stiffened. "This has nothing to do with slavery."

"It has everything to do with slavery. The Confederation wishes to keep men slaves, and President Lincoln wishes for them to be freed."

"And you side with him, I sense?"

"Any God-fearing man should."

"Including your father?"

Her mouth opened then snapped closed.

"So, your father is exempt from pandering to your belief."

"I didn't say that. . . ." She huffed out a breath, red rushing to her cheeks. "It's not about my beliefs, but what's obviously right or wrong."

Flynn shoved a log into the forge and pulled down the handle for the bellows. The fire swelled, sparks flying upward. Sweat tickled his neck and spine. "Obviously. And so it makes perfect sense why you came to live in your father's home, being catered to by all his slaves while siding with talk of legislation against all that."

One look at her face, and Flynn knew he had misspoken. Anger flickered in her eyes, but they glistened with a sheen of moisture.

"It is not my place to judge," he sighed. "Simply consider that there is more than the issue of slavery to consider in this division between states. Freedom, ma'am. The states that have seceded and formed the Confederation want the freedom to make their own decisions as promised them when the Union of States was first organized."

The iron had heated as much as their conversation, and he removed it to his anvil then slammed his hammer down. Only to realize he had not yet inserted the mandrel and risked flattening the barrel.

"Perhaps it is best we leave." Esther pushed to her feet, standing her son in front of her. The boy looked from her to him as though trying to figure out what was happening.

"No. Please. I did not mean to offend you." He blew out his breath, wishing he could keep his confession to himself. "I am more a contradiction than you."

She didn't move, probably waiting for further explanation. One he was not ready to give.

"Let me show Master Charlie what I am doing." He was ready to redirect the conversation before it buried him. He focused on the boy. "Would you like to see?"

An enthusiastic nod was offered by Charlie—and the mother made no protest—so Flynn continued, explaining the role of the mandrel in keeping an even channel through the center of the rod. Later the hole would be smoothed and a groove edged in to encourage the bullet straight. The boy watched in fascination as Flynn demonstrated the swings that brought the sides of the iron to meet, and the use of the swage block. Even Esther's expression relaxed and grew interested as he worked, making it hard not to wonder what it was she saw. A laborer doused with sweat? Or a man with the power to wield iron into something of worth? Able to be something of worth.

⇌

Esther wished there were a subtle way to produce her fan from her reticule. Heat radiated through the smithy and not just from the glowing forge, or the glowing iron. The man. . . Perspiration soaked his shirt, making the worn fabric cling to the contours of his back and upper arms. His forearms, the shirtsleeves rolled to his elbows, revealed the ridging of ligaments and muscles drawn taut with each precise strike against the iron.

How different a man he was from any she had personally been acquainted with—if one could call this an acquaintance. The differences between him and Charles were wide and deep. Charles had also cut a slender figure in his perfectly tailored suits, but his hair had been sandy and his complexion white. Mr. Flynn, on the other hand, appeared almost as tanned as a mulatto, dark brown hair laid across his forehead. His eyes, however, were as pale as a summer sky at noon, and stole glances at her every few minutes. Did he conduct a similar analysis? Did he find her lacking?

What does it matter? He was nothing more than a blacksmith, his place in society decidedly below her own. And an Irishman. A wonder anyone trusted him with their business. Charles had been very careful to avoid any interactions with his kind. And yet, the longer she stood watching him, the more self-conscious she felt. Esther sank back into the chair and allowed Charlie to stand by to watch on his own.

When Flynn finally set the hammer aside, he explained how to tap the spike in the center out and return the iron to the forge.

"That was very kind of you, Mr. Flynn." Esther leaped at her chance to retreat, and set her hands on her son's shoulders, ready to direct him from the smithy. "Say thank you, Charlie."

He cocked his head to look at her with pleading eyes. "I want. . . to stay."

"We mustn't impose too long upon Mr. Flynn's hospitality."

"The boy is no trouble."

Esther felt a renewed wave of heat climb her face. He made no mention of her own presence. "Thank you, sir, but I have errands to attend to before returning home."

Flynn leaned his hip into the anvil and crossed his arms in an all too relaxed manner. "Leave him here then." His focus lowered. "How old are you, lad?"

Charlie held up both hands, fingers splayed.

Esther tucked one finger down for him.

"Not much younger than when I began my apprenticeship in this very smithy."

Esther snapped upright. "Excuse me, sir, but—"

"I wasn't implying that he become an apprentice. No doubt you have a much loftier goal for the lad." His jaw tightened and his eyes glinted. "I only suggested he be old enough to stay and watch."

"I understand what you mean to say, but my son. . ." *is not like other boys.* She clamped her teeth onto her tongue.

Flynn stared her down as though daring her to voice her thought. "If he wishes to stay for a little while longer, he's welcome."

Shame for her unspoken words and the pleading in Charlie's eyes stacked upon her conscience. She couldn't force him away. And she'd already declared she couldn't stay. But to trust this man, a stranger, with her son, when even her family, friends, and trained nursemaids had failed. . .

"It'll be all right." The urge came with a gentleness unexpected from a man of such coarseness.

"You're sure?" She searched Flynn's face for any reason to fear to take Charlie despite his protests.

"I am." An easy smile curved the blacksmith's mouth. One she wanted to trust.

Even still, her hands trembled as she crouched and turned Charlie to her. "You sit down here and mind Mr. Flynn. And don't leave until Mama comes for you. I'll only be a few minutes."

The grin on his face broke through her. "I'll be. . .really good, Mama."

"That's my boy." She pressed a kiss to his forehead, lingering for a moment longer before finding the resolve to walk away. "I'll be right back." She willed herself not to look over her shoulder.

An impossible feat.

$$\leftrightharpoons$$

A few minutes later, Esther paced outside of the dressmakers. She was due for her first fitting, postponed because she could not trust to leave Charlie for that long. How could she do so now? She looked back toward the smithy, unable to calm her mother heart. Not until she saw for sure how her son fared with Mr. Flynn.

Instead of heading to the front where the bell would warn the man of her return, she slipped between the buildings into the alley behind. Three men with stained beards and dirt-ridden aprons loitered, arguing about whether or not Virginia should secede with the other southern states—a common topic now. They eyed her as she hurried past, and her pulse skittered. Despite the brightness of day, unease pressed her faster. Weeds grew without care as did piles of forsaken tools and refuge. She hardly allowed a breath until she reached the back of the smithy. The tat of hammer at work eased her steps. She approached the open door from an angle, attempting to remain out of sight.

"Well done." Flynn's voice rumbled.

She peeked around the corner to spy her son, coat removed, bearing a small hammer. He tapped it against a thin sheet of steel laid across the anvil. The barrel Flynn had been working on was laid aside, its glow diminishing.

"Good." He patted Charlie's back, and Esther could almost see the light beaming from her son's face, though mostly turned away.

She leaned back out of sight. Why couldn't Charles have been as encouraging of his son as this stranger? Not that he'd ever spoken cruelly. . .he simply never said anything. He'd avoided. He'd run. Abandoned. And asked her to do the same.

Charlie's laughter flitted through the open door, a balm over old wounds she no longer wished to dwell on. Her husband had made his decision, and now he was gone. She could only imagine what he'd say to his offspring learning a trade, even for a day. Never mind her own father's disapproval. But her son was happy, he was learning, and he was accepted. For now, that was all that mattered.

Taking a deep breath, Esther turned from the smithy. She would hurry with her fittings, and make sure Flynn was well compensated for his time.

Chapter 5

Y ou can't keep doing this to yourself."

Esther glanced up from the newspaper as her father entered the library. So much for a few minutes of peace. Not that the paper had added much peace with talk of political estrangement between the North and South. South Carolina had already seen battle at Charleston. Fort Sumter had fallen to the Confederates. War was no longer a possibility, but a reality. Though nothing made her quite as distressed as her beloved Virginia. Two days ago, they had abandoned the Union. Secession.

"Esther, are you listening?"

She set the newspaper aside, knowing her father felt quite differently about current events. "I'm sorry?"

Father huffed out a breath. "You never let the boy out of your sight. You have buried yourself in his care, wasting your life." He stalked across the room and dropped into his large upholstered chair before reaching for his pipe. "It's affecting your health. You're exhausted."

Which was why she longed for a quiet moment to herself. Her head and feet ached, and Charlie had not gone to bed easily. Still too excited about his time with the blacksmith, the fourth time they'd taken advantage of the man's patience. Since leaving him there while she finished her fittings a week earlier, Charlie couldn't go a day without begging to visit, and it was becoming harder and harder to deny him. She'd had to pry a rough-hewn spoon from her son's hand after he'd fallen asleep.

"I wish you would reconsider—"

"Father! I have already given you my answer. Please do not mention it again." As exhausting as his care could be, the thought of being separated from Charlie, of her boy being handed over to strangers. . . She shuddered while her heart constricted. "I know what's best for my son."

Father murmured something as he lit his pipe and stuck it in his mouth. "At least leave him long enough to attend some social events with your sister. All I hear from Julia is how disappointed she is. That boy's care is too much for one person."

Yes, it was. Being able to step away for a few minutes was becoming a glorious reprieve. Then to return and see Charlie beaming with pride at his creations. And the twinkle in Flynn's eyes. Despite the brawn of the man, he had such gentleness when it came to her son. He didn't seem fazed by Charlie, that he wasn't like other boys. It was as though she'd finally found a kindred spirit—disguised in sweat-stained clothes, a crooked smile, and blue eyes.

"Esther, have you heard a word I've said?"

She jumped and looked back at her father who frowned at her past his smoking pipe.

"Dr. Kirkbride is a leader in his field, and the superintendent of the Pennsylvania Asylum for the Insane."

"Charlie is not insane!"

"He's ill. Both physically and in his mind. Even you can't deny that."

Oh, that she could. To pretend everything was all right with her little boy. What if her attempts to protect him kept him from the medical care he needed? Her lungs felt constricted by an invisible weight, one that grew, year by year, along with Charlie.

Esther stood and walked to the far side of the room and the wall of books, thousands of stories and facts that her boy might never read. She'd tried to teach him, even hired tutors. She sighed and pressed her hands down the front of her full skirts. "Only you are allowed to examine him. Charlie's been seen by others, ones who couldn't care. But he's your grandson, and my child." Esther turned and faced her father. "Please. . ." *Love him.*

He seemed to consider. "I'll examine him. And *you* will attend tea, or whatever other event your sister was upset about tonight."

She chafed under the firmness of his voice. Just because she had come home did not mean she intended to place herself back under his thumb. In the years she'd been away, she'd forgotten how controlling he could be. So long as she was under his roof. . . "Very well."

$$\backsim$$

The next morning, dark blue hung in the sky when Flynn pushed the back door wide and then hauled a load of coal to his forge. The embers still glowed from when he'd finally succumbed to exhaustion the evening before and stumbled up the stairs to the small loft room and the lumpy mattress he called his own. He could have collapsed on the floor downstairs and slept as heavily. Just enough to take the edge off. At the first cock's cry, Flynn rolled to his knees to ask God to bless the day and his work. He didn't usually give the Lord much thought, but if he was going to get everything done, he needed help. Gaining his feet took a little more effort, but it would be worth the pain.

The flames soon burned hot, and Flynn thrust his iron into the coals. While he waited for the rod to heat, he chewed on bread left over from yesterday. A little crustier than Flynn liked, but he had no time to worry about that. The morning melted away to the clang of his hammer and the spray of sparks.

A Tempered Heart—245

"Excuse me."

Flynn jerked around to Esther Mathews, Charlie at her side with his usual smile in place. Flynn wasn't sure why, but the look on the boy's face warmed him beyond the work or the flames. As the boy released his mother's hand to wrap a hug around Flynn's torso, that warmth penetrated deep into his chest.

"Morning to you, Master Charlie."

The boy grinned up at him, and Flynn tousled his hair.

"Mr. Flynn!"

Flynn glanced to Esther and her pout of protest then back to the boy who also looked concerned at his mother. Flynn stepped away, pushing Charlie to arm's length. "You best keep your distance," Flynn told him. He'd donned clean clothes this morning, but they were already moist with perspiration, and his heavy leather apron had been dusted with soot.

"No, it's. . ." Esther waved toward the child's head. "His hair." She stepped closer to comb the wayward locks straight.

"Oh." Flynn wasn't sure what else to say. Fingers through his shaggy mane was about all the grooming his hair got in the morning.

"It doesn't matter." She looked up, large eyes holding such sadness. . .and just a little bit of something else. A tenderness no doubt meant for her son. "Thank you for being kind."

"I—" Flynn raked his fingers through his hair, suddenly self-conscious. The way this woman looked at him sent an unfamiliar sensation through him. His head had been turned by a pretty face before, but this was different. She was different. And the direction of his thoughts needed to be severed immediately.

Easier said than done as roses bloomed in her cheeks. She stepped back. "Charlie was wondering if he could watch for a little while today. You needn't stop your work for him. He's promised to sit in the chair and watch you. I'll also reimburse you for your time." She ran her hands over her already smooth skirt the color of the Emerald Isle itself. "I should have offered that earlier. I'm sorry."

"Ma'am—"

"No, no, I refuse to take advantage of your time or your debt to my father."

Flynn stiffened. Of course she knew about the debt, knew that her father owned him and this shop. He choked down his pride and managed a tight smile.

Her smile faded. "I understand you must be busy with—" She waved her hand toward the swage block where the half-formed rifle barrel lay. She grimaced, probably recognizing it for what it was. "Maybe this is a mistake."

Charlie looked between them, his expression hopeful.

"No. Not a mistake. He can watch me." Flynn squeezed the boy's shoulder—and glimpsed his father in himself. Thomas Flynn Sr. The morning he had left this very shop for the last time, leaving his son behind with nothing but a squeeze of his shoulder and an order to work hard. "I don't require any compensation. From you or your father."

"Sir, I insist."

"Don't." He nodded Charlie toward the chair and shoved the rod back into the forge. "It's not work if for a friend."

Esther's eyes widened. "A friend?"

"Charlie's a good one." He smiled at the boy, who grinned back.

"Mr. Flynn. . .my friend."

"That's right." Flynn nodded at him.

Esther did not look as pleased. Or perhaps she hadn't expected the sentiment. "Oh." She wet her lips and backed to the door. "You be good, Charlie." She glanced to Flynn but never met his gaze. "I'll be back within the hour."

She slipped away, leaving him with the feeling that maybe Charlie wasn't the only one in need of a friend.

Chapter 6

Flynn laid his hand over the much smaller one, guiding the direction of the hammer. Charlie's visit had become almost a daily occurrence, usually for a few minutes, an hour at most. Often Esther sat and watched with her son, but sometimes she slipped away to complete one errand or another. At the moment, she stood behind him, just returned from the milliners.

Despite the work piling up that he needed to attend to, Flynn enjoyed Charlie's company, found himself smiling more, thinking about the boy. And his mother.

"Any luck with your hats?" He turned the small piece of brass in Charlie's hand, yet another spoon he'd been helping the boy with. This would make number three, each one an improvement on the last.

"Julia is happy, so I suppose shopping was a success."

"She was the one who needed a hat?"

"Hats. Or bonnets in this case. For some reason one is never enough. And no, the bonnets were for my head, but on Julia's insistence. One for each gown." Esther groaned, and he suppressed a smile.

"Gowns and bonnets." Flynn had to admit the color she'd added to her wardrobe suited her much better than the grays and blacks worn upon her return to Charlottesville, but didn't dare guess the cost of such things.

"And ribbons, and gloves, and shoes, and reticules, and. . ." She sighed and rolled her eyes.

Flynn looked away. Again, all the reasons to keep his blinders on. He remembered the simple threadbare dress that hung only as far as his mam's calves. She'd worn the same pair of low boots for as long as he could remember, though the soles had worn through. All money went to feeding the children, not frivolities. "Is there anywhere else you need to go today?"

An airy gasp sounded from behind him. "Are you trying to be rid of me, Mr. Flynn?"

No way to answer that honestly without causing offense. Her presence was becoming a distraction he didn't need. "Charlie wants to stay here a little while longer, so no point in you standing around if you have things you need to take care of." He directed Charlie to start tapping again.

"So, my presence here doesn't disturb you?" He could almost hear the smile in her voice.

"Why should it disturb me?" Other than how self-conscious he felt with her lingering near. And the growing desire to steal a glance at her.

"No reason, I guess." Esther stepped nearer, mere inches from his arm. "That doesn't look so difficult."

Charlie paused to beam up at her. "You like, Mama?"

"Very much so." She brushed his bangs from his eyes. "Almost makes me want to try."

Flynn coughed. "Try what?"

She motioned with her head to the half-shaped spoon. "To make something."

Flynn was still trying to come up with a tactful protest when Charlie moved out of the way, his spoon in hand, and passed the hammer to his mother.

"You can. . .have a turn. My arm tired."

Her smile crept higher while her delicate fingers wrapped around the tool's handle.

Flynn stared for a long moment before finding his voice. "Be serious, ma'am."

Her jaw set. "You don't think I can? Or should?" The last word held an edge.

He held up his hands and stepped away. "Be my guest."

For the first time, uncertainty flickered in her gaze. "What do I do?"

He picked up a small slab of iron from his discarded pile, leftovers from other jobs but still useful, and laid it on the anvil. Then handed her a midsized hammer.

She passed the smaller one to him and stepped to the anvil. "Now I hit it?"

"Go ahead."

She gave a whack. And another. With no effect.

A chuckle broke from him.

Brushing a perfect ringlet behind her ear, Esther cocked her arm back to bring her full strength down on the iron. The head of the hammer landed with a loud clank but barely scored the surface. "Really?"

"Cold iron doesn't like to bend." He took his pliers and clamped the tip of the slab before moving to the forge. He showed her where the coals would heat the iron and how to use the bellows to increase the fire's heat.

"I imagine you can make about anything from iron."

"Within reason." The alloy hot, he set it on the anvil and stood aside. "Now give it a try."

She eagerly stepped up and hammered the slab, which gave way under the force. A giggle bubbled from her. She glanced to him with bright eyes, mirroring her son's despite the darker color. "I'm doing it."

"You are." He smiled with her while she continued, unable to help himself.

She hammered this way and that, shaping the iron until it became too cool to form.

"We should heat it again." He moved the iron back to the forge, but Esther beat him to the long handle of the bellows and began pumping it up and down. Perspiration glowed on her face, giving vibrancy to the smile that had replaced her usual doleful expression. He had thought her handsome before but was unprepared for the beauty he beheld now.

Flynn cleared his throat. "Um, that's good. This fire doesn't need too much encouragement right now." He dragged his gaze from her.

"Can I have another turn?" Charlie moved forward, darting toward the forge.

Esther lunged forward. "Stay back, Cha—" Her head cracked against the handle of the bellows.

⮑

Pain radiated through Esther's head from the burning spot the bar had hit. Something clanked on the floor, and a strong hand gripped her arm. "Are you all right?"

"I'm an idiot. It was in my hands not a minute ago. You would think I'd have stepped around." She groaned but tried to straighten, making sure Charlie had heeded her warning and was not near the oven.

Flynn's hands braced her arms. "Maybe you should lie down a moment." His fingers brushed across her hairline, making her wince as they met the bump already forming.

Thankfully, it was only a bump. She'd be fine—as soon as she shook off the feeling of a fire poker to the brain.

"Stay still."

Her thought to argue died under the throb taking up a rhythm with the beat of her heart. She allowed him to lay her down on the firm floor and then closed her eyes. "I'm such a fool."

"Accidents happen to the best of us." Flynn's voice rumbled from where he sat beside her.

Best of us.

"You are the best, aren't you?" Somewhere in the back of her aching mind she knew she spoke far too freely. But it was true, wasn't it? He was honest and hardworking. Industrious. Kind. He was patient and encouraging with Charlie, and even with her. "The very best," she murmured.

"Do you want something cool for your head? I think you must have hit it hard." A hint of amusement lightened his voice.

Charlie's came next. "Is Mama all right?"

She tried to sit up. "Of course, I—"

Flynn's arms easily braced her down.

For which she was grateful. Her head really did hurt. Why not lie here a little longer, on the floor of the smithy? What a spectacle she must be. How ridiculous all this was. Laughter spilled from her.

"Not quite sure what's so amusing," Flynn said easily, a hint of accent rolling off his tongue.

"Everything. I can't believe I did that." Not just bumping her head but working the bellows in the first place. Wielding a hammer and enjoying the whole experience. Feeling alive for the first time in years.

Moisture pricked her eyes, and she pressed them closed.

"Give it a moment. The pain'll pass." The tenderness in Flynn's voice brought more tears.

"It's not that." Esther kept her eyes closed as the confession leaked from her, the weariness and loneliness that had been building long before she even met her husband. The expectations of her family and society. Holding her son close since his birth had started severing each of those ties. And now look at her. "Do you ever feel like life is hammering away at you? It heats you up and then starts hammering."

Constant. Pounding her into the ground.

The crackling of the fire and the shuffle of Charlie's feet denoted the otherwise silent room. She didn't want to open her eyes, to face Flynn now that she had unlocked a small part of her soul.

"Whatever ya've come through has made ya strong," he said softly. Again with that Irish brogue she'd once looked down on. Now, it eased past her defenses—like she wasn't the only one sharing a bit of herself.

Esther shook her head. The ache there was quickly fading, unlike the one in her chest. "I'm like that piece of iron. Growing softer."

"Only for a short while. Softer doesn't mean weaker. If iron's too hard, it breaks under pressure. With the right temperature, ya can take some of that hardness away, temper it, strengthen it."

She dared a glance and found not just understanding but acceptance in his eyes.

He cleared his throat and the accent vanished. "How's your head?"

"Better." And so was her heart somehow.

"You should lie there a little longer."

She crossed her ankles and glanced to make sure her skirts covered them. "I still feel like a fool. And must look it too."

He shrugged and leaned back on his hands. Charlie climbed onto his lap, leaning into his chest. Almost enough to give birth to another river of tears, but she held them at bay, allowing the image and the feeling to settle into her heart. "This is strangely comfortable."

He chuckled.

The only thing she would change was the pinch of her corset. Smoke saturated the wood floor beneath her, a pleasant aroma. She could happily lie here for hours and forget the world and their criticisms.

"Let me know when you want me to help you up."

To reduce the risk of making a greater fool of herself, Esther offered her hand and let him pull her to her feet.

"Why don't you sit down for a while." He led her to the chair. "I'll let Charlie have another go while you rest."

"Thank you." She wasn't ready for the long walk home. While he worked with her son, she stared at her misshapen piece of iron, cooling on the floor where Flynn had let it fall. She missed the liberation of pounding it into submission, seeing it give to her hand. That and the freedom of speaking her mind. She couldn't remember the last time she had been so honest about her feelings, or felt such acceptance.

Chapter 7

The clink of dainty teacups and saucers and the titer-tatter of gossip grated Esther's nerves. Maybe she was just out of practice mingling with other ladies, submerging herself in society. Up north, she had tried to appease Charles's need to maintain his place among his peers, to attend dinners, balls, and receptions. She had even gone for herself at the beginning when Charlie was little. But as he grew older, and news of his "condition" leaked to the upper crust of Boston, friends fell away, and it became easier to sit indoors with her boy and her books.

No wonder her husband had spent more time abroad.

"Isn't that fabulous, Esther?"

She looked to her sister, trying to make her smile appear genuine.

Her efforts must not have succeeded. Julia gave an exasperated sigh. "Never mind."

"I'm sorry. I was thinking of. . .travel. Europe." She nodded to Mrs. Hurst and Miss Johnson and their raised brows. "My late husband was very fond of visiting the Continent."

"Indeed?" Miss Johnson, niece of the mayor, leaned forward with anticipation raising her delicate features. "I am to take my first tour in another month. Which are your favorite cities to visit? I have insisted on Bath." A blush crept into her cheeks. "I adore Jane Austen's novels, and Bath seems quite the romantic location. Have you been?"

"Uh, no. I did not travel extensively with my husband." Esther felt her own blush rise up her neck. "But I also enjoy Jane Austen. Wonderful stories." Stories that had only made her more lonesome for her husband and what they'd never shared. She'd been enamored with him, and he'd been very kind to her when they were first married. But unfortunately, love was hard to find outside of novels. Especially for a widow in her late twenties with a half-grown son.

The conversation continued with talk of Europe and whether the beginning of hostilities with Washington could hamper travel abroad. Talk of war brought back thoughts of Mr. Flynn and the swing of his hammer against long rifle barrels. She could understand trying to make a living and secure one's future, but what about his duty to his conscience?

She shook the thought from her head. So long as he didn't enlist Charlie to work on the rifles with him, what did it matter to her what he did with his time or talent? He was just a blacksmith, and an Irish one at that. An Irish one with sweat glistening on his brow and a dimple in his cheek. Blue eyes like the ocean on a clear day—and just as much depth. A man strong enough to create beauty out of ordinary iron. And to protect the people for whom he cared.

"Someone has better things to think of." Mrs. Hurst chortled, her smirk aimed at Esther.

"What?"

"Or was that smile for a someone?" the matron finished.

"I. . ." Though they couldn't read her thoughts or know how far they traveled, heat infused her face.

"Oh!" Miss Johnson squealed. "Is there someone you fancy here in our blessed little city? I was saying to Auntie that Mr. Long is a perfect candidate for you since he's a widower for over five years now with no children. It's not him, is it?"

"Not Mr. Long." She'd met the man once briefly after church

and could not imagine marrying someone so stiff. Too much like Charles had become. And the way he'd turned up his nose at Charlie... "There's probably a reason he's not found another woman to marry him."

From the gasps Esther realized she not only vocalized her thought, but no one shared her sentiment.

"He is one of our most eligible bachelors," Miss Johnson said. "He's the choosy one when it comes to selecting a second wife."

"Well then, obviously I shan't do for him." She lifted her cup to find it already empty.

"Would you care for more tea?" Mrs. Hurst asked.

Esther lowered the dainty china with its yellow roses to the end table nearby. "No, thank you. I really should be on my way. But Julia may stay longer if she wishes."

"Esther." Julia's glower drove spikes into her conscience. She had promised her sister a full hour, and they were a good thirty minutes shy of that, but she'd had enough of this idle chitchat. She wanted to see how Charlie fared with Mr. Flynn. Honestly, she was beginning to prefer his company.

"I'm sorry." Esther stood and thanked her hostess before taking her leave. She only made it as far as the hall before their mumbles began.

"...sorry for the girl. She hasn't quite recovered from her husband's passing, has she?"

"I don't think it's that," Julia replied, an edge to her tone.

"Ah, that son of hers. What exactly is wrong with the boy?"

Esther slowed just out of sight, though her brain shouted at her to keep walking, to not listen.

"Who knows," Julia said. "From what I understand, he was born this way."

"Of course. Such a look about him."

"So peculiar," the younger woman piped in. "I've not seen anything like him."

"And yet she takes him everywhere with her, not trusting anyone but the blacksmith to watch her precious boy."

"The blacksmith!"

"Mr. Flynn. Charlie likes him." Julia spat the words.

Esther could almost hear the lady sniff. "The Irishman? I declare. Though, I suppose the boy might be taught to swing a hammer. There's not much else he'd be fit for."

The clock ticked on the parlor wall, denoting a pause.

Please, Lord, let them be through. Esther tried to back away, but her feet remained fused to the oak floor.

Julia's voice broke the silence. "What I wonder is how she'll ever find a husband with the boy around." Her sigh was audible.

"Besides," Mrs. Hurst added, "how are they to know all her children won't be like that?"

The chair legs scraped as they scooted another inch closer, and Flynn smiled. He finished hammering the mandrel from the newly formed rifle barrel and glanced back to Charlie, who had pulled his chair a full three feet closer since he'd begun.

"What do you think?" Flynn asked, showing him the piece. "Do you think it's straight enough?"

"Looks straight. Very straight."

"That's good enough for me." He leaned the hollow iron rod against the wall and glanced to the door—no sign of Esther—then at the small timepiece in his trouser pocket. Already after three. She'd been gone more than two hours, and his stomach pinched as he'd been too busy for lunch before Charlie's arrival. She'd never left him for more than an hour at a time and always returned well before she said she would. Had something happened?

He looked to Charlie's expectant face and sighed. He'd learned a man had to feed his body well if he wanted to survive this business. Flynn waved for Charlie to follow him. "Let's go find something to eat, shall we."

The boy's face brightened, and he shoved to his feet, quickly taking up the path behind Flynn, who led up the steep stairs to the room above. More of a loft, really. The ceiling sloped toward his bed. Two chairs sat with a small table on the opposite side of the room. Ironic that some of his best pieces of work were elegant tables and chairs of iron and brass, and yet his own furnishings had been constructed from wood.

"Welcome to my home, Charlie." He waved the boy toward a chair while he moved to the counter where a fresh loaf of bread from the bakery down the street waited for him along with the chunk of cheese he'd been eating over the past two days. He kept his meals simple during the day to save time and money.

"I wish I. . .lived here."

"What?" Flynn glanced at the boy standing in the middle of the floor. "I'd think you would enjoy living in that big house with all those grand rooms. I bet your bed is twice the size of mine and ten times more comfortable."

"They don't. . . They don't like me."

"Who doesn't?" Flynn brought the bread and cheese to the table along with a knife.

"Family. They never. . .talk to me. Don't look at me."

Flynn set the food aside and stepped to Charlie, wrapping an arm around him. The boy returned the embrace and buried his face in Flynn's side. "They just don't know you as I do. They don't know what a good boy you are."

Flynn slipped to his knee, now eye to eye with the child. "You know what I think?"

Charlie shook his head.

"I think you are the closest friend I've had in a long time. Maybe ever."

Arms wrapped his neck. He returned the hug, soaking up the warmth like sunbeams through a morning window. This child had somehow dug his way deep into his heart.

"Mr. Flynn?" The feminine call was followed by footsteps up the stairs.

Flynn pulled away from Charlie and started for the doorway, arriving the same time as Esther.

"Why aren't you in your shop?"

"I have to stop for dinner sometime."

"Dinner? It's halfway to supper."

He smiled, and her argument stopped.

"I didn't mean to be away so long." Esther brushed past him, tipping her chin away. She hurried to Charlie and pulled him to her, hand lingering on the nape of his neck. She pressed his head closer and shut her eyes a moment. A droplet glistened on her lashes, but she swiped the evidence away.

Flynn proceeded carefully. "He was about to join me for some bread and cheese. Both are fresh. I don't suppose you would want to join us."

"I—no. I should get home. It's been. . .a long day." Her shoulders slumped as though to confirm her statement. A glance at him revealed the red in her eyes.

"Has something happened?"

She shook head, but her chin trembled.

"Mrs.—" That was as far as Flynn got. He had no right to speak her Christian name, but the other sounded so stiff, so distant when all he wanted was to offer her friendship and an ally. "Esther."

Her glistening eyes widened. "I—" She looked at Charlie and

shook her head. "I can't." She mumbled something under her breath and started past him toward the door, Charlie's hand secure inside her own.

The boy staggered behind her, trying to keep up, his eyes concerned when he glanced back at Flynn.

Their feet echoed in the narrow stairway. Flynn groaned. He couldn't let her leave like this. He jogged down the steps, two at a time despite their steepness. She jerked around as soon as she reached the workshop.

"Wait. All I wanted was for you to know you have a friend. If you ever need anything." Flynn clamped his mouth closed against the desire to spout a lot more than friendship. She stared at him with moist eyes. Against his bidding, his went to her equally moist lips. He took another step, under the sudden urge to pull her into an embrace, to let her cry in his arms.

"Thank you. . .Mr. Flynn."

His surname hit him like a hammer, leaving him immobile while she made her retreat. What had he been thinking? Why would she need him? She had a fortune and a family and a house on a hill. While he had this meager shop and enough debt to drown a man. The only thing that burned more than her rejection was what little remained of his pride being smelted away, leaving the raw bones of hurt.

Chapter 8

Esther couldn't seem to catch her breath. She sat on the edge of her bed staring at the intricate handles of her ash broom and shovel. Friendship. That is what he offered. And she'd run.

Friendship with an Irish blacksmith. The thought was laughable!

Yet she didn't feel like laughing. Not even a little. She'd wanted to melt into his arms and cry away the hurt on the shoulder of someone who understood.

A tear trickled down her cheek, and she dropped back onto the mattress. The tear redirected its course toward her ear. She was a grown woman, a mother, a widow—someone who should be in control of her life—or at least her emotions. She shouldn't want to huddle into a ball under a quilt and weep like a child.

Another tear.

She swatted at it and pushed to her feet. No more wallowing in self-pity or confusion. Esther straightened her nightgown. The house slept, allowing her freedom. She stole downstairs and into the library. The flame in her lamp sent a warm glow against the spines of books lining the walls. As a youth, she had never ventured into this room on her own. Books were boring, and she hadn't the patience to discover their secrets. In the past few years, they had become her closest friends. Oh, how she'd needed a friend.

The tender glow in Flynn's eyes again assaulted her thoughts.

What was wrong with her? How could she possibly consider him?

"It's only friendship," she whispered in argument. It wasn't like she contemplated a more intimate relationship. Charlie loved spending time with him and was happier on the days they visited the smithy. What did it matter what people like Mrs. Hurst or Miss Johnson, or even Julia, thought of her relationship with the blacksmith?

Esther turned her back on the library. Her head was in too much of a spin to sit down and enjoy a novel. She walked instead to her father's office. He had examined Charlie almost a week ago, and she still hadn't found the nerve to listen to his prognosis. Easier to avoid him than what she was sure he would say—what everyone else had said.

Damaged brain. Sickly. Addled.

Yet growing uncertainty wrestled in the back of her mind. Charlie was all that mattered and what was best for him, that he received the care he needed.

Deep breaths steadied her while she crossed the thick rug to his large mahogany desk. Several stacks of folders and papers sat on the polished surface. He'd never been much for organizing his papers. Would she even be able to find his notes on Charlie?

She set the lamp on the desk and turned up the wick to better see the ink scrawlings across the documents and ledgers. Esther flipped through them, seeking her son's name. Guilt prickled at the names and private information she unwittingly gleaned. She shouldn't be here.

Esther straightened the papers back into piles and reached to flip a ledger closed when a name caught her in midmotion. "*Thomas Flynn.*"

Thomas?

Could that be her Flynn? Or. . .um. . .the blacksmith? She skimmed down the page, slowing with each line she read. This was absurd! How could a blacksmith possibly be indebted to a doctor close to six hundred dollars? Surely not a mere medical fee. And that was paid down from... She scanned upward. Six hundred and forty-nine dollars. He had already been working to repay the amount for three years.

She quickly tallied. At the rate he was repaying her father, he would be indebted for quite a number of years. Decades. Nausea turned her stomach, and she slapped the ledger closed. Thomas Flynn's affairs were none of her concern. She should never have pried.

Standing, she lifted her lamp and circled the desk. A low light flickered in the hall. Footsteps. She blew out her lamp and edged toward the wall, no desire to face her father tonight, never mind explain what she was doing skulking around his study.

A candle's small flame appeared in the doorway and entered, only it didn't illuminate her father's face, but glowed off a much darker complexion. Eli closed the door and moved to the desk, oblivious to her presence in the shadows. He lowered into the chair she had just occupied and lifted the *Daily Richmond Examiner*. Leaned over it, he flipped through the pages before settling on the article he sought.

"The war?" she whispered.

He jerked to his feet then huffed out a breath. "Miss Esther, what are you doin' there, lurkin' in the dark?"

"Much the same as you." Trying to find information while remaining unseen. "You've been following the politics of the war?" She didn't doubt that was what interested him. He was a brilliant man, taking much quicker to reading than she had. As a young girl, it had been impossible to not pour knowledge into his eager mind. All secretly. Like this.

Eli visibly relaxed but didn't sit back down. He folded the paper and set it back on her father's desk. "Been watching what's goin' on, but I figure we're only getting half the story. What's really happening out there, Miss Esther?"

She sighed. "The Confederation has been busy pulling in more southern states—quite confident with themselves since their victory at Fort Sumter." How long before the fighting reached Virginia? Esther motioned to the paper. "Last week, Arkansas and Tennessee separated from the Union." Bringing the tally to ten southern states. North Carolina would probably follow soon. And then what? More battles? A full-scale war?

"All over slavery, miss?"

"Mostly, I think." She remembered her argument with Flynn—*Thomas*—that the South did have other protests, but how could she look at the man in front of her and consider any of them valid enough to hold him against his will? Every man deserved to choose his life, to have freedom. Eli did.

As did Thomas Flynn.

How did a simple blacksmith build a multi-hundred-dollar debt with a doctor?

Esther shook him from her mind. "What would you do, Eli, if you were free?"

He huffed out a laugh. "I'd join Mr. Lincoln."

"And fight?"

He nodded, his dark brow furrowed. "Whatever they would let me do. I've heard you speaking with Master Allerton. You agree with Mr. Lincoln too."

"But I don't want war." If there was only a way to work out their differences before more blood was spilled. Once they got too far down that course, there would be no turning back. And she wouldn't be able to stay. Thomas Flynn was right to accuse her of trying to ignore her family's position on slavery, but she wouldn't be able to take their side with good conscience. If war reached Virginia, she would return to the North.

Heartsick, Esther took her cold lamp and started the long, dark trek to her room. Strange. It wasn't battles and politics that hung over her heart as she slipped back into bed, but the image of Thomas Flynn, hammering out the long rod that would someday be a rifle. Thomas Flynn and the pile of numbers burying him in her father's ledger.

Chapter 9

Every clank, jangle of harnesses, or approaching footsteps had Flynn glancing up, only to be met with unwitting disappointment. Even customers offering coins for his meager coffer or the praise of his workmanship did little to raise the sinking of his spirits. June already. Over two weeks and no sign of Charlie or Esther. A clear and not so subtle answer to his offer of friendship.

He should have kept his tongue. For Charlie's sake.

Flynn laid his frustration to the bellows. He had orders to catch up on now that the rifle barrels were delivered as agreed to the gunsmith. Payment would be forthcoming as soon as the finished weapons were delivered to the Confederate Army.

Flynn let out a breath at the memory of Esther's anger. She'd convicted him for not being opposed to slavery.

Flames roared with renewed life. The heat from the forge singed his forehead, wetting it with perspiration. Of course he opposed the idea that one man could own another, but what could he do about it so long as his own fetters dug into his flesh? He'd been sold by his own father, compelled to work in this smithy until his twenty-first year. And then what? He'd had nowhere to go—but he should have escaped while he'd had the chance.

Sparks flew as cool iron met the scarlet coals with too much force.

The bell tinkled behind him, and he glanced over. Another customer.

Two weeks and his heart still paused, still hoped.

What a fool he was. He left the iron in the forge and stepped into his shop. "Can I help you, sir. . .Dr. Allerton?" He couldn't remember the last time the doctor stepped under his roof. "What do you want?"

The doctor raised an eyebrow. "You don't seem yourself, Flynn."

"Just surprised to see you. Here." Dr. Allerton always sent Eli to pick up Flynn's payment and the ever-accumulating interest. "I'm a little short today. But in another week, I plan to—"

"I'm not here for money, man!" Dr. Allerton glanced away, brushing his palms across his trim black coat as though he could clean his hands of this whole interchange. "I have been informed by several that my daughter and her boy have made frequent calls here since their return. And not to make purchases."

Flynn narrowed his eyes. "I've seen neither in a fortnight."

A laugh sounded with derision. "But they had been coming regularly."

"Charlie enjoyed watching me work. I may have minded him a few times for your daughter while she ran her errands." The words fell from him like a confession. How did any of this concern the man before him, who glanced out the window as though ensuring his presence went unnoticed?

"You will stay away from Esther. And her son. Being seen with—" His gaze flickered over Flynn. He shook his head. "You are damaging her reputation. As if that child hasn't done enough harm. Now this."

Flynn clenched his teeth against a retort. But what could he say? The man had the ability to do whatever he liked with this shop, with Flynn's life.

"Do we have an understanding?"

He bit his tongue and forced a nod.

"Good." The doctor pulled on his gloves and stepped back out onto the street.

Flynn stood in place for a long moment. Why should he be upset when obviously he needn't worry about Esther and Charlie returning to his shop?

Yet, as Flynn laid his heated iron across the anvil, the last thing on his mind was creation. He pounded the surface, bleeding frustration and other feelings he didn't dare explore. The iron bar became a sheet as thin as paper, ripping with holes. Breathing hard, he thrust it into a pail of water. It met with a hiss and spit. Destroyed. Repairing the damage he'd done might not even be possible.

Seemed fitting somehow.

Flynn pressed his arm over his forehead and wiped away the sweat. He had work to do.

The hours faded into one another with few interruptions. It wasn't until midafternoon that the bell rang at the front of his shop.

Setting his work aside, Flynn met the matronly woman scanning his ready-made lanterns.

"Something you like? Or do you wish one made to your specifications?"

"Oh, these are fine." She spared him a quick glance before turning her gaze back to the iron wrought with his own hands. "I'm just not sure which one I like the best."

She was still making a thorough examination a few minutes later when Lyman Hastings and a larger man pushed into the shop.

"Mr. Flynn."

"Yes?"

Instead of answering, the gunsmith nodded to the woman and motioned his friend to the opposite side of the small room to make a study of decorative hooks. Flynn tried to focus on the lady while she hemmed and hawed, but with his payment for the rifle barrels mere feet away. . .

"Maybe I should come back later and bring my niece. She's much better at making decisions like this than I. She has an eye for such things."

"Whatever you feel is best."

"But I did so wish to make my purchase today."

Flynn unhooked the nearest lantern from the wall. "Why not take one you like home, and if it doesn't suit, bring it back tomorrow and trade for another."

Her face brightened and a dimple appeared in one cheek, wiping away some of her wrinkles. "Wonderful. If my niece is not pleased with this one, she can bring it back and make the switch."

"So long as you are happy with your purchase." Flynn forced a smile and ushered her toward the door, hardly concerned over the two coins she slipped into his palm or that they were slightly less than the named price. "Good day, ma'am."

"Thank you again, young man."

He watched her leave before a woman up the street in a blue gown stole his attention. But there was no boy at her side, and now that he looked closer, her hair was a little too light. He turned back inside.

"Why don't we step into the back to settle business?" Hastings asked, already moving through the door into the smithy.

Flynn stepped in and opened his hand to the small pouch the man extended.

"Costs ran higher than anticipated, and the army didn't pay as well as they'd promised. This will have to do."

Flynn emptied the coins into his palm and his insides clenched. "This is only—" He quickly tallied. "Ten dollars?" His face heated, and his muscles tightened. "Hardly a fraction of what we agreed."

Not nearly enough to compensate for the hours and sweat he had spent to form those rifle barrels. "I need more. You *owe* me more." He'd barely meet his lease, never mind the payment to Dr. Allerton.

Hastings took a step back. "I supplied the iron and the contracts. Be grateful."

"Grateful to be cheated?" Flynn clenched his fist and followed the man's retreat.

"I don't want no trouble." Hastings held up his hands while his friend stepped in, cutting off Flynn's advance. The rancid body of the second man drew Flynn's attention to the sweat-stained clothes, scarred face, meaty fists. The gunsmith had brought a scrapper to keep Flynn in his place.

"Let it go, Flynn," Hastings crooned.

Be cowered into giving up a just wage for his labor? Flynn had worked day and night for weeks, had given up other opportunities. He deserved—he needed—that money. Flynn sidestepped the larger man and gripped Hastings by the collar. "You will give me what we agreed upon or—"

An iron bar cracked down on his arms, breaking Flynn's hold. Hot pain shot up his right arm, and he stumbled. The mangled iron Flynn had left to cool clanged to the floor. By the time he gained his balance, a meaty fist flew toward his head. He didn't have time to even flinch, and the force knocked him into his anvil.

"Take the money." Hastings toed the coins where they had dropped.

No! Flynn's mind screamed the word, but it never breached his throat. He balled his fists to supply them with the answer, but agony momentarily darkened his vision, and he leaned into the unforgiving edge of the anvil. He stared at his right arm, willing the pain to ease. It had not been a fair fight. He could take the man if given the opportunity.

Instead, Flynn sank to the ground, unable to stop the tremble moving through his body. Blood dripped from his nose, splattering on his leather apron. The coins on the floor mocked him. He'd lose everything. Or dig his hole deeper. He'd not be able to swing his hammer with a broken arm.

Chapter 10

Esther tried not to pause, tried not to stare at the door to the blacksmith shop or the sign hanging from its latch.

Closed.

In the middle of the day?

It might not bother her so much if the smithy hadn't worn the same sign yesterday. Charlie pulled at her hand, his desire to stop and visit his friend always foremost on his mind.

As it was on hers.

"Not right now, Charlie." She led him past but found herself glancing to see who watched. Would anyone notice her slipping into the alley? Would it matter if someone did?

Her heart sped. How could she face Mr. Thomas Flynn again after what had transpired between them last time, and with her feelings still unsettled?

"No." She couldn't afford to let her guard down. Charlie was her only focus, all that mattered.

"Mama?"

"Nothing, Charlie. Just that we should hurry home. You know Cook doesn't like when we're not on time for dinner."

She led him away, though very aware of his pout and long glance over his shoulder toward the smithy.

"Why...you don't like Mr. Flynn anymore?"

Her jaw slackened. "It's not that I don't like Mr. Flynn. He's been very kind to us. He's very busy though, I'm sure. We can't keep interrupting him while he's working."

"How about. . .after his work?"

"After?" How long could she stall on that one? "Maybe. But not today, all right, darling?"

"I miss him."

Esther squeezed Charlie's hand. The sentiment settled deep, ringing with truth. She missed their visits too.

She worked hard to put Thomas Flynn from her mind the rest of the way home, and was almost successful until she walked in the front door and heard his name booming from Father's office despite the closed door. She sent Charlie up the stairs to wash. A murmur of voices was punctuated with the latch bobbing downward at the door. She stepped aside and pretended to straighten the arrangement of lilies on a small decorative table. A moment later, Eli slipped out and eased the door closed.

Esther lifted her eyebrows with her unspoken question.

He tipped his head toward the library, and she led the way. "What's going on?"

"Master Flynn sent a message asking for more time before the next payment of his debt. Says there was an accident."

Esther's heart slowed. "What kind of accident? Is he all right?"

"Not sure. Your father's none too happy though. I think he doesn't mean to give him more time."

"What will happen if he doesn't?"

Eli shook his head. "Nothing good."

But Father should be more understanding if there'd been an accident. Was Flynn injured? Did he need help?

"You want me to go look in on him, see what's happened?"

Was she so obvious? "I—I just wouldn't want. . ." She blew out a breath. "I would feel better knowing he is well. It's the Christian thing to do."

"Of course." But the slight upturn of Eli's mouth suggested he read deeper. "I have an errand to run for your father. I'll pause on my way."

"Just don't mention this to—" Esther glanced to the doorway, imagining what her father would have to say about her concern. After Julia suggested she was staining her reputation by visiting the blacksmith so often, Father had had quite a lot to say on the matter.

She chafed at the mere memory of his words. Thomas Flynn was as honorable a man as she'd met—more so than most in the upper circles of society. His occupation was no reason to slander his name, nor was his Irish heritage. A man should be judged on his character alone.

And you judged him any kinder?

Memories of their first meetings scalded her with guilt. What a hypocrite she'd become.

"Mama?"

Charlie's call pulled at her heartstrings. Oh, that her son would be judged for his heart and not his outward appearance or slowness with words.

She squeezed Eli's hand. "Thank you for doing this for me."

Charlie poked his head in the doorway and beamed a smile at them. His gaze quickly wandered to the shelves of books, however, and she realized she'd not brought him in here before.

"Come, Charlie," she beckoned. Esther took his hand and led him to a large stuffed chair. The dark-stained leather held her child as she reached for a copy of *The King of the Golden River*, a children's novel filled with wonderful illustrations. "Why not sit here and look at the pictures while I slip upstairs for a moment? I'll read you the story when I return."

He nodded, not glancing up from the book.

Esther smiled and kissed his head before stealing up the stairs to her room. She set her reticule aside and shrugged off her walking jacket. The silken blouse beneath breathed much easier in the warmth of the house. After washing the dust from her hands and face, she started down the stairs. She had taken longer than she should have, but a few moments of quiet to let the weariness roll off her had been sorely needed.

She stepped into the library and was met by silence. No heels of small shoes bumping stretched leather. No crinkle of pages turning, or the hum of a happy child.

"Charlie?"

The chair sat empty, book abandoned, spine up on the floor.

"Charlie?"

She hurried around the room, glancing under the small tables and behind chairs. The foyer was also empty. Heart climbing in her throat, she tapped on her father's office door as she cracked it open. "Have you seen Charlie?"

Father looked up from his ledgers. "Of course not."

Esther let the door close with no further comment. She checked the kitchen next, but Cook hadn't seen him.

No one had.

⌒

Flynn stared at the stick of iron till his eyes blurred, the end he had mangled taunting him. His forge was stocked and billowed heat enough to fill the smithy. The iron glowed red and lay across his swage block, but he couldn't swing a hammer. Not with his right hand, at least, and his left was clumsy—not much better than when he'd first started out as an apprentice. For the first four years after his parents had given him over to the blacksmith, he hadn't touched a hammer. Only to fetch it for Leighton. All he considered Flynn good for was fetching this or that and stoking the forge. Flynn had also spent plenty of time on the bellows, making those coals glow. Sleeping on a pallet made up in the corner of the smithy and eating whatever and whenever the man remembered to feed him, learning quickly not to complain. If the blacksmith threw him out, he had nowhere to go.

Flynn gripped the hammer in his left hand and chased the memories away with an attempt to smooth a barb. The tip of the rod had been flattened and twisted in his frustration after the doctor's visit, and almost resembled the wilted petal of a rose.

Flynn leaned forward on his stool with a small hammer and clumsily tapped away the burrs, flattened the ridges.

"That's fine work."

Flynn looked up at Eli, who stood in the open back door. Leaving the iron on the swage block, Flynn started to stand. Pain spiked through his bound arm, eliciting a grunt.

Eli frowned at the crude splint Flynn had strapped to his arm. "I heard something about an accident."

"Not so much of an accident."

"A fight?"

"I wish." He'd liked to have finished it. Hasting's goon might have some height on him, but years of molding iron would let Flynn hold his own. "Dr. Allerton send you about my late payment?" He fished the remaining coins from his pocket he'd held back for food. He wasn't so hungry anyway. "This should keep him satisfied for a week or two."

Eli's hands remained at his side. "Dr. Allerton didn't send me."

Flynn stared. "But not a social call." As a boy, Eli had been somewhat of a friend to Flynn, but any bond had faded after Eli started collecting his payments for Dr. Allerton.

"Miss Esther may have been concerned."

"Esther?" Elation at her worry faded quickly. She hadn't come herself for many a good reason. "Inform her I'm fine. She can put me from her mind."

Eli shook his head. "Your arm, how bad?"

Flynn shrugged, trying to ignore the painful throb that beat in time with his heart. "I'll heal."

"Your shop has been closed."

"I just needed a few days. Everything's fine." Flynn walked past Eli to the door, hoping he'd get the hint and follow him out. As much as he liked Eli, right now was not a good time for company—especially anyone tied to the Allerton estate. "I'd rather you didn't say anything to the doctor, but see that he gets these." Flynn pressed the coins into Eli's hand.

A nod and Eli was on his way.

Flynn closed the door and leaned into it, the pain in his arm mounting along with the ache in his head. "What now, Lord?" He'd been raised by his parents to worship God, and Matthias Leighton had insisted Flynn attend church with him every Sabbath, but was that all God was good for? Something to believe in? Someone to thank when all was well, and plead to in times such as these?

A light tapping vibrated the door, and Flynn cracked it open to see what Eli had forgotten to say. Instead, two bright blue eyes stared up at him. Despite the huffing and puffing of his breath, a grin spread across Charlie's face.

"I. . .found you."

Chapter 11

Still several blocks from the smithy, Esther met Eli on his way home. "You haven't seen Charlie?"

Esther's plea was met with widened eyes and a shake of Eli's head. "He was sitting in the library reading that book you gave him."

"Not when I came down. He didn't follow you?"

"I would have seen him."

Esther started past Eli, toward the smithy. If he wasn't with Thomas, how would she find him? He could be anywhere. *Please, God, help me.*

A breeze teasing her loose sleeves and her hair falling from its pins, Esther hitched her hem and jogged across the street. Who cared what anyone thought when her child was missing?

The front latch gave under her hand, and she swung the door open. "Mr. Flynn?" After learning his given name, speaking so formally felt strange. "Hello?"

A shuffle of boots, and a shadow filled the second doorway to the back. Her breath snagged in her throat. She was accustomed to seeing his hair tousled, but the look had spread to the whole of him. His usually smooth jaw wore scruffy whiskers, and dark rings hung under his eyes along with the purple-yellow bruising on the left. Cradled to his abdomen, his right arm had been wrapped in stained rags, short lengths of sticks acting as a splint.

"What happened?"

He replied with a grunt and stepped aside to show Charlie nibbling his lower lip.

"I in trouble?"

"Yes." The word escaped Esther on a sigh as all her fears rushed from her. "Yes, you are."

Charlie stepped to Thomas as though the man could provide a shield from her anger, anger that had fled with her fears. Concern took both their places. "We'll talk when we get home. Just promise me you will never leave without me again."

His head dropped forward. "Sorry, Mama."

She pulled him to her and kissed his head while stealing another look at the man behind him. "Is your arm broken?"

"I'm fine," he grumbled.

"You are not."

He opened his mouth.

"You haven't even sent for a doctor, have you? Just patch yourself back together and hope for the best."

"I don't need a doctor or his spoiled daughter telling me what's wrong."

Esther fell back a step, unable to push past the sting. "That's how you see me." She wanted to make it a question, but couldn't.

He wiped a hand down his neck and retreated. "I just want to be left alone." He started to the stairs, completely dismissing her.

Charlie pulled away and followed him.

Call Charlie back and let the man boil in his stupid pride, or. . .or what?

Forcing her spine straight, Esther charged up the stairs.

Thomas spun, surprise and uncertainty warring in his expression. "What are you doing?"

She froze at the utter disarray of his home. Dirty pots and dishes across the table, a chair shattered on the floor, worn quilt halfway hanging off the side of the bed. "Unwrap your arm while I find better bandages."

He squared off with her, toe to toe, a head taller than her and pure brawn. He had no reason to take an order.

"Please."

His gaze fell with his chest. "Why?"

"Because. . ." Esther hesitated. But there was nothing to give but the truth. "Because I care."

The storm in his dark blue eyes softened. He moved to the one remaining chair, tipped it up, and began unwrapping the rags from his swollen arm.

It still took Esther another minute to catch her breath and the cascade of her thoughts. "Um, Charlie, stay with Mr. Flynn. I'll be right back." She made a mental list of the things she would need from the closet of medical supplies her father kept at home. She went out the back door and tried her best to go unnoticed for the sake of wagging tongues. At the house, she slipped in and out with only one servant noticing her presence.

By the time Esther returned to the room above the smithy, Thomas had his arm unwrapped and laid flat against the table. Sweat beaded on his forehead. Charlie stood at his side, concern mingled with confusion.

"It'll be all right, sweetheart." She cleared the other half of the table of dishes and dried bread crumbs before laying out the bandaging and formed splint. Esther cringed at the swollen arm and black bruising expanding out from a red welt. "How did this happen?"

"Lost a fight."

"Couldn't have been a fair fight then."

Silence lapsed between them as she knelt on the floor and poured witch hazel over the welt. "The bone appears to be straight."

"I set it," he grunted.

The swelling made the splint a little tight, but not enough to impede circulation. The hardest was to wrap it tightly, knowing she caused him pain. When Esther did look up from her task, Charlie had taken up residence on Thomas's knee. Thomas's good arm wrapped him against his chest.

"Are you all right?"

Thomas nodded, but there was little color under his tan.

"Maybe you should lie down."

"I'm fine."

She shook her head at him and started gathering the leftover strips of bandages. She would put them aside for him. "You keep saying that." She smiled, an attempt to lighten the mood in the room. Then set about piling dishes in the basin that already held a stained pot.

"What are you doing?"

Esther kept working, not daring a glance at him lest he see her uncertainty. She had no idea what she was doing, having never washed dishes or done much more than straighten her gowns or tidy her dressing table. But she wanted to be useful. To him.

"You don't have to clean my mess. I can manage."

"You need to rest that arm."

The chair creaked as it was released of its burden. "Esther."

She spun, bringing a hand to her hip. "Thomas."

A moment of surprise faded behind a look of pain in his eyes. He sank back into the chair.

❧

Thomas.

The name echoed in his head, but it wasn't his da's name on his mother's lips. It was his, as her mouth touched his head. *"Be strong, my Thomas, until I have you back in my arms."* A tear had splattered on his cheek, one of hers, before she tucked the newest Flynn baby to her bosom and allowed Da to lead her out of the smithy.

"*Do as you're told, Thomas,*" was all Da said before showing his back, walking away.

Do as you're told. Keep your head low. Be grateful. Do your work. He'd spent his life doing just that, and where had it gotten him? Buried and barely breathing. Even Da had more from life than him. A wife, children. . .a future. All Flynn had was a skill he couldn't use.

"That is your name, isn't it? *Thomas* Flynn?"

He blinked to clear his vision from the haze of memory. "How did you know?"

Esther turned away, and dishes clanked into the washbasin. "Doesn't matter."

"No one calls me that anymore."

She glanced at him, head cocked. "Not even your friends?"

"I have work, not friends."

Charlie tugged on his shirt. "I your friend."

Flynn lowered back to the chair. "You're right, of course." He squeezed Charlie's shoulder but choked on the lump in his throat.

"I'd like to be your friend too," Esther whispered. "If I may. . . Thomas."

He held her gaze, soaking in its warmth despite the warning blaring like a train whistle in his head. What good was her friendship when her father had warned him against letting her near him? He would destroy her reputation and both their futures. "I can't," he heard himself say.

"Why not? Wasn't it you who first offered?"

"I did, but things were different." His legs protested, but he stood again and moved around Charlie. He stepped to Esther as she turned to him. Toe to toe yet again. How beautiful she looked with her cheeks pink and brown eyes flaring with her son's stubbornness. He touched her arm to direct her away, but the motion didn't follow.

"How was it so different a couple of weeks ago? Because I was the one in distress and not you?"

"I'm fine," he murmured. But he wasn't. He was about to do exactly what his father had—push away someone he loved for their own good as well as his own.

One more mouth he couldn't feed.

No choice but to walk away.

Flynn pulled his hand back and set his jaw, again seeing his da in the stance he took, the firmness of his resolve. "I am grateful for your offer, and for all you have done, but I need you to leave. You and Charlie need to go home."

"Thomas—"

"Please, don't come back."

Chapter 12

Weeks crawled by, a strange sort of limbo. Tensions were building across the states and in the Allerton home. Esther avoided her family as much as she could. Why even try to appease Julia? They had never been close, but now the gulf between them seemed uncrossable. And more the pity. Esther would have loved having a confidante to share her tousle of feelings with, to talk late into the night like girls about their latest infatuations. Maybe if she could voice her thoughts about a certain blacksmith, she'd make sense of them. Instead, she sat alone in the library long after the rest of the family retired for the night, trying to read while Thomas Flynn haunted her mind.

"Forget him," Esther murmured, the mantra she had taken up since he'd forced her to leave him half patched together, his home a mess. The man was enough to drive any woman insane. He offered her friendship, only to pull away when she was ready to accept. What had changed?

Forget him!

Easier said than done. She missed how easy she felt around him, how at home—more so than the one she shared with her father and sister.

"You and Charlie need to go home."

If only she knew where that was.

"You wanted to speak with me, Miss Esther?" Eli stepped into the library, candle in hand. Its light joined the lamp she had set on the decorative table at her side.

"Yes. I have a question."

He slipped the door closed behind him and lowered his voice. "I haven't seen Master Flynn since you sent me yesterday with the soup from Cook. He doesn't want anything."

Esther cringed. "Anything from *her*," had probably been Thomas's choice of words. "That's not what I wished to speak with you about."

"I think he's just stuck on his pride. Doesn't like you seeing him broken like he is."

"That doesn't matter."

"Doesn't like needing help."

Esther stood, setting the newsprint aside. "But we all need help. We can't get through this life on our own." She knew better than most. Yet she had no choice but to do it alone. "I didn't ask you here to discuss Mr. Flynn or his pride. I—" She motioned to the *Washington Star*. "President Lincoln has requested five hundred thousand men from Congress. They're not going to back down and neither is the Confederation. This war isn't going to have an easy resolution." Like a flooded river, picking up speed and sweeping away everything in its path. "I can't stay here any longer. Not pinched between the North and South, and with Charlie's poor health."

Eli's mouth opened, but a moment passed before sound followed. "Where will you go?"

"Back to Boston. I still have the apartment there. Though I plan to sell it and find a cottage in the country. The city is no good for Charlie." Nor for her. She was so tired of keeping up pretenses. "And I don't belong here."

"We'll miss you and Master Charlie, Miss Esther."

She shook her head. "You could come with me, Eli. If you wish. You see, Father never owned you. Mother did. You were left to her daughters." A bitter taste crept up the back of her throat. She had been raised with the understanding that a man could own another, but not to speak of it in such crude terms. "I've made the necessary arrangements with my sister." Another sore spot between them. "You are free." She pulled the document from beside the lamp and held it out. "You may do as you please now."

Eli stood silent, staring at the papers in her hands. "I thank you, Miss Esther."

She wiped a sudden trickle of moisture from her cheek. "I'm sorry I took so long."

His arms opened, and she stepped into them. "I have funds set aside for you, whatever you need. Whether you come with me or join President Lincoln's fight, that's your choice. Go with God."

They sat in the dark for another hour, the lamplight flickering ever lower as they discussed plans. She wanted to depart as soon as everything was made ready, before any real conflicts began. Eli agreed to wait the week to accompany her to Boston, where he would leave them and find out where he was needed by the Union. Soon everything was decided and they bid each other good night, though it was probably early morning.

All was settled. By the end of the week she would be on her way north. Strangely, her main regret for leaving was the man who wouldn't let her near him. Oh, how Charlie would miss him. As would she.

Forget him.

$\backsim$

As hard as he tried, it was impossible to push Esther from his mind. Though he had removed her splint from his arm, the memory of her gentle ministrations remained. Along with the image of her standing in his room, stacking dishes to wash. . .

Flynn brought the hammer down with his left hand, his right tucked tight to his chest. Healing, but not ready for the abuse of his trade. He hadn't produced anything he could sell in almost a month, but he needed to keep his mind and body busy, so here he sat, tapping clumsily away at something that only opened the hole in his chest wider.

"Wh—what is. . .that?"

Flynn spun to face the chair in the corner now occupied by Charlie. "How did you get in here?"

Charlie pointed to the open doorway from the mostly bare storefront.

"You surprised me." He set the hammer on the swage block and straightened. "I didn't hear you."

"You were busy." The boy nodded at him emphatically.

A smile teased the corner of Flynn's mouth. He pulled the glove from his hand. "Yes, I was." He glanced around, disappointment and concern battling for prominence. "Where is your mother?"

Charlie shuffled his feet back and forth, looking at the floor. His shoulders lifted to his ears.

"Did you come here on your own? Again?"

A subtle smile stretched his mouth, and he bit his lip.

"Charlie."

"Mama said. . .we couldn't come no more. She. . .she wouldn't listen. . .that I haaaaad to come. You neeeed me."

Swallowing hard, Flynn crouched in front of the boy, but before he could open his mouth, Charlie threw his arms around his neck. Emotion surged up Flynn's throat and misted his eyes. *I do need you.* Despite all his bluster that he could get along on his own, the truth gripped his heart like a vice.

Lord, help me.

"I want to stay. . .with you."

"I want that too. I really do." He gripped Charlie's arms, meeting the boy's ever-welcoming eyes. "But your mama will be missing you. We need to take you home." Even if that meant confronting Esther again. And her father.

Chapter 13

As much as Flynn wanted more time with Charlie, he had to see the boy home for Esther's sake. Even if it meant Dr. Allerton's wrath. Hopefully, they could avoid him altogether.

Flynn weaved through the back streets and alleys to avoid being seen, but the Allerton estate stood on the outskirts of town, making the route lengthy. Charlie breathed hard, and his feet dragged slower with each block.

"Just a little farther," Flynn encouraged.

Charlie gripped his hand, following without a word or complaint. But his breathing. . .

Flynn paused and looked back. "You all right?"

The boy's smile had fled. "I'm. . .good."

A few more steps and his hand slipped away from Flynn's. He leaned over and rested his hands on his knees.

Buggy wheels and hooves against the ground made Flynn glance up. Recognition surged, and he dragged Charlie from the street behind a vine of honeysuckle. The boy's eyes grew wide, and his smile crept out again.

"It's better that your grandfather not see us together."

Flynn looked to the road as the doctor's buggy jostled past. Eli wasn't at the reins. Strange.

"He doesn't. . .talk. . .to me." Charlie's words puffed out on labored breaths, and he clutched his arm. His brows pushed together. "I—"

"Easy, Charlie." Flynn eased him into his arms, bracing him up on his knee. "Catch your breath." Only this was more than just shortness of breath from the exertion or excitement. He was in pain.

His breaths came more rapidly, barely making it past his throat.

"Charlie. . .Charlie, you need to breathe." Panic climbed Flynn's spine. "Come on, Charlie." Flynn held him against his chest and breathed deep. Just as Esther had the day they'd arrived. Which meant Charlie'd had these episodes before and he'd be fine. Right? Still, doubts hung over Flynn. "Breathe, Charlie." What if he wasn't fine this time? Even though there was a doctor just ahead, climbing out of his buggy.

Flynn scooped Charlie's small body against him in his arms, ignoring the sharp ache in the right one as he sprinted up the packed dirt road toward the Allerton estate.

"Dr. Allerton!"

The doctor spun, a curse on his lips as he jogged to meet them. "What have you done?"

"He can't breathe. Why can't he breathe?"

"It's not his lungs, it's his heart." Instead of taking the boy, Allerton fumbled with his case and then with a tiny jar of powder. He forced Charlie's mouth open and spilled some over his tongue. "Come on, boy."

Flynn's own heart thundered in response. If anything happened to Charlie, if he became the cause of any more pain for the child or his mother, he'd never forgive himself. *Please, God, heal his heart. Help him.*

⮑

The smithy sat still and silent. No tatting of hammers or the rumble of Thomas's voice as he explained his work. No laughter or Charlie's happy response. Esther would give almost anything to go back to those happy first weeks here, before they had tried to ignore and deny the affection growing between them.

"Thomas?"

Unease creeping through her, Esther set her hand to the cool forge—she'd never seen it without coals alive within. Where was Thomas? And where was Charlie? When she'd told him they'd be returning north, Charlie became upset and insisted he needed to say goodbye to his friend. Had even asked if Mr. Flynn could come with them.

She'd managed a smile and told him they would say goodbye, but a blacksmith needed to stay with his shop—he didn't fit into their world.

Charlie had given the most confused look, making her question her own words.

Esther stared up the back stairs. Charlie had to be with Thomas. He'd been so insistent they go right away, but she'd been busy organizing their belongings. Honestly, she hadn't been ready to see Thomas. Or to say goodbye.

The upstairs room sat quiet and dim, abandoned. Had she missed them? Was Thomas walking Charlie home?

"Please, let him be with Thomas, Lord," she prayed as she hurried down the stairs and directly into a solid chest.

Thomas grunted in pain and pulled his sore arm out of the way. "Esther?"

"I'm so sorry!"

Thomas stared at her for a moment, not speaking.

"Did I hurt you? Why aren't you wearing your splint? It hasn't been long enough to—"

"You need to hurry home," Thomas started. "Charlie—"

"Then you did see him?"

A nod. Dark hair fell over his brow. "He came to see me. I took him home."

Breath left her. What a relief to know her boy was safe. She was so grateful for this man. And in fact, he'd never looked so well. Hair still a little wild, but his clothes were clean, and he wore a coat that fit his trim stature well. Esther wasn't sure she'd ever seen his attire so complete. But it was his eyes that drew her in. A darker shade of blue than usual with a hint of moisture glinting in them.

"Thank you. Again."

His brow furled. "Again?" he choked. "What have I ever done that has benefitted you?"

Had he no idea how much lighter her burden had become every time she stepped through those doors with her boy? "You can't know how long I hoped someone else could see Charlie the way I do. You looked beyond the things that make him different." She set her palm against his chest. "You have been more of a father to him than even his own. I can't ever repay you enough for that. Thank you, Thomas Flynn, for loving him." If only he could feel something similar—something more—for her.

His eyes misted. "You need to go."

"Why? Why do you keep pushing me away?" When all she wanted was to be pulled close. She wanted to be held. Cherished. Loved. By him.

"Charlie."

"Charlie loves you."

He gripped her hand in his until she met his gaze. "Charlie isn't well. I left him with your father, but his heart is failing. Your father said he could have died."

"What?"

"You need to go home."

Esther blinked. Her baby was fighting for his life while she stood here about to bare her heart like a fool. She spun and raced out the front of the smithy, with only one quick glance back at Thomas and his pained face. Why did it feel as though she were leaving her rock behind while she plunged back into the storm?

Chapter 14

Flynn paced the street in front of the Allerton estate. Even dressed in his best, he felt like riffraff compared to the grandness of the house. He should walk away and not breach the grounds, but five days had passed and he'd heard nothing of Charlie's condition. Or how Esther faired. Did they expect him not to care, to be able to sleep, eat, or even think straight not knowing?

But could he risk everything?

A short laugh tasted bitter. Esther and Charlie *were* everything. The smithy, the shop, the work he'd spent his life mastering had lost any meaning but to prolong his lonely existence. Flynn filled his lungs and started up the narrow walk around the back of the house. Stomach in knots, he tapped on the smaller door that should lead to the kitchen.

A willowy woman, black curls wrapped up in a bandanna, squinted at him. "What you here for?"

"I need to speak with Eli."

"Eli?" She eyed him up and down once more before turning away. "He ain't here anymore. Gone north, he did."

"He's free?"

She nodded. "Best you just leave."

"No. I can't. I need to know. How is Charlie? Is he—"

She folded her arms. "Upstairs sleeping. But he ain't good."

"Will he recover?" *Please, God, give us that much.* Flynn hadn't prayed much in his life, but the plea flowed easily now, directly from his heart.

The woman glanced down. The pause was too long.

"Where's Esther?"

"Sitting with the boy, I reckon."

Flynn gripped her arm until she met his gaze. "I need you to take me to them."

"I don't think—"

"Please."

"I heard 'bout what happened. Master Allerton's already mad as a hornet. If he sees you here—"

"I don't care. I need to see Esther—Mrs. Mathews."

Another pause, and the woman nodded. "Master Allerton's in his office. You'd better hope he stays there awhile. If he sees you, I had nothing to do with letting you inside."

She left the door open and disappeared down the hall. Yeast and onion mingled on the air, another woman busy within the kitchen. He followed the first woman's path through the back of the house, climbing to the second floor. Anticipation grew.

"Charlie loves you, Thomas."

He wished Esther shared her son's feelings. The way she looked at him lent him hope.

Flynn shook the thought from his head. Esther might be grateful for the kindness he had shown her son, but she would never see him as more than he was, more than his station and heritage allowed him to be.

Deep rugs cushioned his footfalls, and he hoped his boots would not mar their ornate designs. Finally, the woman stopped and motioned him to move ahead, through a doorway into a large bedroom. The grand bed in the center appeared all the greater with how small a body lay tucked under a yellow quilt. An appropriate color for a boy who spread sunshine wherever he went.

"Charlie." He breathed the name, stepping into the room.

"Thomas?" Esther stood from the window ledge and hurried toward him. She kept her voice low. "You came."

He couldn't tell whether the pinch in her tone was from surprise or unease. Flynn motioned to the bed. "How is he?"

Water sprang to her eyes, and she shook her head. "I should have paid more attention to the doctors. They warned me he wasn't well, but they wanted to take him from me. I didn't want to hear anything they had to say after that. Now his heart is damaged, and he—"

Flynn braced her arms, and tears tumbled down her cheeks.

"He's dying." She leaned into him, tipping her head against his shoulder. "He's dying, Thomas, and it's all my fault."

"No," Flynn choked. Charlie slept so peacefully in the bed, his chest rising and falling with steady rhythm. He couldn't imagine a child so full of life fading away. "You did everything you could to keep him safe. He couldn't ask for a better mother."

"All I did was love him. He needed more than that."

And yet, Flynn would have given anything for that much. "How long?"

She sniffled and straightened away. "There's no way to know. His heart is doing better, but we were so close to losing him. Father says it's only a matter of time before. . ." She pressed her hands to her face, shaking her head.

Flynn stood silent, not knowing what else to do. He felt as though he'd taken an anvil to the gut. He barely heard the shuffle of feet behind him and the punctuation of a feminine gasp.

Esther looked past him, but he didn't turn. He didn't need to see Julia Allerton's shocked face to imagine her sentiments. And now there was little chance word of his presence would not reach their father's ears.

Esther stepped around Thomas to confront her sister, but Julia hurried from the room and disappeared down the hall.

"I should go." Thomas touched her shoulder, and she set her hand over his fingers to hold him in place. Just for a moment, to soak in his strength.

"Thank you for coming." Esther looked up at him, but her gaze snagged on his mouth and the wistful upturn of one side. As it lowered toward her own. She closed her eyes.

Warmth. Touch. A hint of moisture. The subtle but lingering aroma of smoke and iron that was such a part of who he was. She slid her hands to his freshly shaven face, discovering it again for the first time. The hair at the nape of his neck was thick but soft between her fingers. Fire ignited in her chest, both pleasant and burning. A twinge of pain as her heart opened wide and lodged him in place.

She'd never felt this way with Charles. Excitement at the beginning. Affection. But not this hunger, this need for him.

"Mama?"

Thomas drew away first, Esther's own thoughts in a blur. He released her and stepped toward Charlie, who lifted his head from his pillow. A smile split across her little boy's face and his blue eyes brightened.

"Mr. Flynn!"

"Shhh," Thomas crooned, crossing the distance and dropping to a knee at the bedside. He laid his hand over the blankets, over Charlie's heart. "I don't want ya getting yourself excited on my account." His subtle accent rolled from his tongue, softening his words.

"But. . .I missed. . .you."

"I missed ya too." Thomas wrapped Charlie's smaller hands in his good one.

Heavy boots up the stairs made them all turn. Father appeared in the doorway, his face flushing red. A vein bulged in his neck. "What is the meaning of this?"

Thomas moved to stand, face drawn, as though facing a firing squad. Even Charlie's eyes widened.

Esther hurried across the room and grabbed her father's arm. "Please." She stressed the word, making sure she gained his attention. "Mr. Flynn is here to see Charlie. Give them a few minutes." She waited, but he never looked at her. "Don't risk upsetting Charlie over this."

Her father glowered at Thomas, his jaw working, but finally his gaze fell on his grandson. The pounding of Esther's heart counted the moments before he grunted out a "Very well." One more glare cast in Thomas's direction and he retreated down the stairs.

Esther looked to Thomas, who stood beside the bed, eyes hooded. "Please stay a little longer. For Charlie." *And for me.* His kiss still tingled on her lips and life coursed through her limbs. But Charlie needed his friend more.

After expelling a breath, Thomas lowered to the edge of the bed and leaned back on the headboard. Charlie sat up just enough to recline against his arm. "Grandfather is. . .always grumpy."

"I'm sure he just wants you to rest and get well," Thomas said in return, his speech no longer relaxed.

Esther sank onto the end of the bed. "He does love you, Charlie. He's never been good at showing it." As a child, she had questioned his affection as well. Even now, it was often hard to see. She didn't want to live like that—her feelings buried deep. Time was too short.

Her thoughts wandered as Thomas turned Charlie's mind to other things. They talked about the smithy, all the things they could build someday, and how important it was that Charlie listen to his mother and get well soon.

"I don't feel sick anymore," Charlie insisted, sitting up more.

"My arm is also feeling much better, but if I use it again too soon, it won't heal properly. I could damage it for good."

Esther reached for her son's hand. Oh, that Charlie would heal, perfectly and completely. But Father's prognosis was much grimmer. He might recover now, but be it weeks, months, or a few years, one day his heart would no longer be up to the task of supporting his body. The end would come.

Time was too short.

She glanced at Thomas.

Life was too short to worry about what others thought of an Irish blacksmith. Too short to pass up a chance at happiness for her and Charlie.

After a while, Charlie yawned, and Esther nodded to Thomas.

"You should rest for a while, Master Charlie," he said, helping her son settle back.

"I don't want you to leave yet."

A smile grew on Thomas's face. "I don't want to leave yet either." He put his feet up on the bed and semi-reclined beside Charlie, who still gripped his arm. "You go to sleep again, and I'll sit with you for a while longer."

Minutes later, Charlie's eyes dropped and then closed. Thomas leaned over and kissed his brow. When he finally stood, his shoulders slumped. "What can I do?" he whispered.

About Charlie?

Or about their kiss?

"I don't know." She clasped her hands. "You've done so much already. Thank you." A meager offering for gratitude she longed to show. Would another kiss be untoward?

His gaze brushed her lips as though he'd understood her thought, and she stepped closer. But instead of taking her in his arms again, he shook his head and walked past her.

Rejection. The pain of it burned in her chest, though she recognized the wisdom of his actions. Esther found her feet and started after him. "I'll show you out." The least she could do was see him past the wolves.

"I know the way." His tone suggested understanding, and the desire to face her father alone.

"You're sure?"

He nodded and turned away.

Esther's heart thundered as she stood in the doorway, listening. All she heard was departing steps down the stairs. She closed her eyes and laid a hand over the thudding in her chest. "What now, Lord?"

The murmur of men's voices at the front of the house drew her to the opened window in time to see the local sheriff and his deputy clasping Thomas's wrists in shackles. Head tipped forward, he went without a fight, without a word of protest.

"Father, what have you done?" She spun and raced through the house, almost stumbling on her petticoats. By the time she reached the foyer, her father had closed the front door and was halfway to his office as though nothing had happened.

"Go back upstairs to your boy, Esther. That man is none of your concern."

"*That man?* He has a name. Just as Charlie has a name. Thomas did nothing wrong in coming here. Why are you doing this?"

"Thomas, is it?" He pointed a finger at her. "I know what's best for my family—what's best for you."

"No. I'm not a little girl anymore, Father. I can't stay here and pretend to be who I was. As soon as Charlie is well enough, I will no longer be under your roof or any of your concern."

Chapter 15

Flynn stared past the thick iron bars to the bleak hall beyond. He'd expected a confrontation with Dr. Allerton, but the man had never been one to do his own dirty work. He'd probably sent a runner for the sheriff as soon as he learned of Flynn's presence in the house. They'd been waiting. Trespassing and unpaid debt. He'd go before the judge in the morning, but Allerton had enough leverage to see him rot in prison.

"Is this what you planned for me, Lord?" His whole life seemed one downward spiral. From his birth in famine-stricken Ireland, to his parents walking away for the sake of their younger children. He'd poured his sweat into pleasing his master only to be buried under the man's debt. How could he have let his head be turned by Allerton's daughter? He had nothing to offer her or Charlie.

He leaned his head back against the hard wall, one pleasant memory rising over all the muck. Esther in his arms, his mouth over hers, and her returning his kiss.

Maybe life wasn't so bad after all.

"Thomas Flynn?"

He stood at the deputy's bellow and moved to the barred door as it swung open.

"Come along." The man motioned for him to pass. "There's a lady waiting for you in the office."

Flynn's stomach dropped. Not Esther. He didn't want her seeing him like this, dirty and stinking after three days in that tiny cell. But the deputy prodded him on, so there was no way to go but forward. He stepped into the office, and Esther pushed up from a creaky, wooden chair.

"Charlie?" he asked. What if he'd had more trouble with his heart, what if Esther had come to tell him—

Esther waited until the deputy passed through the room before speaking. "Charlie's well. Up and about more every day."

Flynn nodded and let the relief have its moment. He brushed his hands down the front of his wrinkled shirt. His coat sat back in his cell, too much for this July heat. "You shouldn't have come," he said, though he'd thought of little else than of her and Charlie since he'd been locked up.

"It's my fault you're here in the first place." She waved a hand around the room with its oak desk and simple chairs. Sparse, but clean and brightly lit—unlike the cell he'd come from. Thankfully, this was all she'd seen of the jail.

"You had nothing to do with it," Flynn stated. "Your father warned me."

"My father has no right to dictate my life."

"But he can dictate mine."

Esther crossed the room and gripped his hand, eyes sparking. "Not anymore. Your debt has been paid."

Flynn stared, not quite believing, not quite ready to hope. Freedom? "How?"

"Does it matter?"

"Yes." He tried to swallow, but his mouth had gone dry. Pieces fell into place. First Eli. Now him. "You?"

She stepped back. "Why should I not put my money to good use?"

Humiliation burned through him. "Because I didn't ask you to."

Bought and sold from one Allerton to the next. "I don't need you."

Her expression faltered for a moment then hardened. "Yes, you do. You expected me to leave you here?"

"It was my problem."

"Stop thinking about yourself!" She shook her head and backed away. "I have done what I've done. If you want to stay here and rot, that's your choice." With the swoosh of her full skirts, she walked from the room.

⌒

"Stop thinking about yourself."

Thomas Flynn climbed the steps to the miserable little room where he'd lived the better half of his life. Small. Hot. Smelling of smoke.

"If you want to stay here and rot, that's your choice."

Choice? Did he have a choice now? From apprentice to debtor—had he ever really known freedom?

He wasn't sure he knew it now. He still felt indebted, but now to the one woman he had wanted to impress, to prove himself to.

"Guess she knows what I'm worth." Down to the penny. He groaned and plopped onto the edge of the bed, which creaked in protest. A small rodent scurried along the wall before vanishing down a hole. Flynn worked his right hand. The tips of his fingers tingled and the bone in his arm ached, but less every day. "What am I worth?" To the world, who had both looked down their noses and praised his work. To Esther, who had paid the debt hanging over his head. To Charlie—his friend.

To God above.

He glanced to the dark rafters.

"I have done what I've done. If you want to stay here and rot, that's your choice."

Chapter 16

After a last glance around the room, Esther closed the lid on the last trunk. All that remained were the goodbyes. With news of a major battle between Charlottesville and Washington, near the town of Manassas, waiting was no longer an option. Father agreed that Charlie was well enough to travel by carriage, and she had purchased the most comfortable one she could find. With a small bed made up for him inside, and some medicine for his heart, hopefully their journey would prove smooth and uneventful.

"You ready, ma'am?" the footman asked from the doorway.

Esther nodded and stood back as the driver hauled her trunk downstairs to the carriage. Charlie sat on the window ledge watching the bustle below.

"It's time to go, sweetheart."

He dropped to the floor and took her extended hand. "To go see. . .Mr. Flynn?"

She squeezed his shoulder. "Yes." The goodbye she dreaded the most for so many reasons. Esther had not seen him since she stormed out of the Charlottesville jail over a week ago. Was he still angry? He'd made no attempt to visit her—at least, that she was aware of. No one had been eager to talk to her since that day. Father confronted her once, but backed down as soon as she'd turned the questions back on him.

"How does a blacksmith even have that much debt? With a doctor, no less?"

"I did the boy a favor when he came to me asking for help. The debt was with others. Gambling losses and failed speculation. I was the one who bought him time."

"Thomas gambled?"

Her father had glared, but answered. "No, Leighton was the one."

"Then most of this was his old master's debt?"

Uneasiness flickered in her father's eyes. And maybe a little shame. "The man was dying."

"So you made Thomas sign the loan too." Much of the debt had never been his, and yet he had borne it. Why would he not let her do the same?

Esther turned her thoughts back to the present and slowly guided Charlie down the stairs. Julia waited by the front door and allowed for a brief embrace. "I'm sorry," Esther whispered.

"So am I." Julia's eyes glistened as she touched Charlie's face. "Goodbye."

"Goodbye, Aunt Julia."

Father stood next, face drawn. He'd not argued with her when she'd revealed her plans to return north. Simply nodded and mumbled that it was probably for the best. His farewell was short, but his eyes softened when his grandson stepped near.

"Farewell, Charles." He squeezed the child's shoulder, but Charlie wrapped his arms around his middle. Her father returned the hug.

Esther froze the image in her memory, locking it securely in her heart. If she never saw her father again, this is how she wanted to remember him.

The carriage ride to the smithy seemed to take an eternity. . .and yet was over far too soon. She lifted Charlie to the ground and let him lead the way. He knew it well enough.

The front door sat open, but inside, shelves and displays sat dusted and empty of Thomas's workmanship. The clean window streamed light into the empty storefront. The *swoosh swoosh* of a straw broom beckoned from the smithy. Charlie beat her over the threshold, but stopped just inside.

The man wielding the broom was larger than Thomas, taller by at least half a foot, and broader through the shoulders.

"Excuse me?"

The older man looked up, brows raised.

"Where is Mr. Flynn?"

He harrumphed. "Not here, as you can see. Gave up the lease. Offered him a loan to keep going, but he won't take it. Packed up his things and off he went."

Esther's heart seized. "He's gone? Where?"

"What business is that of mine? But it's not like there aren't any other blacksmiths in this town. I'm sure you'll find someone who can see to your needs."

What she needed was Thomas Flynn. Head spinning, she turned back onto the street, Charlie in tow.

"Mama?"

How to tell him that they might never see his friend again? The thought made her heart sick. How would they find Thomas now? Why hadn't she come sooner? She was well enough acquainted with his pride to know he'd not come to her, not after their meeting at the jail. But her own pride had stood in the way of reaching out again, and now it was too late.

Too late for what? A goodbye?

Maybe it's better this way.

Now if only she could convince Charlie—and her heart.

Charlie tugged away and started up the street.

"Charlie, come back."

"I need Mr. Flynn."

"No, sweetheart." She stepped around him and gently took his shoulders. "Listen to me, Charlie. Mr. Flynn left. He's not here anymore."

"But he's right there." Charlie pointed past her.

Esther spun. Sure enough, Thomas stood speaking with a man in an apron just outside of the mercantile several buildings away. Her pulse skittered out of control and her feet seemed welded to the walkway as Charlie hurried past her, weaving around people, until he threw his arms around Thomas's waist.

Thomas jerked in surprise then dropped to one knee and wrapped her boy in an embrace. His gaze searched until it found her.

She managed to narrow the distance between them. "You lost the smithy?"

"I gave it up." He stood, but held Charlie to his side.

"What will you do?"

One of his shoulders lifted. "Not sure. Hire out to another blacksmith." He lowered his voice. "I hear Mr. Lincoln has called for more soldiers."

She stepped near. "Go north?"

"I need to make a new start somewhere."

"Come north."

His blue gaze locked on hers with a look akin to panic. "You're leaving?"

Two older women brushed by.

"The war has come to Virginia," Esther answered.

A wagon creaked and moaned as it pulled to a stop in front of the mercantile.

"And isn't likely to end any time soon." Thomas took Esther's arm and led her and Charlie to the side of the brick building. "I'm sorry for what I said last time." He mumbled as they moved. His voice was deep and his eyes intense. "I was wrong. About a lot of things. I owe you all my gratitude. For what you did."

Thomas released her to reach into the haversack hanging from his shoulder. A long stem. A threesome of leaves. A rose blossom, shaped from iron. "It's far from perfect."

"You made this?" For her?

"Took some doing without use of my good arm, but I couldn't leave it alone."

She took the rose and opened her mouth to tell him how beautiful she thought it, how much she loved it—loved him—but he was so much nearer now, only a breath away. Enough words, enough burying her feelings and pretending she could get by on her own. Enough worrying about what the rest of the world thought. His lips separated, and she pushed up on her toes to find his with her own.

⇨

Flynn closed his eyes and blocked out the passersby with their expressions of shock and disapproval. He braced Esther's arms and allowed himself to answer her kiss. Nothing had ever tasted sweeter. Her lips. Her mercy. Her love.

Thank Thee, Lord. For who else but God above could have forged this moment? Flynn had planned to say goodbye before he left Charlottesville, but he might have been too late—he might have never seen them again. The mere thought constricted his chest with a throbbing ache. He tightened his hold and deepened the kiss.

At the taste of salt, Flynn glanced to Esther and the tears on her cheeks. He cupped her face and drew back. Words escaped him, so he tipped his forehead to hers and filled his lungs. "Forgive a fool."

"There's nothing to forgive."

"I love ya, Esther." The words rolled from him, refusing to be kept back. None had ever felt so natural on his tongue.

Her lips curved. "I can't forgive that."

"Then I'll be in ya'r debt—I'll swear to love ya for as long as I've breath in me."

Her eyelashes lowered, dislodging more tears. "I accept."

Her choice of words settled into him, and he eased back. "Ya do?"

She bit her bottom lip and nodded.

"Marriage?"

A smile bloomed in her eyes, while Charlie's arms squeezed around his middle. Flynn tightened his jaw against the surge of emotion threatening to spill. He gathered them to him, an arm around Charlie while he pressed a kiss to Esther's temple.

Family.

No one could be certain how long they would have together, but he would take whatever God gave them.

Epilogue

Thomas Flynn thrust the long rod of iron into the forge. Another round of tempering and the barrel would be ready to be set aside with the others due to the gunsmith. He tried not to think about the lives his work might take, no longer able to sit on the sidelines while war ripped the states apart.

"That one is. . .very. . .straight."

Thomas glanced back at his son—his dear, precious Charlie—in his wheeled chair watching on. They had almost lost him several times over the past two years, and he had never fully recovered, but by some miracle his heart kept beating.

"That's good enough for me." He smiled at his boy before turning back to work. "Give me a few more minutes, and we'll head in for dinner."

Once the barrel was finished and the fire was banked, Thomas pushed Charlie's chair out of the barn they'd transformed into his smithy, toward the two-story brick cottage Esther had made their home. She stood on the porch, little Betha on her hip, speaking with an officer in blue. Had the army sent for the rifles already? He'd told them the barrels would not be ready until the end of the week.

Quickened pace brought him up the path, but conversation faded before he reached them. The officer stepped closer, emotion in eyes to match his uniform.

"Thomas?" he asked, tentatively.

Familiarity buzzed in the back of Thomas's brain. He looked to his wife for an explanation.

Esther smiled. "I didn't want to say anything, not until I knew for sure. But that detective we hired found a lead." She motioned to the young man. "I asked Captain Ewan Flynn to come meet us since he was posted near."

The veil of years faded, and Thomas glimpsed his seven-year-old brother in the grown man before him. "Ewan?"

" 'Tis me, though I'd not recognize you but for how you look like our da."

Thomas crossed the distance and crushed his brother in an embrace. He'd agreed when Esther suggested a search, but hadn't expected—hadn't allowed himself to hope—they'd have success. Too many years separated them. He pulled back but gripped his brother's uniform. "What of Da and Mam?"

"Da passed 'bout ten or twelve years back. Worked himself into a grave, he did. But Mam is well. Lives with Declan and his wife. The three youngest girls are there as well." Ewan shook his head, brow furrowing. "Guess ya'd not know of lit'l Caitlin. She wasn't born till after ya left us."

Thomas allowed the news to penetrate. A sibling he'd never met. And Da gone. The last sank through him with keen regret. So much he'd wanted to say to the man, to ask him. So much he understood better now.

Esther moved to stand beside him. "You will stay for dinner, I hope, Captain Flynn." She smiled. "Ewan. I'm sure there is much you and Thomas would like to discuss. It's been so long for both of you."

Ewan nodded. "I'd like that. I only have today before I return to my posting, but I know the rest of the family will be so glad for a visit." He grinned at Thomas. "Ya've done fine for yarself. Da would be proud. He prayed and talked of ya all the time, saying that now ya'd have a chance at something better than he could offer."

Thomas swallowed hard but couldn't quite press down the regret. All the years he'd hated his da, or considered himself unloved. If only he'd recognized the truth.

"Da!"

Little Betha reached out her pudgy arms and wrapped them around Thomas's neck. Hardly more than a year old and already walking and talking like she'd kissed the blarney stone. Esther's concerns with her pregnancy had come to naught. Betha was as healthy as they came, a large, happy girl who adored her older brother like nothing else.

"And ya named this youngster Betha, yar wife says?" Ewan asked.

"We did." The name had fit so well—meaning *life* in Irish.

"Think Mam will be right happy to know a grandchild carries her name." He then nodded to Charlie who watched the whole exchange with interest.

Thomas returned his hand to the chair's handle. "This is Charles, our eldest."

Ewan smiled and saluted the boy, whose grin was ready. Always ready.

The conversation continued as they made their way into the house, Ewan asking questions and answering in kind. Memories unfurled from the tangles of the past, bringing healing, granting light.

⌐

Esther laid Betha in the center of their bed, as no crib would hold her, and headed down the stairs to find Thomas sitting alone at the table.

"Ewan's retired for the night?"

He nodded.

She slipped into the chair beside him and stretched her hand out. There were dishes to wash and a house to tidy, but she wouldn't allow this moment to pass. He twined his fingers through hers and squeezed.

"I wish I knew your thoughts, Mr. Flynn."

"Just marveling, *Mrs. Flynn*."

She raised her brows and waited.

" 'I have done what I have done.' "

The phrase rang with familiarity. "I'm not sure I understand."

"A wise woman once said those words to me and demanded I make a choice."

She shook her head at the memory of that day in the Charlottesville jail. "I was upset."

"Understandably so. Ya gave me a gift, and I spurned it."

Esther winced and started to stand. "It's been a long and wonderful evening. What good does it do to rehash the past?"

Thomas pulled her back down and took both her hands in his. "My da did the same. Gave me a gift and prayed I'd make the most of it. He's not the only one."

"I don't understand."

"God gave me His own Son. And it took me how long to fully accept Him?"

Esther squeezed her husband's hands, considering the gifts she too had received. Her husband. Her children. She wasn't aware of the tears until they spilled down her face. She tried to steal a hand back to wipe the moisture away, but Thomas held fast.

"Charlie?" he said softly.

She nodded. Another gift from God Himself. One she hadn't always seen for what it was.

"We don't get to choose what life we're given. Only whether or not to embrace it."

She gripped Thomas's hands and let the tears fall freely. He leaned forward and kissed where each tear ran. One. After. Another.

They would embrace every day the good Lord gave them, and every child He sent into their arms.

Angela K. Couch is an award-winning author for her short stories and has been published in several anthologies. She was also semi-finalist in ACFW's 2015 Genesis Contest with her Colonial romance, *The Scarlet Coat*, book one of the Hearts at War series that was released by Pelican Book Group in 2017. As a passionate believer in Christ, Angela's faith permeates the stories she tells. Her martial arts training, experience with horses, and appreciation for good romance sneak in there as well. Visit her at www.angelakcouch.com.

A MALLEABLE HEART

by Jennifer Uhlarik

Dedication

To Kerry J.
Girl, you stepped in when I was dealing with
some tough stuff. My creative well was dry,
and you helped me look past the difficulty
to find the story I needed to tell.
From the bottom of my heart, thank you!
Love you, my friend!

Acknowledgments

To Pegg: Thank you for inviting me to be a part of this cool story collection! It's one of my favorites so far.

To the wonderful critique partners who have continued to help me with my stories: Cindy, Michele, Ruth, Sarah, and Shannon—thank you all for your invaluable feedback and encouragement.

To my family: There were a lot of nights I was an MIA wife and mom while getting this one done. Thank you for your understanding and grace. I love you all!

To my fabulous editor, Ellen Tarver: Woman, you ROCK! Thanks for helping me make my stories so much better in the end.

To Becky Germany: Thank you for the continued faith in me and my stories.

And most of all, to Jesus Christ, my Lord and Savior: Thank You for allowing me to touch some small part of the world through these words and stories. May You be magnified in my meager attempts.

Chapter 1

Elverton, California—1870

Leah Guthrie wrapped a wisp of hair around her finger as she stared at the wagon wheel. Broken. Sighing, she looked across the town in the valley down the road.

"Was it too much to ask that this rickety wagon hold together until I finished my trip, Lord?" At least she'd broken down on a flat spot, rather than on the steep incline.

The wagon had seen hard use in and around Elverton these last five years. The nagging thought that *something* would soon go wrong had plagued her, though she'd prayed the fear was unfounded. Unfortunately not.

And, unfortunately, there was no money for its fixing. She'd already pulled her younger brother and sister from school so they could work while she continued their lessons each evening at home.

A slow shiver inched up her spine. "All right, Father." Leah forced her gaze to the tall white steeple peeking over the valley's treetops. "You've allowed this. I trust You have a plan how to pay for it."

Leah gave the wisp of hair another twist as she considered options. Her wagon was loaded with her customers' dirty laundry. She'd needed to collect only three more batches before she could return home and check on Mae. Dare she walk to the blacksmith shop on the far edge of town and risk someone stealing something from the bed? Little else she could do. She must get home, so she gave her big horse, Samson, a pat and descended toward Elverton.

She was nearly to the bottom of the road when a wagon turned and started the climb. As it drew nearer, neighbors Tom and Grace Peterson came into view. Mr. Peterson slowed his team as he drew alongside.

"Leah." He nodded. "Everything all right?"

She offered the grizzled, salt-and-pepper-haired man a crooked smile. "The wagon wheel broke. I am going to ask the blacksmith for help."

"Have you had any dealings with Bo Allen before, darlin'?" Mr. Peterson asked.

"No, sir."

"Why don't you let my Tom go in your stead?" Mrs. Peterson asked. "Once he's talked to Mr. Allen, we'll drive you on home."

"I appreciate the offer, but. . ." After Papa's passing, she'd tried to ask as little of her neighbors as possible. Caring for her younger sisters and brother was *her* responsibility.

"Darlin', Bowdrie Allen's an ornery cuss," Mr. Peterson continued. "I'd feel a heap better if I at least went with you."

She'd heard the stories—how he argued with customers and even broke a man's nose during one altercation. Despite her apprehension, she would talk to the reclusive blacksmith herself. "If you really want to help, would you allow me to put the laundry orders I've got in your wagon, then wait while I gather the last three?"

Their reticence obvious, they nodded.

After going back to her wagon, transferring everything into the Petersons' wagon, and tying Samson to the back, they descended into Elverton and stopped near the smithy.

"Thank you both. I'll be back soon."

Long before Leah reached the building, the loud, rhythmic clang of hammer against anvil punctuated the quiet street. Her heart pounded as she reached the wide double doorway and looked inside. The forge's red glow lit the far side of the room where the blacksmith worked, back to the door. The pungent odors of burning coal and hot metal gave an eerie stench, as if she stood at the gaping maw of Hades itself.

"Mr. Allen?" she called over the clanging.

The rhythm didn't change, nor did Mr. Allen flinch.

"Pardon me, sir."

When no answer came, Leah huffed and stepped inside. "Helloooo?"

Finally, the cadence stopped. The broad-shouldered man laid the hammer aside and dropped the long, narrow piece he'd been hammering into a bucket. A mighty *hiss* filled the sudden silence as steam rose around it.

"Excuse me, Mr. All—"

"I heard you." The blacksmith snatched a rag from his back pocket.

"Then why didn't you answer?"

Mopping his face, he turned and approached her. "Didn't you hear me hammering?"

Was he joshing? His intense hazel-eyed glare didn't indicate any humor.

Leah planted a fist on her hip. "Rather hard to miss that, don't you think?"

"Yeah, I woulda thought. . ." He ran the cloth over his sweaty blond locks then shoved the rag into his pocket again. "But you just kept yammerin', despite all the signs that I was busy just then."

Leah's jaw hinged open, but she quickly snapped it shut. "Forgive me for *yammering* at you, sir. How would you suggest a potential customer alert you when she arrives and you appear to be *busy just then?*"

Mr. Allen stepped past her and rapped soundly on the silvery wooden slats of the door. "She could knock and wait to be acknowledged."

Leah's ire sparked, and she marched to his anvil. "And you, sir, could answer like this." She picked up his hammer, clanged it twice, and spoke as she turned to face the door. "I'll be with you in a m—"

Bowdrie Allen's solid chest, covered in a tight-fitting gray Henley, blocked her view. She slowly looked up, gaze traveling past his muscled shoulders and blond beard to his stern expression.

"Give me the hammer."

Whether the heat filling her cheeks was from the forge or something else, she wasn't sure, but she wished to be standing near the door and its nice cross breeze. She passed the tool to its owner.

"Now, what do you need?" He made no attempt to step away, leaving her pinned between him and the anvil.

He towered over her, so meeting his eyes required craning her neck at an uncomfortable angle. It was hardly proper to stare at his broad chest. She finally pinned her focus on his Adam's apple.

"I have a broken wagon wheel I was hoping you could fix."

"Sure—either fix it or replace it. It'll be ready in five days."

"I can't go that long without my wagon."

"You want it sooner, you can pay double, and I'll put you to the front of the line."

"Double?" She gulped. This felt all too familiar. "Please let me pass."

He folded his arms, hammer resting against his shoulder. "Do you want me to do the work or not?"

Overly warm and a bit claustrophobic, she darted a glance to the open floor space beyond. If she could just get there. . . "Please, Mr. Allen, let me pass."

"Is that a no then?"

Heart pounding, she drew another breath to quell her panic, but the feeling only grew. She shoved both hands against his solid biceps and forced him backward by half a step. Just enough. Head spinning,

Leah escaped the confined area into the open, only to stumble once free.

Lord, please don't let me pass out. . . .

⪼

The woman sank to the floor, dress billowing around her as she gulped for breath. Bo's chest seized. Was she sick? He dropped the hammer and grabbed a straight-backed chair from the corner then dragged it to her. He gently took her elbow.

"Here. Sit." He applied gentle pressure until she took the offered seat.

Rocking, she wrapped her arms about her middle. A low whimper peppered her rapid breaths.

"You need a doctor or something?"

Her eyes clamped tight.

"Ma'am?" His heart ratcheted into a staccato rhythm.

Distant memories niggled at his mind of his own mother's ministrations. Bo hurried to the corner and dunked a clean rag in the pail of drinking water. As he returned, he squeezed the excess from the rag then gathered her loose red-blond curls and draped the cloth across the back of her neck. She flinched but continued to rock. Holding the rag in place, Bo squatted to peer up at her high cheekbones and porcelain skin.

Concern froze him to the spot. Should he fetch Doc Bates? Probably, but if he left her alone, he risked that she might stumble the wrong way toward the forge. He could saddle Diego and take her to the doc's office, but again, he'd have to take his attention from her for too long.

Only then, a second recollection came to mind, of his ma whispering prayers for almost everything, particularly when she was worried.

God? The name formed in his thoughts about as easily as opening a severely rusted gate. *It's been a long time. If You hear me, I could use some help. . . .*

What on earth would God's help look like? He hadn't any idea, nor did he know how long to wait, but within a moment, her breathing slowed and her rocking stopped. He kept his hand clamped against the wet cloth until, finally, her eyes fluttered open. Only then did he release his grip.

"Ma'am? You all right?"

She stared blankly for another moment before finally releasing her grip on her midsection and blinking a few times. Slowly, she pulled the cloth from under her hair.

"Hey." Bo brushed the back of a hand against her knee.

The woman turned his way, her light brown eyes sparking with. . .was it ire or humor? "I heard you, sir, but I couldn't answer. I was *busy just then.*"

Her pointed words lodged like a well-aimed arrow. Definitely a sharp-witted humor. Few women ventured into his shop, and fewer still stood up to his ornery nature. He rather liked it.

"Reckon I deserved that."

"Good of you to notice." She handed the rag back. "Thank you. The cool cloth helped."

"You sure you're all right?"

Her pretty features pinked, and she nodded sheepishly.

"What was that?"

Pink turned to crimson. "I sometimes grow overly anxious. My heart races, I struggle to breathe, the room spins."

"You *sure* I shouldn't fetch Doc?"

"Yes." Her throat worked furiously. "It would only be another bill I can't pay."

The last words were spoken so softly he almost missed them.

She stood. "Thank you for your kindness, Mr. Allen." Her soft voice shook. "I won't keep you." She brushed past him.

Him. . .kind? Few, if any, had ever said as much.

"Wait!"

Her feet faltered.

Bo stepped in front of her. At the sight of her brimming tears, his heart sank. Had *he* caused them?

His mind blanked. Why on earth had he called after her? "I don't even know your name."

She blinked furiously. "Leah. Guthrie."

"Mrs. Guthrie, I wasn't looking for trouble. I'd be obliged if you didn't tell tales to your husband that I reduced you to tears."

Oh, for Pete's sake. Had he truly just thrown out such obvious bait?

Get her out of your shop before you make a complete fool of yourself.

She patted her cheekbones dry. "No need to worry. The only Mr. Guthrie is twelve and stands half your height. He may be a rapscallion, but I can't imagine my brother picking a fight with you."

"You're not married?"

Why in heaven's name was his tongue wagging so?

Miss Guthrie's chin jutted. "No, sir. I've been busy raising my younger sisters and brother since our pa died. There's been no time to wed."

She was raising her kin. . . .

The silence grew awkward. "I'll go."

Right. She should before he opened his—

"How old are they? Your family."

Oh, blast!

"As I said, my brother's twelve. My sisters are fourteen and eighteen."

Miss Guthrie looked to be about twenty-two. As beautiful and spirited as she was, surely she'd attract a man's attention. "Why haven't you left the young ones with your eighteen-year-old sister and gone your own way?"

He cursed himself roundly for the question.

Her eyes flashed. "Not that it's any of your concern, but Mae's health is such, she needs care herself."

He furrowed his brow at that.

"Besides, what member of a loving family would abandon everyone to seek her own happiness? That would be the height of selfishness."

"Yes, miss, but I've seen it before." One too many times.

She folded her arms. "You won't see it here. As hard as it's been to feed four mouths on a laundress's income, I'll not leave my family to seek my own happiness."

He'd overstepped. "Forgive me. I didn't mean to offend, and I wasn't purposely casting aspersions on your character." Yet he'd done exactly that, blast it all. There were reasons he kept to himself, and this was one. "Don't reckon a caring woman like you would abandon her kin."

"Never. Speaking of, it's past time I get home." She nodded to the rag still in his hand. "Thank you again for the cool cloth." Miss Guthrie turned.

Bo groaned inwardly. He'd angered her. His customers often left upset, so why he cared whether this one was flustered, he couldn't quite explain. "Um, about your wagon—"

She rounded on him. "The truth is, Mr. Allen, I can't afford to pay *single*, much less double. I'm sorry I wasted your time."

"You said you're a laundress?"

She nodded. "Yes."

"You the one I heard picks up and delivers the clothes to her customers?"

"Yes."

"Then you really can't do without your wagon, can you?"

Her voice softened. "No."

"How 'bout a trade? In exchange for you doing my laundry, I'll charge you the going rate for a wheel repair or replacement—whichever it takes—and I'll have it ready by tomorrow afternoon."

Her eyes widened. "You would do that?"

For a woman who'd willingly saddle herself with three younger brothers and sisters? "Yeah. Just don't tell anyone." He shrugged. "I've got a reputation to uphold, y'know."

A smile blossomed on her lips, and she giggled. "So I've heard." The smile faded all too soon for his liking. "You have a deal."

Chapter 2

"Where have you been?"

"You're late!"

Leah cringed at her sisters' gentle chidings. "I'm sorry. The wagon wheel broke." She moved aside, allowing Mrs. Peterson room to enter. "Please set the laundry in the corner, Mrs. Peterson. Thank you."

The woman placed two bags along the wall and hurried outside for more.

Once alone, Leah put down the basket she carried and looked again at her sisters. "I'll tell you all about it once we get the orders in. Where is Ethan? He can help."

Hope shook her head. "He said Mr. Tallis had work for him at the mercantile. But I'll help." The girl scurried outside after Mrs. Peterson.

Leah turned to Mae. "I didn't leave you in too bad a way, did I?" Today had been one of Mae's weaker days.

The girl shrugged. "I did all right alone. I was starting to worry, but Hope arrived home and kept me company." Using both hands, she hoisted her useless right leg down from the footstool—a milking stool with a pillow atop it—followed by her weakened left. "I'll start supper."

Once Mrs. Peterson and Hope filed through with more of the laundry orders, Mae pushed up onto her crutches and shuffled to the kitchen table.

Leah discreetly watched as Mae hobbled to the nearest edge of the table and all but collapsed into a chair. The girl breathed deep, the short jaunt having obviously taxed her. After a moment, Mae hoisted herself onto her elbows and, shifting all her weight to one side, dragged the basket of vegetables and the knife from the far side of the table.

"Go on, Leah." Mae settled again in the chair, never turning to see that her sister was truly there. "I'm fine."

Leah went to the wagon for one of the baskets. Mae had been nothing if not brave in the face of the illness that stole the use of her legs. Perhaps even braver than Leah herself. How many nights had she cried over Mae's deteriorating condition, begging God for a miracle? Let her sister walk again like the stories of miraculous healings in the Bible. . .only, so far, the prayers hadn't worked.

If her sister had such thoughts, she'd locked them deep inside and never shared them. There were days when Mae grew moody and withdrawn. At such times, Leah wondered whether Mae was lamenting the loss of her ability to walk—and all that meant. The end of her formal schooling. The fact she was mostly homebound. That people gawked when she did go out in public or gushed effusively when they saw her, only to spread false tales later.

Mae's beauty shone through despite her condition. Her thick brown hair and striking blue eyes complimented her shapely figure. She had a quick wit and a sweet spirit—all the things Leah imagined a young man might want in a wife. But at the time Mae ought to be thinking of suitors, instead, she lived in their rickety house, barely able to move from one side of the cabin to the other without falling. Any young men who'd expressed interest before the illness disappeared afterward.

"That's the last of it." Mrs. Peterson deposited the final basket along the wall.

"I can't thank you enough for your help." Leah gave the woman a hug.

"You know we'd do anything to help."

Mr. Peterson appeared. "Samson's watered and put up in the corral. Can we do anything else whilst we're here, darlin'?"

There was a list of twenty things she might ask his help with, but most were chores that couldn't be accomplished in a few minutes, even if her pride might allow her to ask. "No, thank you."

After brief goodbyes, Leah herded Hope toward the kitchen to assist with dinner preparations.

The girl took a seat and plucked a potato from the basket. "All right. Tell us what happened with the wagon."

Leah stirred the potbellied stove's coals to life with a long piece of kindling. "I was just descending into Elverton when the wheel broke on the east road. I was worried about leaving the fully loaded wagon untended." Tiny flames sprouted, and she fed more wood in.

"So, what *did* you do?" Mae pinned her with a questioning look as Leah stood.

She explained about the Petersons' timely arrival and her visit to Bowdrie Allen's smithy, leaving out the details except that he'd agreed to fix the wheel.

"Is he as much of an ogre as everyone says?" Hope's eyes sparkled with morbid interest.

Mae dropped a peeled potato into the pan. "I've heard he's mean as a bear startled out of hibernation." She bared her teeth and snarled at Hope.

At the younger girl's frenetic giggles, shame spiraled through Leah. "Stop!"

Her sharp word brought both girls up short.

"You're not to speak so uncharitably toward Mr. Allen again. Am I understood?"

Repentance tinged Hope's expression. "We were just joshin', Leah, like we've done a hundred times before."

That was it. They *had* poked fun. All of them, Leah included. But the man wasn't near as curmudgeonly or mean-spirited as he liked to be thought. At least he hadn't acted so with her. "We needn't be unkind, so I'll thank you to stop."

Mae arched her brows. "There's something you're not telling us."

She shook her head. To tell them of the episode she'd had would only worry them. They'd seen Leah's attacks a time or two, and the heart-pounding incidents only caused them to fret.

"We're waiting." Mae pinned her with a look.

Hope also pressed for details.

Leah sighed. "Yes, there is more." *Lord, please don't let this upset them.* "Mr. Allen *was* rather rude at first." She told of their tiff over his not acknowledging her when she'd entered. "So I walked to his anvil to demonstrate how he could've called out to me, but he followed me there." She avoided the detail of his muscles. "When I turned, he had me pinned in a tight space and was pressing for an answer on what to do about the wheel, and—"

"And *what?*" they chorused.

"It felt a lot like the day that awful banker kicked us out of our house."

Hope's eyes widened in understanding. Not quite ten when it happened, she'd had nightmares after watching her eldest sister almost lose consciousness.

"You didn't pass out, did you?" Mae prodded.

"I was close."

"Are you all right?" The tightness in Hope's voice told her she'd better turn the conversation in a happier direction.

"I am, thanks to Mr. Allen. He brought a chair, a cool rag, and stayed with me until it passed."

"Bowdrie Allen?" Mae's mouth dropped open.

"Yes. He was very kind in his gruff way."

And so very handsome.

⟿

One week later

Bo stood under the old oak tree between his corral and smithy, enjoying the cool evening breeze. His arms ached and his feet throbbed after long hours of work. It would be nice to sit, kick off his boots, and relax. With the horses fed and settled for the night, he'd soon turn in himself in his small quarters behind the smithy. Perhaps draw a little, if he wasn't too tired. However, as was his custom, he gave Diego, his dun, a few minutes of attention before he turned in.

Despite his rubbing the horse's neck vigorously, Diego nudged his chest playfully.

"What?" Bo laughed. "Isn't this enough for you?"

It probably wasn't. He'd not had time to ride in a week, and Diego liked to run. Surely by now, he needed to stretch his legs. Maybe he should take the spirited horse for a run before starting his day tomorrow.

He *could* ride to Leah Guthrie's and deliver his laundry since he'd missed her that afternoon. Before she'd showed up, Bo had gone to ask the butcher, Sal Harper, if he could help with a two-man job. He returned to find a paper crammed between the locked doors. Unable to read, he'd had to wait until Sheriff David Yeldin made his afternoon rounds to discover what the note said. It took work to hide his disappointment at missing the feisty gal.

Yes, indeed. Maybe he needed to drop off his dirty clothes. . . .

As he considered the plan, all his horses' heads came up, and their ears pricked toward the smithy. Bo also focused in that direction. The sound of breaking glass shattered the stillness, followed by pounding feet and laughter.

Bo launched himself toward the corner of the smithy in long strides. Before he reached it, a shadowy shape darted around the building and slammed into him hard. Bo staggered back but kept his feet, unlike the small figure who tumbled into the dirt with an *oof*. Bo hauled him up by the shirt collar, able only to tell it was a young boy.

"Let me go!" The kid squirmed.

Two smallish shadows darted to the far side of the street.

"Move, you idiot!" one called.

"But what about Red?" came a second voice.

Bo gave the captured boy a rough shake. "Red, huh? Is that your name?"

The brat kicked, his foot landing square against Bo's kneecap. Pain lit his senses and, grunting, he hoisted the kid over his shoulder and limped into the shop. All the way, the boy squirmed, driving bony knees and elbows into Bo's chest and back.

Inside, a fist-sized rock and shards of glass littered his desk and the plank floor, glittering in the forge's glow. Bo huffed. He crunched past the glass shards and dropped the kid none too gently.

"Thought it'd be fun to bust my window, did ya?"

The boy, lanky with an overgrown mop of auburn hair, stared, wide-eyed.

"Answer me, *Red*."

The kid tried to inch backward, not uttering a word.

"Where you going?" Bo snagged him by the shirtfront. "We got a long talk ahead of us."

Red's eyes narrowed, and he spat in Bo's face.

Shock rattled through him, though he schooled his expression. Deliberately, he wiped the spittle from his cheek with the rag he kept in his back pocket then pinned the little hoodlum with a glare.

"You want to handle things this way, let's go."

Bo hoisted Red to his feet, clamped a firm hand around the scruff of his neck, and guided the boy toward the wide doorway.

"Where are you takin' me?" Red grappled to free himself.

At the wide double doorway, Bo dragged one sliding door closed then the other, laced the chain through the handles, and clicked the padlock shut. Then he roughly pointed his young charge toward the cross street a half block away.

"Let me go!"

Bo dragged him to a halt. "You ready to talk?"

Despite the darkness, the narrowing of Red's eyes was unmistakable. This time, Bo was ready. At the slight shift in the boy's weight, as if he prepared to kick again, Bo also shifted—and swept the kid's legs out from under him. Landing flat on his back with a *whoosh*, Red gulped air like a dying man.

Bo knelt beside the kid. "You want to keep testing me, you do that. I'll keep knocking you on your backside until you understand the way of things."

Red finally caught his breath. "What're you planning to do with me?"

He hoisted the kid to his feet. "Since you ain't talkin', I'll just press charges and let the sheriff deal with you." He reasserted the vise grip and maneuvered the kid toward the next street.

"Press charges? You gotta be joshin', mister!"

"Do I act like I'm joshin'?"

The kid's feet slowed. "No."

"So. . .you ready to talk, or do I haul your sorry hide down to Sheriff Yeldin?"

"What do you want to know?"

He steered the kid toward a bench. "Sit."

Shifty-eyed and anxious, Red did as he was told.

"Why'd you break my window?"

The kid eventually lifted a slim shoulder. "Dunno."

"Who were you with?"

Silence.

"What's your last name?"

Red's heel began to tap at a clipped pace.

Bo clenched his jaw at the lack of answers. "Where do you live?"

Somewhere down the street, a door squeaked, but Red made no attempt to speak.

Frustration coiled in Bo's chest. "Last question, kid. Who are your parents? Answer me, or I'm hauling you to the sheriff."

The tapping of Red's heel continued, though he finally piped up. "Audie and Mary."

"That's more like it." The coil loosened slightly. "Audie and Mary *who*? I need a last name."

Red gave a slight shake of his head.

"Let's go." He dragged Red from the bench by the upper arm.

The kid went limp.

Bo bit back a curse as he crouched low to keep a grip on the boy. "You little troublemaker. Stand up, or I'll thrash you then drag you the rest of the way, and I won't be gentle."

"I'm not going to the sheriff," Red shouted.

"Then tell me what I've asked, and I won't make you. Audie and Mary *who*?"

"*Guthrie*. They're dead!"

Chapter 3

Heat radiated from the potbellied stove, leaving Leah in a sweat as she ironed. Mae sat at the table nearby, sound asleep with her chin cupped in one hand and pencil poised over the ledger in her other. Leah grinned.

"Mae."

No response.

She placed the iron on the stove's burner to reheat then moved to her sister's side.

"Hey." She shook Mae gently.

The girl came awake with a sharp inhale.

"You're tired. Why don't you go to bed?"

She blinked heavily. "We aren't done yet."

"I can tally the rest of this order." Leah plucked the stubby pencil from Mae's grip. "Go rest."

With a sigh, Mae reached for her crutches. "Yes, *Mother*." She giggled softly.

"You watch that, young lady, or—"

A sharp knock at the door stalled Leah's words. Deep darkness pressed at the windows. Not the usual time for visitors. "Who on earth is that?"

"I haven't the faintest idea."

A tingle crawled down her spine, and she suddenly wished either

Hope or Ethan were home so she could position them with the rifle near to hand. Both were spending the night at friends' homes.

"Stay here."

Wide-eyed, Mae nodded.

As Leah stepped past Mae, her gaze strayed to the rifle above the door.

The firm knock came again. "Miss Guthrie?" The muffled male voice was familiar.

"*Mr. Allen?*" What was the blacksmith doing on her doorstep at this time of night?

"It's me."

"Is something wrong? I don't usually expect visitors so late." Particularly handsome male visitors.

"Yeah. There's a problem."

Her heart stuttered. What problem would require him to knock at her door? Surely not… "Sir, if this is about my missing you in town today, my note said I would return for your clothes."

"Would you *please* open your door?"

Boots scuffed on the porch, and then a hushed but scolding voice followed.

"Is someone with you?"

"I'd be happy to show you, if you'd open the door."

Was the man drunk? Typically a solitary man, it was all too unusual why he'd be at her door.

"Leah, open up!" This time, it was another voice.

"Ethan?"

She snatched the rifle from its pegs and opened the door. Leah leveled the gun barrel at a stern-faced Bowdrie Allen, whose meaty hand engulfed her little brother's shoulder.

The infernal man looked at the rifle, calmly pushed the barrel aside, then nudged Ethan forward. "Is this your brother?"

The rifle barrel dipped toward the ground. "Yes." Leah tried to drag the boy inside. "What is he doing with *you*?"

Mr. Allen held Ethan in place.

When she pulled at her brother's forearm, both his hands came up in awkward unison, revealing a narrow cord bound his wrists.

"You've tied his hands?" She stepped back and hoisted the gun again, aiming for the man's broad chest. "Explain yourself and fast, Mr. Allen."

No more concerned than if he'd shooed a gnat, the blacksmith brushed aside the gun barrel again. "He and his friends busted the front window of my shop tonight." He drew a knife from his belt and cut the cord. "In trying to deliver him to you, he kept attempting to make off with my horse. So I tied him to the saddle horn."

Her ire withered. "Ethan?"

The boy rolled his eyes, a behavior he'd displayed with increasing frequency. Her heart sank. His impudence was growing as fast as his body, and she felt helpless to stop it.

"Your sister asked you a question, boy." Mr. Allen shook Ethan. "Answer her."

"Or what?"

Mr. Allen spun him so they faced each other. "Or you'll deal with me."

"Are you her protector now?"

The blacksmith's jaw grew rock-hard, and he grabbed Ethan's arms. "No. Just a man who'll not abide your mouth anymore."

Leah's breath caught as the big man dragged Ethan toward the edge of the porch. The boards creaked as Mr. Allen sat heavily on the step and pulled Ethan, belly first, over his knee.

The boy flailed. "What're you doing? Let me go, you big—"

Ethan's next word humiliated Leah.

"This is for my window." Mr. Allen's hand connected with Ethan's backside, and the boy cried out.

Leah gasped.

"And this is for kicking me." Another firm strike, and another pained cry.

As Mr. Allen's hand rose for a third time, she moved toward the door, but something blocked her path. Beside her, Mae leaned hard on her left crutch as she blockaded Leah with the right.

"Don't you dare stop him." Mae's voice trembled. "You know this is exactly what Ethan needs."

"This is for spitting on me." Another thunderous swat, punctuated by Ethan's now-muffled grunt.

Mae sidled up close. Whether for physical support, to bolster Leah's resolve, or to sustain her own, Leah wasn't sure, but she set aside the rifle and clung to her sister, thankful for her presence.

As Mr. Allen doled out several more swats, Leah gulped. Her composure flagged as this stranger addressed her brother's rotten behavior. Spitting? Kicking? Cursing? Breaking another's property?

When the paddling ended, Ethan burst past them, all but bowling Mae over. Leah held her as he stomped toward his room. An instant later, Mr. Allen rose to face them.

His eyes widened as Mae extricated herself from Leah's grasp.

"Didn't realize there was an audience."

She cleared her throat. "Mr. Allen, my sister, Mae. Mae, meet Bowdrie Allen."

"Sir." Mae dipped her chin. "If you'll both excuse me, I'll look in on Ethan and head to bed."

"Thank you." As her sister hobbled off, Leah stepped onto the porch and pulled the door partially shut.

"Thank you for returning my brother to me, Mr. Allen. Tell me what we owe you for your window, and I'll be sure to—"

"*You* don't owe me anything. That defiant brat in there does."

She bristled, though he was right. Ethan was defiant—and a brat. She'd been so consumed with caring for Mae, working to provide for her family, and keeping this rotting roof over their heads, she'd not realized just how rebellious her brother had become.

"He can work extra at Tallis's Mercantile to earn what he owes." He was already working to pay down their large line of credit at the store. Hopefully Mr. Tallis would agree.

"Fine then. Just make sure it ain't your household money. Ain't your place to pay for his wrong choices."

He made it sound so simple. If he only knew how thin a thread they lived on, always wondering when it might break.

"Thank you again, sir." Exhaustion pulled at her. "Good night."

"Night, Miss Guthrie."

She backed toward the door. As she bumped it open, light fell across the porch.

"Miss?" The blacksmith scrubbed the back of his neck. "I'm real sorry about the hullabaloo. I *do* hope you can settle yourself and rest."

"Thank you, Mr. Allen."

The way her heart pounded, it might take some time. But was it pounding from anger at Ethan's behavior? Perhaps at Mr. Allen's firm treatment of the boy?

Or—was it the odd feeling that for the first time in five years, she wasn't alone in seeing her younger brother and sisters to maturity?

⌁

Bo's hammer strikes fell into a familiar rhythm. Strike, strike, tap. Strike, strike, tap.

You're a fool.

The rhythm faltered with the accusing thought.

Strike, strike, tap. Strike, strike—

She won't speak to you after the thrashing you gave her brother.

He struck the metal with too much force and immediately cringed. The strike had misshaped the barrel of the hinge he'd crafted. It was the third mistake he'd made in the last two hours. His mind was *not* on his work. Rather, it was soundly focused on Leah Guthrie and her kin. But he shouldn't be worried about whether she spoke to him again or not. Few enough in town bothered, and he got along fine.

So why did he look forward to bantering with her?

"Yep, you're a fool."

He paced to the forge, buried the misshapen hinge in the coals, and pumped the bellows to stoke the fire. As he did, a sharp knock came at the door. Bo glanced over his shoulder, ready to offer the intruder a "be right with you," like Leah Guthrie had suggested.

Only it *was* Leah Guthrie.

He made sure only the barrel of the hinge was buried then crossed toward the door.

"Morning." He nodded. "Reckon you're here for the laund—" His words dissolved when she turned red-rimmed eyes his way. "You all right?"

Of course she wasn't. He'd walloped her kid brother.

"Do you have a moment?" Her voice shook.

"For. . . ?" Here it came. She would tell him to steer clear of her.

"I was checking on the cost of a new window for you at Mr. Tallis's Mercantile."

"You what?"

"I said I was—"

"I heard you fine. What about it?"

"Some time ago, I made arrangements with Mr. Tallis that Ethan would work at the store so we could pay down the credit he's extended us."

"All right." What did this have to do with him?

"When I asked for Ethan to work more hours, Mr. Tallis informed me he fired Ethan more than two weeks ago."

"Why?"

"He was stealing. Dime novels, candy. . .I don't know what else." The woman's cheeks flushed. "Ethan never told me he'd been fired, so I've no idea what he's been doing these past few weeks."

"So you're saying he won't be paying me until he finds another job?"

Her expression turned hopeful. "That, and. . ."

His stomach knotted. "And?"

Leah Guthrie shrugged a bit sheepishly. "I was told by the butcher that your assistant quit abruptly. Nor do you have an apprentice."

Blast Sal Harper's mouth. "No!"

"No, you don't have an assistant or—"

"I'll not take on your kid brother as an apprentice." He shook his head. "Just. . .no."

"Mr. Allen, please. This is not easy for me." She glanced toward the doors then beckoned him farther into the smithy.

For some unknown reason, he followed and bent his head close when she spoke in a whisper.

"I've not seen Ethan so. . .subdued as he was last night and this morning. Not since my father was alive. He needs a firm hand, one that I have struggled to provide."

"Grief, woman! You're asking *me* to provide it?" Given this request, being ignored would be preferable.

"Not like you did last night, no. But you need a helper, and Ethan needs a job—and I suspect he'll thrive having a man to teach him manly things again. How does this not benefit us all?"

It was a workable plan except that he didn't need—or want—to apprentice *anyone*, much less a green kid full of anger and disrespect. He'd been that kid, and under the harsh tutelage of his guardian, he'd only grown more angry. He'd not be the cause of some boy turning out just like him.

"Please?" She fluttered her long lashes.

His resolve turned to mush. "Fine. But only until he's paid me what he owes." He'd pressure the kid to give up his friends' names so Bo could make them pay their fair share too. That would cut the time down as well.

A broad smile spilled across her face. "Thank you so much. Ethan? Come inside, please."

The boy shuffled in, hands shoved in his pockets. He glanced around before finally looking at his sister.

"You're going to work with Mr. Allen until you've paid for a new window. Understand?"

"Yes." The boy wouldn't look at Bo.

"What time should I return to collect my brother, Mr. Allen?"

He thought an instant. "Does five work for you?"

"Yes. I'll see you both then." She turned that beautiful smile on him then swept out of the smithy, leaving him staring at the kid.

"What do I call you? Ethan, or Red?"

He shrugged. "Red, I guess."

"All right then." He waved toward several heavy aprons hanging near the door. "Find yourself an apron that fits."

Red rolled his eyes as he turned away.

"Listen here, boy. You're not saying it, but the way you're carrying yourself screams how much you don't want to be here. Keep it up, and I'll give you more of last night's medicine, haul you back to your sister, and you can carry the shame of letting your family down. Or we can put aside our differences, you can act like a man, and we can get to work. Which is it?"

Red plucked an apron from a hook and looped it around his neck, attitude changing none at all. "I'll work."

Blast. This was going to be a long few weeks.

Bowdrie Allen, you're a fool.

Chapter 4

Four days later

Crouched under the tarpaulin she'd rigged for shade, Leah wrung Bo Allen's gray Henley and shook out the garment. Standing, she found the shoulder seams and gave it a firm *snap*. The hem cracked, drawing Mae's attention from the new book they'd borrowed from Doc Bates's wife.

From the nearby quilt where she sat, Mae's blue eyes sparkled with mischief. "That Mr. Allen certainly has strong shoulders, doesn't he?"

His shirt draped over her forearm, Leah arched her back and stretched, then massaged her aching muscles. "I hadn't noticed." She tried to sound disinterested.

Grinning, Mae jabbed Leah's hip with the end of a crutch. "*Liar.* You can't help but notice one so handsome as him."

"Mae Elizabeth Guthrie!" She threw the wet garment at her sister.

The girl dropped the crutch to catch the gray fabric and shook it out again. "You know it's the truth." Sighing, she gave an appreciative once-over glance as if Mr. Allen filled out his shirt presently. "If you don't notice, you're tetched in the head." Mae lowered the shirt to tap her skull.

Leah frowned. "You're shameless." She crouched again, draw-ing the last garment from the water, this time, her own blouse. As she reached for the bar of soap, Mr. Allen's wet shirt sailed back and smacked her hard in the face.

"And you're acting like an old maid." Mae glared.

She set his shirt in the basket and began to scrub her blouse. "I am twenty-three years old, Mae. Heavens, I've never even been kissed. The moniker applies."

Truth was, since Pa died, few had paid her a lick of attention. Any remaining male interest stopped after Mae's illness robbed her of the use of her legs and any remaining inheritance they might have had.

Mae turned serious. "But it doesn't have to for you. One old maid from the Guthrie clan is more than enough, sis—and I was the lucky one to draw that straw."

The blunt words knotted Leah's throat. *Why, Lord? Why my beautiful sister Mae?*

Mae wouldn't let up. "But with your reddish-blond hair and fun personality, you'll make a fine wife. All that's required is a little effort."

Leah continued to scrub. "I haven't the energy for more effort, Mae. I scour the skin from my hands every week to keep the roof over our heads. You and Hope have been easy to raise, but Ethan? Honestly, some days I wonder if I can deal with even one more of his antics. There's nothing left after all that to seek a husband."

Mae shot her a sympathetic look. "Maybe it won't take much extra effort. We have to eat, don't we?"

"What are you talking about?"

"Why not invite Mr. Allen to dinner? Men lose their hearts to good cooks—and you're a fine one." Her expression turned almost pleading. "Invite him and see what happens."

Leah blew out a long breath. "You make it sound so easy, but the little I know of Mr. Allen, he's *not* an easy man." She rinsed the suds from her blouse.

"Yet you think he's a *good* man, don't you?"

She pondered her sister's words as she wrung the blouse. "There's goodness in him, yes." Buried under a tough veneer of hard living, anger, and hurt. Could she muster the stamina to seek the goodness out?

"Leah, you'd be asking him to dinner. That's all."

She carried the basket toward the clothesline. "That's not all. The gossips in town will talk."

"So? They already talk because of my affliction. Don't let them bother you."

Leah sighed and plucked her blouse from the top of the basket. "It feels very forward, like I'm throwing myself at the man." She applied the clothespins to her blouse before retrieving Mr. Allen's Henley. Removing the right pin, she lapped the shoulder of his shirt over hers and reapplied the fastener.

"It's not if you invite our brother's boss to say thank you for hiring him. That's called being neighborly."

Leah pinned the second shoulder and faced Mae. "I'll pray about it. Now, are you going to read me some of that book like you promised?"

"Of course." Mae cracked the cover. "*Pride and Prejudice* by Jane Austen. Chapter one. 'It is a truth universally acknowledged, that a single man in possession of a good fortune, must be in want of a wife.'"

Oh, good heavens above. She rolled her eyes.

Mae read on, and Leah grabbed the next piece of clothing from the basket. *Lord, what man would want me with my little brother and two sisters in tow?*

A strong breeze caught the two garments on the line, fluttered their hems, and released them again. As they settled, the arm of her blouse twined around the arm of Mr. Allen's.

Bo stepped out into the afternoon sun and turned toward the corral. Some fifteen minutes earlier, Red had excused himself to use the outhouse but hadn't returned. The fact Bo had seen a couple boys skulking near the livery across the street, easily in view of the smithy door, had him wondering. Were *they* the pair who'd been with Red the night his window was broken?

A quick check of the outhouse proved Red wasn't there. After Bo had watched the street awhile, one of the kids he'd seen stumbled out of the alley beside the stable then darted into the narrow space again, laughing.

That was where he'd find Red.

Bo angled across the street and crept to the corner, listening.

"...been there a week, and all he lets me do is dump more coal in the fire and pump the bellows. It's stupid."

Red.

"He's prob'ly making you do the boring stuff so's you can't pay him back for that window too fast." This voice was deeper than Red's. "Using you for free labor."

"Yeah." The third voice was high-pitched and chirpy, like from a younger kid.

"He keeps pesterin' me to tell him who you two are, but I ain't gonna." Red again.

"You do and I'll pound you." This from the deep-voiced kid.

The threatening tone irked Bo, and he rounded the corner then. Red and the smaller of the two boys—perhaps eight years old—stood nearest to him. The third—half a head taller than Red—stood a few paces beyond. The minute Bo grabbed Red and the smaller boy by their arms, the third one's eyes bulged, and he charged down the pathway.

Bo dragged both squirming boys out of the alley and wrestled them to the bench near the livery's entrance.

"Quit your caterwaulin' and sit." He pushed them toward the wall, and their bodies folded against the bench.

Bo looked the little boy over. White-blond hair, small frame, maybe seven or eight. "So. . ." He looked toward Red. "He helped you bust my window?"

Red's expression turned stony. If the size of the towheaded boy's eyes was any indication, he was scared witless. *Good.* Maybe he'd think twice about destroying someone else's property again.

"Am I to assume that boy who abandoned you in the alley was in on it too?"

"Burl didn't abandon us," the blond boy growled.

"Burl. That his name?"

The boy's eyes widened even more.

"Burl and. . .who are you, kid?"

"Jess."

The answer came from the livery's entrance, where prospector Sean McCready stared him down. The taller boy, Burl, stood slightly behind.

"His name's Jess McCready, and he's my nephew." The elder McCready folded his arms.

Bo inwardly grinned at the unnatural hook to the prospector's nose, a hook he'd given McCready a year earlier when the miner walked into his smithy and demanded Bo drop everything to do a job for him.

"You got an issue with these boys, Allen?"

"What I got issue with is my smithy window getting broke. I caught this one running away just after it happened." He nodded at

Red. "The other two ruffians ditched him to take the punishment alone, and that ain't right."

"And you're sayin' my nephews are those. . . *ruffians?*"

"Red just said as much."

"When did this window get broke?"

"A week ago."

At McCready's beckoning, Jess darted off the bench and raced to his uncle, who bent to look each boy in the eye. "Is what he's sayin' true?"

Burl—about age fifteen, judging by his size—gave an emphatic shake of his head. "No, sir."

Little Jess appeared less sure but also shook his head after seeing Burl's response. "No."

McCready faced Bo, trying to rein in a smirk. "Figure you got the wrong kids, Allen. Easy mistake to make, but from now on, come to me with any issues you got with my kin. Do we understand each other?"

Bo itched to wipe the sneer from McCready's mouth, but he kept himself in check.

"Red, you got anything to add?" he said, never breaking eye contact with the elder McCready.

Bo thought he caught a discreet head-shake from Burl, aimed in Red's direction.

"Nope," the boy muttered.

Sean McCready's smirk only grew. "Think we're done here."

"For the time being." Bo stepped close and dropped his voice. "But if I ever get the idea you're sending those little boys to get back at me for breaking your nose, there'll be trouble."

"When or if I choose to get back at you, you'll know."

A shot of lightning coursed through Bo's veins at the threat. "Stay away from my smithy—you and any McCready spawn." He waved

Red toward the shop. "Let's go. Now."

Sighing, Red started across the street, his twelve-year-old body ramrod straight and screaming his displeasure. Once they reached the shop, the boy whirled. "Are you trying to drive away all my friends?"

"What're you talking about?"

"Burl and Jess! They might never speak to me again after what you just did."

Bo arched a brow. "It surprises me that you're still speaking to them."

"They're my friends." He enunciated each word.

"Some friends. They let you take the blame for their actions, threaten to pound you if you tell, and make you pay to replace my window. Seems to me, you're getting the raw end here."

"Am not!" Despite the rebuttal, Red deflated, his mind obviously churning.

"Go on believin' that, kid." He jerked a large, sturdy crate off a low shelf and slid it across the floor. Selecting a piece of scrap metal, he walked to the anvil and beckoned to Red. "Got a project for you."

With a frustrated groan, Red walked to the bellows and started pumping.

Bo split the air with a sharp whistle. "Over here." He turned the sturdy crate upside down in front of the anvil.

Surprised, Red approached as Bo measured and marked a spot on the piece of iron. "What're you making?"

"I'm not. You are. It's about time you start doing something useful."

He instructed Red on heating the small metal piece, and once it was glowing, the boy grabbed the tongs from the wall hook and brought it to the anvil.

"We'll start simple and work our way to more difficult techniques. You're gonna take this and taper the end into a point."

"How?" Red held the tongs out to Bo.

"Don't give it to me. You said I don't let you do nothing interesting, so you're doing this one."

Understanding lit the boy's eyes. "All right. Which hammer?"

Bo handed a small cross peen to Red, who stepped onto the crate. From behind, Bo nudged the boy's feet wider.

A memory flashed—of some twenty-odd years earlier when he'd begun learning blacksmithing techniques at age seven. His taskmaster had been harsh, abusive. He'd berated Bo often, struck him for even the smallest mistakes.

"What do I do?" Red's question snapped him back from his contemplations.

Before he found his voice, he thought of pretty Leah Guthrie. She'd asked him to extend the firm hand she'd struggled to provide the boy. But firm and harsh were two very different things, and finding that balance was suddenly important to him.

God, I ain't sure how to do this. Please, if You're listenin'. . . If You care. . .help me get this right.

He stepped up behind Red. "Hold the metal at an angle, like this. . . ." Bo took Red's hands, positioning them, his touch far gentler than his mentor's ever was.

Chapter 5

The following morning

A
s Mr. Allen unlocked the sliding doors, Leah halted Samson outside the smithy. Almost before she'd stopped, Ethan vaulted to the ground and hurried toward the shop.

"Morning, Mr. Allen," he called, his tone cheery.

Confusion etched the blacksmith's features as his gaze followed Ethan. Inside, the boy looped an apron around his neck and tied it at his waist.

"What's with him?" Mr. Allen hooked a thumb in Ethan's direction.

Leah set the brake. "I was going to ask you that question. He was worn out last night but woke with a smile and seemed anxious to get here. What did you have him do yesterday?"

"It was a slow afternoon, so I let him pound some scrap metal. Showed him a few techniques." His flummoxed expression accentuated his handsome features.

Beside her, Mae and Hope stifled giggles, and she gave her youngest sister a discreet elbow to the ribs.

"Ask him." Hope employed an elbow of her own.

"Hush!" Leah glared at the youngest girl.

"Ask me what?" Mr. Allen looked at each in turn.

"Oh, you already know. I've asked every day this week, but if I must say it again—"

"We want you to come to supper tonight," Mae blurted.

"Please?" Hope stretched the word across a full two seconds.

A flush crept up his neck. "Now that ain't fair. You brought reinforcements."

She quirked a brow at him. "I did."

"I, uh. . ." He scrubbed the back of his neck. "I ain't got clean duds for something so fancy."

Leah handed the reins to Hope and swung down. "Not true." She plucked a paper-wrapped package from the wagon bed. "It's all washed and pressed. The brown plaid would be quite appropriate for tonight. Is six too early?"

When he motioned her toward the corner of the building, out of earshot of the others, she followed.

"What's wrong?"

"You *sure* you want me to come to supper?"

"You don't bite, do you, Mr. Allen?"

The man ducked. "Most everyone in this town—including me—says I do. You *sure* you want to give folks fodder for the gossip mill?"

Remembering Mae's suggestions, she smiled. "What fodder are you talking about? We've invited my brother's boss to supper. Is there something untoward about such an invitation?"

Mr. Allen loosed a sardonic laugh. "Not much wrong with it unless it's me you're inviting. People in this town think I'm a belligerent, stubborn cuss, ill-tempered and not suited for polite society. And they're right."

"Perhaps they wouldn't think that if you'd allow them to see the side you've shown me. You're not a *pure* ill-tempered curmudgeon. You've shown me wonderful kindness, so that side of you is in there." She again extended him the paper-wrapped package. "So. . .six tonight, and wear the brown plaid shirt."

He scowled as he received the parcel. "You don't hear *no*, do you?"

Leah lifted her chin, a coy smile on her lips. "There are some stubborn parts in me too. You'll become accustomed to them eventually. See you at six."

⁓

Heart pounding, Bo knocked on the door.

God, how in blue blazes did I get roped into supper at the Guthrie house?

He'd turned Leah Guthrie's invitations down all week, but she'd outsmarted him by bringing her whole family that morning and by completing his washing two days earlier than expected. The troublesome woman deflected his every attempt to scare her off.

When no one answered the door in a reasonable time, he knocked again.

"Just a moment."

The muffled voice didn't sound like Leah's. The next-oldest, perhaps. What was her name?

Before he thought of it, the door cracked open, releasing the savory scents of the meal they'd prepared. Bo's stomach growled.

"Mr. Allen?" The middle sister squinted, as if unsure.

He swept his Stetson off. "It's me."

She grinned and shuffled around on her crutches until she could swing the door wide. "Welcome. Have a seat. The others will be out momentarily."

He ducked through the doorway.

"You're welcome to hang your hat on the peg." The young woman nodded in the direction.

"Thanks." He left it where indicated and chose a seat on the far side of the room but became painfully aware of the struggle the younger Miss Guthrie had in closing the door and traversing the crowded room.

"I'm not taking your spot if I sit here, am I?" He indicated the chair he'd chosen.

"No, sir. I prefer this one." She nodded to the worn chair with a milking stool nearby.

He waited to sit until she'd situated herself, and no sooner did he settle than Leah Guthrie swept into the room. His breath caught as he rocked back to his feet.

Her beautiful sage-colored dress, dotted with clusters of pink flowers, made her red-blond hair stand out all the more.

"Good evening." She dipped her chin in his direction.

"You look right pretty."

Oh, blast it all. Get a hold of yourself, man. He'd meant only to say a pleasant good evening, but his brain turned to mush around her.

The younger Miss Guthrie stifled a giggle as the elder Miss Guthrie smiled.

"You look nice yourself."

Before he could fumble for more words, Red and the youngest Miss Guthrie entered.

"Mr. Allen, you obviously know Ethan, and you've met Mae."

Mae. That was it.

"I don't believe you've been formally introduced to Hope." She drew the youngest girl forward.

"Miss Guthrie." He nodded to her.

"It's a pleasure, Mr. Allen."

"If you'd do us a favor," Leah Guthrie said, "we'd be obliged if you'd call us by our given names. With three Miss Guthries in the room, it'll be easier."

It would at that. "All right then. Y'all can call me Bo."

She nodded. "I hope you're hungry. Supper's ready."

Hope helped Mae up as Leah led him toward the kitchen. As he passed, Red fell in beside him, and Bo shook his hand.

"Thanks for coming," Red whispered. "It's nice not being the only fella in the house."

Bo grinned at that. He already felt awkward and out of place, exactly why he'd not wanted to come.

After a blessing, they passed the venison stew, and the conversation started. Hope chattered about sewing a wedding dress with the town's seamstress, Mrs. Nagle. Red filled his sisters in on the things he'd learned at the smithy that day, and Mae and Leah peppered Bo with questions about his work. By the time their bellies were full, any reservations he'd had about coming had dissolved.

Leah caught the two youngest with a pointed look. "Ethan and Hope, please wash the dishes. Mae can dry."

"Me?" Red balked. "I worked all day. I'm tired."

Bo snapped his fingers, the sound loud in the sudden stillness. "Boy, you best rethink that attitude. What do you think your sisters did today?"

"Women's work. I was doing man stuff."

"Oh. I see." He turned to Leah. "Just wondering. . .who hunted the meat for the stew?"

"I did." Leah twisted a strand of her hair around her finger.

"You dressed the meat and cooked the meal, I reckon?"

She nodded.

He asked a litany of questions about the work she did every day. "So has Red here ever done his own laundry?"

"No." She released the curl, which brushed her soft cheek. His heart stuttered. How soft her skin must be. . . .

Blast it all. He shoved the unbidden thought aside but held her gaze intently. She stared back until he gave her the slightest quirk of a brow and a discreet glance toward Red.

Leah smiled as understanding dawned. "But perhaps it's time he learn. Since women's work is so easy, right?"

Bo winked discreetly at Leah. "A fine idea. He oughta be able to get his wash done before work tomorrow morning. Don't you think?"

What in thunderation was he was doing? This was *her* kid brother, and it wasn't his place to suggest she implement chores. But hearing the boy shrug off Leah's hard work rubbed him wrong. Perhaps a taste of her daily efforts would silence the boy's complaining.

Her smile grew. "I'll see he does."

The intense sparkle of her eyes tightened his chest, and he was suddenly aware of the other girls' attention too.

Red folded his arms. "That ain't fair. I'm a kid."

Bo laughed. "You just told us you were doing a man's work. You can't have it both ways, boy." He nodded toward the sink. "Now, be the man you say you are and help your sister. And when you come to work tomorrow morning, I better hear a report that you've done your laundry."

Leah nodded. "Oh, he'll do every step, from hauling the wash water to pressing the clothes once they've dried. Ethan, go help Hope then get to bed. You've an early start tomorrow."

Red slumped. "What're you gonna do?"

Hope pulled him from his chair, a knowing grin on her face. "None of your business, nosy boy. Now, come along."

With a coy smile, Leah nodded toward the front door. "Would you join me on the porch, Mr.—Bo?"

While neither looked his way, Mae and Hope exuded an eager anticipation.

Blast it all. Being watched by all these womenfolk was unnerving. Bo rose, all too happy to escape their scrutiny.

As they exited the house, the kitchen erupted in whispers and giggles.

Chapter 6

Leah's steps faltered. Could her sisters not hold their excited chatter even two more breaths until she and Bo were outside? She faced her guest as he grabbed his hat and closed the door behind him.

"Thank you." And please overlook the giggling.

"For?"

For coming to dinner. For giving her a reason to dress up. For making her feel alive and feminine and not so very alone. At least for tonight.

"You're really good with Ethan. . .and with helping me see how to handle him."

A cockeyed smile tugged at his mouth. "Then you ain't angry at my pushing more chores on him?"

"Not at all!"

"Red ain't a bad boy, Leah. But he's at a hard age. If you don't get him going in the right direction now, he could wander into real trouble."

She cocked her head. "Why do you call him *Red*?"

"It's what he asked to be called."

"Really? Why on earth—"

"I think it's the name the McCready brothers call him."

The kitchen window's gingham curtain rustled, and three faces peeked out.

Leah craned her neck. "Dishes. *Now.*" She spoke loudly enough to be heard inside.

The curtain fluttered again, the faces disappearing.

Bo chuckled, the sound low and warm. "Got us a spy, do we?"

"More like three." She chuckled herself. "We so rarely entertain company, it would appear the exhilaration of this unusual experience has caused my brother and sisters to forget their manners."

He squinted at her. "An unusual experience. Is that what you call it?"

Her cheeks warmed. "I suppose so." Truth was, the anticipation had caused her and her sisters to lose their ever-lovin' minds as they prepared, but she wouldn't admit that.

"Why don't you? Entertain more, I mean. You've a fine family."

"Thank you." She drank in the intensity of his gaze. "Many reasons, I suppose." Leah dropped her voice so as not to be overheard in the kitchen. "Mainly, Mae's condition."

"What *is* her condition?" He matched her tone.

His bluntness took her aback. Few asked such pointed questions. Then again, those who tiptoed around the issue were often those who stared or met Mae with such effusive greetings, only to gossip about her as they left. Perhaps more pointed questions were preferable.

"About three years ago, we all came down with an illness. Our heads ached, our throats hurt, body stiffness, fatigue."

"Influenza?"

"So we thought. The illness lasted about a week, but as Ethan, Hope, and I began improving, Mae took a turn." Her throat knotted. "She struggled for breath, and her body grew weak. Her legs began to waste." Leah brought the back of her hand to her mouth then cleared her throat roughly.

"I'm sorry," Bo whispered. His boots scuffed. "Reckon I'm nosin' into things that don't concern me."

She looked up, startled to find herself staring at his solid chest. His hands hovered near her shoulders, as if to give her a comforting caress or maybe a hug, though once he saw her eyes open, he stepped back without contact.

Leah cleared her throat again. "I don't mind your questions." And oh, how she'd have welcomed his touch. "The memories of that time are. . .difficult. I was terrified I would lose her. Even three years later, the illness has its effects. She has no use of her right leg, and her breathing remains somewhat weakened. Doc Bates calls it a debility of the lower extremities. He gives no hope for improvement."

"This happened after your parents died?"

"Yes. Mama died giving birth when I was Hope's age. We lost her and our baby brother both. Papa left us five years ago after a rattler bite."

He was quiet a moment. "You ain't had it easy, have you?"

She hadn't, though she didn't desire sympathy. Only friendship. "We're all born with a set of difficulties to endure. Those are mine." A moment passed. "But then, you don't strike me as a man who's led the easiest life either."

Something in his eyes darkened. "I haven't."

"Do you have family?"

He snorted. "Maybe somewhere. Ma's dead. Died in Texas when I was six. Pa never stuck around long enough to get to know. And my older brother, Reese, sold me into indentured servitude to a cruel cuss of a blacksmith months after Ma's passing." He shrugged and jammed his hands into his pockets. "If either of them are still alive, I got no use for 'em."

Leah's jaw went slack. "Your brother *sold* you?"

"To Paul Cooper, a harsh, uncaring, often brutal man. Apparently, Reese sold fourteen years of my life to Coop. What he got for the promise of my serving this man, I have no idea. I never saw any money, and Reese dumped me with Coop and his wife and never looked back."

"Oh Bo." She laid a hand on his forearm. "I am so sorry. How could he do that?"

He squirmed from her grasp and pinned his attention on his horse tied nearby. "Like you said earlier, it's pure selfishness, dumping your kin to seek your own happiness." His voice shook.

She settled a hand over her aching heart. "That's why you asked me why I hadn't left my family to get married—"

"Yeah." He slapped his hat against his thigh, the sound startling her.

"You've not seen Reese since?"

A muscle along his jaw popped. "Don't care to."

"And you've had only this man Coop's influence. No motherly figure since your own ma—?"

"Coop's wife, Anna, was good to me, but she died when I was nine." He inhaled, the breath shaking as he released it. Whether from anger or pain, she wasn't sure. "Coop and I packed our belongings and headed to California just after that. Didn't realize it at the time, but in hindsight I think he might've murdered her and used the Gold Rush as an excuse to leave before anyone pieced it together."

"Oh my word, Bo. And you stayed with this man fourteen years?"

He shook his head. "Eleven. I was seventeen years old when he came at me with a knife for some mistake I'd made. When the scuffle was over, I was the one left standing. Sheriff Yeldin's uncle was the lawman in that town. It was his duty to arrest me for murder, and I stood trial. Fortunately, he also testified on my behalf. I got off on account of it being self-defense."

Leah could find no words, only the desire to pull him into her arms and ease away the emotion etched in his features.

Before she could, Bo turned, his hazel eyes stormy. "I think I've spewed enough of my troubles. I should be heading back now before it gets too much later." He tugged his Stetson into place. "Thank you for the tasty supper. It was a real nice evening until me and my big mouth ruined things."

Thunderstruck, Leah stared.

"Bo, wait." She found her tongue as he mounted his horse. "You've not ruined anything. You don't have to leave."

"Best if I do." He scowled. "Thinking about Reese and Coop puts me in a foul mood."

With a touch of his hat brim, he rode toward town.

⌒

Blast it all, why had he shared so much with Leah? He barely knew her, and he'd dumped his darkest secrets, all at once. Idiot!

Thoughts circling like vultures, Bo descended into Elverton and steered Diego toward the Sierra Gold Saloon. About the only thing that stopped his thoughts from swirling was whiskey. Tonight, he'd need copious amounts of it.

The Sierra Gold was an upscale establishment. No saloon girls or women of ill repute. Just billiard tables and whiskey. Forget the billiards. He'd take a bottle, a glass, and a quiet table in a corner.

He tied Diego to the hitching post, entered, and sounding a sharp whistle, caught the owner, Orrin Jagg's, attention. Without a word, the man nodded, grabbed a half-filled bottle and a glass, and handed them over.

"Thanks," Bo mumbled. The crowd was sparse, so he parked himself at an out-of-the-way table and poured a drink.

"To Reese and Coop. May you both rot." Bo tossed back the contents then poured a second glass.

As he reached for it, Sal Harper stumbled up and sat. "Don't you know by now, it ain't right, a man drinkin' all by his lonesome." The butcher wrenched the bottle from Bo's hand and tipped it toward his mouth.

Bo caught his wrist. "Put it down."

His friend's smile faded. "Ease up there. I'm just funnin' ya." The slur to Sal's words clued Bo in to just how long his friend had already been drinking.

"Ain't in the mood."

"Feeling fractious, are you?"

"Oh, shut up." Bo swirled the liquid in his glass then drank.

"What's eatin' you?"

"Got things on my mind."

Sal offered a sympathetic smile. "You want the respectability of company, or are you determined to drink alone?"

Disinterested, Bo waved a hand. "Stay if you want, and help yourself to the bottle. But if you do, get a glass."

The portly man lumbered toward the bar then returned. After pouring himself a glass, he looked Bo's way. "A customer give you problems?"

Silent, Bo shook his head.

"One of your jobs go wrong?"

"Nope."

The man thought. "Then what ruint your day?"

Bo swallowed another mouthful of whiskey.

Sal snapped his fingers. "I know." A smirk rolled across the man's face. "It's that new kid. Red somebody. Heard he's a little hellion."

Bo smacked the table hard enough to rattle their glasses and cause the bottle to teeter. "Red Guthrie ain't a hellion," he growled.

Sal's brows arched in surprise.

"He's…confused, is all. Made a few bad choices." Bo leaned across the table. "And if you think the kid's a hellion, why'd you suggest he come ask me for a job?"

"Are you blind?" Sal leered. "Thought you'd like that pretty thing he calls a sister coming into your shop. She's a looker—"

Bo's right hand tightened around the glass. "She ain't a *thing*. Her name's Leah Guthrie, and you'll show her respect."

Irritation flashed on Sal's face. "Who's disrespecting her? I just like the view. Thought you'd appreciate such finery yourself." He paused an instant then swore. "If it weren't for all them kids she's raisin', especially that one with the crutches, I'd consider—"

Bo swung. As his fist connected, the whiskey glass, still in his hand, shattered on impact. Sal reeled backward in his chair, as pain lit Bo's arm clear to the shoulder. Air rushed from his lungs as blood and glass covered his palm.

An oath dripped from his lips. What had he just done?

Several men rushed up, two ushering Sal a few steps away while more came to Bo's side. Orrin Jagg dashed up then, cloth in hand, and wrapped the rag around Bo's bloodied hand.

"We best get you to Doc's place, Bo. That's gonna need attention." The barkeep nodded to the others, who guided him past the table.

As they passed, Sal grabbed Bo's shirt, dragging him close. "You hit me."

The men attempted to break them up, though Bo lunged closer. "I told you. You show that woman respect, *especially* because she's raising her kin."

Strong hands shoved him toward the door. Suddenly light-headed, he turned toward the barkeep. "What do I owe you, Jagg?"

The saloon owner nearly guffawed. "We can settle up next time."

Chapter 7

Fatigue pulled at Leah as she guided Samson into Elverton. She'd slept little after what Bo told her of his past. That and the worry that he'd left in a bad frame of mind. Was he angry at her for dredging up the memories? She wouldn't have asked if she'd known it would spark the anger or hurt or. . .whatever she'd seen in his eyes. Yet he hadn't been forced to tell her anything. She'd inquired, but he could've declined to answer if he wasn't ready to tell her the harder details of his life.

Surely they weren't *all* so hard. . .were they?

Leah drew the wagon to a stop outside the smithy, where bleary-eyed Ethan swung down from the bench. She remained on the seat, foot still poised on the brake as she stared at the shop's double doors. Still closed. Her stomach knotted. They'd arrived thirty minutes later than anticipated, given Ethan's laundry chores. Bo should've been to work by now.

Halfway to the doors, Ethan took notice and stopped. "Where's Bo?"

She looped the reins around the brake and scrambled down, striding to the newly replaced window. Hands cupped around her eyes, she peered into the smithy. Dark. Still. No fire in the forge. The work space still tidy, with his various hammers, tongs, and other tools in their proper places. A shiver traced her spine.

Something was wrong.

"Where do you think he is?" Ethan peered through the bottom of the high window.

She paced to the corral to the left of the building. The handsome dun he'd ridden to the house the night before was missing. "Not here, it would seem."

"You two ganged up to make me do my laundry before work, and now he doesn't even have the decency to *be* here?" Ethan heaved a big breath. "He's gonna get an earful from me."

"Leah? Leah Guthrie." The faraway call drew her attention toward the corner, where Rosalind Bates hurried toward them.

As Doc's wife approached, Leah hurried to meet her, Ethan keeping pace. "Is everything all right?"

Winded, Mrs. Bates drew up next to Leah. "He was so worried about you last night. Just kept asking for someone to be sure and tell you."

"Who? Tell me what?"

"Mr. Allen." She gulped a deep breath. "He was in a fight last night. Despite his pain, he wouldn't settle until someone promised to tell you and Ethan where he was this morning."

"Is he badly injured?"

"Just his hand, dear. Doc worked on it for hours last night."

Ethan stepped forward. "Can we see him?"

"Of course. He's asleep now, but I expect he'd like the company." She leaned discreetly toward Leah. "Most men do, don't you know."

She didn't. But if Bo was half as adamant as Mrs. Bates described, she would be there when he awoke.

⌐

Bo roused slowly, his mind all too willing to stay adrift in the haze. Several times, he pried his eyes open, only for them to close of their own volition.

"You figure he'll wake soon?"

At Red's quiet question and the answering whisper Bo couldn't quite grasp, his mind lurched. Strange images of himself laid out on the smithy floor formed in his thoughts, and his heart pounded. Had something happened?

Red better not be standing over him with Burl and Jess McCready—

"I'm awake." Bo pushed up onto his right elbow, causing lightning to shoot through his hand and up his arm. He sagged.

"Ethan, get Doc. Quickly!"

Hurried footsteps punctuated the stillness as warm hands guided him onto his back. "Easy, now. Don't tear your stitches."

He cradled the offending hand against his chest. Stitches? Bo forced his eyes open. Leah Guthrie looked down on him, but this was *not* the smithy, and *not* his house. Didn't look like a room in the Guthrie household either.

"You're at Doc Bates's office." Leah spoke as if reading the questions in his mind. "You cut your hand."

"Right." Memories took shape. He'd hit Sal Harper with his whiskey glass in his hand. *Idiot.*

Pain still racing through his right side, he gingerly freed his arms from the quilt. The covering shifted to the middle of his chest, and Leah gasped. Bo traced her wide-eyed gaze to his bare chest—straight to the mark inflicted on him years earlier.

Leah shook. "Coop *branded* you?"

He covered the three-inch mark with his hand. "It doesn't hurt—"

She gulped a breath, looked as if she might speak, but Red and Doc entered, Doc carrying a couple short, narrow lengths of wood.

"You'd better not have torn any of your stitches, Allen," Doc growled. "I spent half the night repairing that hand, and I'm in no frame of mind to repeat the process."

Half the night? He remembered being brought to Doc's door, and Doc suggesting he'd need surgery. But once he was stretched on the table, Mrs. Bates administering ether, he remembered nothing more until now.

Leah stepped back and beckoned Red. Doc moved into her former spot and, after laying aside the wood he'd carried in, helped Bo sit up, propped up by pillows.

Awkwardness threaded through him as he tried to cover Coop's mark. To his credit, Doc pretended not to notice, though Leah still shook after seeing it. When Red's gaze fell on the scar and he turned questioning eyes on his sister, Leah shoved the boy toward the door.

"Ethan and I are going to run an errand. We'll return shortly."

As they departed, Bo sank back, tension draining from him.

Doc flicked a glance toward the door then to him. "Something going on between you two?"

"No."

"You look like a man trying to impress someone, Allen."

"I ain't trying to *impress* anyone." More like trying not to scare her off completely. But when had that changed? Only a morning or so ago, he'd told her how wrong she was for inviting a man like him to supper.

"Mmm-hmm." Doc unwound the bandages and, cradling Bo's hand so his wrist remained bent, cautiously peeled back the dressing.

"How bad?" Bo cringed.

"You didn't tear any stitches. That's good."

Bo risked a look. His badly swollen palm was crisscrossed with angry cuts held together with more thread than he cared to think about.

"But you won't be swinging a hammer anytime soon," came the response he'd been waiting on. Doc slid a pair of spectacles from his pocket and put them on, squinting. "Depending on how it heals, you may never again. At least, not with that hand."

His stomach churned. "Please tell me you're joshin'."

Compassion flashed in the doctor's features. "I wish I could, but you cut several tendons last night. I tried to put them back together, but the healing will take months. If I can splint your hand so your wrist and fingers stay bent, it might allow the work to hold until things mend." He shook his head. "I was out in the barn attempting to come up with something when Ethan told me you were awake."

How was he supposed to work? Months without being able to pick up a hammer? Folks in town would start taking their jobs to neighboring Grass Valley, just as they did before he came to Elverton. And if his hand *didn't* heal right? He had no other skills than blacksmithing.

"For now, we'll use this." Doc picked up the wooden contraption—a couple of sturdy boards nailed together at their ends.

"You expect me to wear *that—for months?*" It was large and unwieldly.

"Only until I can find something less cumbersome. But you *will* wear it, or you'll lose all use of that hand. Understand?"

He bit back a curse. "Yeah."

His touch delicate, Doc redressed the wounds and applied fresh bandages. "I'm sorry it's not more promising news, Bo."

He rolled a look toward the ceiling. "It's my own stupid fault."

Doc was kind enough not to agree.

Bo's thoughts roiled over the what-if's until fear began to build in his chest. To alleviate the uncomfortable feeling, he forced his mind to another topic.

"Can I ask you something?"

Bates tied off the bandage ends and slipped the splint into place. "What's on your mind?"

"Mae Guthrie. Leah says she won't get better. That right?"

Doc tied the splint in place with several strips of bandages then sat back. "It's not my practice to share a patient's information with anyone outside of their family. I hope you understand."

Bo shrugged. "Just wondered if there ain't somethin' to help her."

Doc grew thoughtful. "Let me answer you this way. What Mae needs most are things to help her get around."

"Any ideas on what those are?"

"Maybe..."

Chapter 8

Why are you upset?" Ethan pressed.

Leah glanced at her brother then hurried on. "I'm worried for Bo." It wasn't a total lie.

"Then it's not about that scar he was covering up?"

The direct question brought her up short. When she didn't answer immediately, Ethan stepped in front of her. "You always do this."

"What?"

"Treat me like I'm too young to understand. You send me out to feed the chickens or check on Samson, or whatever gets me out of earshot so you can whisper to Mae and Hope. I ain't a *little* kid anymore, Leah. I'll be thirteen soon. Stop treating me like I'm five."

Conviction constricted her lungs. Had she been treating him so? They'd all been young when Papa died—Ethan seven, Hope nine, and Mae thirteen. At first, she'd kept the overwhelming truth of their circumstances to herself. However, when the banker foreclosed on their house, she could no longer hide the truth. It was then Mae became her confidante and ally. They'd recently begun sharing the heavier circumstances with Hope, which left Ethan as the only one in the dark. Without realizing it, they'd excluded him as they huddled together.

Papa's death forced them all to mature fast. It was time she started treating Ethan as the young man he was.

She led him around the corner toward the bench near an empty storefront.

"Ethan, I'm sorry. I haven't meant to discount you. You were so small when we lost Papa, I didn't want to worry you with things, but you're old enough now to know more, help us make decisions."

The boy folded his arms. " 'Bout time you realized it."

"It is."

"You gonna tell me about Bo's scar?"

"Yes." She gulped. "That mark is a brand, like you'd put on cattle or horses, and it says *Coop*." Her stomach knotted afresh. The pain he must have endured from just that *one* incident...

Ethan's eyes rounded. "Why's he got a brand like that?"

"He said last night, he was raised by a very cruel man named Coop, but I don't know exactly why Coop branded him." She folded her hands in her lap to keep them from shaking. "It breaks my heart to think what he must've endured."

Her brother looked away, obviously chewing on the information. She also sat, staring mindlessly at Mrs. Casselroy's boardinghouse across the street.

Minutes ticked by before Ethan looked at her. "I like Bo."

"He's a good man." Underneath all his rough edges.

"He's good for you, sis."

"For me?"

Ethan nodded. "You smile more when you're around him."

Did she? Realizing Ethan was right, warmth spread through her like honey on fresh biscuits. "I hadn't realized I wasn't smiling."

"Probably because you're sore at me all the time." His tone turned apologetic. "I haven't been doin' right lately."

The quiet confession was all the apology she needed. To lighten the mood, she elbowed him in the ribs. " 'Bout time you noticed."

He chuckled but sobered quickly. "I'll do better. I promise."

Leah looped her arm around his shoulders and planted a sisterly kiss on his head. "I appreciate that. Now do me a favor and go to the post office. See if we've received any mail." She rubbed his arm.

"Back in two shakes." He scurried off.

Oh Lord Jesus, please. Let Ethan truly be turning a corner. He's worn me down lately. It would answer months of her prayers if he would act better. And. . .dare she hope that his better behavior might ripple through other areas and ease the difficulties? Maybe.

Her thoughts ricocheted back to Bo. Was Ethan right? Was Bowdrie Allen good for her? The blacksmith was having a positive effect on her brother, it seemed. And her sisters. . . Hope and Mae both had chattered about the previous night's visit, despite his abrupt departure.

And yes—Bo Allen *did* make her want to smile.

A fine carriage pulled by two beautiful bays interrupted her thoughts. The fancy conveyance stopped in front of Mrs. Casselroy's, where a man, tall and blond, wearing a sharp suit and an immaculately groomed beard, stepped down and rounded the carriage. There, he helped a dark-haired woman down, followed by two beautiful blond girls around Ethan's age or younger. The girls between them, father and mother walked toward Mrs. Casselroy's door.

Leah's heart ached at the picture. *Lord, dare I hope to think I might be part of such a loving image someday? And does that image include Bowdrie Allen?*

~

"Grief, Doc. No. It's not proper." Bo glowered as the healer helped him thread his injured hand through his shirtsleeve. "I can take care of myself."

"Under normal circumstances, I would agree. But you've got no kin, and I had you on my operating table under the influence of ether for hours last night. Between that and the blood you lost, someone really should look in on you every few hours, at least until tomorrow. And since the missus and I have another emergency to attend to some distance away, you can't stay here."

Blast it all—why'd Doc have to be summoned now?

"Leah's already agreed. You'll stay with her."

This was getting worse by the minute. "What happened to keeping a patient's condition private except for their closest relatives?"

"I hardly shared intimate details. Besides, Leah's been sitting with you all morning as we've discussed your condition. You haven't seemed overly worried about her knowing things."

He hadn't been—but her hearing about his hand was a far cry from him staying in her house.

Doc held the other side of the shirt as Bo slid his arm through the sleeve. "Now finish getting dressed. Mrs. Bates and I need to go. It's urgent." He departed, leaving the door ajar.

Bo blew out a frustrated breath. As he tried to align the button with its proper hole, a soft knock came at the door.

Leah peeked in. "I overheard your conversation. We don't mind you staying, Bo."

"I have no intention—"

"Why on earth not?" Leah planted her fists on her trim waist. "Need I remind you? You're not able to work with your hand in that shape."

The button slipped from his fingers.

"And heavens, Bo. You're barely able to dress yourself."

"It ain't appropriate. You've got plenty on your plate already." He tried again to slip the shell button through its corresponding hole one-handed. He nearly had it until the tiny disc escaped his fingers again. Bo swallowed his mounting anger and lined up the two sides of his shirt. "I'll make do."

"Stop being so stubborn." She crossed to where he stood. "You don't have to *make do*. Let us help you."

Leah reached to fasten his shirt, but he shoved her hands away and backed up a step. The room weaved with the sudden movement, so when his calves hit the edge of the bed, momentum carried him down to the mattress.

"Stop!" He stood, towering over her. "I'm a thirty-year-old man. I been taking care of myself since I was nine. I'll not be mollycoddled by you or anyone else."

"Mollycoddled—" Hurt flashed in her eyes, only to dissolve into a stubborn glare. "You've taken care of yourself for so long because you *had to*. You no longer *have* to do this on your own." She took a step back and folded her arms. "Not unless you're trying to prove just how stubborn, prideful, and bullheaded you really are. If that's the case, Bowdrie Allen, then you're not the man I think you are."

The words struck like a slap across his cheek. "Just what kind of a man do you *think* I am? 'Cause I'm betting you're wrong."

"I *know* you to be a kind, good-hearted man, but you hide yourself behind your hurt and fear. You act so bullheaded to keep people from getting close, but you've let your guard down enough to show there's a gentle soul inside."

Her words stabbed straight to his heart, leaving him as exposed and vulnerable as if he stood without a stitch of clothes in a crowd. He shoved past her, fumbling again to fasten his buttons so he could pull his hat on and leave.

"Tell me I'm wrong." A challenge sparked in her tone.

He scrambled for something—anything—to deflect the truth, yet for all his mental flailing, he came up empty.

"Blast it all, Leah! What do you know—" He spun to face her, bringing on another wave of dizziness. He reached for something with which to brace himself.

Leah was immediately at his side. "Step back." She guided him toward the large comfortable chair in the corner. Once more, as the backs of his legs hit the furniture, he toppled, pain lancing his wounded hand.

When finally he looked up at her, she looked back with great compassion and understanding. "I know more than you're giving me credit for, so please stop pretending you're something you're not. At least with me." She eased onto the arm of the chair and reached for the buttons.

This time he didn't resist. "Are you prepared for what people will say?"

"What do you think they'll say?"

"It ain't right, you having a man who ain't your husband, staying in your house."

She pursed her lips but didn't respond.

"Leah, I've defended your honor once, and I'd do it again—but how am I s'posed to do that when everyone's gonna assume it's me who's stolen it?"

A quizzical expression contorted her features. "When did you defend my honor?"

Blast. What was wrong with him? He got anywhere near this woman's red-blond curls and his tongue flapped like a creaky gate in a gale wind. "What do you think happened to my hand?"

She sobered. "I heard you were in a fight. What really happened?"

"After I left you, I went to the Sierra Gold Saloon. Sal Harper was mouthin' off, and I didn't like what he was saying about you and your kin."

Her lips parted a little. "Isn't Sal your friend?"

"I don't know what he is right now."

"Oh Bo. You could lose the use of your hand. Because of *me*."

"No. Pretty sure it was my own stupid thinking to hit him with that glass clenched in my fist." Stupid didn't begin to cover it. Downright fool-headed idiocy.

"I feel terrible," Leah whispered. "This is my fault."

"No, it ain't." He gritted the statement through clenched teeth then softened and began to rub the knuckles of his left hand along her arm. "Leah, men fight. Leastways the ones I know. Stay around me long enough and you'll come to understand. I do a lot of stupid, angry things." His words stalled. "Defending your honor ain't one of 'em though. You're a good woman. Reckon if I'm gonna lose the use of my hand, it oughta be fighting for someone like you."

She twisted a strand of hair around her finger. "I think you just proved my point. Your heart is kind and good."

He shook his head. "You haven't answered my question."

"About people gossiping? Nothing to worry about there. First, Doc's mandating this. Second, you'll share Ethan's room, and my sisters and I will share the other—as we always do. And third, there are three chaperones who can clarify things for anyone who questions the arrangements." She emphasized it with a nod.

Between his frustration, dizziness, and pain, he didn't have the will to keep arguing. "Fine. You win. But at least take me by my place so I can get some clean clothes and walk my horses across to the livery."

"Doc already sent Ethan to take care of your horses. And I'd be glad to let you collect a few things." Once Leah stood from her perch on the arm of the chair, Bo rose as well. She reached for his hat and handed it to him.

He snugged the hat on his now aching head. "Grief, woman, do you spend all your time thinking how to win arguments with me, or are you just gifted like that?"

Leah chuckled. "Gifted, I suppose."

Chapter 9

Leah stifled her grin as Bo wandered from Ethan's bedroom, gray Henley rumpled, blond hair mussed, and feet bare. Her sisters exchanged amused glances, certainly due to the almost boyish look clinging to him.

"Evening, sleepyhead. Hungry?"

Arm cradled against his body, he glanced around the room. First at Mae, mending a dress, then to where Hope coiled the yarn looped around Ethan's hands into a ball, and back to Leah where she sat darning a sock.

"I could eat."

"Good." Sock still in hand, Leah led the way to the kitchen table. "I hope you don't mind. You were sleeping so well, we ate without you." She motioned to a seat then set the sock down across from him.

Bo took the offered chair and looked out the window. "It's near dark." Surprise laced his words. "Guess I *was* sleeping good."

Leah poured coffee and dished a bowl of hearty soup. She set both down in front of him then took the chair across the table.

Bo nodded his thanks, but after a moment, stood again. "Where are the spoons?"

"Oh—" Leah lurched to her feet.

"I can get it myself if—"

"Don't be silly. You're hurt—and a guest." She retrieved the utensil and slid it across the table.

"Thank you." A perplexed look crossed his face as he settled.

Fumbling, Bo chased a chunk of venison around the bowl. Leah ached to help but clasped her hands in her lap instead.

"Did you want sugar for your coffee?"

"Black is fine." He abandoned the meat for a potato instead and awkwardly shoveled the spoonful into his mouth. Some broth dribbled to the table in the process, and Leah rose to retrieve a dish towel.

When she offered it to him, he hesitated then self-consciously wiped his beard and the table. "Thanks."

Don't be overzealous, Leah. Let the man eat. She resumed her darning.

He cleared his throat.

"So you're the one who absconded with my socks. Couldn't find 'em when I woke."

"I didn't *abscond.* I planned to return them." A wave of self-consciousness settled over her. "Ethan's hard on socks, so I darn his often. I'd noticed yours were thin when I washed them, and I didn't think you'd mind my mending them as well." The explanation sounded nosy and intrusive when spoken aloud.

At his silence, she pressed on. "How's your hand?"

"Tolerable. Throbbing. If Doc Bates thinks I'm wearing this contraption for the next few months"—he waved at the clunky wooden splint—"he's mighty wrong."

"For your hand to heal properly, you must keep it splinted."

"I plan to. But not with this. 'Bout near took my eye out with it twice already." Bo took another spoonful of soup and a swallow of coffee. "Reckon I can make something in the smithy."

"How?"

"You got some paper? I want to try and draw an idea out."

"But aren't you right-handed?"

One brow arched. "Yeah. Didn't say it'd be pretty."

"Of course." She nodded. "I'll find you some paper, but how will you do anything in the smithy when you can't hold a hammer?"

His jaw popping, Bo laid aside the spoon. "Is this how we're gonna be whilst I'm here?" He spoke in a near-whisper.

"I don't understand."

"If you're gonna treat me like an invalid, always reminding me why I can't or shouldn't do things, I'll thank you to return my socks so I can walk myself back to town."

Shock and embarrassment roiled through her. *Lord, I've overstepped.* Just like always. She often smothered Mae with her helpfulness. Hope— and especially Ethan—complained about her mother-hen tendencies. What in heaven's name made her think she could bring Bo Allen home and *not* strangle him with her care?

"I'm sorry. You said no mollycoddling, but that's all I'm doing." She rose and pushed in her chair. "I'll let you eat in peace. Help your- self to more soup, if you'd like." She swept past him toward the door.

"Leah, wait," he called, his voice low. "I shouldn't—"

She hurried through the front door and charged toward the tree-lined streambed that marked the far edge of their yard. The stream, nothing more than a dry bed at this time of year, would be a good place to hide. Weaving between the trees, she stepped down into the sandy creek bed.

Lord, why do I overwhelm everyone I care about?

The question didn't require a divine answer. She was painfully aware.

She'd never *asked* to take Mama's role when she passed, but Papa had needed help, and she was the oldest. When he also died, it fell to her to become Ma *and Pa* to her family. In those early days, they'd needed the reassurance that she was there, guiding and protecting, even if their parents no longer were. Then, when they'd nearly lost

Mae, she'd poured out constant attention on her sister, anticipating her needs and thinking how to make her life easier. Meanwhile, she'd become bossy and strict with the youngers, both in attempting to keep them safe and to provide Mae a quiet environment to heal.

No wonder they balked at her overbearing ways. At some point, she'd taken up the unbearable burden to see her kin survive to adulthood and make something of their lives, as if their success or failure was her doing.

And she was treating Bo—a grown, capable, successful man—in the same way.

"Goodness, Lord, if I were him, I'd threaten to leave too," she said, continuing her prayer in a whisper. "I'm a domineering, meddlesome fussbudget."

Why couldn't she be like Mrs. Bates—full of concern and grace, rather than nagging and cajoling.

"A domineering fussbudget?" Bo's voice cut the silence.

She spun, heart thudding mercilessly at the sight of his huge form.

He stepped down into the streambed. "Is that really how you see yourself?"

"I smother everyone. Ask my family." Her voice quavered. "Or look at how I've been treating you."

"The problem's not you." He stepped nearer. "It's that the person you're trying to lavish that caring on ain't used to such attentions. Don't mean you did wrong."

"No, you're right about me. All I know how to do is mollycoddle. You have every right to be upset."

"I'm not upset." His voice was husky.

"Angry then."

He shook his head. "Not angry." Stepping closer still, he ran his fingertips along her jaw then cupped her cheek in his hand. His expression contorted as if something pained him. *"Scared."*

At the vulnerable admission, she reached for his trembling hand, pressing it between her palm and her cheek.

His eyes clamped shut. "What you said at Doc's this morning was spot on. I've used my hurt and fear to keep people away." He shook his head. "Trust doesn't come easy for me. Anyone I've ever trusted has died. . .or turned on me."

"I don't plan on doing either of those things, Bowdrie Allen. So maybe you could try trusting me?"

He dragged her to him and twined his fingers in her hair. "Blast it all, woman." His thick words rumbled in his chest. "I been doin' everything I can to push you away since you barged into my smithy. Ain't none of it worked."

Timidly, Leah wrapped her arms around his waist. "If Papa were alive, he would tell you—"

Bo's splinted hand circled her back, and she melted against him, mind dulling to everything but the security of his embrace.

Lord, this feels good. Bo feels good. Dare she dream he might hold her like this forever?

"What would your pa say?"

She struggled to latch on to the thought again. "If what you're doing isn't working, try a different approach."

"That's what scares me." The words, whispered softly against her hair, were nearly lost in the rustle of the trees. "But I *want* to trust you."

She looked up at him. "I promise I won't ever purposely hurt you, Bo."

Despite the darkness, the emotion in his eyes was unmistakable. Her heart thudded as his gaze intensified. Bo hesitated for half a breath then pressed his lips to hers almost roughly, his fingers sinking deeper into her curls.

Startled by the suddenness of her first kiss, she went rigid, emotions surging.

Bo pulled away, grip loosening in her hair. "I'm sorry," he whispered. "I shouldn't have done tha—"

"Yes." She twined her fingers into his shirt, holding him in place. "You should have."

Leah stared for the briefest instant then rose on her toes, seeking his lips. For a split-second, he too went rigid, then pulled her close again, returning the affection more gently this time. A full-body shiver overtook her, and her world turned topsy-turvy. She clung to him, aware only of his nearness, his strength, and the delicious tenderness of his lips.

When finally he broke the kiss, Leah leaned against him, completely unsure if she could trust her legs to hold her weight. She held him until her heart slowed to a more regular rhythm.

"We probably ought to go back inside," he finally said.

"Should we?" It would ruin the moment. . . .

"I've a compelling reason to say yes."

Concern threaded through her. Was his hand hurting? Or perhaps the ether was still affecting him. "What reason?"

"My feet."

"Your feet?" She pulled back to look.

"Yeah." He wiggled his bare toes then maneuvered behind her. "They're cold. Some domineering ol' fussbudget absconded with my socks."

Leah's jaw dropped, and she spun to give him a playful swat. "Bowdrie Allen, you're a beast!"

⌐

"I'll start the forge." Red scrambled from the wagon bench, smithy keys in hand, and headed to the door.

"Looks like he's ready for work." Bo smiled in Leah's direction, glad for the kid's enthusiasm.

"Are you sure *you* are?" Since their kiss, Leah's brown eyes held a new level of concern. "Doc said to rest *at least* a day."

"I'll be fine." He climbed down, thankful she'd suggested a sling. The wooden splint wasn't quite so unwieldy tucked against his body. Hopefully by evening, he'd have a less cumbersome splint. If things went *very* well, they'd have a good start on their next project.

"What if you get tired? Or hungry? Or—"

"Leah. . ."

She hung her head. "I'm mollycoddling again."

"You're worrying, and I appreciate it." Things had changed for him also, after admitting his fears. "Let me put your mind at ease. C'mere."

Confusion creased her brow, but she descended.

As they neared the corner of the smithy, Bo whistled sharply to Red. "Toss me the keys."

Red did. Bo caught them then guided Leah behind the building. "Where are we going?"

He unlocked the door of his small house.

"Take a look." He pushed the door open.

"At?"

He stepped through the doorway. She stopped at the threshold. "There's a bed, a stove in the corner, even food in the pantry. Check if you'd like. I can sleep if I need to, Red and I won't starve, and I promise not to work us into the ground."

She gave him a sheepish grin. "In other words, I'm overly concerned."

"Just a little." He scuffled nearer and tipped her chin up. "But thank you." As foreign as it was, there was something pleasant, knowing someone cared.

When he traced his fingers along her jaw, Leah's eyelashes fluttered. He drank in her porcelain skin and red-blond curls. Heaven's sake, she was beautiful. His heart thudded with anticipation as he brushed her lips with his.

A sharp rap on the wall outside caused Leah to pull back. They both turned toward the sound, though Bo couldn't see who was there.

"Morning, Miss Guthrie."

Sal Harper's grating voice set Bo's teeth on edge.

"You're lookin' mighty fine this morning."

"Mr. Harper." Her face flushed crimson.

Bo stepped through the door between her and the butcher, every nerve primed. "You need something?"

Sal's gaze flicked to the sling, concern in his expression. "We still fightin', are we?"

"Depends on you. You abide by what I told you—show this woman and her kin respect—and we'll be square."

Harper nodded. "Then we're square."

Trouble was, after what he'd heard in the saloon, Bo didn't trust him. "What can I do for you?"

"Just a neighborly visit to tell you a couple kids were hauntin' around your place last night. Saw 'em from down the alley, jigglin' door handles and such." The butcher shrugged. "Thought you'd wanna know."

He did. "The McCready kids?"

"Ain't sure who they belong to, but they had the look of trouble. Older one, especially. Seen him skulkin' about the town a few other nights too."

Bo nodded. "I'll keep an eye out. Thanks."

Again, the man's gaze flicked to the sling. "You hurt bad?"

"It'll heal." He wouldn't tell Sal he might never use the injured hand again. "Now if you'll excuse us, Miss Guthrie and I both have work to do."

"All right then." Harper waved and meandered off.

Once he was out of sight, Bo found Leah hiding inside the doorway.

She turned an apologetic expression his way. "I'm sorry. I know he's your friend, but I never have liked him much."

"After the other night, I got issues with him myself."

"You're not upset with me?" Hope permeated her expression.

"No." He tugged her into his arms.

He bent again to kiss her, but the sudden distant clang of hammer against anvil drew him up short. "What on earth?" Bo strained to hear.

"What's wrong?"

A second clang, then more.

"Red shouldn't be hammering on anything yet. The forge hasn't had time to get hot."

Leah's eyes widened, and they both scrambled outside and toward the front of the smithy. As they rounded the last corner and stepped into the building, Red tussled near the anvil with Burl McCready.

"Give it, you big oaf!" Red swiped the air, grabbing at one of Bo's many hammers clenched in the bigger boy's fist.

Bo charged into the smithy and rammed into the McCready boy's back. Burl slumped over the anvil, and Bo lodged the elbow of his injured hand against the boy's back. Lightning bolts coursed through his forearm and hand, but he gritted his teeth to fend them off.

"What're you doing here, kid?" He jerked the hammer from Burl's fist and handed it off to Red.

"Let me go!" Burl squirmed, his writhing further jostling Bo's hand.

He leaned harder, pinning Burl more soundly. "Not until you state your business."

Burl's answer was a stream of foul words unfit for polite company.

"Let my brother go!" The squeakier voice came from behind him, and he turned as Leah snatched Jess McCready up by his arms.

While she struggled to hold the rambunctious boy, Bo dragged Burl toward Leah.

"Sit!" He swept Burl's legs out from under him, forcing the young man onto his rump. Bo turned on Jess. "Sit, you little imp, or I'll make you."

Jess plummeted to the floor of his own accord but punctuated the action with his brother's curses.

When the boy's foul mouth didn't stop, Bo hauled the kid from the floor by one arm. The action silenced the ruffian.

"There's a lady present. Watch your mouth or I'll knock some manners into you." Bo gave him a single rough shake. "Understand?"

Jess tried to squirm free, to no avail.

Turning, he kicked Burl's boot. "And you ought to be ashamed, teaching your little brother such words."

The elder boy only glared.

"I hate you!" the younger brat squealed.

"After you broke my window, I'm not real fond of you either." He released the boy, and Jess tumbled backward with a thump. "Sit, and don't move."

"Red?" Bo worked not to show how much his hand throbbed. "What're these two doin' in my smithy?"

A slight hesitation preceded Red's answer. "They saw me setting up for the day and came to chat."

"That all?"

"No, sir. Two things. One...when I wouldn't leave with 'em, Burl started calling me names and throwing your tools. I tried to stop him, but, well, you saw."

"And two?"

Red glared in Burl's direction. "Think I'd rather be called Ethan, not Red."

"Yes, sir, Ethan." He turned back to the McCreadys. "Where's your uncle?"

Both sat in sullen silence.

"Fine then. Leah, need you to drive us on over to Sheriff Yeldin's office. It's about time we all had a chat."

Chapter 10

It was far later than usual when Leah arrived to collect Ethan and—she hoped—Bo. She stopped the wagon near the wide doorway and swung down. Inside, Ethan stood at the forge, Bo nowhere in sight.

She hurried in. "I'm sorry I'm late."

Ethan turned and brought a finger to his lips. "Shhh."

Leah crossed to him. "Why?" she whispered.

Her brother motioned toward the door. Beside the opening, Bo sat at a small desk, chair pushed back as he rested his head on his good arm. His injured hand rested on a stack of folded rags.

"He fell asleep about twenty minutes ago while I shut down the forge."

Leah couldn't help her amusement, though concern tempered her mirth. Bo hadn't admitted it, but she'd caught a hint of pain in his eyes at the sheriff's office earlier. "Did he rest today?"

"He sat with his hand propped up." Ethan indicated a chair near the anvil.

Leah envisioned Bo straddling the seat with his elbow resting on the top rung of the chair's back as he guided her brother's efforts at the anvil.

"He told Doc Bates his hand hurt a bunch."

"Doc came by?" Hopefully he'd not mentioned about her visit to his office, requesting he see their patient.

"Yeah. He changed Bo's bandages and said he's healing all right then helped Bo put on the new splint."

"It's done?" She hurried to see. The clunky wooden piece was gone. In its place, four small-gauge iron rods traced the bone structure in Bo's hand. Each curled around Bo's fingertips, down the back of his hand, and ended at the middle of his forearm. They'd been driven through several larger-gauge cross-pieces, which held them in alignment, and it was secured to his hand with strips of soft buckskin.

She returned to Ethan. "You made that?" she whispered.

"Bo measured everything, marked the holes." He shrugged. "Even used his left hand to show me how hard to strike with the hammer."

"But you got it done. I'm so proud of you. How long did it take?"

"We finished about midday then started on another project."

"Are you about done tonight? I'm hoping dinner will be ready when we get home."

"Let me finish shutting down the forge."

He continued his task, and Leah drank in the sight of her rapscallion brother taking pride in his work.

Lord, thank You—a thousand times over.

She went to Bo's side and touched his shoulder. "Bo?"

After a second call, his eyelids fluttered open and his tired gaze fell on her. "I could get used to waking up to you."

Oh my. Heat cascaded through her, and she pretended she'd not heard.

"I'm sorry I'm late."

Bo sat up and mopped his face. "How long was I asleep?"

"Ethan said about twenty minutes. I hear Doc stopped by?"

"Yeah. Says my hand's healing good."

"Is it hurting?"

"Aching something fierce."

"Isn't the laudanum Doc gave you helping?"

"Didn't take any until a bit ago. A blacksmith shop ain't the place to be when your mind's dull. People get hurt that way."

Leah folded her arms. "Bowdrie Allen, I don't appreciate being lied to. At breakfast, you said you were well enough to come to the shop—and you promised to rest. If you were hurting that much, you didn't need to be here."

His jaw popping, he stood. "Woman, I didn't lie. The pain was mild until Burl McCready required my attention. And I didn't work. *I sat.* Ask your brother."

"He's told me. But was anything you did today so all-fired important that you suffered hours of pain for it?"

"I happen to think it was." He lifted his splinted hand.

Her ire sparked. "Ethan says you were done with that around noon. Was your next project so necessary that it couldn't wait?"

Bo stepped nearer, hazel eyes storming. "I don't know. It felt plumb important to me, but you decide. Your brother was building a pair of leg braces to help your sister get around."

Leg braces? All the air left her in a *whoosh*, as if she'd been gut-punched. With it, her anger fled as well.

"You *told* her?" Ethan yelped from across the shop. "You made me promise I wouldn't say—"

"Hush, now!" Bo growled. "Finish shutting down that forge."

Leah couldn't look away from the man before her.

"You were helping Mae?" Her voice nearly squeaked.

"Trying." Bo gave a curt nod. "After I hurt my hand, I asked Doc what could make Mae better. He said leg braces." Another brief pause. "Now. . .in your estimation, is that worthy enough to endure some pain to get it done?"

Throat knotting, Leah clamped a hand over her mouth and nodded.

"Good." His voice softened. "Seems it is possible to win an argument with you now and then." He pulled her into his grip, and she buried her face against him, overcome with the gesture.

Besides Doc Bates, no man had shown any inclination to help sweet Mae—until Bo. It was the kindest, most considerate thing anyone had ever done for her family.

"I'm sorry. I should've trusted you. You know your own limits."

"Yes, I do. But given time, I might could get used to a domineering fussbudget of a woman looking after me."

Leah gave him a playful shove. "You're incorrigible."

With a laugh, he motioned her toward the chair as he leaned against the desk. However, with the growling of her stomach, she realized how late it must be. "We need to get home. I wasn't sure whether to assume you were returning with us."

He offered a tired smile. "I appreciate the hospitality, but I don't want anyone saying I've sullied your reputation. Besides, Sheriff Yeldin turned the McCready boys over to their uncle earlier today. I don't trust 'em."

"I don't like the idea of you staying alone tonight, but I appreciate you wanting to protect my honor."

It took a moment for Bo to speak. "Ethan looks mighty irked that I told you about Mae's braces."

She turned to find Ethan glowering in their direction. "Oh, yes, he does. I'll talk to him."

"No. Leave him here with me. Reckon that'll ease your mind some, and it'll give me time to smooth things over with him."

A smile sprouted. "That's a fine idea." Tomorrow was Sunday. She'd bring Ethan's go-to-meeting clothes in the morning, and hopefully, she'd convince Bo to attend service as well.

⌐⌐

"You want me to go to church with you?"

Through the haze of laudanum, Bo looked at Leah across the threshold. It was far too early for the swirl of anxiousness that settled in his belly.

"Yes." She fluttered her eyelashes his way. "Didn't you tell me before that you believe in God, Bo?"

"Ma taught me about Him." He did believe, and he'd been praying more regular since he'd met Leah. But he'd not set foot in a church since his mother died.

"Then come with us." Again, she employed the fluttering eyelashes.

He grasped for any logical reason to say no.

"They're having a picnic dinner after service, Bo." Ethan poured two cups of coffee from the pot on the stove.

"He's right." Leah smiled. "It's always enjoyable when they do dinner on the grounds."

Maybe for someone who liked people. But he'd spent his adult life avoiding them. The thought of facing the judgmental stares of Elverton's residents in such a public place set his heart to pounding.

"I don't know, Leah. Let me think on it."

Disappointment glinted in her eyes, but she nodded. "Don't think too long. Service starts in an hour." She turned toward the smithy where her horse and wagon were parked.

He shut the door to find Ethan holding out a coffee cup to him. "You look like you could use this."

He received it silently and sipped it, hoping to clear the cobwebs.

"Services don't last too long," Ethan explained as he washed up. "They sing a couple songs, and Reverend Danby preaches. That's all."

"I don't know, kid." He took another drink. "Think I might just stay and rest."

Ethan exchanged the washrag for the towel and dried his face. "C'mon, Bo. Please? You have to—"

"Why on earth do I *have* to?"

He replaced the towel and gave his fiery hair a couple quick swipes with Bo's comb, then turned toward the bed where the clothes Leah brought waited. "It'd mean a lot to me if you did." Ethan slipped into his tan shirt. "And don't forget. My sisters are just outside. I guarantee they're plotting how to convince you."

Bo puffed out his cheeks with a frustrated breath. After a long silence, he finally shook his head. "Fine." His stomach knotted. "I'll come to the service, but no promises I'll stay for the picnic."

"Deal."

Chapter 11

"Breathe, Bo," Leah whispered as they stood beside the wagon. Most parishioners had already gone inside, including Mae, Hope, and Ethan. Fewer to witness the near-panic in Bo's eyes. "You'll know a lot of these people."

He fiddled with the sling, as if it choked him. "That's what's worrisome."

"They're *good* people."

He drew a deep breath and blew it out. "Like I told you, folks in this town see me as an ill-tempered, stubborn cuss."

"Since when did you start caring what people thought?"

"Since I met you."

The whispered statement brought a knot of emotion to her throat.

Please, Father, give me something to calm him down. And please let the church be welcoming.

"Blast it all. They're probably staring out, wondering why a man like me is about to darken the church door."

She swallowed around the knot. "Some *may* think that. They'll be the very same ones who gush over Mae to her face, only to gossip behind our backs. What do they matter, Bo? They won't change my opinion of you."

The words seemed to calm him some.

"Also, no one inside that building is perfect, so don't think you're unwelcome here because you've had hardships in your life. This is God's house, and He welcomes everyone."

He closed his eyes and breathed deep. His clenched jaw loosened, and his shoulders slowly uncoiled. "Thank you. That helps some."

Leah smiled, captivated by his eyes. Perhaps it was the deep green of his shirt, or maybe the bright sun at just the right angle, but...*Lord, I might never tire of looking at this man.* She threaded her arm through his, praying he wouldn't reject the small intimacy. When he didn't, she leaned close. "Shall we?"

With his solemn nod, they walked toward the entrance. As they neared, Tom and Grace Peterson approached.

"Leah." Mrs. Peterson met her at the staircase with a hug. "We haven't seen you since your wagon broke down. How have you been?"

"Very well, thank you." She nodded to Mr. Peterson, who gave her a fatherly peck on the cheek.

"I believe you both know Bowdrie Allen?" At their nods, she turned to Bo. "The Petersons are my nearest neighbors. They were the ones who gave me a ride home the day I first came to your shop."

Recalling Tom Peterson's warnings about Bo, Leah whispered a quick prayer.

"Allen." A smile lit Mr. Peterson's grizzled face. "Glad you're joinin' us."

"Thank you, sir."

Mr. Peterson continued. "I'd offer to shake your hand, but—" He nodded toward the sling. "You break it?"

Bo cleared his throat. "Cut it six ways to Sunday."

Tom Peterson cringed in sympathy.

"It'll be a couple months before it's healed."

"What about work?" Mrs. Peterson asked.

"Leah's brother's working in the smithy now, so I'm not shut down completely."

"Ethan's working for you. That's good." He shot an approving glance Leah's way. "That brother of yours'll learn a heap more practical skills working in a smithy than filling orders in a mercantile."

Leah gave Bo's arm a squeeze. "I agree. I'm forever grateful Bo hired him."

Mr. Peterson unbuttoned his shirtsleeve and pushed it up. "See that scar?" He indicated a jagged line from elbow to wrist where the muscle was misshapen. When Bo nodded, the grizzled man turned up the stairs and motioned Bo to walk with him.

"Gored by a bull. Oh, it was nasty—and the pain? Hurt like the dickens."

At the top step, the men disappeared inside.

"Well, now." Mrs. Peterson looped her arm in Leah's, her tone low and conspiratorial. "I've been praying off and on for three years for Mr. Bowdrie Allen. Maybe, my dear, *you* are the answer to those prayers."

⤳

Tom Peterson led Bo to several of the men prior to the start of service, among them Doc Bates, Sheriff Yeldin, and a few of Bo's past customers. Each had been friendly and welcoming, though a few of the nearby women had met him with icy frowns, looking none too pleased at his attendance. With them, Bo reminded himself Leah said her opinion wouldn't change.

God, I hope it never does. Having Leah and her kin in my life feels like a steady rain on dry, cracked earth—even if she *did* rope him into uncomfortable situations like going to dinner or attending church.

Or baring his soul.

When Reverend Isaiah Danby called the service to order, Bo took his place beside Leah on the bench at the back of the room.

He leaned close. "Hope you ain't sittin' back here because of me."

She shook her head. "The reverend keeps that chair there for Mae." She indicated a wooden armchair with padded back and seat, placed in the center of the wall between two benches. "From there, she can see the podium whether people are sitting or standing. And it's easier for her to get in and out of the building."

Getting out quicker suited him fine.

The service began with prayer and singing. After several verses of "The Old Rugged Cross," which Bo knew none of the words to, Danby asked everyone to turn to Psalm Thirty-Two. Ethan passed a thick book to Leah, who flipped to the middle. When a weight settled on his left thigh, he found Leah's book resting halfway on his lap. She smiled at him.

"Let them read it." He nodded toward the younger Guthries.

"We have this Psalm memorized." She nudged the book toward him, as if expecting him to take it.

He reluctantly did, though he put all of his attention on Danby's reading.

Apparently following along, Leah reached over and turned the page, drawing his focus back to the book. When she tapped the upper left corner and smiled, her gaze expectant, Bo enveloped her hand with his own.

"Stop." He hissed the whispered word.

Eyes clouding, she matched his tone. "What's wrong?"

Shame spread in him like a tree's roots. His chest tightened. Teeth clenched, he whispered again. "I can't read."

Eyes wide, she pulled back. "Oh Bo..."

He glared. He could imagine what she was thinking. An illiterate failure. A stupid blacksmith. Too dumb for anything more noble. Bo set his jaw and faced front, shaking.

A moment passed before she leaned nearer, but Bo shifted away with a discreet shake of his head. He swore silently. Thankfully, their whispered exchanges hadn't attracted attention. Still, his heart pounded and the blasted sling felt as if it might choke him. He tugged at it and tried to inhale, only his lungs wouldn't fill.

When next she made an advance, she reached for his hand—twining her fingers between his. He brushed away her touch, gripping the bench instead.

If only he'd insisted he stay home. He'd still be in his bed.

Leah discreetly slid the book from his lap and closed the cover.

That was it. He could take no more. Rocking to his feet, Bo slipped into the vestibule but stopped short at the unexpected sight of a family of four—husband, wife, and two daughters—in the space.

"Pardon," he mumbled then snatched his Stetson from its peg and slipped outside.

Bo flew down the steps. He gulped several breaths and pulled at the sling. At Leah's wagon, he extracted his injured arm from the offending material then crammed his hat on and turned toward the street.

"Excuse me," a male voice called softly.

The man from the vestibule descended the steps, his raven-haired wife and two girls following.

"You wouldn't be the town's blacksmith, would you?"

Stress rooted him to the spot. "I would."

The man glanced at his family with an odd expression then faced Bo again. "Is your name Bowdrie Charles Allen?"

If his chest had eased even a little, it tightened again. "What if it is?"

The other man hung his head, a sad smile on his lips. "Then I'd say I'm glad I've found you."

Irritation blanketed him. "Mister, you got something to say, spit it out. What's your business with me?"

"Bo." The man's voice grew thick. "It's Reese."

His insides turned cold. "Reese. . ."

"Your brother?" He stepped closer, brows arched as if willing him to remember.

"I know who you are."

"I've been looking for you for eighteen years."

"Have you now?" Doubtful.

"I went back to Texas, but I was told the Coopers had moved. I didn't know where to find you. But ask Katie." He nodded to the dark-haired woman standing at the base of the steps. "I've never stopped looking."

Seeing Leah on the steps, he shook his head. "Is this why you wanted me to come to church? So you could spring this on me?"

Confusion etched her features. "Spring what? I don't know what you mean. Who is this?"

"Bo." Reese stepped nearer and lowered his voice. "I stopped by the blacksmith shop several times, but it was closed. Someone said you'd hurt your hand and wouldn't be back until next week. But today we happened to pass each other in the church." Reese settled a hand on Bo's shoulder. "God *wanted* us to find each other."

Fast as lightning, Bo grabbed his brother's suitcoat and hauled him nose to nose, knocking his own hat off in the process. "You're so proud of yourself, aren't you?"

Eyes wide, Reese gripped Bo's wrist, and Bo settled the back of his splinted hand against Reese's chest.

"Bo, don't hit him!" Leah shrieked.

Both little girls started crying.

"I don't claim to know God very well, *brother*, but I'm betting He would say it's wrong to sell your kin in the first place. Especially to the likes of Coop."

"What do you mea—"

Bo slammed his skull hard into Reese's face, dropping his elder brother to the ground.

"Don't come near me again. I got nothing for you!"

Head buzzing, he scooped his hat from the dirt and stalked toward the street.

Chapter 12

Horror blanketed Leah as she stared at the downed man, the same one she'd seen outside Mrs. Casselroy's boardinghouse days earlier. Why in heaven's name had Bo attacked a man in front of his family? Had he been so angered by her mistake in the service he'd taken it out on a perfect stranger?

His wife and daughters rushed to his side.

"Please," the woman pleaded. "Is there a doctor in this town?"

"No." The man pawed the air, his hand settling on his wife's shoulder. He attempted to sit up. "I'm all right."

Only he toppled back into the dirt, blood soaking his beard and mustache.

Leah raced into the church and, rounding the vestibule wall, pinned Reverend Danby with a wide-eyed look. The preacher stopped.

"I'm sorry, Reverend." She faced the direction of the Bates family. "Doc, you're needed outside, please. *Quickly.*"

Doc lunged up, medical bag in hand, Mrs. Bates with him. Leah hurried to rejoin the family.

"Doc will be here momentarily."

The door creaked open, but it was Ethan, not Doc, who exited. Following him, a couple others spilled outside, staring.

Her brother bounded down the stairs, but before he could insert himself into the scene, she pointed him toward the wagon. "Stay out of the way. Stand over there."

"Where's Bo?" he asked.

Leah's stomach knotted. She *must* find him, but first—attend to the emergency. "He headed that way." She waved toward the smithy. "Now, sit."

"Make way!" Doc bellowed as he descended the stairs.

The crowd spilled down the steps like cascading water and surrounded the scene. Doc found a clear path to the man's side and stripped off his coat to use as a pillow. "Do you know where you are, sir?"

From his place on the ground, the man blinked. "Elverton." His Adam's apple bobbed. "California."

Doc produced a handkerchief and pressed it against the injured man's nostrils. "Hold this under your nose." The fellow did as instructed. "Do you know what day it is?"

"Sunday."

The doctor lifted the gentleman's right eyelid then his left, taking a long look at each eye. "What's your name, friend?"

"Reese Allen."

A murmur rippled through the crowd, and Leah's heart stuttered.

"Bo's brother." Her stomach clenched so tight it hurt. *This* was the man who'd sold Bo into servitude to Coop. . . .

The dark-haired woman approached her. "I'm Katie Allen. Are you Bo's wife?"

Leah shook her head.

"His intended then?"

Mind spinning, Leah backed up. "Excuse me. I need to find him." She turned to tell Ethan where she was going, but the boy was gone.

"Please, wait." Katie touched her arm.

On the street, Ethan darted out of view, headed toward the smithy at a full run.

"I have to go." Leah stalked away.

Reaching the street, she turned toward Bo's smithy.

Lord, please help. I need You.

They were the only words that would come as she grappled with all that had transpired. How had she not thought—or realized—that Bo couldn't read? As she'd looked around his modest home, there'd not been a single book. He drew pictures, but she'd not seen him write. If Coop were half as cruel as Bo described, it made sense he'd not have educated Bo.

Her cheeks burned again at the memory of his expression painted with anger, hurt, and betrayal.

Lord, help.

She'd wounded him. Unintentionally, but she had.

But he'd hurt her too. Rejecting her attempts to soothe his raw feelings. Charging from the service and leaving her to look the fool. Far worse, he'd run into his brother, a man who'd *truly* betrayed him, and he accused *her* of orchestrating the run-in.

Had she not told him she'd never intentionally hurt him? Could he not allow himself to believe her?

Lord. . . She sighed. *Help Bo see, please.*

By the time she reached the smithy, a boulder almost crushed her chest. Ethan stood at the doorway, face pale as a cacophony erupted from inside. Leah dashed to her brother's side to see Bo jerk a wooden box from a shelf and fling it with all his might. Metal pieces scattered across the workbench, floor, and shelves. It obviously wasn't the first he'd hurled.

Box empty, he slammed it on the ground and leveled a vicious kick to the container. It crashed into the wall and splintered.

"Bo!" Heart pounding, she waded inside, careful not to slip on the cluttered floor. "Stop, please."

As if he didn't hear, he jerked another box, this one larger, from a shelf.

"Bowdrie Allen, talk to me!"

He turned, eyes flashing. "I got nothing to say right now, woman. Get out."

"Don't you speak to my sister like that," Ethan roared. He charged across the room and slammed into Bo, managing to knock him down, though Ethan landed on his backside.

The man drew his wounded hand to his chest and swore under his breath. "Stupid kid."

Before she could stop herself, Leah landed a hard smack to his cheek, and for one horrifying moment, they locked gazes. His jaw clenched, his eyes smoldered, and he almost shook—but he didn't lift a hand against her.

Her eyes brimmed. "Don't you *ever* say such a thing to my brother or sisters again. Ever."

As she turned to help Ethan to his feet, the boy's eyes grew huge. "No, Bo! Not—"

Leah turned to see him hurl something—long and cylinder-shaped—at the far wall. It struck with a clang and clattered into pieces.

Looking like he'd been gutted, Ethan rose. "I made those! I made that brace, and you destroyed it."

All the fire in Bo's demeanor drained then. "Oh God. Oh God in heaven, what have I done?"

"You ruined it." Ethan backed away. "You ruined everything."

"Ethan." Bo choked his name. "Wait. Please!"

The boy ran, leaving her to face Bo alone.

"Leah, I'm so sorry." He breathed the apology, reaching for her hand.

"Don't."

At the vigorous shake of her head, he pulled back. "Tell me what I can do to make it up to you."

"I don't think you can."

⌒

Bo sat in the smithy, the brace he'd thrown lying on the desktop in pieces, it's unblemished mate beside it. For hours, his thoughts had swirled from the incidents at the church to his rage in the shop to Ethan and Leah running out.

"God, I really messed up." And there was no fixing it. No sense even asking for a miracle. He should've tried harder to push her away—saved them both this painful outcome. It was a false hope that he'd ever be capable of true friendship or love.

A sharp rap at the entrance drew Bo's attention, and Sheriff Yeldin stepped into the doorway. The lawman's gaze traveled the room.

"Something happen in here?"

It figured Yeldin would stop by. He always seemed to show when things turned bad.

"*I* happened." The admission heaped more shame across his shoulders.

"You busted up your own place?"

"I was angry. Reckon you know why."

"I do." Yeldin paused. "You still angry?"

"Reckon not." Not since he saw the hurt in Ethan Guthrie's eyes. Hurt *he'd* inflicted. In its place grew shame, embarrassment, hatred of just how broken and ugly his life truly was, but no, the fight was gone.

The sheriff nodded to the chair near the anvil. "Mind if I sit?"

Bo waved at the chair.

Yeldin picked his way over, dragged the chair back, and sat. "Need you to hear me out on something."

Bo closed his eyes. "Go on."

"I know you as well as anyone, don't I?" At his nod, Yeldin continued. "You've told me about your upbringing."

"Yeah." Where was the lawman going with this? Not in the direction Bo had thought. He'd expected to be run out of town, but that didn't appear to be the sheriff's direction.

Yeldin started to speak. "I, uh, I talked to your brother, and the story he told is different than yours."

His insides went numb. "You sayin' I lied?"

"No, sir." His friend's tone was firm but compassionate. "As a lawman, I find the truth amongst all the various stories people tell me. I listened to the tale Reese told then tried to marry it up to yours. I think you're both saying what you believe to be right, but I think there's an angle neither of you considered."

"Yeldin, I'm tired. Spit it out."

"Will you talk to your brother—with an open mind?"

Anxiety knotted his muscles. "You're asking a lot."

"It's important, Bo."

A war waged in Bo's thoughts. Reese didn't deserve any more of his time. But Yeldin hadn't steered him wrong yet. If he said it was important. . .

"If anybody other than you asked me, I'd say no."

"Then you'll say yes?"

Could this day get any worse? "Not happily. Where do I find him?"

The sheriff walked to the smithy door, only to return with Reese and his wife.

At their approach, Bo stood, nerves zinging.

"Bo." Reese nodded.

His brother's eyes were rimmed with black and his nose was badly swollen. Bo had expected to take satisfaction in that, but it only brought sadness. "Reese. Ma'am." He cursed Yeldin silently. Today was *not* the day for this. Of course, no day was.

"I'm Katie. Your sister-in-law." She smiled, though her eyes were wary.

He wouldn't tell her it was a pleasure—not when it was so awkward. Instead, he lifted his chair and placed it next to the other. "Sit, if you want."

As they took the chairs, Bo opened one of the desk drawers and tossed a folded gunny sack to Yeldin. "Open that, would ya?"

Puzzled, the lawman did so. Bo dropped the leg braces and all their broken parts into it. "Set that beside the desk for now."

Yeldin knotted the top and set it aside. Then Bo sat on one corner of the desk, the lawman leaning against the other.

"Reese, go ahead." Yeldin nodded.

"You said something earlier that I didn't understand."

Bo wasn't an educated man. Didn't know a bunch of highfalutin words. What could his brother possibly have misunderstood?

"Your exact words were 'God would say it's wrong to sell your kin. Especially to the likes of Coop.' What did you mean by that?"

Bo squinted at the man. "Has your memory gone soft in the last twenty-four years?"

"You think I *sold* you to Coop?"

Bo leaned toward his brother. "He told me so himself, right before he marked me."

"Marked you?" Reese shook his head. "I don't understand your meaning."

"I'll make it real clear." He stood, untucked his shirt, and drew the garment over his head, revealing Coop's brand.

Just like Leah had, Katie gasped. Pain flashed in Reese's eyes.

"A month after you walked out on me, I ran away, figuring to find you. Coop caught me a day later, hauled me back, and beat me. I tried again about three months later. Coop beat me again—worse that time. When I was able to stand upright once more, he burned his name in my chest and told me I belonged to him, that you'd sold fourteen years of my life into servitude in his smithy." He narrowed his eyes. "I always wondered. . .what was fourteen years of my life worth to you?"

Reese paled. "I didn't sell you to him. Six months after Ma died, her friend, Anna, came to our house. She'd been away awhile, had married Coop, and they'd moved back to town. She wanted to introduce Ma to her new husband. Hearing of Ma's death and what we were facing, Coop offered to take you in." He pinned Bo with a firm stare. "*He offered*, Bo. I never tried to pawn you off on anyone."

"Maybe not, but when the opportunity presented itself, you jumped at the chance."

"Bo. . ." Yeldin warned. "Keep an open mind."

He fell silent.

"Coop said they'd raise you until I could take over the job. It was the best chance we had to survive and make something of ourselves. But I was *paying* Coop and Anna for your upkeep. I started sending five dollars a month. A year later, Coop wrote, said he needed more. So I sent seven, then ten."

Bo chewed on that, his irritation growing. "That ain't what Coop told me. I was forever reminded just how dear he paid for me." Bo pulled his shirt back on then sat, fatigue stealing through him. "He'd always tell me how bad I musta been for my own kin to sell me like that. And how it cost him to *save* me from you."

Yeldin cleared his throat. "Here's what I think. Coop saw two green kids who'd be easy to swindle. Reese, you were desperate for a way to keep your family alive. When Coop and Anna showed up, you took their help, not knowing Coop'd continue upping the money he required for Bo's keeping. And Bo, he probably figured you'd grow up strong like your brother. Once Reese was out of the way, he could spin a few lies and have free labor for years."

Reese groaned. "I feel like such a fool. He played us, Bo."

"What were you paying him for?" Bo asked.

"Clothes, shoes, food, doctoring. Whatever you needed."

"I never saw that money. I wore rags most of my youth. If I asked for anything, I was told how much they'd already spent for me."

Reese's voice shook. "Of course you didn't. He kept it." He rocked to his feet and paced. "If I'd known, Bo, I never would've left you there. Please believe me."

"I don't know what to believe. He said you sold me. You say you were paying for my upkeep. Either way, you abandoned me with no word."

Reese spun on Bo. "No. Not without word. I wrote you—one letter before I left to explain why I had to go. Then two a month. He promised to read them to you."

"He never read me nothin'."

Reese fairly shook as he paced again. "I knew you'd fight me if I told you I was leaving, so I left while you were asleep. Before I went, I took a piece of Ma's pretty stationery—you remember, that pink paper she got so angry at you drawing on?"

Bo's recollection sparked.

"I wrote you a letter on that stationery because I knew you'd recognize it. I said I was going to find a way to support us, but I'd be back, and that I loved you. That I'd write you as I got settled. I always wrote on Ma's pink paper. At least until it ran out. Then I bought yellow."

Bo jerked. "Yellow?"

Reese nodded. "I remember writing on that first yellow sheet—explaining why it wasn't pink."

"Yellow. . ."

Katie stood. "That means something to you, doesn't it?"

He moved toward the door. "Wait here, please." He pinned Yeldin with a look. "All of you."

Bo nearly ran to his house and, barging through the door, opened the chest in the corner. He unloaded the top layers of clothing and blankets until he reached the treasures underneath. There, he opened the wooden box Ma gave him the Christmas before she died, and extracted its contents. Pink and yellow papers in hand, he stalked back to the smithy and thrust them toward Yeldin.

"You *did* get them!" When Reese rushed forward, Bo leveled his splinted hand against his brother's chest.

"Those would show up every few weeks at Coop's place, usually in the tinder bin. He never said they were letters for me. Neither Anna nor I could read, so we didn't know what they were. But the pink paper reminded me of Ma, so when I could, I sneaked 'em out of the bin and hid 'em." He shrugged. "It felt like finding a little piece of her." He glanced the sheriff's way. "Yeldin, I trust you. Please take any one of those and tell me what it says."

The lawman unfolded the top letter. "It says, 'Bo, I hope you'll understand someday. I have to leave for a while. I don't want to, but there are no jobs here, and I have to find a way to support us. That'll be harder if I have to keep watch over you while I'm doing it. That's why I'm leaving you with Coop and Anna. They've promised to keep good care of you until I can take over that job. Things have been hard between us since Ma passed, but I hope you know how much I love you. I'll write soon. Love, Reese.'"

A boulder sat on his chest. He shot an awkward glance at each, ending with Reese. "You're telling me the truth."

"Yes. The next letter I wrote said I'd found work in a factory in St. Louis. Later, how I got to know an attorney for the company, and he took a shine to me. Two years later, I came into his office and read the law. After four years of study, I became an attorney myself.

Ever since, I've been trying to find you. Writing letters, making trips—"

Katie sidled up next to Reese. "He wouldn't rest until he found you. We even gave up our St. Louis home to travel the West these last few years, taking work where we could as we looked."

Bo could scarcely breathe. When Reese settled a gentle hand on his shoulder, a cry tore from Bo's lungs. Reese pulled him close, settling their foreheads together as years of pain broke free in great body-shaking sobs.

When he finally drew back from his brother and dried his eyes, they were alone, the nearest smithy door pulled partially closed. He must've looked confused.

"Katie and the sheriff stepped out to give us some privacy."

Bo stared at his brother. "Never in a hundred years would I have thought we could stand in the same room without me wanting to kill you."

A lopsided smile crossed Reese's lips. "Didn't you try that this morning?"

Laughter boiled from Bo's gut, though it dissolved into another knot of emotion. He gulped several deep breaths to calm himself. "I am so sorry," he whispered once he could trust his voice.

"If a broken nose is the price of regaining my brother, I'd endure it again." His gaze flicked to Bo's hand. "What about your hand? Is it broken?"

"I hit someone." He relayed the details, and Reese cringed.

"What possessed you to hit him?"

He scuffed a boot on the floor. "I didn't like what he was saying about a lady and her kin."

"Would that be the redhead at church? Katie thought she was someone special to you."

"Leah Guthrie." His chest tightened. "I hoped she was becoming someone special, but I messed up pretty bad with her earlier."

"What'd you do?"

Before he could answer, Sheriff Yeldin peeked in. "Bo? Ethan's missing."

Chapter 13

Hello, Mrs. Kelso." Leah smiled at the barber's wife. "You haven't seen my brother Ethan today, have you?"

She hoped for a more favorable reply than at the previous homes she'd checked.

"No, dear," the gray-haired woman said. "Not since church this morning."

The rock that filled the pit of her stomach grew by half. She'd checked every house on Mrs. Kelso's street, and Hope was canvassing the next. Dusk was upon them, and no one had seen Ethan since he ran from Bo's shop.

One of the foul words the McCready boy had uttered rumbled through her thoughts, and her cheeks burned.

Lord, forgive me that thought, and please. . .help me find Ethan.

"Thank you for your time." She turned toward the street, but Mrs. Kelso called out.

"Quite a kerfuffle at church today, wasn't it?"

She shuffled to a halt. Was she about to be blamed for disrupting the service? It wouldn't be the first time. While the disruptive actions were Bo's alone, there was that element in the church that cast blame on her for inviting him.

"It was something. Now if you'll excuse me, I—"

"That Bowdrie Allen near ruined dinner on the grounds."

Oh, he'd done more than ruin the picnic. He'd made her love him when he'd made Mae's braces, then he'd shattered her heart when he broke one.

She smiled. "I understand why you'd think that, ma'am."

The woman's sanctimonious *tsk-tsk* grated on Leah's nerves, and she lifted her chin. "However, I would think one so upstanding as you would be more concerned about his interrupting the fine sermon, not the dinner."

The woman's eyes rounded. "Well. Believe you me, I was."

"As I suspected." Leah gave a syrupy smile.

"Rumor is you've been keeping company with Mr. Allen."

Her hackles rose. She wouldn't defend her actions to this old busybody. Particularly since she wouldn't continue to keep company with Bowdrie Allen.

She mustered her sweetest tone. "Now, Mrs. Kelso. The book of James says anyone who thinks themselves religious but doesn't bridle their gossiping tongue, their religion is in vain." She smiled again. "I wish I could stay, but I *must* find my brother."

The woman gasped as Leah marched toward the street again.

With a sigh, she turned at the corner to find Hope.

She'd left the awful scene at the smithy in tears but had somehow managed to collect herself enough to return to the church and gather her sisters. They'd searched town in hopes of finding Ethan, but he'd disappeared. She'd not panicked then. The boy was plenty capable of walking home. But when the Petersons stopped by late that afternoon, her worry had reached a fever pitch. Mr. Peterson accompanied them into town to tell Sheriff Yeldin while Mrs. Peterson stayed with Mae in case Ethan returned home.

Rounding the corner, she found Hope walking her way.

"Anything?" she called out.

Her sister scowled. "No sign of Ethan, but that Burl McCready is awful."

"Why? Did he hurt you?"

"He threw a rock at me."

"He what?" Leah looked her sister over. "Are you okay?"

"I'm fine. Those boys were prowling around, so I tried to ask 'em about Ethan. They darted into an alley without answering me, so I followed, and when I got close, I could hear Burl urging little Jess to do something he obviously didn't want to do. Jess kept asking what would happen if they were caught."

Leah frowned. "What were they planning?"

Hope shrugged. "I've no idea. I rounded the corner, scolding Burl for bullying his little brother, and the brat yelled an obscenity at me, threw a rock at my head, and told me to leave. So I did."

Leah's shoulders knotted. "Lord, please don't let Ethan be with those boys!"

"To put your heart at ease, I didn't see him. Nor did I hear Ethan mentioned in the conversation I overheard."

That was only mildly comforting, especially since in the few minutes they'd stood talking, evening had fallen. Darkness was upon them, and searching for Ethan would become infinitely harder.

Lord, help me. Where is my brother?

A chilling thought took shape. "You don't think they could've done something to Ethan, do you? Was *that* why Jess was worrying about being caught?"

Hope's jaw went slack. "I don't know."

"Show me where they were."

Hope hurried toward the alley, Leah fast on her heels. Nearing the backs of the buildings, Hope slowed.

"They *were* just to the left." She held her voice to a whisper as she indicated the direction.

Without a thought, Leah brushed past her sister and barged into the connecting alley. Gone. Hope molded herself against Leah's back as Leah scanned the narrow passageway.

"How long ago were they here?" she whispered.

"Ten minutes ago."

Frustration wound through her. *Lord, am I following a rabbit trail, or do those boys know something?* She didn't want to waste time if they couldn't provide clues.

"Come on. We'll make a pass through the alley then try the livery. Maybe someone there knows something." Taking Hope's hand, she led her sister into the adjoining alley and headed first toward Elverton's center. When no sign of Ethan or the McCready boys turned up, they hurried in the opposite direction, straight toward Bo's property. As they neared, a strange orange glow grew on the horizon, and the breeze carried the strong sent of smoke.

Leah's footsteps faltered. "Something's burning!"

She began to move, slowly at first then faster. Her heart pounded as she hit a full sprint. A few doors lining the alley opened, people stepping out to crane their necks in the direction of the glow.

"Fire!" she shouted as she raced past. "Something's burning!"

Near the end of the alley, Mr. Harper burst out and charged toward Bo's place. She, Hope, and the butcher reached Bo's property at nearly the same time—just in time to see Burl McCready throw something toward the roof of Bo's home. Glass shattered, and flames leaped into the air.

"Hey!" Mr. Harper sprinted toward Burl. The young man took off, Harper in pursuit.

For a stunned moment, Leah scrambled to assess the situation. Flames flew from both the smithy and Bo's house. A frightened wail from the direction of the large oak tree drew her attention. There, Jess McCready stood near the trunk.

More townsfolk had come to the scene, several racing to the front of the shop while someone pounded on the front door of the house.

"Mr. Allen? Fire!"

Leah grabbed Hope's hand and dragged her toward the tree. Reaching Jess, she braced a hand against the trunk as she squatted beside him. Perhaps it was her own body shaking, but it felt as if the tree quivered.

"Are you hurt?" she asked the boy.

Eyes huge, he gave a faint head-shake, then his face twisted into a mask of fear. "I didn't want to set anything on fire. Burl made me come."

"Don't worry about that now." Turning to her sister, she joined Hope's hand with Jess's. "Take him and go to the church. Ring the bell until the whole town comes out. Do you hear me?"

Her sister nodded, and both raced away from the danger. Thankfully, the boy didn't resist, but kept pace with Hope.

Lord, keep them safe.

Leah's thoughts shifted instantly. Where was Bo? If he'd taken a dose of laudanum and gone to sleep, would he rouse? Heartbroken or not, she had to be sure he was safe.

She took a step toward the house, but a sudden cascade of leaves and branches showered her. Covering her head with her arms, she shrieked and raced away, turning back as a large shadow jumped from tree limb to rooftop. Stunned, she straightened.

"Bo?" She squinted at the roofline.

The form, nowhere near large enough to be Bo, neared the flames, his red hair giving him away.

"Ethan? No! Get down from there!"

She watched in horror as her brother shook out what appeared to be a blanket and began to swat the flames.

"Ethan. Come down. Now!" Leah raced to the back of the building and pounded on the wall to get his attention. "Get down! Jump!"

A bucket brigade had formed, and those people too shouted for

Ethan to descend. As the flames raced down the back wall, someone pulled Leah away from the building just in time to see the roof collapse, taking Ethan with it.

~

"Ethan Guthrie!" Bo's voice shook the silence as he stood in his stirrups, lifting a lantern into the falling dusk. He and Reese had searched the road to the Guthrie home in the two hours since learning of the boy's disappearance. Finding no sign of him, they'd widened the search to the areas surrounding the pathways on their return.

"Ethan!" Reese's voice echoed not far off.

"Answer me, boy!" *Please.* Bo swiveled in every direction. "You got folks worried about you."

After a long scan of the area, he slumped in the saddle.

Reese came alongside him. "I know you don't want to hear this, but we should go back."

He didn't want to hear it, though his brother was right.

"C'mon. We'll rest and start fresh again at dawn. Besides, he might've been found by now."

Or he could be lying injured somewhere, unable to call for help. "I won't forgive myself if anything happens to that boy." His voice was husky.

"This isn't your fault, Bo. That boy ran off of his own volition."

"It's *all* my fault."

"How do you figure that?"

His gut knotted. "After our run-in in the churchyard, I was so angry at seeing you, I tore my smithy apart."

"I saw it." Reese's expression held only compassion.

"Ethan and Leah showed up, and Leah tried to calm me down...." He relayed the words he'd spoken, the way he'd acted, his destroying the leg brace, then hung his head. "I've never let myself get close to people. Not before the Guthries. Always been too afraid I'd do something like this—wind up hurting people I care for because of my temper. That boy ran because of the way I spoke to them and what I did to his sister's brace."

Reese reined his horse around, facing Bo. "Do you still hate me?"

"No." The knowledge that he'd *not* been abandoned, and in fact was sought after, went far to quench that. "But my anger has been a constant companion, and everyone in Elverton knows it. How do I assure myself it won't get the better of me again? I'm tired of holding myself away from everyone. These last weeks with the Guthries have shown me I don't want to go back to how I've been living."

When Reese spoke, his voice was husky. "First of all, you aren't alone anymore. You've got me and Katie and our girls, and that won't change."

Bo's throat knotted.

"Second, there's nothing wrong with being angry. The Bible says, 'Be ye angry, and sin not.'" He shrugged. "Like me, you just have to find better ways to release it when it comes."

"Like you?"

Reese nodded. "After I became an attorney, I went out to Texas to collect you, only you were gone with no word where. The more dead ends I ran into, the angrier I got. After months of searching, I was out of money and needed to return to St. Louis. That just fueled my anger. It overtook my life for a while. I became sullen, argumentative. Then I met Katie and her parents, started going to church with them, meeting with their preacher, reading the Bible. God didn't do it overnight, but He changed me."

Bo's thoughts churned. "You think He could change me too?"

A grin sprouted on Reese's lips. "I know He can. Just ask Him."

At Reese's expectant look, Bo squirmed. It would be a welcome thing if God could take the anger from him. But too much had happened too quickly. He needed time to process it all. "I think you're right. Let's head back."

"All right."

Silent, they turned down the steep east road into Elverton. As they neared the bottom and the outskirts of town, a glow like the first rays of sunrise lit the night sky. Down the street, panicked voices sounded an alarm. Almost as one, he and Reese spurred their horses toward the commotion.

As they drew nearer, Bo's heart sank. Flames leaped from the smithy roof. A lone figure stood atop the building, beating at the fire with. . .a blanket?

The fool. Who was up there?

He steered Diego to the hitching post several storefronts down and, sliding from the saddle, blew out the lantern's flame. He stashed it near the edge of the boardwalk and sprinted toward the shop.

"Get off the roof! Get down!" He shouted the words as he raced beside the building. Rounding the tree, an eerie groan split the air, and the figure disappeared, swallowed in a swirl of sparks.

"Ethan!" Leah's terrified shriek rose above the roar of the fire.

"Oh God. No." Leah ran past, and Bo caught her. "That was Ethan?"

She fought free of his grasp and charged toward the front of the building. Heart hammering near out of his chest, he followed.

God, help.

He rounded the front corner and someone called out: "Allen, your keys. We gotta unlock these doors."

Bo patted his left hip, but they were gone. His mind scrambled for an answer, gaze darting to Diego. He'd stashed 'em in his saddlebags.

"This corner." He lurched toward the nearest corner of the door, and several men gathered around. "Lift from the bottom and pull out. I'll slip through the space you create."

Sal Harper stripped off his apron. "Douse that and wrap it around your nose and mouth whilst we get this door wrenched free."

Behind him, Leah pounded on the wall beside the window. "Ethan! Oh Lord. Ethan."

Grabbing her by the waist, Bo dragged her toward the livery.

"No! Ethan's in there. I have to get him!" She flailed at him.

At the front of the stable, Bo took her face in his hands. "I'll get him. Stay here."

With that, Bo left her and sank, full body, into the horse trough then surged up and flew across the street. He looped the dripping apron around his face as he went.

"Someone make sure Leah stays put," he shouted. Then, with the left door partially lifted from its track, he pulled himself through the narrow opening.

Thick black smoke and flames filled the space. The heat immediately brought a sweat to his skin.

"Ethan!"

A spate of coughing drew his ear. Bo tried to stand, to move toward the sound, but his foot hit something and went out from under him. He crashed to the floor, pain jolting his injured hand. Gritting through the agony, he rolled up and crawled, one-handed, toward the coughing, shoving the clutter from his earlier rage out of his way.

"Ethan!"

"Help." The voice was weak, muffled.

"Come to me. Now."

"Can't. My leg. . ."

Putting on speed, he surged toward the sound. "Keep talking."

"By the quench—" Coughs overtook him again.

The quench bucket. Near the anvil. His own lungs burning and eyes smarting, he kept going.

"Say something."

"Here."

Bo reached toward the sound and found the boy huddled under a blanket. A very *wet* blanket.

A fit of coughing overtaking him, Bo adjusted the apron around his face then hauled Ethan into his arms. Whispering a prayer, he lunged up and ran. In four giant strides, they reached the door, and he slammed into it with his shoulder. From outside, the door pried outward, and he shoved Ethan's head and shoulders into the tight space.

"Take him."

As quickly as the men jerked Ethan through, Bo slid his feet into the opening. Hands grabbed at his ankles and pulled. Before they pulled him from the building, he snatched the gunny sack beside the desk, dragging it with him.

Chapter 14

Two days later

A soft knock roused Leah. She'd managed to sleep a little in the large corner chair of Doc Bates's recovery room while Mae kept watch over Ethan and Hope returned home for fresh changes of clothes.

"Come in," Mae called.

Lord, please let it be Bo. She had so many things she needed to say to the man, but almost two full days after the fire, he'd not come.

Reverend Danby peeked in. "Afternoon."

Disappointment wound through Leah. Not Bo.

"Good afternoon, Reverend." Mae waved him into the room.

He stepped inside. "How's the patient?"

Leah took the other cane chair beside Mae. "He's improving. Doc's giving him morphine to keep him still for a bit, but his breathing is easier. Of course, his leg will take time to heal."

Reverend Danby grinned. "Everyone says it's a miracle he survived."

Mae nodded. "From what we've gathered when Ethan is awake, he landed near the quench bucket beside the anvil. Despite everything, he had the presence of mind to wet the blanket he'd used to beat out the flames." Mae's voice quavered. "Doc says but for that, he'd have died before anyone got to him."

Leah's stomach knotted. How close they'd come to losing their only brother. And how grateful she was that he was spared. "You don't happen to know where Bo Allen is, do you, Reverend?"

"No. No one seems to know where he is. Once he's found, though, I'd like to discuss something with him."

If he was found. . . .

Lord, Bo wasn't injured in the fire, was he? He'd been in that same smoky room. Had he rescued her brother only to succumb to the smoke himself? Sheriff Yeldin had assured her they'd searched and not found his body. In fact, they'd found nothing. All but two of his horses were still at the livery, which might indicate he hadn't gone far, but she was fearful.

Leah shook off her thoughts. "I hope it's not to take him to task for the scene at church."

"Not at all. I simply meant to give him the news that we called a town meeting. Many from the community have offered their help."

"That's very kind of everyone."

"In fact," he continued, "that's why I've come to see you. With Ethan's injuries, it may be difficult for you to work until his condition improves. We've taken a collection, and several have pledged meals, offers to stay with Ethan if you must leave, that sort of thing." He withdrew an overstuffed pouch and a folded paper from his shirt pocket. "Here's the money collected and a list of those who've offered other assistance."

Leah hesitantly took the offered pouch, loosened the drawstring top, and tipped the uppermost layer into her palm. Out spilled several coins and even a tiny gold nugget. Wide-eyed, she and Mae looked at each other.

"Reverend, I'm humbled by Elverton's generosity, but given that Bo lost everything, perhaps this should go to him. We'll make do until Ethan's well again." Hands shaking, she returned the coins to the bag and offered it to him.

The man smiled but shook his head. "If you prefer it to go to him, I think it's best if you tell him yourself. But the community took two collections—one for each of you. He'll have a good start on rebuilding."

She wrapped her arms about her middle. "Then please pray, Reverend, because after all that happened Sunday and the fact that no one knows where he is, I fear he's picked up and moved on."

Two days later

"Have you given any more thought to rebuilding?" Reese asked.

Bo roused from his thoughts. He'd be returning to ashes. And not just the remains of his smithy and house. His chances for even a friendship with Leah had burned up hours before the fire claimed everything else.

Lifting his canteen, Bo uncorked it and took a slow sip before answering. "Reckon if I had to make a decision right now, I'd move on." He recorked the canteen and hung it from the saddle horn again.

"Are you *sure*?"

He ducked at the pointed question. "Not real sure of anything right now."

"Would you like some brotherly advice?"

Bo shrugged. "Couldn't hurt."

"You've lived and worked in this community for the last three years."

"Yeah, but I told you, I was pretty standoffish. My list of friends is short."

"Whether you count them as friends or not, Elverton residents are used to having a blacksmith in town. They're not going to want to ride to Grass Valley to avail themselves of another blacksmith's services. They *need* you."

A valid point—but did he have the guts to stay when he'd made such a public scene in front of the community's most upstanding citizens at church? Surely by now, the town was talking, and none of their chatter would be good.

"Just seems easier, packing up and moving on." Especially since he had nothing to pack.

Reese gave him a sidelong glance. "Sure, it's easier. And if that's really want you want to do, we'll move with you. *One time.* But I promised Katie that once we found you, we'd settle down for good. Hazel and Violet deserve the chance to grow up with friends, attend school, do all the things that little girls ought to do. And between you and me, I think Katie finds this little town charming. You might just break her heart if you choose to move on."

It was a strange and unfamiliar thing, thinking about what was best for somebody other than himself. That would take getting used to. Did he have it in him to try?

"Somebody once told me that if things aren't working to try a different approach."

"Wise advice." Reese grinned.

"Maybe if I'm hoping to change, I need to quit running every time things get difficult."

"That's a shrewd assessment. Who told you that—about a different approach?"

"Leah."

Reese gave him a hard look. "You're convinced things are dead with her?"

Bo removed his hat and wiped his forehead with his sleeve. "I asked her what I could do to fix things, and she said I couldn't." Tugging the hat back in place, he stared down the hill into town. "Feels pretty convincing to me."

"But since she said that, you risked your life to save her brother's.

Don't you think that might change something?"

"I didn't pull Ethan out so's I could win his sister's heart back." He nudged Diego down the hill toward town.

Reese drew alongside. "I didn't think you did. In fact, the way you speak of them, I'd say you've grown sweet on the whole family."

So true, but that had gotten him nothing but an aching, empty heart.

Lord, how do I stay in town if there's no chance with Leah and her kin?

As they rode between the first buildings, people's quiet conversations waned, and they slowed to watch them pass. Even a man driving a heavily loaded wagon in the opposite direction turned to look as he passed. He and Reese exchanged glances as the uncomfortable tightness he'd experienced in the church settled in his chest again.

Bo tugged his hat low over his eyes. "Figured I'd be the talk of the town, but this is worse than I expected," he grumbled under his breath.

A block down, a young man with a dirt-streaked face and filthy clothes stepped off the boardwalk toward them. "Mr. Allen?"

Both he and Reese slowed.

"There's a whole lot of people looking for you, sir."

Looking—for him? "Why's that, kid?"

His eyes widened. "You been missing since the fire. Sheriff Yeldin's had people out searching for you."

"That explains the stares," Reese whispered.

He glanced around the street again then nodded to the young man. "Thank you. I'll visit him directly."

When they drew up outside Yeldin's office minutes later, the sheriff burst out, scowling.

"Where in thunderation have you two been for the past four days?"

He and Reese looked at each other. "Grass Valley," they answered in unison.

Utter consternation crossed the lawman's face. "Get in my office." They dismounted and entered, Bo feeling like a chastised pup.

"You couldn't have said something before you left—tell someone where you were going? Instead, you watch your place burn then decide to ride to Grass Valley on a whim?" He stabbed a finger in Reese's direction. "And you. What married man tells his wife he's leaving but doesn't say where he'll be or when he's returning?"

Bo's hackles rose. "Leave Reese out of this. He told Katie we needed time to work through some things, and she trusted him enough to let him go without further explanation. Aside from that, I didn't know I needed to explain myself. My comings and goings have never concerned anyone before."

"Your place never burned before either. Folks have been concerned, and as your friend, I'm chief among 'em. Are you all right?"

He ducked his head. "Reckon so, for having lost everything. And…I'm sorry, Yeldin. I didn't know my leaving would cause anyone worry."

"Didn't know— I think you need to see something. C'mon." He motioned them through the door but stopped. "Jess McCready, where are you?"

Bo's ears perked at the name. "Those boys makin' trouble again?"

Yeldin pulled the door closed. "I don't know whether to tell you this or not."

"Tell me *what?*"

He spoke in a confidential tone. "Leah, Hope, and Sal Harper all saw Burl McCready start that fire."

His insides turned cold. "Tell me you caught that little—"

"Sean and Burl McCready have disappeared. They made a hasty getaway, if their shack at the McCready claim is any indication. I got a posse hunting Burl, but so far, he hasn't turned up. I've only got Jess, and between what Hope, Leah, and the boy himself have said, I don't think he lifted a finger in helping that good-for-nothing brother of his burn your place. In fact, I think his brother, and maybe his uncle, forced him to be an unwilling accomplice in a lot of things. But that kid doesn't have the same temperament as the older McCready men."

Bo nodded thoughtfully. "Will you let me talk to him?"

"Not if you're gonna pounce on him. He's a frightened little boy."

"Blast it all, Yeldin, I've been that frightened little boy. I ain't gonna pounce."

Yeldin hesitated then pushed the door open. "I'm trusting you, Bo."

Inside, Bo scanned the room. The only place anyone might hide was under Yeldin's desk, so he headed to it. Pulling the chair out, he sat and settled his elbows on his knees. There, Jess McCready peered out, face as pale as his white-blond hair.

"Come on out, boy, so we can talk."

With his saucer-eyed gaze riveted on Bo, Jess shook his head.

"Please?"

Again, only a shake of the boy's head.

"All right. Then we'll talk here. I understand it was your brother that lit up my place. Is that right?"

Little Jess gulped but didn't speak.

"Listen here, boy. You and I have had our problems lately. The broken window, you and your brother messin' with my tools, cursin' in front of Miss Guthrie. But I'm thinkin' maybe you did those things because your big brother told you to, or you were followin' his example."

Jess nodded, the movement so small Bo almost missed it.

"Three different people saw Burl set that fire, so I know it was him. Will you tell me, from your perspective, what happened?"

The boy was silent so long, Bo figured he wouldn't answer. Then. . . "Uncle Sean and Burl said we should get you back for lockin' us in the jail. I didn't know what they was plannin' till after Burl stole some whiskey bottles from another miner. I kept telling him I didn't think it was right, and I didn't want to do it. But he said they wouldn't lock me up on account of I was a kid. He made me go, tried to get me to throw the first bottle. When I wouldn't, he shoved me down, set your place on fire, and ran off and left me."

Bo considered all Jess said. Then he said, "I believe you."

"You do?"

"I do." More importantly, he believed the boy didn't share the same temperament as his uncle and older brother. "You make me two promises, and you and I will get along just fine."

The boy's fear dissolved. "What promises?"

"Promise me you'll stop using those ugly words you were spoutin' the other day. And—promise you'll start respecting other people's property—windows and tools and the like."

"I will, Mr. Allen."

Bo extended his left hand to the boy. "Then c'mon, kid. We're about to take a ride."

Outside, the men mounted, and Yeldin pulled Jess up behind him then led the way to Bo's property.

Chapter 15

With Ethan sleeping and her sisters catching a breath of fresh air, Leah curled in the corner chair. She balanced Mrs. Bates's copy of *Pride and Prejudice* on her lap, yet every time she tried to delve into the opening line of the story, her mind drifted to the day Mae began reading it to her. The day her blouse sleeve twined so perfectly with Bo's Henley on the clothesline.

That day, it all had been a sign of things she dared not dream for. Today, it was the memory that mocked her unanswered hopes.

She closed her eyes, her last haunting memory of Bo scrolling through her mind. The fire raged, devouring his smithy. He had promised to get Ethan out, and she'd stood across the way, watching, praying until men pulled a small limp form from behind the door. In that instant, she'd run to see. As she'd neared, they unwrapped a sopping blanket from around Ethan's listless body. He was so still. So small. Horror enveloped her. Was he—?

No! A spate of coughing overtook him. He was alive! Thanks to Bo.

She'd huddled next to Ethan, stayed by his side until a wagon rumbled up to ferry her brother to Doc's office. As the men loaded his battered body into the wagon bed, Leah scanned the faces, looking for her brother's rescuer and her hero. Only she couldn't find him. Not until they rumbled past him seated on the edge of the boardwalk.

Soot-covered. Shoulders slumped. A broken man watching his life burn. How she'd wanted to go to him, to cling to him and cry, but Ethan had needed her just then. And no one knew where Bo'd gone after that.

Surely if Bo were going to return, he'd have made contact by now. Wouldn't he, Lord?

"Leah?" Ethan's sleepy voice cut into her thoughts. "I'm thirsty."

She moved to the straight-backed chair beside his bed and, settling the book in her lap again, tipped a glass of water to his lips. "How's that?"

He swallowed. "Better." Ethan settled back into his pillow, blinking up at the ceiling. "When's Bo gonna come?"

She pushed his unruly red locks off his forehead. "I don't think he's—"

"Leah?" Hope's shrill call stopped her short. "Leah!" The girl skidded into view, eyes wide.

She lurched up, book tumbling open onto the bed. "What? Is it Mae?"

Hope shook her head as Mae hobbled into view an instant behind her.

Thank God. Not Mae. "What is it?"

Both girls looked at each other then faced her, and in unison, spoke.

"Bo's back!"

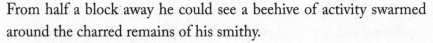

From half a block away he could see a beehive of activity swarmed around the charred remains of his smithy.

"What is this?" Bo stared.

Yeldin flung a hand toward the plot of land. "Ride on up there and see."

As he neared the action, everything stopped, and the men approached. Among them were area ranchers, miners, business owners, and total strangers—all falling in behind Sal Harper. Once he'd dismounted, they gathered around.

"Where you been, Bo?" Harper asked.

Heat crept through him at the memory of Yeldin's stern rebuke. "Rode over Grass Valley way. The sheriff tells me I worried some of you. If that's the truth, I'm sorry." He took a long look at the men surrounding him then at the wagons standing at intervals around his property. "What're you all doing?"

"What do you think?" someone from the group called. "We can't start rebuilding until the land's clear."

"Rebuilding?"

"The town met after the fire." A stranger spoke. "By and large, the men agreed we'd work in teams to clear the debris."

Another man, a customer he'd had a few angry words with just after he'd opened shop spoke up. "We'll rebuild your house first, then the smithy, so you can get back to work once your hand's healed enough."

"We're putting any tools and supplies over here as we find 'em, Mr. Allen." The young man who'd stopped them on the street pointed to a collection of boxes and crates. "Figured you'd want to go through 'em, see if anything's salvageable."

His lungs would only half fill. "I don't understand. Why're y'all doing this when I've been so—?"

"It's the neighborly thing," one of the older men said. "That, and a bunch of us realized after church on Sunday that we ain't done the best job reaching out to you. We'll be changing that."

Bo rubbed the back of his hand across his mouth. They were extending him kindness, even friendship, in spite of everything. "Thank you. Truly." He looked around at the lot of them. "I wasn't expecting any of this."

"We wouldn't've done it if you were expecting it," someone called from the back of the bunch, and a laugh rippled through the group.

Reese sidled up and gave him a shove. "Does this help you answer that question I asked you?"

Rather than address his brother directly, he offered a lopsided grin to the group. "Reckon I oughta introduce my brother, Reese. He and his wife and daughters are planning to settle here."

"Brother?" Sal Harper pinned him with a questioning glance. "Thought you didn't have kin."

"I didn't either, but I got proved wrong. I'll have to tell you about it sometime."

"Will you tell *me* about it now?"

Leah. Heart thudding, Bo turned.

She stood a short distance off, breathing as if she'd run a mile.

Lord, please—if there's any way we might rebuild the trust I broke...

"Reckon our break is over, men," Harper called. "Let's go. We're burnin' daylight."

She approached him almost timidly as the men filtered back to work. "You and your brother are speaking?"

"More than." He crammed his left hand into his pocket. "We're healing."

For a moment, they faced each other. Then Leah launched herself into his arms. He caught her, pulled her close, and held on as if his entire life depended on it.

Lord, please. Reese said You'd help me overcome my anger if I asked. I'm not asking. I'm begging. I don't ever want to hurt those I love because of my anger again. Especially Leah. Show me how to change.

She drew back all too soon for his taste, "I'm so happy for you both. I'd like to hear all about it, if you're willing to share."

"There's a whole lot I need to share with you. I don't even know where to start."

"There much I need to say too, but—Ethan's begging to see you. Would you come to Doc's office and look in on him?"

"Are Mae and Hope there too?"

"Yes. Why?"

"I paid the Grass Valley blacksmith to finish Mae's leg braces, fix the damage I caused." He patted the oddly shaped bedroll tied behind his saddle. "I thought everyone might want to be there when she gets 'em."

"They weren't destroyed in the fire?"

"Like I said—I got a lot to share. And if you think Ethan's up to it, I'd like Reese and his family to come by and meet you all too."

Epilogue

Six months later

W e're gonna be late," Ethan griped.

"Usually *you're* fussin' at us to hurry up." Jess McCready flopped on his bed in the corner.

Bo rinsed his face and chest then grabbed the towel to dry. The boys were dressed in nice shirts, their hair combed. Ready to go, except—

"Jess. Find a pair of pants that don't have a hole in the knee."

"Sorry." Cheeks flushing, he dug into the trunk at the foot of his bed.

Ethan loosed a frustrated growl. "C'mon. It's Leah's birthday."

"We won't be late." Bo dried himself off. "I sent you both in to clean up a full twenty minutes before I closed up shop, just to keep us on time."

He replaced the towel and combed his hair then pulled on a red shirt. As he fastened the buttons, he flexed his right hand. The wounds had healed, and he'd kept use of the appendage, though his hand was still stiff and clumsy at times. Thankfully, he'd taught himself to do some blacksmithing skills left-handed as he'd healed.

Bo tucked in his shirttails. "One of you dump the dirty wash water, and we'll be on our way."

Both flew past him, laughing and shoving.

"Careful, now! No messes." Last thing they needed was to slosh water down their good clothes or across the floor.

In the instant Ethan jerked the door open and Jess flung the water out, both boys went ramrod stiff.

"What is the meaning of this?" an unfamiliar voice boomed.

Bo hurried to the door. Outside stood a stately gentleman in a fine suit, now dripping from chest to knees. Ire sparked in the man's expression.

"I am so sorry." Bo fought to stifle his laughter. He reached for a clean towel hanging on the washstand then handed it to the man. "I assure you, that was an accident."

Fuming, the man snatched the towel, patted his face dry, then rubbed at his flabby midsection. His eyes widened, and he withdrew a pocket watch and held it to his ear.

"That little brat ruined my watch."

"I'm sorry." Bo spoke the words deliberately. "The boys didn't realize anyone would be there. Now, may I help you?"

"Are you Allen Bowdrie, the blacksmith?" He continued to rub at the water.

"I'm the blacksmith, yes." It wasn't worth correcting him, given the circumstances. "What can I do for you?"

"I have need of your services. Immediately."

"Tonight?"

"That is the meaning of immediately, isn't it? Without delay. . .at once."

"Reckon it is, Mr.—"

"Richard Shenley, hotelier."

"I'm sorry, Mr. Shenley, I'm about to be late for an important evening appointment."

"I doubt whatever you're doing is that important."

Irritation skittered down his spine. "Come back tomorrow, and I might be able to accommodate your needs on an immediate basis.

But it'll cost double my going rates."

"Double—" He tapped his foot. "That's robbery."

"No, sir. That's standard."

The man looked first at Ethan then Jess. "Are these your children?"

Bo looped his arms around the boys' shoulders. "They're kin. What of 'em?"

"The little one ruined a very expensive timepiece when he doused me with water. If you don't want to be sued for the cost of its replacement, then I expect you'll reopen your shop and take care of this work for me. *Tonight*."

The old familiar stir of anger began in Bo's belly. "You expect that, do you?"

"I demand it."

"Demand?" The urge to plant his fist in the man's nose bubbled to the surface.

"That is what I said."

Both boys stiffened as Bo pushed past them.

"Bo—" Ethan's tone held a hint of warning.

Images of Leah and her kin, Jess, Reese and his family, and the various friends he'd made in Elverton—far too many he'd disappoint by losing his temper over one sanctimonious dolt. "I told you I'm closed for today. You want to sue me for that watch, there's a fine attorney here in Elverton. I'm sure he'll listen with interest to your complaint." He mustered a smile. "Now if you'll excuse us, we've somewhere to be."

Bo shut and locked the door in Shenley's face and snatched his hat from its peg on the wall. He stalked to the door leading to the alley. "Let's go."

"We're off to set the table." Hope scurried through the door between

Katie and Reese's kitchen and dining room, carrying a stack of plates.

Leah grinned as Mae plucked the basket with napkins and silverware from the counter then followed, leaning on a single crutch as she shuffled toward the door.

"I'll get your other crutch." Leah reached for it.

"I don't need it for this." Mae slid her arm through the basket handle and pushed the door open. "It'll just be in the way."

Leah's throat knotted as her sister exited the room.

Katie sidled up next to her, wrapping an arm about Leah's shoulders. "Seems to me, Mae moves better every time I see her. I think those braces are helping her regain her strength."

"Or her confidence," Leah whispered, fighting to swallow her emotion. "Either way, it's good to see my sister more able to participate in life again."

"It is, at that." Katie gave her a sisterly hug then nodded toward the oven. "Biscuits should be about done."

"I'll get them."

Just as Leah withdrew the pan of golden biscuits from Katie's oven, a single knock sounded at the back door. Both she and Katie turned as the door opened, and Bo's big frame filled the space. Her heart fluttered fiercely at the sight of him in his new red shirt.

"Oh, no you don't, Bo Allen." Katie jabbed a finger toward the door. "Out! You wipe your boots before you come in from that alley."

Wearing an impish grin, Bo locked eyes on Leah just before he turned back to his sister-in-law. "Yes, ma'am."

He backed up, deliberately wiped his boots, then entered again. "Better?" He smiled at her across the room.

"Better," Katie confirmed, "but why on earth are you three coming in my back door?"

"We were avoiding someone at our front door." Jess dashed in and gave Katie a hug.

"What was that about?" Leah squatted to give the boy a hug of her own. He'd changed after Burl and Sean McCready had disappeared out of his life. Sweet, charming, and completely loveable. She'd enjoyed watching both Jess and Bo blossom into different people once Bo took him in.

"Well, first, I threw water on this fella, then he demanded Bo open the shop back up and do something for him, and when Bo said no, the fella said he's gonna sue Bo because I wrecked his watch."

"What?" Mind reeling from the whirlwind description, Leah rocked to her feet. "Someone's going to *sue* you?"

Bo stepped over and hoisted Jess up by the arms until he was at Bo's eye level. "Thanks, kid. You weren't supposed to worry her on her birthday."

"Sorry. . ."

"Go find Hazel and Violet. They're probably anxious to see you." Bo lowered the boy again, and Jess darted away.

"Happy birthday, sis." Ethan circled past for a hug before heading into the dining room to greet Mae and Hope.

With only Bo and Katie in the room, Leah faced him. "Is this something serious? Do you need to be concerned?"

"I don't know. The fella was dressed in an expensive-lookin' suit. But him getting doused was a stupid accident. And he walked in demanding I drop everything to work on something for him. Even went so far as to say whatever my plans were tonight couldn't be as important as what he needed done."

Leah's eyes widened. "That didn't go well, did it?" *Oh Lord, please don't let him have punched the man.*

"Don't look so frightened. I told him Elverton's got a fine attorney if he wanted to sue me. Then we left out the back door."

Katie giggled. "You know my husband won't help the man sue Bo. In fact, that'll be a conversation Reese will have a lot of fun with."

Leah shook her head and turned her attention to the biscuits.

"Happy birthday," Bo whispered as she transferred the first from pan to a plate.

"Thank you. How was the rest of your day?"

"No complaints. Got several projects done." Bo hovered near her shoulder as she worked. "Those biscuits look mighty tasty." He reached for one.

Leah smacked his hand away. "They're for the meal, not before."

He pulled his hand back but continued to hover. "You're really beautiful. You know that?"

Her face grew hot, and she elbowed him. "Give me some room to work, please. Go find your brother."

Katie giggled at them. "Reese walked back to his office for a minute. He shouldn't be long."

"Then make yourself useful. Carry those platters to the table." Leah pointed at the serving dishes.

"Oh, fine then." Bo turned as if to leave but reached around and snagged one of the biscuits from the perfectly arranged plate.

"Bowdrie Allen!" She dropped the table knife she'd been using to extract the biscuits and made a grab for it. He lifted it high overhead and walked out of the kitchen.

"Give me that." She chased him into the dining room. "I have exactly the same number of biscuits as people."

"Come take it from me." He looped around the big table, pausing long enough to give both Mae and Hope a peck on the top of the head before he moved toward the door to the hallway.

"Bo!" Leah hopped along after him, trying to reach the biscuit.

At her sisters' delighted tittering, Leah shot both a withering glare. They were only spurring him on.

As he neared the door to the entry hall, Bo caught her hand and drew her across and into the sitting room, out of everyone's view.

"What are you doing? I have to help with dinner."

He set the biscuit down on an end table then pulled her into his arms. "It's your birthday. I bet they can do without you for a minute."

Leah braced her hands against his chest and pushed away, trying to break his grip. But when he sank his fingers into her curls and pulled her to his chest, she gave up with a contented sigh. This was where she liked to be—safely wrapped in his embrace.

"I have something for you." His words rumbled against her ear.

She shook her head. "I told you I didn't need anything."

"Reckon you did, but I thought maybe you'd need this. Or. . .*want* it." Bo drew a yellow paper from his back pocket.

Still wrapped in his embrace, she unfolded the paper and smoothed it against his chest. She squinted then turned the page right side up. There, a beautiful pencil drawing of a rambling one-story house with a wide wraparound porch captivated her attention, followed by the words:

Will you be my wife and live here with me?

A happy little giggle bubbled out of her.

"What? You're laughing. Did I spell something wrong?"

"You spelled everything perfectly."

"Then why're you giggling?"

"That house looks big enough to sleep an army."

Understanding lit his eyes, and he set the drawing aside. "Well, we'll need space for the two of us. Mae. Hope. Ethan. Jess. And I'm hopin' at least a few more. . . ."

Leah's cheeks flamed. "I might be prone to mollycoddle you."

"I'm counting on it." He sank his fingers into her curls once more and trailed kisses along her jaw to her lips. Her heart thundered as she melted into him. Oh, heavens, she loved this man.

She wasn't sure how long they'd kissed before the soft clearing of someone's throat intruded on the moment. Bo broke the kiss, though she clung to him, not wanting the heady feeling of his lips to leave.

"Did you ask?" Reese grinned.

Bo ducked his head. "After a fashion."

"And?"

Their family pressed into the doorway, led by a grinning Mae.

"I think that kiss was a yes." Bo pulled back enough to look at her. "That's what that meant, right? Yes?"

Leah giggled. "It was a resounding yes."

Jennifer Uhlarik discovered the western genre as a preteen, when she swiped the only "horse" book she found on her older brother's bookshelf. A new love was born. Across the next ten years, she devoured Louis L'Amour westerns and fell in love with the genre. In college at the University of Tampa, she began penning her own story of the Old West. Armed with a BA in writing, she has won five writing competitions and was a finalist in two others. In addition to writing, she has held jobs as a private business owner, a schoolteacher, a marketing director, and her favorite—a full-time homemaker. Jennifer is active in American Christian Fiction Writers and is a lifetime member of the Florida Writers Association. She lives near Tampa, Florida, with her husband, teenage son, and four fur children.

Coming Soon. . .

Carousel Dreams (Releasing June 2020!)
Experience the early history of four iconic carousels—Oak Bluffs in 1889 Martha's Vineyard, Crescent Park in 1895 Rhode Island, Conneaut Lake in 1910 Pennsylvania, and Balboa Park in 1922 California—that draw together four couples in whirling romances full of music and charm.

Paperback / 978-1-64352-470-2/ $14.99

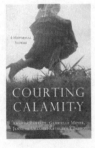

Courting Calamity (Releasing July 2020!)
Join these romantic adventures as four women of bygone days face challenges in which a hero would be welcomed to retrieve a stolen deed, to help at the family mercantile, to endure society rules, and to bring justice for a loved one. But can four men live up to heroic expectations?

Paperback / 978-1-64352-412-2 / $14.99